Over My Dead Body

Over My Dead Body

Jeffrey Archer is one of the world's bestselling authors, with sales of over 275 million copies in 97 countries.

Famous for his discipline as a writer who works on up to fourteen drafts of each book, Jeffrey also brings a vast amount of insider knowledge to his books. Whether it's his own career in politics, his passionate interest in art, or the wealth of fascinating background detail – inspired by the extraordinary network of friends he has built over a lifetime at the heart of Britain's establishment – his novels provide a fascinating glimpse into a range of closed worlds.

A member of the House of Lords, the author is married to Dame Mary Archer, and they have two sons, two granddaughters and three grandsons. He splits his time between London, Grantchester in Cambridge, and Mallorca, where he writes the first draft of each new novel.

Also by Jeffrey Archer

THE WILLIAM WARWICK NOVELS

Nothing Ventured
Hidden in Plain Sight
Turn a Blind Eye

THE CLIFTON CHRONICLES

Only Time Will Tell
The Sins of the Father
Best Kept Secret
Be Careful What You Wish For
Mightier than the Sword
Cometh the Hour
This Was a Man

NOVELS

Not a Penny More, Not a Penny Less
Shall We Tell the President?
Kane and Abel
The Prodigal Daughter
First Amongst Equals
A Matter of Honour
As the Crow Flies
Honour Amongst Thieves
The Fourth Estate
The Eleventh Commandment
Sons of Fortune
False Impression
The Gospel According to Judas
(with the assistance of Professor Francis J. Moloney)
A Prisoner of Birth
Paths of Glory
Heads You Win

SHORT STORIES

A Quiver Full of Arrows
A Twist in the Tale
Twelve Red Herrings
The Collected Short Stories
To Cut a Long Story Short
Cat O'Nine Tales
And Thereby Hangs a Tale
Tell Tale
The Short, the Long and the Tall

PLAYS

Beyond Reasonable Doubt
Exclusive
The Accused
Confession
Who Killed the Mayor?

PRISON DIARIES

Volume One – Belmarsh: Hell
Volume Two – Wayland: Purgatory
Volume Three – North Sea Camp: Heaven

SCREENPLAYS

Mallory: Walking Off the Map
False Impression

Jeffrey Archer

Over My Dead Body

HarperCollins*Publishers*

HarperCollins*Publishers* Ltd
1 London Bridge Street,
London SE1 9GF

www.harpercollins.co.uk

HarperCollins*Publishers*
1st Floor, Watermarque Building, Ringsend Road
Dublin 4, Ireland

First published by HarperCollins*Publishers* 2021
1

A catalogue record for this book is available from the British Library

ISBN: 978-0-00-847427-0 (HB)
ISBN: 978-0-00-847428-7 (TPB)
ISBN: 978-0-00-847637-3 (US/CA)
ISBN: 978-0-00-847640-3 (IN)

Typeset in New Caledonia LT Std by
Palimpsest Book Production Ltd, Falkirk, Stirlingshire

Printed and Bound in the UK using 100% Renewable Electricity at CPI Group (UK) Ltd

MIX
Paper from
responsible sources
FSC C007454

This book is produced from independently certified FSC™ paper
to ensure responsible forest management.

For more information visit: www.harpercollins.co.uk/green

To Jack

CHAPTER 1

'ARE YOU A DETECTIVE, SIR?'

William looked up at the young man who'd asked the question. 'No, I'm the assistant manager of the Midland Bank in Shoreham, Kent.'

'In that case,' continued the young man, not looking convinced, 'you'll be able to tell me what the exchange rate was between the dollar and the pound when the currency market opened this morning.'

William tried to recall how much he'd received when he changed a hundred pounds into dollars just before he joined the ship the previous evening, but he hesitated for too long.

'One dollar and fifty-four cents to the pound,' said the young man, before he could reply. 'So, forgive me for asking, sir, why aren't you willing to admit you're a detective?'

William put the book he was reading on the table in front of him and took a closer look at the earnest young American, who seemed desperate not to be thought of as a child, although he hadn't started shaving. The word 'preppy' immediately came to mind.

'Can you keep a secret?' he whispered.

'Yes, of course,' the young man said, sounding offended.

'Then have a seat,' said William, pointing to the comfortable chair opposite him. He waited for the young man to settle. 'I'm on holiday and I promised my wife that for the next ten days, I wouldn't tell anyone I was a detective, because it's always followed by a stream of questions that turn it into a busman's holiday.'

'But why choose a banker as your cover?' asked the young man. 'Because I have a feeling you wouldn't know the difference between a spreadsheet and a balance sheet.'

'My wife and I gave that question some considerable thought before we settled on a banker. I grew up in Shoreham, a small town in England, in the sixties, and the local bank manager was a friend of my father's. So I thought I'd get away with it for a couple of weeks.'

'What else was on the shortlist?'

'Estate agent, car salesman and funeral director, all of which we were fairly confident wouldn't be followed by never-ending questions.'

The young man laughed.

'Which job would you have chosen?' asked William, trying to regain the initiative.

'Hitman. That way no one would have bothered me with any follow-up questions.'

'I would have known that was a cover immediately,' said William with a dismissive wave of his hand, 'because no hitman would have asked me if I was a detective. He would have already known. So, what do you really do when you're not a hitman?'

'I'm in my final year at Choate, a prep school in Connecticut.'

'Do you know what you want to do when you leave school? That's assuming you're not still hoping to be a hitman.'

'I shall go to Harvard and study history, before going on to law school.'

'After which, no doubt, you'll join a well-known legal practice, and in no time be made a junior partner.'

'No, sir, I want to be a lawman. After I've spent a year as editor of the *Law Review*, I shall join the FBI.'

'You seem to have your career well mapped out, for one so young.'

The young man frowned, clearly offended, so William quickly added, 'I was just the same at your age. I knew I wanted to be a detective and end up at Scotland Yard when I was eight years old.'

'What took you so long?'

William smiled at the bright young man, who no doubt understood the meaning of the word precocious without realizing it might apply to him. But then William accepted that he'd undoubtedly suffered from the same problem when he was a schoolboy. He leant forward, thrust out his hand and said, 'Detective Chief Inspector William Warwick.'

'James Buchanan,' replied the young man, shaking William's outstretched hand firmly. 'Dare I ask how you reached such a high rank, because if you were at school in the sixties you can't be more than . . .'

'What makes you so sure they'll offer you a place at

Harvard?' asked William, trying to parry his thrust. 'You can't be more than . . .'

'Seventeen,' said James. 'I'm top of my class with a grade point average of 4.8, and I'm confident I'll do well in my SATs.' He paused before adding, 'Should I presume you made it to Scotland Yard, Chief Inspector?'

'Yes,' William came back. He was used to being interrogated by leading counsel, not teenagers, although he was enjoying the encounter. 'But if you're that bright, why haven't you considered becoming a lawyer, or going into politics?'

'There are far too many lawyers in America,' said James with a shrug of the shoulders, 'and most of them end up chasing ambulances.'

'And politics?'

'I wouldn't be any good at suffering fools gladly, and I don't want to spend the rest of my life at the whim of the electorate or allowing focus groups to dictate my opinions.'

'Whereas, if you were to become the Director of the FBI . . .'

'I would be my own master, answering only to the President, and I wouldn't always let him know what I was up to.'

William laughed at the young man, who clearly didn't suffer from self-doubt.

'And you, sir,' said James, sounding more relaxed, 'are you destined to become the Commissioner of the Metropolitan Police?' William hesitated again. 'Clearly, you think it's a possibility,' James continued before he could reply. 'May I ask you another question?'

'I can't imagine what would stop you.'

'What do you consider are the most important qualities needed to be a first-class detective?'

William gave the question some thought before he responded. 'A natural curiosity,' he eventually said. 'So you immediately spot something that doesn't feel quite right.'

James took a pen from an inside pocket and began writing William's words down on the back of the *Alden Daily News*.

'You must also be able to ask the relevant questions of suspects, witnesses and colleagues. Avoid making assumptions. And above all, you have to be patient. Which is why women often make better police officers than men. Finally, you must be able to use all your senses – sight, hearing, touch, smell, and taste.'

'I'm not sure I fully understand,' said James.

'That must be a first,' William replied, immediately regretting his words, although the young man laughed for the first time. 'Close your eyes,' said William. He waited for a moment before saying, 'Describe me.'

The young man took his time before replying. 'You're thirty, thirty-five at most, a shade over six foot, fair hair, blue eyes, around a hundred and seventy pounds, fit, but not as fit as you used to be, and you've suffered a serious shoulder injury at some time in the past.'

'What makes you think I'm not as fit as I used to be?' said William defensively.

'You're about six or seven pounds overweight, and, as this is the first day of the voyage, you can't blame the never-ending meals they serve on board ships.'

William frowned. 'And the injury?'

'The top two buttons of your shirt are undone, and when you leant forward to shake hands, I noticed a faded scar just below your left shoulder.'

William thought as he so often did, about his mentor, Constable Fred Yates, who had saved his life only to sacrifice his own. Police work wasn't always as romantic as some authors would have you believe. He moved quickly on. 'What book am I reading?'

'*Watership Down* by Richard Adams. And before you ask, you're on page hundred and forty-three.'

'And my clothes, what do they tell you?'

'I admit,' said James, 'I found that a bit of a mystery. It would take me several subtle questions before I came up with an answer, and then only if you told the truth.'

'Let's assume I'm a criminal who won't answer your questions until I've phoned my legal representative.'

James hesitated for a moment before he said, 'That in itself would be a clue.'

'Why?'

'It would suggest you've been in trouble with the law before, and if you know the telephone number of your lawyer, you certainly have.'

'OK. Let's assume I don't have a lawyer, but I've watched enough TV programmes to know I needn't answer any of your questions. What have you been able to work out without asking me any questions?'

'Your clothes aren't expensive, probably bought off the rack, yet you're travelling first class.'

'What do you deduce from that?'

'You're wearing a wedding ring, so you could have a rich wife. Or perhaps you're on a special assignment.'

'Neither,' said William. 'That's where observation ends, and detection begins. But not bad.'

The young man opened his eyes and smiled. 'My turn, I think, sir. Please close your eyes.'

William looked surprised, but continued with the game. 'Describe me.'

'Bright, self-assured, but insecure.'

'Insecure?'

'You may be top of the class, but you're still desperate to impress.'

'What am I wearing?' asked James.

'A white button-down cotton shirt, possibly Brooks Brothers. Dark blue shorts, white cotton socks and Puma trainers, though you rarely, if ever, visit a gym.'

'How can you be sure of that?'

'I noticed when you walked towards me that your feet were splayed. If you were an athlete, they'd be in a straight line. If you doubt me, check the footprints of an Olympic runner on a cinder track.'

'Any distinguishing marks?'

'You have a tiny birthmark just below your left ear that you've tried to hide by growing your hair, although that will have to be cut short when you join the FBI.'

'Describe the picture behind me.'

'A black and white photo of this ship, the *Alden*, sailing out of New York harbour on May twenty-third, 1977. It's being accompanied by a flotilla, which suggests it was on its maiden voyage.'

'Why's it named the *Alden*?'

'That isn't a test of observation,' said William, 'but of knowledge. If I needed to know the answer to that question,

I could always find out later. First impressions are often misleading, so assume nothing. But if I had to guess, and you shouldn't as a detective, as this ship is part of the Pilgrim Line, I'd say that Alden was the name of one of the original pilgrims who set sail from Plymouth to America on the *Mayflower* in 1620.'

'How tall am I?'

'You're an inch shorter than me, but you'll end up an inch taller. You weigh around a hundred and forty pounds, and you've only just started to shave.'

'How many people have passed us while your eyes have been closed?'

'A mother with two children, one a little boy called Bobby, both American, and a moment later one of the ship's officers.'

'How do you know he was an officer?'

'A deckhand passing the other way called him sir. There was also an elderly gentleman.'

'How could you tell he was old?'

'He was using a walking stick, and it was some time before the sound of tapping faded.'

'I'm half blind,' said James, as William opened his eyes.

'Far from it,' said William. 'Now it's my turn to ask the suspect some questions.' James sat bolt upright, a look of concentration on his face. 'A good detective should always rely on facts and never take anything for granted, so first I have to find out if Fraser Buchanan, the chairman of the Pilgrim Line, is your grandfather?'

'Yes, he is. And my father, Angus, is deputy chairman.'

'Fraser, Angus and James. Rather suggests a Scottish heritage.' James nodded.

'No doubt they both assume that in the fullness of time you'll become chairman.'

'I've already made it clear that's not going to happen,' said James without hesitation.

'From everything I've read or heard about your grandfather, he's used to getting his own way.'

'True,' James replied. 'But sometimes he forgets we come from the same stock,' he added with a smirk.

'I had the same problem with my father,' admitted William. 'He's a criminal barrister, a QC, and he always assumed I'd follow him in chambers and later join him at the bar, despite my telling him from an early age that I wanted to lock up criminals, not be paid extortionate fees to keep them out of jail.'

'George Bernard Shaw was right,' declared James. 'We are separated by a common language. For you, the bar means courts and lawyers. For an American it means high stools and drinks.'

'A sharp criminal will always try to change the subject,' said William. 'But a thorough detective won't allow himself to lose the thread. You didn't answer my question about your grandfather's feelings about you not wanting to be chairman of the company.'

'My grandfather, I suspect, is worse than your father,' said James. 'He's already threatening to cut me out of his will if I don't join the company after leaving Harvard. But he'll never be allowed to do that as long as my grandmother's alive.'

William chuckled.

'Would it be too much of an imposition, sir, to ask if I might be allowed to spend an hour or so a day with you during the voyage?' James asked, without displaying his previous confidence.

'I'd enjoy that. Around this time of the morning would suit me, because that's when my wife will be at her yoga class. But there's one proviso: should you ever meet her, you won't tell her what we've been talking about.'

'And what have you been talking about?' asked Beth, as she appeared by their side.

James leapt up. 'The price of gold, Mrs Warwick,' he said, looking earnest.

'Then you will have quickly discovered it's a subject about which my husband knows very little,' said Beth, giving the young man a warm smile.

'I was about to tell you, James,' said William, 'that my wife is far brighter than I am, which is why she's the keeper of pictures at the Fitzmolean Museum and I'm a mere Detective Chief Inspector.'

'The youngest in the Met's history,' said Beth.

'Although should you ever mention the Met to my wife, she'll assume you're talking about one of the finest museums on earth, rather than London's police force.'

'I was so glad you managed to get the Vermeer back,' said James, turning to Mrs Warwick.

It was Beth's turn to look surprised. 'Yes,' she eventually managed, 'and fortunately it can't be stolen again because the thief is dead.'

'Miles Faulkner,' said James, 'who died in Switzerland, after suffering a heart attack.'

William and Beth looked at each other but said nothing.

'You even attended the funeral, Chief Inspector, presumably to convince yourself he was dead.'

'How can you possibly know that?' said William, once again on the back foot.

'I read *The Spectator* and the *New Statesman* every week, which keeps me up to date on what's happening in Britain, and then try to form my own opinion.'

'Of course you do,' said William.

'I look forward to seeing you again tomorrow, sir,' said James, 'when I'll be interested to find out if you think it's possible Miles Faulkner is still alive.'

CHAPTER 2

MILES FAULKNER STROLLED ACROSS THE dining room of the Savoy just after eight o'clock the following morning, to see his lawyer already seated at his usual place. No one gave him a second look as he weaved in and out of the tables.

'Good morning,' Booth Watson said, looking up at his only client, a man he neither liked nor trusted. However, Faulkner was the one person who made it possible for him to enjoy a lifestyle few of his colleagues at the bar could hope to emulate.

'Good morning, BW,' Miles replied, as he sat down in the seat opposite him.

A waiter quickly appeared, notebook open, pen poised. 'What will you have this morning, gentlemen?' he asked.

'The full English,' said Miles, without looking at the menu.

'And will you be having your usual, sir?'

'Yes,' confirmed Booth Watson, as he peered more closely

at his client. He had to admit the Swiss plastic surgeon had done a first-class job. No one would have recognized him as the man who had escaped from prison, attended his own funeral, and recently risen from the dead. The man seated opposite him bore no resemblance to the successful entrepreneur who had once owned one of the great art collections in private hands, but now looked every bit the retired naval captain and veteran of the Falklands campaign, who answered to the name of Captain Ralph Neville. But if William Warwick were to discover that his old nemesis was still alive, he wouldn't rest until he was back behind bars. For Warwick it would be personal, the man who escaped from his clutches, the man who made fools of the Metropolitan Police, the man who'd—

'Why did you need to see me so urgently?' Miles asked once the waiter had left.

'A journalist from *The Sunday Times* insight team called yesterday and asked me if I knew anything about a Raphael that had recently been sold by Christie's and turned out to be a fake.'

'What did you tell him?' asked Miles, nervously.

'I assured her that the original was part of the late Miles Faulkner's private collection, and is still hanging in his widow's villa in Monte Carlo.'

'Not for much longer,' confided Miles. 'Once Christina found out she wasn't a widow after all, I had no choice but to move the entire collection to a safer location before she could get her hands on it.'

'And where might that be?' asked Booth Watson, wondering if he would get an honest reply.

'I've found somewhere that doesn't have any locals to spy

on me, and only the passing seagulls can shit on me,' was all Miles offered.

'I'm glad to hear that, because I think it might be wise to leave England for a few weeks before you once again reappear as Captain Neville, and no better time than while Chief Inspector Warwick and his wife are enjoying a holiday in New York.'

'A holiday that was arranged for them by Christina to make sure they're both well out of harm's way when my wife and I get married for the second time.'

'But I thought Beth Warwick was going to be Christina's maid of honour?'

'She was, but that was before Christina discovered why I couldn't afford to be seen on board the SS *Alden*.'

'You have to admit your ex has her uses,' said Booth Watson, 'and one of them is to take advantage of the close relationship she's formed with Mrs Warwick.'

'Frankly, BW, I would have been better off if Christina had never discovered I was still alive. So please explain to me why I have to marry the damn woman a second time?'

'Because, in the end, it solves all your problems,' said Booth Watson. 'Don't forget she's the one person who can keep an eye on Detective Inspector Warwick without him ever becoming suspicious.'

'But if she were to switch sides?' said Faulkner.

'That's unlikely while you still hold the purse strings.'

Faulkner didn't look convinced. 'That wouldn't be the case if they discovered who Captain Ralph Neville was, and I ended up back in prison.'

'She'd still have to get past me, when Christina would quickly discover which side I'm on.'

'But you also don't have a choice,' said Miles, 'because you'd have to explain to the Bar Council why you've been representing an escaped criminal for the past couple of years, when you were well aware he was your former client.'

'All the more reason,' suggested Booth Watson, 'to make sure Christina signs a binding agreement that if she were to break she'd have just as much to lose as either of us.'

'And be sure she signs it before she marries Captain Neville, and certainly before the Warwicks return to Blighty.'

'Blighty?' said BW.

'That's Captain Neville-speak, old chap,' said Miles, sounding rather pleased with himself. 'So when are you seeing Christina?'

'I have a meeting with her in chambers tomorrow morning, when I intend to take her through the agreement clause by clause, stressing the consequences of her failing to sign it.'

'Good, because if she ever thought she could get her hands on my art collection simply by telling her friend Beth that Miles Faulkner is still alive and kicking . . .'

'You'd end up having breakfast in Pentonville and not the Savoy.'

'If that were to happen,' said Miles, 'I wouldn't hesitate to kill her.'

'I've already made that painfully clear,' said Booth Watson as the waiter returned with their breakfast. 'Though I confess, I haven't spelt it out quite that explicitly in the final agreement.'

• • •

'The full English breakfast, madam?'

'Certainly not, Franco,' said Beth, looking up at the name badge on his jacket. 'We'll both have cornflakes with melon and a slice of brown toast.'

'We can offer three types of melon, madam: cantaloupe, honeydew or water.'

'Water, thank you,' said William.

'A wise choice,' said Beth. 'I read somewhere that the average person puts on a pound a day during a sea voyage.'

'Then let's be thankful,' said William, 'that we're going to New York and not Sydney.'

'I'd be quite happy to go to Sydney on this floating palace,' admitted Beth as she glanced around the room. 'Have you noticed the little touches they've done so exquisitely? Fresh sheets, tablecloths and napkins every day. And when you return to your cabin, the bed has already been made with yesterday's clothes hung up and tidied away. I also love the way our laundry is returned each evening in those little wicker baskets. They must have dozens of people slaving away to make it all run so smoothly.'

'Eight hundred and thirty Filipinos are hidden below, madam,' chuckled their waiter, 'who serve our one thousand two hundred guests. However, nowadays we have an engine room, so the galley slaves no longer have to row.'

'And is that the slave master seated at the top of the table in the centre of the room?' asked Beth.

'Yes, that's Captain Buchanan,' said Franco, 'who, when he's not whipping the slaves, is chairman of the Pilgrim Line.'

'Captain Buchanan?' queried William.

'Yes, the chairman served as a naval officer during the

Second World War. It may also interest you to know he was a friend of the late Miles Faulkner and his wife Christina, who, incidentally, called to tell us you would be taking their place and asked us to take special care of you.'

'Did she indeed?' said William.

'Is that the chairman's wife sitting at the other end of the table?' said Beth.

'Yes, madam,' replied Franco. 'Mr and Mrs Buchanan are almost always the first to arrive for breakfast,' he commented, before leaving to fulfil their order.

'He looks every bit as formidable as Miles Faulkner,' said Beth, taking a closer look at the chairman, 'although he's obviously deployed his talents to achieve something far more worthwhile than robbing his fellow man.'

'Fraser Buchanan was born in Glasgow in 1921,' said William. 'He left school at the age of fourteen, and joined the merchant navy as a deckhand. When the war broke out, he transferred to the Royal Navy as a rating, but ended up as a lieutenant on HMS *Nelson*. Despite being made up to captain in 1945, he resigned his commission a few days after the armistice was signed. He returned to Scotland and bought a small passenger and car ferry company that operated from the mainland to the island of Iona. He now owns a fleet of twenty-six vessels, and the Pilgrim Line is second only to Cunard in size and reputation.'

'Information no doubt picked up from young James while I was at my yoga class?' suggested Beth.

'No, you can read the history of the company in the *Ship's Log*, which I found on my bedside table,' said William, as Franco placed two bowls of cornflakes and a slice of watermelon in front of them.

'Who's that who's just sat down next to Mrs Buchanan?' whispered William.

'Forgive my husband, Franco,' said Beth, 'he's a detective and for him life is one endless investigation.'

'That's Hamish Buchanan,' said Franco, 'the chairman's eldest son. Until recently he was the deputy chairman of the company.'

'Until recently?' prompted William. 'But he can't be a day over forty.'

'Behave yourself,' said Beth.

'If the press are to be believed,' confided Franco, 'he was replaced at the last annual general meeting by his brother Angus, who's just walked in with his wife Alice and their son . . .'

'James,' said William.

'Ah!' said Franco. 'You've already come across the boy wonder.'

'And the lady who's just sat down on Mr Buchanan's left? I notice she didn't even bother to say good morning to the chairman.'

'That's Mr Hamish's wife, Sara.'

'Why would she agree to come on this trip if her husband has just been sacked?' asked Beth.

'Replaced by his brother Angus, is the official line,' said Franco, as he poured her a steaming cup of black coffee. 'And as Mr Hamish is still a director of the company, he'll be expected to attend the board meeting that is always held on the last day of the voyage.'

'You seem remarkably well-informed, Franco,' said William.

Franco made no comment before moving on to the next table.

'What a fun trip this is turning out to be,' said Beth, stifling a yawn while still looking across at the chairman's table. 'I wonder who the woman is who's just joined them.'

'You're worse than I am,' said William, as he watched James and Hamish stand as an older woman took her place at the table. 'She looks about the same age as the chairman and, as they both have red hair, I wouldn't be surprised if she's his sister.' William continued to study the seating plan, noting that every place had been carefully allocated by the chairman to make sure he was always in control.

'You can always ask James who she is while I'm at my yoga class. But let's forget about the Buchanan family for a few moments, while I tell you what I've got planned for us during our week in New York.'

'The Met, I presume, will be at the top of your list,' said William, 'and I've no doubt it will require more than one visit.'

'Three,' said Beth. 'Everything before 1850 on Saturday, Indigenous Art on Monday, and on Wednesday I want to see the Impressionist collection, which Tim Knox assures me is second only to the Musée d'Orsay.'

'Phew . . . do we get pit stops on Tuesday and Thursday?' asked William after taking a sip of coffee.

'Certainly not. We'll visit the Frick on Tuesday, where . . .'

'. . . we'll see a remarkable Holbein of Thomas Cromwell, and Bellini's *St Francis in Ecstasy*.'

'I sometimes forget that you're a semi-educated caveman.'

'By my wife since leaving university,' responded William. 'And on Thursday?'

'On to the MoMA. A chance to see the finest examples

of the Cubist period: Picasso and Braque, when we'll find out if you can tell the difference.'

'Won't their names be on the bottom of the pictures?' teased William.

'That's for tourists, who won't be joining us in the evenings.'

'Then who will be?'

'We have tickets for the Lincoln Center. The New York Symphony Orchestra, playing Brahms.'

'It has to be the second piano concerto in B Major,' said William, 'one of your favourites.'

'And I haven't forgotten one of your favourites,' retorted Beth, 'because on Friday evening, the night before we fly home, we have tickets to see Ella Fitzgerald at Carnegie Hall.'

'How did you manage that? It must have been sold out for months!'

'Christina fixed it. Seems she knows someone on the board.' Beth paused for a moment before adding, 'I'm beginning to feel guilty about her.'

'Why? The reason she couldn't make the trip to New York is because she's getting married to Ralph, and she was only too delighted to find someone to take her place at the last moment.'

'It's the marriage I'm feeling guilty about. Don't forget she originally asked me to be her maid of honour. But because we took up her generous offer, I'll miss the wedding.'

'Didn't you find that a bit of a coincidence?'

'Not really. August fifteenth was the only Saturday before the end of September when they could get married at her parish church in Limpton-in-the-Marsh, which left her stuck with the tickets. We shouldn't look a gift horse in the mouth.'

William decided this wasn't the time to tell Beth it had taken him only one phone call to discover that Christina's parish church had been available a fortnight before, after which she and Captain Ralph Neville could easily have taken their honeymoon on the ship. However, if he'd refused to join Beth on the voyage so he could keep a closer eye on Christina and her new husband, his own wife might well have sailed off into the sunset without him.

'Have you noticed that Sara Buchanan hasn't spoken one word to the chairman since she sat down?' said Beth, still staring at the captain's table.

'Possibly because he sacked her husband as deputy chairman,' suggested William, as he buttered a second piece of toast.

'What else have you spotted while you pretended to be listening to me?'

'Hamish Buchanan has been deep in conversation with his mother, while James is feigning not to be interested, although he's taking in every word.'

'Which he'll no doubt report back to you, now you've recruited him as your undercover agent for the trip.'

'James appointed himself. And as he's the chairman's grandson, he's well-placed to supply endless pieces of inside information.'

'For a man, it's information,' commented Beth. 'For a woman, it's gossip.'

'James has already warned me that he wouldn't be surprised if an all-out row broke out at some time during the voyage,' added William, ignoring Beth's comment.

'I'd like to be a salt cellar on that table,' admitted Beth.

'Behave yourself, or I'll take a closer look at the young man who's in charge of your yoga class.'

'His name's Stefan. All the other middle-aged women in the class fancy him,' she sighed, 'so I'm not in with much of a chance.'

'You are not middle-aged,' said William, taking her hand.

'Thank you, caveman, but I've already had two thirtieth birthdays, just in case you hadn't noticed, and the children will soon be off to nursery school.'

'I wonder how our parents are coping with them.'

'Your father will have Artemisia doing torts . . .'

'. . . while your mother will be teaching Peter to draw.'

'Lucky children,' they both said simultaneously.

'Still, back to the present,' said Beth, picking up a copy of the daily cruise programme. 'There's a talk in the lecture theatre this morning that I'd like to go to.'

William raised an eyebrow.

'Lady Catherine Whittaker on the operas of Puccini.'

'I just might give it a miss. Mind you, if she's the wife of Mr Justice Whittaker,' said William, looking around the room, 'it would be fascinating to have a chat with him.'

'And there's a different show in the theatre every evening,' continued Beth. 'Tonight it's Lazaro, a magician, who will apparently shock and surprise as he makes objects and even passengers disappear before our eyes. We can go to either the seven o'clock or the nine o'clock performance.'

'Which sitting would you prefer for dinner?' asked Franco, when he returned to their table and began to pour them a second coffee.

'What time do the chairman and his family come down in the evening?' asked William.

'Around eight thirty, sir, when they have cocktails before dining.'

'Then we'll take the second sitting.'

'What are you up to?' asked Beth, looking closely at her husband.

'I have a feeling that if we attend the second sitting, we'll have more shocks and surprises, and possibly see more people disappearing before our eyes, than Lazaro will manage in the theatre.'

CHAPTER 3

BOOTH WATSON ROSE FROM BEHIND his desk when his reluctant client entered the room. Mrs Christina Faulkner sat down opposite him, without bothering to shake hands with her husband's lawyer.

Booth Watson looked across at the elegantly dressed lady who had been married to his client for eleven years, before they both decided to go their separate ways.

Both of them had had countless affairs, long before she'd issued divorce proceedings. However, after Miles was convicted of the theft of a Caravaggio and sent to jail, Christina felt on stronger ground until he died, when she assumed she had lost everything. That was before she turned up at the funeral to discover that her late husband was very much alive, and would have to cut a deal with her if he was going to be allowed to stay that way. Christina didn't need to be told it was a game changer.

But the merry widow had also worked out that Miles

Faulkner – or Captain Ralph Neville as he was now – was better alive than dead, because that way she could lay her hands on at least half of Miles's fabled art collection, which she had signed away in their original divorce settlement.

Booth Watson was well aware of the shifting sands he was tiptoeing over, but still had one ace up his sleeve. Christina's love of money.

'I thought we ought to have a word about what will happen after the wedding has taken place, Mrs Faulkner,' said Booth Watson.

'Am I allowed to ask what you and Miles have decided on my behalf?' asked Christina.

'There shouldn't be a great deal of difference from the present situation,' parried Booth Watson, ignoring the jibe. 'You will retain your home in the country, along with the Belgravia apartment. However, in future Monte Carlo will be out of bounds.'

'Found someone else, has he?'

Somewhere else, Booth Watson could have told her, but that was not part of his brief. 'You will continue to receive two thousand pounds a week for expenses, while retaining your housekeeper, maid and chauffeur.'

'And have you two decided where you'll be spending my honeymoon?' asked Christina, making no attempt to hide any sarcasm.

'Miles will not be spending a great deal of time in England during the next few months, so it will in effect be a marriage of convenience. To that end I have drawn up a binding agreement, which is ready for you to sign. Just remember, you get far more than you could have hoped for in return for your silence. You needn't bother to read it as there won't be any amendments.'

'So we won't be living together?' said Christina, pretending to sound shocked.

'That was never the plan, as you well know. Miles has no objection to you continuing your present lifestyle, but he would ask you to be a little more discreet in future, and to be available to accompany him as Mrs Ralph Neville on what we might describe as formal occasions.'

'And if I'm not willing to sign?' said Christina, sitting back, despite the fact that Booth Watson had already taken the top off his pen, turned to the last page and planted a forefinger on the dotted line.

'You will be destitute, and end up living in sheltered accommodation.'

'While Miles will be back in jail for a very long time, unless . . .'

'Unless?' repeated Booth Watson.

'Unless he gives me the additional million I was promised in the original divorce settlement. I don't have to remind you, Mr Booth Watson, that Miles is dead. Like you, I attended his funeral in Geneva, where I was touched by your moving address. If the police were to discover those were not his ashes I was presented with by the compliant priest, it might be a lot more than a million he ends up having to sacrifice. However, if Miles feels unable to keep his word, you can send back the wedding cake and cancel the caterers.'

A long silence followed, during which both sides waited for the other to blink.

'And do remind him I've still got his ashes, which is no more than my insurance policy should he fail to deliver.'

'Life insurance policies usually only pay out when you die.'

'I left the urn to Detective Inspector William Warwick in my will, which I think might help him to make up his mind.'

• • •

'Beware,' said William, as he took a seat in the corner of an alcove opposite the fledgling detective. 'If I were a contract killer, I would have known exactly where to find you at this time of day, which would make bumping you off that much easier. If you're going to be a detective, you can't afford to be a creature of habit. In future, James, I'll expect you to find me. And I'll never be in the same place twice.'

'But a contract killer isn't likely to be on board a luxury cruise liner.'

'Unless his victim is on the way to New York, leaving us with over two thousand suspects.'

'I saw you having breakfast with your wife this morning,' said James, wanting to move on.

'Never assume anything,' said William. 'Always open any investigation with a blank page.'

'But you introduced her as your wife.'

'Proves nothing.'

'She was wearing a wedding ring.'

'Married women have been known to have affairs.'

'I don't think a mistress would have ordered breakfast for you,' said James, fighting back.

'A fair assumption, but not beyond reasonable doubt. What's the equivalent legal term in America?'

'On the balance of judgement,' replied James. 'I also noticed that your wife appeared to be more interested in our table than yours,' he continued, not allowing him to change the subject.

'That's called marriage,' said William with a chuckle. 'But I confess, she's already turned your family into a gothic novel, with the juicy details supplied by our waiter.'

'Franco,' said James. 'He's served on my grandfather's ships for over thirty years. No one knows the company, or the family, better. My grandfather offered him the chance to be the maître d' on *The Pilgrim*, our flagship vessel, but he turned the old man down.'

'Why would he do that?' asked William.

'He told me he didn't want to lose contact with the passengers, but I suspect it's more likely he didn't want to forgo the tips he picks up on every trip.' James paused. 'I doubt if Franco is his real name, and he sure isn't Italian by birth.'

'Proof?' demanded William.

'The accent slips occasionally, and I once asked his opinion of Caruso, and it was clear he'd never heard of the great tenor.'

'Reason for suspicion, but not proof. Although I do think he's hiding something.'

'What makes you say that?'

'I've seen that look before when someone discovers I'm a copper.'

'He did a short spell in prison before he joined the company,' said James. 'But even my grandfather doesn't know about that.'

'How did you find out?'

'I was once on a voyage out of Southampton, when he asked to change tables.'

'Did you find out why?'

'One of the passengers came from somewhere called Hackney, and I saw a look of recognition on his face when he spotted Franco. I arranged for him and his wife to sit at the captain's table one evening, in exchange for information. Even Franco doesn't know I know. Mind you, there but for the grace of God goes my grandfather. Several well-chronicled near misses and one appearance in court, when the jury concluded "Not proven".'

'A less than subtle Scottish judgement. It usually means that both the judge and the jury aren't in much doubt that the accused is guilty, but there isn't enough evidence to convict. However, if you want to scale the heights your grandfather has reached, I suspect you'll have to take the occasional risk along the way, especially when you start out with nothing.'

'Grandpa started out with less than nothing. When his father died, he left his wife and two children with debts of around a hundred pounds. Just imagine how much that would be in today's money. It took her years to pay it off, which was probably the reason she died so young.'

'It may also explain why he's so tough on his own children.'

'Evidence?' demanded James, imitating his tutor.

'Franco told me that your uncle Hamish was recently sacked as deputy chairman of the company at the recent AGM. To be fair, I think the word he used was "replaced".'

'That's common knowledge,' said James. 'It was well covered by the press on both sides of the Atlantic. I heard my father telling Mother that only the laws of libel prevented the papers from publishing the whole story.'

Franco appeared carrying a tray with a coffee and a hot chocolate.

'Shall I tell the Chief Inspector the whole story about why my father became deputy chairman, Franco?' said James, as the hot chocolate was placed on the table in front of him.

'As long as you leave me out of it,' said Franco, before disappearing even more quickly than he had materialised.

'I doubt if you, or your father, know the whole story,' said William. 'I suspect the chairman has secrets he intends to take to his grave.'

'Great-Aunt Flora will know the whole story,' said James confidently.

'Great-Aunt Flora?' asked William, leaving her name floating in the air, in the hope it would induce the young man to even greater indiscretions.

'After Grandfather left home to join the merchant navy, his sister Flora became the first person in our family to go to university. After graduating from Glasgow with an honours degree in math, she studied accountancy, where she came top of her year. Well, top equal. It seems they weren't quite ready to admit that a woman might be brighter than any man from her intake. That all happened around the time Grandpa was discharged from the Royal Navy, having served King and country with distinction, as he never stops reminding us. He then somehow raised enough money to buy a clapped-out – his expression – ferry company that transported vehicles and passengers from the mainland to the island of Iona.'

'I've sailed on one of those boats myself,' said William.

'Great-Aunt Flora told him he was bonkers, but as there weren't many firms offering women serious jobs after the war, she reluctantly joined the company and took charge of the books. Her favourite expression remains: "While he raised the pounds, I took care of the pennies." However, despite her natural caution and shrewd common sense, the company nearly went under on more than one occasion.'

'What self-made millionaire hasn't had to face that problem at some time in their career?'

'On one occasion, Grandfather was within twenty-four hours of declaring bankruptcy, and would have done if the Dundee Bank of Trade and Commerce hadn't come to his rescue. Even I haven't worked out how he pulled that one off. All I know for certain is that when his first cruise ship was being built on the Clyde, at the end of one particular week he couldn't afford to pay the dockers' wages, and they threatened to go out on strike. He once told me he didn't sleep for a week, and this is a man who slept soundly every night during the Battle of the Atlantic.'

'I read all about the role he played in that encounter in the *Ship's Log*.'

'Not to be relied on,' said James, tossing a ball in the air.

'Why not?' asked William, genuinely curious.

'Grandfather wrote it himself. Or to be more accurate, should I be called to give evidence in court, he dictated every word of it to Kaye Patterson, his private secretary.'

'Who, I suspect, was the lady seated next to you at breakfast.'

'Not bad, Chief Inspector. But if I told you my

grandfather has two secretaries, one who can spell and one who can't, which is Kaye?'

'The one who can.'

'What makes you so sure of that?'

'Your grandmother appeared to be having an animated conversation with her, which she was clearly enjoying,' said William, as Franco reappeared by their side.

'Anything more, gentlemen?' he asked.

'No thank you, Franco,' said James.

'Why does Franco want the passengers to think he's from Italy?' asked William once the waiter had left them.

'He once told me you get better tips if the passengers think you're Italian.'

'I didn't realize you were meant to tip the staff,' said William, feeling slightly embarrassed.

'Not until we dock in New York,' James reassured him. 'Small brown envelopes will be left in your cabin for your maid and your waiter. One hundred dollars each is the going rate, unless you feel they've done a particularly good job.'

'You adore your grandfather, don't you?' said William, not letting him off the hook.

'Unashamedly. He's the reason I'm confident I'll be offered a place at Harvard.'

'Because of his money and connections?'

'No, I don't need those. Something far more important. I've inherited his energy and competitive spirit, although I lack his entrepreneurial genius.'

'I suspect he still hopes you'll become chairman of the company one day, by which time it will need a safe pair of hands to replace his entrepreneurial genius.'

'That's never going to happen. My father may well succeed him, but not me.'

'How does your uncle Hamish feel about that?'

'Still thinks he's in with a chance of becoming chairman, otherwise he wouldn't be hanging around, humiliating himself and his wife by joining us on this voyage.'

'That bad?'

'Worse. I think he'd do anything to stop my father becoming chairman. And if he wouldn't, Aunt Sara certainly would.'

'But by replacing him with your father as deputy chairman, your grandfather couldn't have made his position any clearer.'

'True, but don't forget, Uncle Hamish is still on the main board, and nobody can be sure which way Great-Aunt Flora will jump when the time comes to appoint the next chairman; she may well have the casting vote. Not that the word retirement is one I've ever heard cross Grandfather's lips.'

'How do you know so much about what's going on when you're just a . . .'

'School kid? That's something else I've turned to my advantage. When I was growing up, my parents didn't realize I was listening to every word they said at the breakfast table. But they've all become a lot more cautious recently, especially Uncle Hamish, so I'm going to have to be far more cunning in the future. That's where you come in.'

William was once again taken by surprise, but he didn't have to ask James what he had in mind.

'I'll tell you everything I know about my family, if you'll show me how to take advantage of it. With your knowledge and experience, I may be able to stay a yard ahead of Uncle Hamish.'

'But why bother, if you have no interest in joining the company?'

'I still want my father to be the next chairman, so that in time I'll end up owning the Pilgrim Line.'

'You can add being devious to the gifts you inherited from your grandfather,' said William, giving James a warm smile.

'Possibly. But I still need to be even more cunning than my uncle Hamish, and more devious than Aunt Sara, if I'm going to have any chance of inheriting the company. Don't forget they also have children who are only a little younger than me.'

'In which case you're going to have to stop thinking like a detective, and start thinking like a criminal.'

CHAPTER 4

'SHE DEMANDED WHAT?' SAID MILES, as the waiter poured them both a steaming black coffee.

'The million she was promised in the original divorce settlement,' said Booth Watson.

'But unfortunately I died before the decree nisi was signed.'

'And she's got your ashes to prove it.'

'So what?'

'You clearly haven't heard of Crick and Watson,' said Booth Watson, 'because they've made it possible for her to prove you're very much alive.'

'Not if she's dead she can't,' said Faulkner.

'If Christina were to suffer an untimely death,' said Booth Watson, choosing his words carefully, 'the first person they'd question would be her new husband, Captain Ralph Neville RN. It wouldn't take them too long to work out his true identity. So I'm recommending you hand over the million if you want to remain a free man.'

'Over my dead body,' said Miles emphatically.

'Which is precisely what I expect Christina has in mind, if she were to tell her friend Beth Warwick who she's actually about to marry.'

'If she did, she'd be penniless overnight.'

'I'm not sure that's a gamble you can take. Heaven knows what she'd get up to while you were back in prison and safely out of harm's way. I'm bound to ask, is a single painting worth a life sentence?'

Miles didn't respond while the waiter served them both and only said 'possibly not' after he'd left.

'All the more reason for you to be out of the country for the next few weeks while I make sure Christina keeps to her side of the bargain, and that Captain Ralph Neville can safely return to these shores whenever it suits him.'

'I'd always planned to move into my new home immediately after the wedding,' said Miles. 'Somewhere, I can assure you, BW, where neither Warwick nor Christina will ever find me or my paintings.'

'I'm glad to hear it. But in my opinion we need to keep Christina on our side while she's still able to supply inside information on the Warwicks. Don't forget how close she is to Beth Warwick, who innocently passes on information about what her husband is up to.'

'Or not so innocently,' suggested Miles.

'With that in mind, I'm planning to put Superintendent Lamont back on the payroll to keep an eye on her.'

'Ex-Superintendent,' Miles reminded him. 'Don't forget he's no longer on the inside and, more important, that man will do anything for money while he has a "trophy wife" who keeps his bank balance in the red, not to mention his genius for backing horses that can't find their way to the winner's enclosure.'

'That might well be the case. But don't forget that the ex-Superintendent was once Commander Hawksby's second-in-command.'

'Until he had to resign.'

'But he still knows a lot of people on the inside, and one in particular.'

'Do I know him?'

'Her. She's part of William Warwick's inner team, and, more important, she isn't averse to receiving the occasional brown envelope.'

'Then keep supplying them. That way we can stay ahead of both Christina and the Warwicks.'

'So you're willing to cough up the million she's demanding?'

Miles smiled as he picked up his knife and fork. 'On one condition,' he said. 'Make it clear that if Christina ever breaks the agreement, I'll dock her monthly allowance until the million is paid back.'

• • •

'So how was the lecture?' asked William, pulling back Beth's chair before she took her place at their table.

'We listened to different arias from *La bohème*, after which Catherine explained the dramatic realism of Puccini's operas. I can't wait for tomorrow.'

'*Tosca* or *Madame Butterfly*?' asked William as Franco handed him a menu.

'*Madame Butterfly* – want to join us?'

'I fear I'll be otherwise occupied with a chrysalis who's

hoping to become a butterfly. Did you find out if she's the wife of Mr Justice Whittaker?'

'The same, and Charlotte has invited us to join them for dinner tomorrow evening,' said Beth. William became distracted when Fraser Buchanan entered the dining room with his wife on his arm. He was dressed in a smart double-breasted dinner jacket that disguised his weight, while she wore an elegant long cream gown which caused several women in the room to take a second look, including Beth.

The chairman took his place at the top of the table. All the men stood and waited for his wife to take her seat at the other end of the table – a cricket pitch away.

'Who's the man sitting next to the chairman's sister, Flora?' asked Beth, once Franco had taken their order.

'Andrew Lockhart,' said William. 'He's the company's doctor and sits on the main board. He's also the chairman's personal physician. Buchanan had a heart attack a couple of years ago and since then Lockhart has accompanied him on every trip.'

'I'm not surprised,' said Beth. 'He must be two or three stone overweight.'

'I'd be two or three stone overweight,' said William, 'if I spent half my life on a cruise liner.'

'Would you like to order, madam?' said Franco.

'Two consommés followed by Caesar salads,' said Beth without looking at the menu.

William smiled as he closed his menu and handed it back to Franco.

'Are you married, Franco?' he asked innocently.

'Only for fourteen weeks a year, sir.'

'About the same as me,' said Beth, taking William's hand.

• • •

The British have many qualities and even more failings, George Bernard Shaw once told the English Speakers' Union, and one of those qualities is to ignore an altercation that's taking place in front of them. The Italians can't resist watching from a distance, the Germans want to take sides, while the Irish just have to join in.

Beth pretended to be unaware of the raised voices coming from the chairman's table, while continuing to eat her consommé.

'I thought tonight's magician . . .' began William.

'Shh,' said Beth. 'As you've got a far better view of what's going on than me, you can give me a blow-by-blow account.'

William suppressed a smile, and began taking a closer interest in the Buchanans' table.

'It looks to me as if the chairman is having a heated discussion with his former deputy chairman, while the rest of the table is studiously ignoring both of them.'

'They don't want to get involved,' suggested Beth.

'A shrewd observation.'

'So what's the row about?'

'Not sure. I can only catch the odd word. But don't despair, James will give me a blow-by-blow account in the morning.'

'I can't wait until then,' said Beth, sounding exasperated. 'They might all have murdered each other by the time you next meet up with James. I want to know now.'

'It seems to be something to do with Hamish Buchanan's drinking habits,' said William, but he stopped in mid-sentence when Franco reappeared with their main courses. He placed the two Caesar salads in front of his guests as if nothing untoward was happening just a couple of tables away.

'I presume you've seen all this many times before,' said Beth, looking up at him.

'Not quite this bad, madam,' Franco admitted, as he poured them both a glass of white wine.

'Perhaps it was unwise for the whole family to travel back to New York together,' suggested Beth, 'after what took place at last year's AGM.'

'James tells me his grandfather insisted on it,' said William, 'despite the bad feeling between him and his son Hamish. I suspect it's no more than background noise to the old man.'

'I'm only glad I'm not serving on that table this evening,' said Franco, before placing the wine bottle back in its ice bucket and leaving them.

'I wish I was,' said Beth, as she watched Hamish Buchanan take a silver hip flask from an inside pocket and pour the contents into his coffee.

• • •

'I thought you told me you'd stopped drinking!' barked the chairman from the top of the table.

'Indeed I have,' replied Hamish as he screwed the top back on the flask. 'This is no more than a mild sedative prescribed by Dr Lockhart to help me sleep, because as you well know, Father, I'm not a good sailor.'

'The sea is as flat as a pancake tonight,' retorted the chairman. 'Not to mention the fact that I've spent a fortune on stabilisers to ensure that every passenger is guaranteed a smooth voyage. Once you're safely tucked up in bed you wouldn't even know we were at sea.' Hamish took another sip from his hip flask. 'I'd like to taste that so-called sedative.' Fraser held out his hand, as if it were a command, not a request.

'As you wish, Father,' said Hamish, who handed the silver flask to his aunt Flora, who in turn passed it up the table to the chairman. Several passengers, including Beth and William, watched as Fraser unscrewed the top, put the flask to his lips and took a long swig. They all waited for an explosion.

The chairman paused for a moment. 'Foul stuff,' he announced, before screwing the top back on the flask.

'Would it be too much to ask for an apology?' asked Hamish's wife, as Fraser passed the flask back down the table. Everyone turned to see how the chairman would react to Sara's suggestion.

'I don't think so, my dear,' replied Fraser coolly, 'because no one believes for a moment that Hamish has given up drinking. If you doubt me, I suggest you check the contents of your drinks cabinet when you return to your cabin after dinner.'

Hamish didn't respond, but unscrewed the top of the hip flask and took another long gulp, before screwing the top back on and placing it in an inside pocket.

• • •

Commander Hawksby sat at his desk, thinking about his next meeting and the potential consequences of getting it wrong. He knew they called him 'The Hawk' behind his back, which he considered a compliment – but it wouldn't be too long before he retired and he didn't want his reputation to be damaged so late in his career. DI Ross Hogan was the missing piece in the jigsaw that would complete the picture.

William Warwick was the natural leader of the team but DS Adaja, impressive though he was, was not ready to take on the role of second-in-command. DS Roycroft wouldn't have wanted the job, while DC Pankhurst would in time overtake both of them, but not yet.

The Hawk didn't need to check Ross Hogan's record. He'd served four years with the SAS, before joining the Met. He'd spent only a couple of years on the beat before taking his detective's exam and joining the murder squad. Four years later he was among those chosen few to go undercover, where he found his calling. If a group of rebels had formed a gang, he would have been their leader. He had a Queen's Gallantry Medal, three official warnings, and a suspension for sleeping with a suspect to complete his CV. However, The Hawk knew he couldn't leave him undercover for much longer. If Ross was ever to return to the real world and still be capable of obeying an order, it had to be before it was too late for him to change his ways. Was it already too late? Would he resign?

Ross had already played a crucial role in gathering enough evidence to convict Miles Faulkner and get him sent down, even going to prison himself to gather the necessary evidence. Even risk-takers considered him a risk-taker.

When Faulkner escaped, Ross had gone AWOL and become even more determined to snap the handcuffs back on him, because he never believed for one moment that Faulkner was dead.

There was a knock on the door.

'Enter,' said The Hawk.

Anyone who'd seen the man who walked into Commander Hawksby's office that morning would never have believed he was a police officer. Dressed in a grubby T-shirt, torn jeans and a leather jacket, Ross Hogan looked more like a bother boy than an upholder of the law.

'Good morning, sir,' he said as he sat down.

The Hawk stared at his secret weapon, wondering how he would break the news, but Ross came to his rescue.

'As you called me into the Yard for this morning's meeting, sir, should I assume my days as an undercover officer are numbered?'

'Over,' said The Hawk. 'You've been in the field for far too long, Ross. Although you'll be almost impossible to replace, I've decided it's time for you to rejoin the human race.'

'Which humans did you have in mind, sir?'

'I've recently set up a small cold case unit to deal with unsolved murders, some of which have been gathering dust for years.'

'Who'll be the SIO in charge of the unit?'

'Chief Inspector Warwick.'

Ross nodded. 'I've watched him at close quarters over the past couple of years, and I wasn't surprised by his promotion. How exactly would I fit in?'

'The rest of the team consists of DS Paul Adaja, DS Jackie

Roycroft and DC Rebecca Pankhurst, all fine officers. But I want you, Detective Inspector Hogan, to act as William's second-in-command.'

Ross smiled. 'Is there an alternative, sir?'

'Yes, you could return to your old patch in Chiswick, as a traffic warden.'

'Or I could resign.'

'You're unemployable,' said The Hawk, unable to resist a smile. 'Unless you plan to end up as a seedy private eye, eavesdropping on errant husbands, which is hardly your style.'

'When do I start?'

'Chief Inspector Warwick will be back in ten days' time. He's presently having a well-earned holiday on the high seas, so I suggest you also take a break until he returns. Just make sure you've shaved and have a bath before you meet the choirboy.'

'No one will recognize me,' said Ross.

'That's all part of my plan,' said the commander.

• • •

Franco was pouring hot chocolate sauce over a large portion of vanilla ice cream when a woman's shrill scream echoed round the dining room. Beth swung around to see Fraser Buchanan leaning forward, shaking and gasping for breath as he clung to the edge of the table.

Dr Lockhart leapt up and was quickly by his side. He untied the chairman's bow tie and loosened the collar of his dress shirt. Franco rushed across to join him.

'Is there anything I can do to help?' he asked.

'I need a stretcher immediately,' said the doctor calmly, 'and get my medical bag from the infirmary.'

Franco ran out of the room, while all the other diners abandoned their meals and became an uninvited audience to the drama taking place in front of them.

Mrs Buchanan had left her seat at the other end of the table and took her husband's hand. She was trembling, but seemed otherwise remarkably calm, allowing the doctor to carry out his calling while everyone else stared on in shock. Well, not everyone. William's eyes never left Hamish Buchanan, who showed no emotion, while his brother Angus joined their mother and placed an arm gently around her shoulders.

Suddenly, Fraser Buchanan turned white, and his head dropped to the table. The doctor tried desperately to revive him, but William knew it could only be a matter of time before he confirmed that the chairman was dead.

Mrs Buchanan sobbed as she knelt down beside her husband and took him in her arms. James burst into tears, a child once again. From a distance, William studied the faces of those seated at the chairman's table. His eyes moved slowly around the rest of the family as he searched for clues, quite forgetting he was on holiday. Not all of them displayed grief, and two of them didn't even appear to be surprised by what had taken place. The dining room door suddenly swung open and Franco came rushing back in clutching the doctor's bag. He was followed by two young ratings carrying a canvas stretcher.

William found himself instinctively getting up from his place and walking across to the chairman's table to see if there was anything he could do to help.

'We don't require your assistance, Chief Inspector,' said Hamish Buchanan as the ratings gently lifted his father onto the stretcher. 'You have no authority aboard this vessel.'

An unprompted and unnecessary comment, was William's first thought, which made him wonder if this tragic event might not be quite as straightforward as it appeared. He recalled The Hawk's advice when investigating an untimely death: *Listen, listen, listen. If you give people enough rope, sometimes they'll hang themselves.* However, William knew Hamish Buchanan was correct, and was about to return to his table and reluctantly mind his own business when Angus Buchanan intervened, saying, 'Unless I give him that authority.'

'I think you'll find, Angus, that I'm now head of the family,' countered Hamish, glaring at his brother.

'I shouldn't have to remind you, Hamish, that I am now deputy chairman of the Pilgrim Line, and this tragedy has taken place on one of the company's ships.'

Both men continued to stare belligerently at each other, until Hamish said, 'Perhaps we should seek Dr Lockhart's opinion.'

'Your father has suffered a massive heart attack. As we all know, it wasn't his first.'

William couldn't help feeling that the doctor's words sounded a little too well rehearsed. Even more strange, he showed no sign of grief at the death of his old friend, as if he were a professional onlooker, no more.

'As I said, we have no need of your services, Chief Inspector,' prompted Hamish, turning to his aunt for support. But she didn't reply immediately.

'I think it might be wise to allow the Chief Inspector to

carry out a routine inquiry,' said Flora, struggling to compose herself in her new role as the grand dame of the family. 'We wouldn't want anyone to suggest that the family was involved in a cover-up.'

No one contradicted her.

Even Hamish remained silent as the body of the late chairman was carried out of the dining room by the two ratings, accompanied by the doctor and Mrs Buchanan.

'What do you want us to do, Chief Inspector?' asked Flora, who seemed to have taken over command.

'With the exception of James, I'd like you all to return to your cabins, and remain there until I've had a chance to speak to every one of you. Mr Buchanan, before you go, perhaps you would be kind enough to leave your hip flask on the table.'

Hamish hesitated for a moment before removing the silver flask from an inside pocket and placing it on the table. A smile flickered across his face when he saw the commodore entering the dining room with Franco following a yard behind.

'Ah,' he said. 'The person who has ultimate authority on his own ship. Perhaps you could tell Chief Inspector Warwick that we no longer have any need of his services.'

'Mr Buchanan is correct to remind you, Chief Inspector, that I am the master of this vessel,' said the commodore gravely, 'and that my decision is final.'

'I accept your authority without question,' said William.

Hamish picked up the silver flask and put it back in his pocket.

'With that in mind, Chief Inspector,' said the commodore, 'I would be grateful if you felt able to carry out a preliminary investigation. While I have no doubt that you'll find the chairman died of a heart attack, your confirmation will settle the matter. How would you like to begin your inquiry?'

'By asking Mr Hamish Buchanan to put his silver hip flask back on the table.'

CHAPTER 5

EX-SUPERINTENDENT LAMONT WAS AT HOME reading the *Racing Post* when Mr Booth Watson QC's clerk called to inform him that the head of chambers required his presence at ten o'clock the following morning. It was the first time Booth Watson had been in touch since the police corruption trial at the Old Bailey when Jerry Summers, a Detective Sergeant who'd taken one risk too many, had ended up going down for ten years because Lamont had failed to remove a vital piece of evidence that would have got Summers off. Lamont had rather assumed after that particular balls-up, Booth Watson wouldn't be requiring his services again. Although he intensely disliked the oleaginous QC, the expression 'Beggars can't be choosers' ensured that he would be on time for the appointment.

During the past few weeks, he'd also done a couple of jobs for Mrs Christina Faulkner, and wondered if Booth Watson might consider that a conflict of interest. After he'd checked his bank balance, he decided not to mention his double-dating to either party. Lamont made sure he was sitting in the waiting room of No. 1 Fetter Court at ten to ten the following morning. He was kept waiting.

When the Head of Chambers eventually called for him, he didn't mention Summers or the key piece of evidence Lamont should have switched, but got straight to the point.

'I need to know what your old friend Warwick is up to at the moment.'

'Warwick's no friend of mine,' said Lamont, almost spitting out the words.

'I'm glad to hear that,' said Booth Watson. 'In which case it should make your task even more enjoyable. I can tell you that the Inspector and his wife are currently sailing first class to New York aboard the *Alden*.'

'A holiday that must have been paid for by his father, because he certainly couldn't afford to travel first class on a Chief Inspector's salary.'

Booth Watson knew exactly who had paid for the trip, but satisfied himself with repeating the words, '*Chief* Inspector?'

'Warwick was promoted following the success of the Summers trial,' said Lamont, who immediately regretted the word 'success', as it produced a scowl on his paymaster's lips.

'Can you tell me anything about this new squad he's heading up?'

'Unit,' said Lamont.

The scowl returned; Booth Watson didn't like to be corrected, even by a judge.

Lamont ploughed on. 'Warwick has four officers under

his command. DS Paul Adaja, who isn't one of us, DS Jackie Roycroft, she's already on my payroll, and DC Rebecca Pankhurst, who's still wet behind the ears. They'll be joined by DI Ross Hogan, but not before Warwick returns from his holiday.'

'I don't know Hogan,' said Booth Watson. 'What can you tell me about him?'

'Tough, resilient, but a bit of a maverick, who's not averse to taking the occasional risk. He's been working undercover for the past three years, but Hawksby must have decided to bring him in from the cold.'

'Why?' demanded Booth Watson.

'Needed to bolster the team with a little sharp-end experience would be my bet. So we'll need to keep an eye on him because maverick he may be, but his loyalty to Hawksby is not in question.'

Booth Watson took his time before asking his next question. 'Do you think Hogan could be tempted into an indiscretion?'

'Never. If that man found a wallet on the London Underground stuffed with fifty-pound notes, he'd hand it in to the nearest police station and not expect a reward.'

'Money may well be the root of all evil, Superintendent, but it's not the only sin Moses found etched on the tablet he brought down from Mount Sinai.'

Lamont thought for some time before he responded. 'Hogan's had on-off relationships with several female officers in the past, and even with a suspect on one occasion, for which he was temporarily suspended. His latest conquest is DS Roycroft, but I'm pretty sure that's coming to an end.'

'So, if we could find the right Eve,' said Booth Watson, 'he might be tempted to bite the apple.'

'I'm not a pimp,' said Lamont acidly.

'Of course you're not, Superintendent. But fortunately, I have a client who swims in those particular waters, so you can leave Hogan to me, while you concentrate on DS Roycroft.'

'Is there anything in particular you want me to find out, when I next see her?'

'The names of everyone under investigation by Warwick's new unit.'

'That shouldn't prove difficult, but it won't come cheap.'

Booth Watson opened his desk drawer, withdrew a thick brown envelope and pushed it across the table, confident in the knowledge that if the ex-Superintendent found a wallet stuffed with fifty-pound notes, he wouldn't hand it in to the nearest police station.

• • •

'I can only imagine what you must be going through,' said William, as he sat down next to James and placed an arm around the young man's shoulder. 'But I'm not convinced your grandfather died of a heart attack.'

'Neither am I,' said James, tears streaming down his face. 'Even if he did, I'd still want to know what was in that flask.'

'Then I'll need you to be at your sharpest for the next forty-eight hours, because once we dock in New York the NYPD won't be interested in what I have to say, unless I can show reasonable grounds for suspicion.'

'Just tell me what you want me to do.'

'I need a detailed table plan that shows where everyone was seated during dinner. And, more important, I want you to write down what you remember of the conversation that took place between your grandfather and your uncle Hamish concerning what he was drinking.'

'That would be hard to forget,' said James. He gathered up half a dozen menu cards, turned one over and began to draw a rectangle on the back of it. He had filled in the last name by the time Franco reappeared, carrying three pairs of white gloves. He handed one pair each to William and James, keeping the third for himself.

'What next, sir?' asked Franco.

'I want this whole area roped off and the doors locked. No one is to be allowed to enter the dining room unless I say so.'

'Understood, sir.'

'I'm off to question Dr Lockhart and Hamish Buchanan. I need to interview them before they go to bed, although I suspect Hamish already has his story well prepared. I should be back in about an hour. Meanwhile, Franco, remember to make sure none of the passengers come into the room.' He touched James on the shoulder and said, 'Make your grandfather proud.'

William didn't need to ask where the chairman's stateroom was. James had already informed him that his cabin was on deck seven along with the rest of the family, and there were no other passengers on that deck.

When William stepped out of the lift, he was greeted by the eerie silence of mourning. A crew member was standing guard outside a door at the far end of the corridor that William assumed must be the chairman's stateroom.

The tall, heavyset man opened the cabin door before William had a chance to knock. On entering, he found Mrs Buchanan seated by the body of her late husband, still holding his hand. She didn't look up.

Dr Lockhart was standing on the other side of the bed. Without a word passing between them, he motioned William towards an adjoining room and closed the door quietly behind them.

'I'm sorry to intrude on your grief, Dr Lockhart,' said William, 'but I need to ask you if there's any doubt in your mind as to what caused the chairman's death.'

'None whatsoever,' said Lockhart firmly. 'In fact, I've already signed the death certificate, which I'll hand in to the coroner as soon as we dock in New York. I'm only surprised it didn't happen earlier. Frankly, Fraser Buchanan was a time bomb waiting to explode.'

'You may well be right,' said William. 'However, there are one or two matters I still have to clear up. Hamish Buchanan claimed the flask he handed to his father only contained a mild sedative that he had been prescribed by you.'

'That's correct. One or two of the family, including Hamish, occasionally suffer from seasickness, so I always have something at hand to help them sleep. In any case, everyone saw Hamish and Fraser drink from the same flask, so there's no reason to suspect that his death was due to anything other than natural causes.'

Once again, someone had delivered a sentence that wasn't necessary. William wondered what else the doctor had to hide.

'Do you have any more of that medicine, doctor?'

William asked. 'As I don't suppose I'll be getting much sleep tonight.'

'Of course,' replied Lockhart, who opened his leather bag, took out a half-empty medicine bottle and handed it to William. As he did so, William spotted something else in the bottom of the bag that answered a question he would no longer need to ask.

'I'll leave you now, doctor,' he said. 'I'm sure Mrs Buchanan will be grateful for your company. But before I go, can you tell me which is Hamish Buchanan's cabin?'

'Number three. It's the first door on the left as you go out.'

'Thank you, doctor.' William opened the cabin door, stepped back into the corridor and walked slowly across to number three. He took a deep breath and knocked on the door.

'Enter,' said a voice that sounded wide awake.

William walked into the cabin to find Hamish Buchanan seated in a large, comfortable chair, a goblet of brandy in his hand, a half-smoked cigar in the other. There was no sign of his wife.

'I'm sorry to disturb you at such a late hour,' said William, 'but I need to ask you a couple of questions before you go to bed.'

'No need to waste your time, Chief Inspector,' said Hamish, not bothering to offer him a seat. 'I've already spoken to my lawyer in New York and he's advised me not to answer any of your questions until he can be present. He felt sure I wouldn't have to remind you that this vessel is registered under an American flag. A country in which you have no jurisdiction.'

'Nevertheless, I do have the commodore's authority to carry out an investigation into your father's death,' responded William. 'I can't imagine my questions would worry someone who has nothing to hide.'

'You won't get me to rise quite that easily, Chief Inspector, so please leave me to mourn in peace.' Hamish flicked a piece of ash into an ashtray by his side before adding, 'My lawyer also advised me that once we enter American territorial waters you will no longer have any authority on board this ship, whatever the commodore says. Therefore, may I suggest you go to bed and try and get a good night's sleep.'

'I will,' said William, producing the bottle Dr Lockhart had given him, which at least produced a flicker of concern on Hamish's face. 'Meanwhile, I would ask you to remain in your cabin while I continue with my enquiries.'

'And if I don't, Chief Inspector, what will you do? Have me clapped in irons before walking the plank? I don't think so. Why don't you run along.' He raised his glass in a mock toast.

William left, convinced that, like the doctor, Hamish Buchanan had something to hide. But both of them in their own way had made him aware of just how little time he had to find out what that something was. 'During the first forty-eight hours of a murder inquiry, you only go to sleep if you fall asleep' was one of The Hawk's favourite mantras. And then only after you've made an arrest.

William quickly made his way back to deck three, where he was pleased to find Franco posted centurion-like outside the entrance to the dining room.

'Any ideas yet about who the guilty party is?' whispered Franco as he opened the door.

'It may just have been a heart attack,' said William, without conviction.

'Fraser Buchanan had the constitution of an ox. He's never had a heart attack in the past that I'm aware of, despite what the doctor claimed. So whatever was in that flask killed him.'

William suspected Franco might be right, but intuition wasn't proof. When he entered the dining room he found James, head down, writing furiously. William sat next to him and studied the seating plan he'd drawn. He then turned over several other menus one by one and began to read the conversations from earlier in the evening that James had meticulously chronicled. Words had been crossed out, replaced, but the tenor of the conversation was clear for him to see.

He'd reached the back of the third menu when he stopped and reread a paragraph, not twice, but three times.

'Are you sure about this?' he asked, pointing to half a dozen lines James had underlined.

'Certain,' said James, not looking up. 'I have no evidence of course, so I can't prove it. But I'm sure I know where you'll find the other flask.'

'I've already seen it,' said William.

• • •

They lay back exhausted. It was some time before she spoke.

'I suppose this can't go on for much longer,' Jackie said as she pulled the sheet up to her chin.

'We won't have a lot of choice,' said Ross, as he lit a cigarette. 'If we don't end it now, I have a feeling The Hawk will.'

'I'll miss you,' she said quietly.

'We'll still be seeing each other every day.'

'It won't be the same,' she said, nestling up against his shoulder. 'Do you think The Hawk knows about us?'

Ross inhaled deeply before he replied. 'Of course he does. Nothing gets past that man. Out of interest, how do you get on with the choirboy?'

'He's the only person I've come across who just might be capable of taking over from The Hawk,' she said with undisguised respect.

'That good?'

'Possibly better. The Hawk already treats him as an equal.'

'And the rest of the team?'

'A great bunch of guys to work with. You're going to have to be at your best just to keep up with them,' she teased.

'Anything else I ought to know before I show up next week?'

'I've already briefed you on the five cases we're working on, and The Hawk's saved the worst one for you. But you should also know I'm still in touch with Bruce Lamont, and I'm being handsomely rewarded for my trouble.'

'With whose money?' said Ross. 'Lamont is still living way beyond his means, so someone has to be backing him.'

'William thinks it must be Booth Watson.'

'What further use would that quilted criminal have for Lamont now that Summers is safely locked up in Pentonville?'

'Miles Faulkner.'

'I thought you attended his funeral.'

'But not his burial it would seem, or at least that's Warwick's opinion,' said Jackie.

'Not a hope,' said Ross. 'If Faulkner's still alive, Lamont

would be the last person Booth Watson would confide in. I suspect he holds that man in the same high regard as the rest of us.'

'We don't have any other leads at the moment,' admitted Jackie, 'except for Christina Faulkner, who's a friend of William's wife.'

'That woman will only ever do what's in her own best interests.' Ross blew out a large circle of smoke, before adding, 'I wish I was still undercover, because nothing would give me greater pleasure than to nail Faulkner and put all three of them behind bars.'

'All three of them?'

'Faulkner, Booth Watson and Lamont.'

'Not Christina?' said Jackie, teasing him.

'She's not my type,' said Ross, as he climbed back on top of her.

CHAPTER 6

'I THINK I'VE SOLVED THE fingerprint problem,' said James, as he sat down for breakfast the following morning.

'How,' asked William, 'when we don't have a forensic lab at our disposal?'

'Don't need one when there's a shop selling toys on deck four,' he announced, looking rather pleased with himself.

'Stop showing off,' said William, grinning.

'It didn't take much research to discover that one of the most popular items in the shop is a Sherlock Holmes kit for aspiring detectives. I bought the last three sets,' said James, producing one of them from below the table with a flourish. 'They contain a fingerprint pad, special paper, dusting powder, a tiny brush and a magnifying glass. What more could you want?'

'Well done, Detective Constable Buchanan. Thinking outside the box.'

'Inside the box, actually,' said James, removing the lid to reveal several small compartments.

'Pathetic,' said William, 'but bravo.'

'Whose fingerprints do you want to check, Chief Inspector?' he asked as he took a sip of orange juice.

'You can begin with your uncle Hamish,' said William, checking James's table plan. 'Start with his silver hip flask, and then his coffee cup, so you have matching prints. Then move on to your great-aunt Flora, who was sitting on his left, next Dr Lockhart, followed by your mother, and finally your grandfather.'

'What about those who were sitting on the other side of the table?'

'We don't need theirs.'

'Why not?'

'Think about it, detective, and let me know when the penny drops.'

'Do you know where that expression originates?'

'Yes, I do,' said William.

'So, where should I start looking for prints?'

'The water tumblers, the wine glasses and then the coffee cups, remembering the waiters wear gloves, so that eliminates them.'

'And after I've done that?'

'I'll double-check the prints you find on Hamish's hip flask. Once I've identified all of them, we'll know if your theory stands up.'

'And if it doesn't?'

'Then your grandfather died of a heart attack, and I shall inform the commodore that I have no reason to suspect foul play.'

'And what if Grandfather's prints aren't on Hamish's flask?'

'Then I'll need you and Franco to carry out a surveillance exercise for me.'

'What do you have in mind, sir?' asked Franco, as he poured William a second cup of coffee.

'When Dr Lockhart comes down for breakfast this morning, I'll go straight to deck seven. If he looks as if he might be returning to his cabin, James, you come up as quickly as possible and warn me. Meanwhile, Franco, you try to delay him even if it's only for a few moments.'

'I'll tell him about my dodgy knee that's been playing up again.'

'How do I get my hands on a pass key for the cabins on deck seven?' asked William.

'No problem, sir.' Franco took a large bunch of keys from an inside pocket, removed one with the number '7' stamped on it, and handed it to William, who said, 'I hope this won't get you into any trouble.'

'Not a chance,' said Franco. 'I had clear instructions from the commodore to give you every possible assistance, so I'm doing no more than obeying orders.'

A few moments later the first guests entered the dining room for breakfast. They stared at the chairman's table, now roped off, while Franco led them to their usual places.

'Got it,' said James. 'I've just worked out why you don't need the fingerprints of anyone who was sitting on the other side of the table.'

Franco looked suitably puzzled.

'Time for me to get moving,' said William, as Hamish Buchanan and Dr Lockhart strolled into the dining room. William was not surprised to see them together. 'Start work on their fingerprints immediately,' he whispered. 'Although time isn't exactly on our side, don't hurry and make sure you're thorough,' he added, before slipping out of the dining room.

James waited until his uncle and Dr Lockhart had sat down for breakfast before he took a seat on the other side of the table and turned his back on them. He picked up the silver hip flask and sprinkled a light layer of dusting powder over its surface.

• • •

'Captain Neville, what a pleasant surprise to see you in Paris,' declared an elegantly dressed, middle-aged woman who Miles had known for many years; she'd even sent flowers to his funeral. 'Unfortunately, none of my ladies will be available until around nine o'clock this evening.'

'I came early,' said Miles, 'because I need to have a private word before your first client arrives.'

'Then let's go to my office where we won't be disturbed.'

Miles entered a Victorian boudoir he'd known long before his physical appearance had been altered beyond recognition. But he sometimes wondered if Blanche had her suspicions about the captain who didn't quibble over the price, although she'd never seen the one part of his anatomy that hadn't changed.

'I need something a little out of the ordinary,' he said, as he sat down on the sofa next to the madam. It was a request Blanche was familiar with, but when he told her exactly what he had in mind, even she was taken by surprise.

He took out several large photographs from his briefcase

that had been supplied by Lamont and handed them to Blanche, who studied them carefully. 'The police uniform is very convincing,' she said. 'If this girl's ever in Paris, I can find work for her.'

'She was the mark's present girlfriend,' said Miles, without elaboration. 'I'm hoping you can provide her replacement.'

'Let me see what I can come up with, captain.' Blanche rose from the sofa and walked across to a large filing cabinet. She pulled open the second drawer, which was labelled 'Blondes, European, fluent English', and extracted two files.

Blanche sat down at her desk and turned the pages slowly, occasionally glancing at the image Captain Neville had supplied. After some consideration she chose three candidates whose photographs she placed on the desk in front of him.

Miles studied the three young women Blanche had selected.

'What else will she be expected to do,' she asked, 'besides seduce him?'

'The mark has the energy of ten men, but it's not his sexual prowess I'm interested in.'

'Any one of them should be able to handle that. After all, they're professionals. But what other skills are required?'

'She needs to be bright as well as irresistible. A combination of Mata Hari and Becky Sharp. It's the pillow talk that's going to matter.'

'Then I'd go with Josephine rather than Avril or Michelle,' she said, pointing to one of the photographs. 'Why don't you come back around midnight, captain, then you can judge for yourself which one of them fits the bill?'

'Quite a large bill, I suspect,' said Miles, 'as I may be needing her services for some time.'

• • •

'What do you think?' asked Beth.

'Quite magnificent. It would look even better if it were hanging around your neck,' said William, as he admired the exquisite necklace displayed in the window of the ship's jewellery shop. 'Dare I ask how much?'

'Way out of your price range, caveman. I should have married a banker.'

William took a second look at the necklace and felt guilty. This was meant to be a break from work, but he'd hardly seen Beth from the moment they'd stepped on board. Yoga, followed by the morning lecture, and a film in the afternoon with her new best friend, Catherine Whittaker, had almost got him off the hook, but not entirely.

Beth straightened his bow tie. 'You need to look your best tonight,' she said, brushing a hair from the shoulder of his dinner jacket. 'Catherine is such fun, and I can't wait to meet her husband.'

'The last time I saw Mr Justice Whittaker,' mused William, 'I was in the witness box when he told me he wasn't interested in my opinions, and to stick to the evidence.'

Beth laughed as he took her hand and they made their way to the dining room on the deck below. William smiled to himself when they passed a window full of toys and spotted an empty shelf.

They entered the dining room, where Franco was on hand to escort them to their table. The chairman's table was no longer roped off, but it remained unoccupied. The Buchanan family were now sitting at separate tables on the other side of the room, the two brothers conspicuously seated apart from each other. Franco accompanied William and Beth to the Whittakers' table, where the judge rose to greet them.

'William, it's good of you to join us after what must have been a gruelling couple of days. I don't imagine you've had much sleep.'

'Not a lot, sir,' said William, as they shook hands.

'George, please. I don't think you've met my wife, Catherine.'

'Beth's already told me about your fascinating talk on Puccini.'

'And I can't wait to visit the Fitzmolean again,' said Catherine, 'now that I have my own personal guide.'

'That's how we met,' said William, as Franco appeared and handed them each a menu.

'Tonight's special is the rump steak,' he declared, 'while there's the finest smoked salmon for the more abstemious.'

William ordered the steak, confident that Beth wouldn't overrule him, although she did frown. Once they had all placed their orders, Beth told them about the morning lecture she and Catherine had attended, entitled, 'The Big Apple: why not take a bite!' given by Professor Samuels of Columbia University.

'The professor has made me think again about how we should spend our time in New York,' Beth commented. 'I now want to drive across the Brooklyn Bridge, walk around Central Park and—'

'Not at night,' said William.

'—and visit the Bronx zoo,' continued Beth.

'Not to mention catching a Broadway show,' said Catherine. 'He told us we should get tickets for *La Cage aux Folles*, if we possibly can,' she added, as Franco reappeared with their first course.

Beth and Catherine continued to chat enthusiastically about the lecture, while the judge ate his asparagus, commenting only on how delicate the hollandaise sauce was. It wasn't until their plates had been cleared away, to be replaced with the second course, that he turned to William and said, 'May I ask how your investigation is proceeding?'

'It's complicated. However, I can tell you I've handed in my report to the commodore,' said William, as he cut into his steak and watched the blood run. He looked up to see that all three of them had put down their knives and forks and were staring at him in anticipation.

'Did the chairman die of a heart attack?' asked the judge, cutting to the quick.

'He may well have done,' said William. 'But I'm more interested in what caused that heart attack.'

Once again, all three of them waited impatiently while William placed a little mustard on the side of his plate.

'Are you going to tell us the answer,' Beth finally demanded, 'or do we have to wait until our food's gone cold?'

William put down his knife, wiped his mouth with a napkin, and said, 'I'm able to tell you how the murder was committed, as long as you don't breathe a word to anyone.'

'And that includes you, my dear,' said George, smiling at his wife.

William waited until Franco had refilled their wine glasses before producing James's seating plan and placing it in the centre of the table.

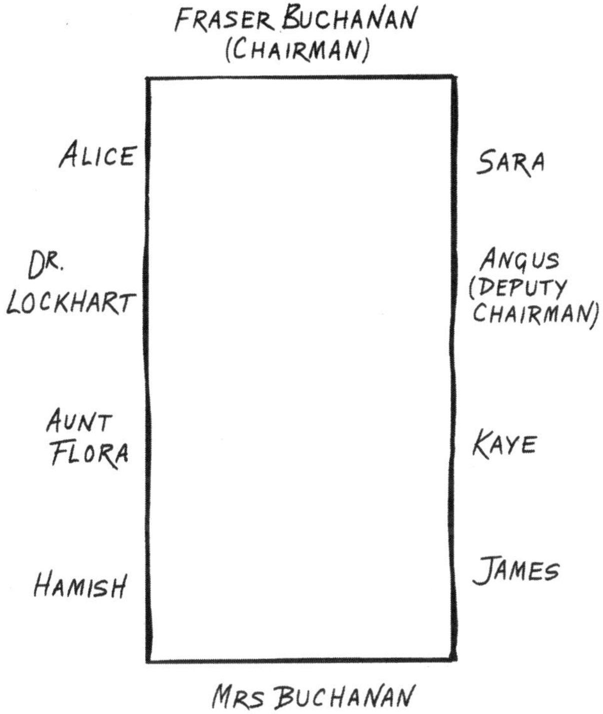

He allowed them a few moments to study it, before he continued. 'First, note that Hamish Buchanan is seated on the left-hand side of the table, between his mother and Flora Buchanan on his left.'

'Who's she?' asked Catherine.

'Fraser Buchanan's sister. The formidable grande dame of the company, who the rest of the family are in awe of.'

'And next to her?' enquired the judge, peering down at the plan.

'Dr Lockhart, whose sole purpose in life was to keep the chairman alive. But not on this occasion.'

This revelation silenced the three of them for a moment, giving William the chance to enjoy a forkful of steak.

'And on his left?' asked Beth.

'Alice Buchanan, James's mother and the wife of Angus Buchanan' – he moved his finger across to the other side of the table – 'who recently replaced his brother Hamish as deputy chairman of the company.'

'I have a feeling that side of the table isn't going to be important,' said the judge.

'A shrewd observation,' said William, 'but you'll still have to concentrate if you're to work out what Hamish Buchanan was up to. Everyone saw him take a drink from his hip flask during dinner, which caused his father to pointedly ask what he was drinking, as he suspected it was whisky or brandy, despite Hamish having just assured him he was on the wagon.'

No one interrupted as William put down his knife and fork.

'Hamish claimed the flask only contained a mild sedative that had been given to him by Dr Lockhart to help him sleep. But the chairman demanded it was passed to him so he could check for himself. Their first mistake.' William paused to allow Franco to refill their wine glasses.

'Where was I?' he said once Franco had put the wine back in the ice bucket.

'Hamish was passing his hip flask to his father, who was seated at the top of the table,' Beth reminded him.

'Ah yes,' said William. 'So, Hamish handed the flask to Great-Aunt Flora, who passed it on to the doctor, who in turn gave it to Alice, who finally handed it to the chairman.' He took a sip of wine while they continued to study the table plan. 'The chairman swallowed a long draught from the flask,' he continued, 'and although he found it tasted unpleasant, it clearly wasn't alcohol, and therefore he assumed it must be the medicine Dr Lockhart had prescribed. He then passed the hip flask back to his son at the other end of the table.'

'Down which side of the table?' asked the judge.

'That's the point,' said William. 'The same side.'

'As I thought,' said the judge. 'But I'm still only half-way there.'

'When the flask was returned to Hamish, he made a great show of taking another swig from it. His second mistake.'

'I'm lost,' said Beth.

'Patience,' said William. 'Concentrate on the seating plan and all will be revealed. James Buchanan, my recently promoted Detective Sergeant, spent this morning identifying all the fingerprints he could find on the tumblers, wine glasses and coffee cups of everyone who had sat on the left-hand side of the table, while I carried out the same exercise with Hamish's hip flask.'

'You're still a yard ahead of me,' said Catherine. 'If Hamish's flask was passed to his father at the top of the table, everyone's fingerprints on that side of the table had to be on it.'

'But they weren't,' suggested the judge, 'because someone had switched the flask for a similar one before it reached the chairman at the top of the table, and that person will be the only one whose fingerprints were on both flasks.'

'Not a bad summing up, m'Lud,' said William with a grin. 'So in order to decide who is the guilty party, the jury must first consider the evidence. Flora took Hamish's flask and passed it on to the doctor like a baton in a relay race, and when the chairman sent it back down the table, the same exercise was carried out in reverse. Simple and well planned, except the accomplices made two mistakes. First—' William stopped mid-sentence as Franco reappeared to clear their plates.

'Would you like to see the dessert menu?' he asked.

'No, thank you,' said Catherine, not even looking up.

'A digestif, perhaps?' ventured Franco.

'No, thank you,' repeated the judge a little more firmly, his eyes still fixed on the place settings on James's drawing. Franco left, having served no purpose.

William waited to see if anyone had worked out what those mistakes were.

'Whose fingerprints did you find on Hamish's hip flask?' asked the judge. 'And, more important, whose fingerprints were missing? Because that will tell us who switched the flasks.'

William acknowledged the judge with a slight bow, as if they were in court. 'The only fingerprints I could identify on Hamish's flask were Flora's, who was seated next to him, the not so good doctor Lockhart, and of course Hamish's.'

'Got it,' said Beth.

'Then you'll be able to explain what they were up to,' said William.

'It had to be Dr Lockhart who carried out the switch both times,' said Beth. 'Otherwise, the chairman's fingerprints would also have been on Hamish's flask when it was passed back to him.'

'As well as those of James's mother, who was sitting

between the doctor and the chairman, and passed the flask to him.'

'Have you found the second flask?' asked the judge. 'The one Fraser Buchanan must have drunk from?'

'Yes,' said William. 'I first saw the other flask in Dr Lockhart's bag when I questioned him last night, and then again this morning when I searched his cabin while he was at breakfast. But the only fingerprints I found on that particular flask were his.'

'He'd had more than enough time to wipe it clean,' said the judge, 'leaving just his fingerprints for you to find. But what about the contents?'

'The ship's doctor confirmed it was nothing more than a mild sedative, just as Hamish had claimed,' replied William.

'They saw you coming,' said the judge, 'and have made it almost impossible for you to prove that Hamish Buchanan and Dr Lockhart were working together as a team.'

'That would have been the case, if it hadn't been for the resourceful and observant James Buchanan, who some of them still think of as a child, rather than a young man who plans to become the Director of the FBI, not chairman of the Pilgrim Line.'

'And what did he observe?' asked Catherine.

'Before I answer that, you need to take another look at the seating plan that night. You'll see that young James was placed opposite his uncle Hamish, from where he had a perfect view of everything that was going on, including when Hamish drank from his hip flask. But it was only later that "the penny dropped", to quote him, when he realized his uncle wasn't drinking from the same hip flask as his grandfather.'

'What made him think that?' asked Beth.

'Hamish had placed his flask on the table during dinner for everyone to see,' said William. 'A foolish mistake, because James noticed the initials "HB" engraved on one side, whereas the one the chairman drank from had no such engraving, as I was able to confirm when later I found it in the doctor's cabin.'

'Bright young man,' said the judge. 'However, it still may not be enough to convict them.' He stopped and pondered for a moment. 'If I was representing Hamish Buchanan, I would suggest to the jury that they could not rely simply on missing fingerprints, and the uncorroborated testimony of a minor, to send two men down for a life sentence.'

'I agree,' said William. 'But don't forget we still have the body of the late Fraser Buchanan. I've already called ahead to the NYPD to let them know I have reason to suspect a murder has been committed, and they've agreed to meet me on the quayside when we dock tomorrow morning. I'm confident an autopsy will show the chairman was poisoned, and end up convicting both of them.'

'Bravo,' said the judge. 'You are indeed the son of Sir Julian Warwick.'

'Not to mention the formidable Lady Warwick,' suggested Beth.

'They would have got away with it if I hadn't had young James Buchanan to assist me,' admitted William, as Franco served them coffee and poured the judge his usual brandy, before handing William a sealed envelope.

'A signed confession?' suggested Catherine, as William tore open the envelope.

'I don't think so,' he said, after extracting a voucher for one thousand pounds. He read out the accompanying letter.

THE PILGRIM LINE

Dear Chief Inspector Warwick,

On behalf of the board of the Pilgrim Line, I would like to thank you for taking on the unenviable task of investigating the death of our late chairman.

The board regret that as a consequence, you have been unable to fully enjoy your holiday, and accordingly feel some form of compensation is appropriate.

The enclosed voucher will be honoured by the company should you and your wife wish to take another voyage on one of our liners, or to purchase something from one of our gift shops.

Yours sincerely,

Flora Buchanan

Acting Chairman

'It was my holiday that was spoilt, not yours,' said Beth. 'In fact, I've never seen you happier,' she added, as she grabbed the voucher and dropped it into her bag.

'I wonder what time the jewellery shop opens in the morning?' said Catherine innocently.

CHAPTER 7

THE LOUD BANGING ON THE door persisted. At first William wondered if it was just part of his dream, but he woke to find it hadn't stopped. Someone was disturbing the first decent night's sleep he'd had in days.

He reluctantly got out of bed, put on his dressing gown and opened the door to find James standing in the corridor.

'Come quickly,' he said, 'you're the only person who can stop it.'

'Stop what?' asked William, but James was already on the move. He closed the cabin door quietly, but heard Beth groan as she turned over. Still half asleep, he followed James along the corridor and down a flight of steps to deck one, where he held open the door and waited for his mentor.

William walked out onto the lower deck, where he found the commodore in full dress uniform solemnly addressing a small gathering.

'Unto Almighty God we commend the soul of our brother departed, and we commit his body to the deep . . .'

William was horrified to see the Buchanan family, heads bowed, surrounding a coffin that rested on a small raised platform.

'. . . *in the certain hope of the resurrection unto eternal life through our Lord Jesus Christ . . .'*

'Can't you do something?' whispered James hopelessly.

'Nothing,' William replied, shaking his head, all too aware that the commodore's authority prevailed over everyone on board his ship.

'. . . *at whose coming in glorious majesty to judge the world, the sea shall give up their dead . . .'*

William remained on the edge of the gathering, a spectator of the game being played out in front of him.

'. . . *and the corruptible bodies of those who sleep in him shall be changed and made like unto his glorious body . . .'*

He took a closer look at the burial party to see Mrs Buchanan was weeping quietly, while her son Angus tried to comfort her. Flora Buchanan stood a pace back, calm and dignified, the mantle of power now resting on her shoulders. Hamish Buchanan, tight-lipped, stood next to Dr Lockhart, whose expression gave nothing away.

'. . . *according to the mighty working whereby he is able to subdue all things unto himself.'*

The commodore closed his prayer book, stood rigidly to attention and saluted. Two young officers stepped forward and raised one end of the platform on which the coffin was resting. The funeral party watched as it slid slowly down its determined path into the sea, before sinking to a salty grave below the waves.

Chief Inspector William Warwick might have been able to convince a coroner to exhume a body that had been buried a few feet below the earth in a graveyard, but not one that rested on the bottom of the ocean. The Buchanan family had buried not only their dead, but the one piece of evidence that would have condemned his murderers.

A minute's silence followed, after which the commodore saluted once again before issuing a command. Moments later, the propellers began to slowly rotate, allowing the ship to continue on its journey to New York.

William stood aside as the family departed: Mrs Buchanan on Angus's arm, silent and resolute; Hamish and the doctor a pace behind, chatting, making a mockery of mourning. They were followed by the rest of the family, with Flora Buchanan and the commodore bringing up the rear. When the new chairman saw William, she broke away and approached him.

'I feel I owe you an explanation,' she said calmly. William couldn't think of an appropriate response and he felt slightly embarrassed by the fact that he was wearing a dressing gown and slippers while the others were all dressed somewhat formally. 'At our board meeting yesterday,' she continued, 'the directors made the decision to carry out Fraser's last request – as specified in his will – to be buried at sea.'

'Even though you must have suspected it was one of those directors who was responsible for his untimely death,' said William pointedly.

'We considered that possibility,' said Flora. 'But as Fraser's personal physician had already signed the death certificate confirming he had died of a heart attack, the family, and

Mrs Buchanan in particular, decided we should carry out his final wishes rather than face a long investigation by the police. One that would have given the press enough ammunition to cause irreparable damage to the company's reputation – the last thing Fraser would have wanted.'

'I would suggest the last thing he would have wanted was to see his son punished for the crime he had committed.'

'I can understand how you must feel, Chief Inspector,' said Flora. 'So you may be interested to know that among the other decisions the board took was to sack Hamish as a director and cut him adrift.'

'To somehow survive on a vast inheritance,' said William bitterly.

'Unfortunately not,' said the chairman. 'The only thing his father left him, as he will discover when the will is read later today, is a compass, a metaphor I'm sure you will appreciate.'

'And the good doctor?'

'Resigned before he could be sacked. I will also personally make sure he won't be employed by anyone who asks us for a reference.'

As Flora turned to leave, William asked quietly, 'When did you discover the truth?'

'Young James is a great admirer of yours, Chief Inspector, as I'm sure you're aware. However, after a little coaxing he couldn't resist letting me know how you were able to prove that my brother didn't die of a heart attack.'

William should have realized that, in the end, blood is always thicker than water. In this case, sea water.

'Don't blame the boy,' said Flora. 'We've all learnt a great deal about ourselves on this journey.'

'What did you learn?'

'That given time, James will make an outstanding chairman of the Pilgrim Line. Which is exactly what his grandfather, may he rest in peace, would have wanted.'

• • •

William returned to his cabin and crept back into bed, relieved to find Beth fast asleep. He was woken a few hours later by a light tap on the door.

Beth, who was already dressed, opened the door to be greeted by a young ensign. He saluted and said, 'Good morning, ma'am. The commodore wondered if you and Chief Inspector Warwick would care to join him on the bridge at around ten o'clock, when we will be sailing into New York harbour.'

'You bet,' said Beth, unable to hide her excitement. 'How kind of him.'

William sat up in bed, and was about to protest when he saw the look on Beth's face.

• • •

'You're a shameless hussy,' said William, as he came out of the bathroom to see his wife looking at herself in the mirror.

'I know,' said Beth, 'but I couldn't resist it.'

'How much?' asked William, who despite himself couldn't help admiring the necklace he'd last seen displayed in the gift shop window.

'Nine hundred and ninety-five pounds,' said Beth without any suggestion of shame.

'And what did I get with the five pounds left over? A Rolex Submariner perhaps, or an eighteen-carat-gold eternity ring?'

'I'm afraid not. All they could manage was a pair of plastic collar stiffeners, top of the range, the sales assistant assured me. I considered the necklace a small compensation for a woman whose husband had deserted her during the day and then disappeared in the middle of the night,' Beth said as she wrapped her arms around his neck.

'That doesn't stop you being a shameless hussy.'

'And where did you go in the middle of the night?'

'To witness Fraser Buchanan's burial at sea.'

'But I thought—'

'So did I.'

'How clever of them,' said Beth, as William pushed a collar stiffener into his shirt. 'That way there'll be no autopsy, no trial and no adverse publicity.'

'And no justice,' said William.

There was a knock on the door, and Beth opened it to find the young ensign had returned. 'The commodore asked me to accompany you and your husband to the bridge, ma'am.'

'Thank you,' said Beth, as she linked arms with the ensign, leaving William to grab his jacket and close the door before catching up with them.

'If I may say so, Mrs Warwick, what an exquisite necklace you're wearing.'

'A gift from my husband,' said Beth, which at least caused William to smile.

William might have only reluctantly accepted the commodore's invitation to join him, but the moment he stepped onto the bridge he changed his mind. He was mesmerized by the sheer size of the control panels that stretched from one side of the deck to the other, allowing the commodore a panoramic view of everything going on around him, including a bank of flashing signals that the alert young officers were studying intently. William listened to the quiet and efficient orders being given by the officer of the watch to the engine room below.

He also noticed that everyone on deck was wearing a black armband.

'Everything's electronic nowadays,' said the ensign, interrupting his thoughts. 'Though we still have two serving officers, including the commodore, who began their maritime careers with a steamship company.'

'Who's in charge?' he whispered to the ensign.

'Captain Maitland, the officer of the watch.'

'Not the commodore?' asked William, who had noticed he was standing a few paces back, passive, eyes never still, arms behind his back.

'Certainly not. He would only take over if there was an emergency.'

'Like what?' asked Beth.

'A gale force storm, or if the officer of the watch was drunk, or a member of the royal family were present. I've never seen him take over command during my four years on the *Alden*.'

'When will you become the officer of the watch?' she asked.

'Not for some time yet, ma'am. Occasionally I get to replace the second officer in the middle of the night, but only if we're a long way off shore, the sea is calm and there's no sign of another ship. The *Titanic* still serves to remind every sailor that the sea must be treated with respect, so when I'm left in charge even the navigator keeps a watchful eye on me. That reminds me, Chief Inspector: the senior navigator, who's at the wheel this morning, was keen to meet you, as it seems you have a friend in common.'

'I wonder who that can be,' said Beth, as the ensign accompanied them across to the wheel and introduced them to Able Seaman Ned Turnbull.

The senior navigator took one hand off the wheel, shook hands with William and said, 'Welcome to the bridge, sir.'

'I understand we have a mutual friend,' said William.

'Yes, we do. I think you know Ee by gum,' said the navigator, which only brought a puzzled look to William's face, which caused the navigator to add, 'Captain Ralph Neville, who I was looking forward to seeing again. We served together on the *Illustrious*, during the Falklands crisis. Mind you, he was only an able seaman back in those days.'

'Ee by gum?' repeated Beth, none the wiser.

'That was his nickname below deck, on account of his broad Yorkshire accent, and the belief that Sir Leonard Hutton was without question the greatest living Englishman. We lost touch after he married an Australian girl and went to live in Perth. Be sure to pass on my best wishes should you come across him again.'

'I most certainly will,' said William.

'You mustn't miss the Statue of Liberty,' the ensign said, as he guided Beth and William across to the starboard side of the ship.

They both stared in the direction of the iconic statue, but they weren't looking at her.

'I've made such a fool of myself,' whispered Beth. 'I should have listened to you in the first place.'

'You've always been a trusting soul,' said William. 'It's one of the many reasons I adore you. And to be fair, Christina must have been lying through her teeth for the past year.'

'I'm missing something, aren't I?' said Beth. 'What's Ralph Neville got on Christina to make her fall into line so conveniently?'

'Wrong question.'

'Then what's the right question?'

'Why was Christina so willing to part with her tickets for this voyage?'

'And the answer?'

'Ralph couldn't afford to be seen on board by someone who'd served with the real Captain Neville.'

'But Christina told me they were getting married.'

'She is, but to whom?'

Beth stared at William for some time before she said, 'How long have you known?'

William checked his watch. 'Ee by gum. I've only been certain for about ten minutes.'

• • •

Beth wanted to fly straight back to England so she could confront Christina before the wedding took place, but William talked her out of the idea. He knew it would only give Faulkner another opportunity to escape, and if he did, it would be the only thing anyone remembered about his short and undistinguished career. It helped that Catherine had stepped in and insisted Beth stay with them while she was in New York.

'The Met, the Frick and the MoMA with our own personal tour guide?' said Catherine. 'What more could a girl ask for?'

Mr Justice Whittaker nodded sagely, but didn't comment when his wife said she would be only too happy to accompany Beth to Carnegie Hall and take William's seat for the Ella Fitzgerald concert. The judge didn't complain, but then he'd never heard of Ella Fitzgerald. He couldn't wait to return to England and preside once again over the trial of Miles Faulkner, and had already decided on the length of his sentence.

'What about Christina?' Beth asked him.

'Assisting an offender,' pronounced the judge, 'although Mr Booth Watson wouldn't find it difficult to get her off that charge, as long as she doesn't visit Captain Ralph Neville in prison.'

William couldn't wait to get back to England.

• • •

'How many murders were there in London last year?' asked Commander Hawksby, as he took his place at the head of the table for the first meeting of the newly formed Unsolved Murders Unit.

'One hundred and eighty-one, sir,' replied Detective Sergeant Adaja.

'How many of those were domestic?' asked The Hawk, switching his attention to the other side of the table. Although the room was large compared with the rabbit warren the rest of the team worked in, the table in the centre could just about seat six. A photograph of the Queen hung on the wall behind The Hawk's desk, and a silver cup on the bookshelf reminded them that he'd once been the Met's middleweight boxing champion.

'Thirty-four,' said Jackie.

'And how many of those ended up with a conviction?'

'Twenty-nine. Most of them were waiting for us to turn up, while the remainder were arrested within twenty-four hours.'

'That's the secret. Most domestic murders are solved in the first twenty-four hours, forty-eight at the most,' said The Hawk. 'After that, they begin to think they've got away with it, and become more and more confident as each day passes.'

'Which is certainly true in the case of Mr Clive Pugh,' said Jackie, opening her case file. 'He murdered his wife a couple of months after taking out a million-pound insurance policy on her life, and was handsomely rewarded for his trouble.'

'Why wasn't he convicted?' demanded The Hawk.

'We didn't have enough evidence to charge him, so he literally got away with murder.'

'Then find the necessary evidence, DS Roycroft,' said The Hawk. 'Because if there's one thing that makes a potential murderer think twice, it's the thought that he won't get away with it. That still leaves us with a hundred and forty-seven murders that can't be described as domestic. DC Pankhurst, how many of those resulted in arrests?'

Rebecca didn't need to open the file in front of her to answer the commander's question. 'One hundred and forty-three, sir.'

'How many of those ended up in prison?'

'One hundred and thirty-nine, and, of the other four, we know who the murderers are, but we didn't have enough solid evidence to convince the Crown Prosecution Service they should be put on trial.'

'Details?' demanded The Hawk.

'One of them, a Max Sleeman, is a particularly nasty piece of work,' said DS Adaja, opening his case file. 'He's a loan shark, and if you don't pay up on time, you end up with a broken arm or leg. And if you still fail to deliver, he rents a hearse, but doesn't cover the funeral costs.'

'I want Sleeman arrested,' said The Hawk, 'and preferably before the next poor sod is eliminated.'

'Already on it,' said Paul.

'Three to go,' said The Hawk. 'DC Pankhurst, what can you tell me about a certain Darren Carter?'

'He's a bouncer at the Eve Club in Soho,' said Rebecca. 'Pleaded guilty to manslaughter and got off with a two-year sentence. Though I've no doubt it was a premeditated murder that he carried out on behalf of the club's owner.'

'Then I want him back in jail. Double jeopardy doesn't apply if fresh evidence can be produced,' The Hawk reminded her. 'And, DC Pankhurst, I also want the club shut down and to make sure that the owner never gets another licence. That should keep you occupied for the time being. Which leaves the final two cases that have been gathering dust for far too long.'

Everyone seated around the table knew exactly which cases the commander was referring to: Ron Abbott and Terry Roach. Two hardmen from rival East End gangs, who were conducting an ongoing dispute about who controlled the gambling, protection rackets, prostitution and distribution of drugs on their patch.

'I know you'll be glad to hear that I've saved those two particularly unsavoury characters for DI Hogan to deal with when he joins the unit next week as DCI Warwick's second-in-command.'

Paul looked disappointed.

'However,' continued The Hawk, 'don't imagine even for one moment that you're off the hook, because I expect detailed reports, including course of action, to be on my desk before we meet again in a week's time.' Biros didn't stop scribbling. 'And if you want to hear the bad news, I've just had a call from DCI Warwick, whose plane touched down at Heathrow about an hour ago.'

'I thought he wasn't due back for another week,' said DS Adaja.

'He wasn't. But he intends to be the officer who arrests Miles Faulkner in person.'

'That might prove a little difficult,' said Jackie, 'as we both attended Faulkner's funeral in Geneva and witnessed his cremation.'

'Attended is the key word,' said The Hawk. 'But whose ashes were in the urn when the priest handed them over to Mrs Faulkner remains a mystery.'

'What makes you think they weren't Faulkner's?' asked Jackie defensively.

'A Raphael which we know Faulkner considered the star of his collection recently came up for auction at Christie's, and was sold for £2.2 million.'

'That doesn't prove he's still alive,' said Paul, playing devil's advocate.

'I would agree with you, DS Adaja, if DCI Warwick hadn't seen the painting hanging in Faulkner's home in Monte Carlo not so long ago. Which suggests that the one sold at the auction was a copy, and because the seller had the authentic paperwork to prove its provenance, even the experts were fooled.'

'Who would pay £2.2 million for a fake?' asked Jackie.

'Someone who doesn't want us to know he's still alive.'

'That's hardly beyond reasonable doubt—'

'Until you consider,' interrupted The Hawk, 'that it was none other than our old friend Mr Booth Watson QC who purchased the painting,' he paused, 'on behalf of a client.'

'Who might have been Mrs Faulkner,' countered Paul.

'Unlikely,' said The Hawk. 'Christina Faulkner has never shown any interest in buying paintings, only selling them.'

'I'd need a little more proof than that if I were sitting on a jury,' said Paul, as the door swung open and William marched in.

'Talk of the devil,' said The Hawk. 'I was just about to explain to DS Adaja and DS Roycroft why you're now convinced Miles Faulkner is still alive.'

'Ee by gum, I am,' said William, taking the only empty seat at the table. 'So if you lot have any plans for next Saturday morning, cancel them, because you'll be attending the wedding of Captain Ralph Neville, RN Rtd, and Mrs Christina Faulkner, widow of the said parish, despite the fact that they're both already married.' He paused. 'To each other.'

CHAPTER 8

SIXTEEN OFFICERS, UNDER THE COMMAND of DI Hogan, surrounded the Norman parish church of Limpton-in-the-Marsh that Saturday morning. None of them were in uniform. Several of the CROP officers were armed.

The banns had been announced in the parish magazine and proclaimed from the pulpit for the past three Sundays by the local vicar. He declared that the service would take place at two o'clock on Saturday August fifteenth. Several uninvited guests turned up for the betrothal unannounced between seven and eight that morning, but none of them entered the church.

The first official guest to make an appearance was Mr Booth Watson QC, a friend of the groom – in fact the only friend of the groom. He entered the west door of the church just after one, but then he charged by the hour.

Christina was the next to arrive, just before two. Unusual for the bride to turn up before the groom, but then this was an unusual wedding. She was dressed in a smart turquoise suit, silk scarf and matching long coat, more of a 'going-away' outfit than a bridal dress. Not that she was planning to go anywhere with her husband.

Miles was running a few minutes late, despite his chauffeur keeping the needle nearer eighty than seventy mph while they were on the motorway. He took exit 13 and headed for Limpton.

'Don't look back, boss, but I think we're being followed.'

'What makes you say that, Eddie?'

'A taxi I spotted on the motorway came off at the same exit as us, and I don't think he's one of your guests.'

'Is there another route you can take to the church?'

'Yes, but it will take far longer, especially if we get held up at the railway crossing.'

'Take it. That way we'll find out if he's following us.'

At the next crossroads, Eddie turned right, and a few moments later the taxi once again appeared in his rear-view mirror.

'He's still with us. What do you want me to do?'

'Keep going for a while, I think,' said Miles. The lorry in front of them slowed down as the barriers were lowered at the railway crossing.

'We got our timing wrong, boss,' said Eddie.

'I think we may have got our timing just right. What I want you to do . . .'

• • •

'Do you think they've spotted us?' said William as the taxi joined a short queue waiting for the train to leave the station and the barrier to rise.

'Possible, sir,' said Danny. 'A taxi's always a bit conspicuous on a motorway and having to do eighty didn't help.'

'Perhaps we should have used an unmarked squad car for this particular job, and not a taxi.'

'Why don't we arrest him while he can't get away?'

'No, we'll stick to the plan, while he's still driving straight into a trap.'

'He's on the move!' shouted Danny as the passenger door of the Mercedes shot open. 'He's heading for the station.'

'Dump the car, then follow me,' said William, as he threw open the back door, jumped out and ran towards the station. By the time Danny had manoeuvred the taxi onto the grass verge his boss was already charging across the pedestrian bridge. William raced down the steps on the far side of the track and leapt through the only door of the train that was still open just as it began to move off.

He yanked down the window and shouted to Danny, who had just reached the platform, 'I want a dozen officers waiting for me at the next station. And call DI Hogan to let him know the groom won't be turning up.'

• • •

'He's going to be late for his own wedding,' said Christina, checking her watch once again.

'And I have another ceremony at three o'clock,' the vicar gently reminded her.

'Something must have gone wrong,' said Booth Watson.

All three of them continued to stare at the entrance to the church, but there was still no sign of the groom.

• • •

William walked slowly down each carriage, double-checking the first-class compartments, in search of Captain Ralph Neville, although he intended to arrest Miles Faulkner. By the time he had reached the back of the train, he assumed Faulkner must have locked himself in one of the lavatories. However, as there were no windows in the toilets, he couldn't hope to escape.

• • •

'I'm so sorry, Mrs Faulkner,' said the vicar. 'But some of the guests for my next wedding are already waiting outside. I can't put them off for much longer.'

'This particular groom won't be getting to the church on time, vicar,' said Booth Watson, 'so I think we should call it a day. Especially as some of those people waiting impatiently outside are not guests for this or any other wedding.'

'How can you possibly know that?' asked Christina.

'They're all over six foot, dressed in the same trademark suits, and not one of them is wearing a carnation.'

• • •

'I've got a dozen officers in place, Chief Inspector,' said a voice William didn't recognize.

'Which station?'

'Tunbridge Wells, where you're due to arrive in about fifteen minutes.'

'How many platforms are there?'

'Just two.'

'Be sure to cover them both, because if there's a way to escape Faulkner will find it. I'll be the first person to get off, and tell the guard the train doesn't leave until I say so.'

'Understood, sir.' The line went dead.

William began the slow journey back down the corridor, double-checking each carriage even more carefully a second time. He thought one man who was studiously looking out of the window at the passing countryside looked familiar, but he'd arrested so many people over the years he couldn't immediately place him.

Five of the eleven toilets were engaged. However, by the time the train pulled into the next station, he suspected only one would still be occupied. The train wouldn't depart until its door opened.

• • •

'We won't waste any more of your time, vicar,' said Booth Watson, checking his watch, 'because I can assure you, the groom will not be turning up.'

'So what am I meant to do?' snapped Christina.

'I'll be in touch,' said Booth Watson, 'just remember you've already signed a binding contract, and there's no get-out clause.'

'I'm very sorry, Mrs Faulkner,' said the vicar. 'You must be so disappointed.'

'Relieved, actually,' admitted Christina.

'No doubt there's a simple explanation,' said the vicar, still trying to comfort her.

'The one thing it won't be is simple,' said Christina, as she headed back down the aisle, unaccompanied.

As Booth Watson left the church, he noticed that one of the tense-looking young men he'd spotted earlier was wearing a Metropolitan Police tie.

Christina walked out of the church a few moments later. Several women who were waiting to take their places for the next ceremony admired her going-away outfit, even if she didn't seem to know where she was going.

• • •

The 14.43 pulled into Tunbridge Wells on time, and William was the first person off the train. He joined the little posse awaiting him. An Inspector Thomas stepped forward and introduced himself. 'I've got every exit covered,' he assured him.

'Put three or four of your men on board the train, and make sure they check the lavatories. If one of them is occupied, that's where he'll be hiding. You'll also need some officers on the far platform, just in case.'

'They're already there, sir.'

'Good. The moment I spot Faulkner, move in and detain him, but leave me to arrest and caution him.'

'Understood sir,' said the Inspector, who barked out some orders while William took up a position by the exit, carefully checking every passenger as they left the station.

Ten minutes later, William and the Inspector were the

only people left standing on the platform. William reluctantly allowed the guard to blow his whistle.

As the train departed, William switched on his radio. 'Put out an all-points alert for a dark blue Mercedes, registration number MF1. The driver will be wearing a chauffeur's hat.'

That was when William remembered where he'd seen him.

• • •

Miles smiled as he watched the train move out of the station.

When the barrier finally went up – the longest four minutes of his life – he checked his rear-view mirror and was relieved to see the taxi was still parked on the grass verge and there was no sign of its driver. He drove slowly across the tracks, knowing it wouldn't be long before the train arrived at the next station, by which time he would need to have ditched the car and the chauffeur's hat. He stuck to quiet country lanes until he spotted an old lady standing at a bus stop looking as if she knew when the next bus was due to arrive.

He parked the car in a layby and tossed the chauffeur's hat over a hedge, before hurrying across to the bus stop, a briefcase his only luggage.

'Run out of petrol, have we?' asked the old lady as a bus came into sight. He didn't bother to reply.

Once he'd climbed on board, he realized he had no idea where the bus was going. He only hoped it wasn't back to Limpton.

'Where to, luv?' asked the ticket collector.

'Where are you going?'

'Sevenoaks,' she said, a puzzled look on her face.

'Then it's Sevenoaks,' he replied.

'That'll be sixty pence,' she said as she printed out a ticket.

He handed her a five-pound note.

'Do you have anything smaller, luv?'

'No. You can keep the change.'

'Thank you!' said the ticket collector, as if she had won the pools.

Miles looked cautiously out of the window, in case he had to move quickly. A police car sped past on the other side of the road.

• • •

When Eddie got off the train at Tunbridge Wells, he spotted Chief Inspector Warwick deep in conversation with a uniformed officer, while his eyes double-checked every passenger. He walked straight past them and crossed the bridge to the other platform, where there were far more policemen than passengers. The next train to Charing Cross was due in twelve minutes. When it pulled out of the station, he was tempted to wave and smile at Chief Inspector Warwick, but only tempted.

• • •

Miles got off the bus at Sevenoaks. The final stop was opposite the train station, and there was a cab rank in front of it. Time was against him, so he would have to take a risk. He crossed the road and got into the back of the first taxi.

'Where to, guv?'

'Luton airport.'

The cabbie looked surprised and delighted.

'I'm in a hurry,' said Miles, 'but don't break the speed limit.'

• • •

'Start by checking out the airports, train terminals and bus stations within thirty miles,' said William. 'We can't afford to let him escape a second time.'

'We just don't have that many coppers available,' said Ross. 'It's a Saturday afternoon and most of them are already out policing football matches.'

'You can be sure he'll have taken that into account,' said William, 'and built it into his escape plan.'

• • •

The taxi came to a halt outside Luton airport just as the crowds were streaming out of football grounds all over the country.

Miles handed the cabbie two twenty-pound notes and didn't wait for the change. The first thing he did as he walked into the concourse was check the departure board. He was interested only in flights departing in the next hour. There were just three: one to Newcastle at 5.40, another to Moscow at 8.30 and the final one to Brussels at 6.10. He opened his briefcase, checked the three passports and selected the Canadian one: Jeff Steiner, Company Director. He walked across to the check-in desk, booked a ticket and paid in cash. Mr Steiner didn't have a credit card, only cash and a passport.

He boarded the plane thirty minutes later. After taking his seat, he considered the worst possible scenarios as he waited for the stewardess to pull the exit door closed. At last, the engines began to turn and the aircraft taxied towards the runway. Another interminable wait before it finally took off. As the plane rose high into the sky, he looked out of the tiny window at a green and pleasant land, and wondered when he'd see England again.

He sat back and began to go over the next part of his plan.

Once the plane had touched down in Brussels, he ditched his Canadian passport in favour of a French one, in the name of Thierry Amodio, architect. During the two-hour stopover, he visited an airport barber, who was surprised by his request.

Thirty minutes later, a bald-headed man made a phone call before he joined a small queue of passengers waiting to board the flight for Barcelona. This time he presented a Dutch passport to the immigration official. Ricardo Rossi, dress designer. Once Rossi had fastened his seatbelt, he skipped the plastic meal, closed his eyes and fell asleep.

The plane landed in the Catalonian capital just after midnight. The start of another day. Miles was pleased to see his Spanish driver waiting for him by the exit barrier.

'Good evening, señor,' he said. 'I hope you had a pleasant flight.'

'Several,' Miles said, as he climbed into the back of an anonymous black Volvo.

Another forty minutes passed while he was driven deep into the Spanish countryside, until they reached a recently acquired property that even Booth Watson didn't know about. A smartly dressed butler had opened the front door before he reached the top step. ‘Good evening, Mr Faulkner,’ he said.

‘Good evening, Collins,’ he replied. ‘Some things never change.’

CHAPTER 9

'YOU DID WHAT?' SAID THE commander.

'I lost him, sir.'

'Then you'd better find him, or I might have to lose you.'

William was about to ask The Hawk what he had in mind, when it became a rhetorical question.

'Remind me, Chief Inspector Warwick' – not a good sign; 'William' would have suggested he was in with a chance – 'do you still have another week's leave?'

'Yes, I do, sir.'

'Then you've got seven days to find Faulkner. Should you fail to do so, Chief Inspector, that will give me more than enough time to appoint a replacement as the team's new SIO, and to decide what your next job will be, and the appropriate rank to go with it.'

The phone went dead.

'That didn't sound too friendly,' said Danny.

'It could have been worse,' William responded. 'He might have addressed me as Constable Warwick.'

'Then I wouldn't have to call you "sir",' quipped Danny.

'But until then,' said William, 'you can take me home.'

'Yes, sir.'

• • •

William picked up the phone by his bedside, assuming it would be The Hawk calling to deliver a second volley.

'Hello, caveman. Do you miss me?'

'More than you realize,' admitted William. He wanted to tell Beth why, but satisfied himself with, 'How's New York?' There was a buzz of boisterous laughter in the background.

'Splendiferous! We went to the Frick this afternoon, and you were right about the Bellini, stunning. But I couldn't wait to find out how the wedding went. Did you arrest Faulkner before or after he said "I do"?'

'After,' said William, hoping he would have done so by the time Beth returned.

'How did Christina react?' she asked, sounding like The Hawk.

'Not over the phone, my darling. I'll tell you everything as soon as you get back. What are you up to this evening?' he asked, desperate to change the subject.

'We're going to *La Cage aux Folles*. Had to buy scalper's tickets. But then, a deserted woman can't afford to hang around. I miss you.'

'Miss you too.'

'And congratulations.'

'On what?'

'On your triumph. Can't wait to hear all about it. I have to go now, the curtain's about to go up. Sleep well, miss you.'

William didn't sleep well; in fact he didn't sleep at all. He would have liked to discuss the problem with Beth and seek her advice, but it would have ruined her holiday. In fact, he suspected she would have been on her way to JFK before the curtain had gone up. By the time the first suggestion of morning announced itself through a crack in the curtain, William had already taken a cold shower, dressed, had a bowl of cornflakes and made two phone calls: one to Danny and the other to DI Ross Hogan.

He was about half-way through briefing his new second-in-command when he remembered what time it was. He began to apologize, when he heard a muffled voice in the background, which he thought he recognized. He'd clearly woken both of them.

'I'll be there as quickly as I can, sir,' said Hogan, before putting the phone down.

'Do give the chief my best wishes,' said Jackie, as Ross leapt out of bed. 'And don't forget to thank him for ruining our last weekend together.'

• • •

Danny pulled up outside DCI Warwick's house forty minutes later. William climbed into the back of the car to join Ross, who looked far more awake than he felt.

DI Hogan was clearly a man who wasn't quite ready for plainclothes work. He was dressed in a pair of light blue jeans, a creased T-shirt that looked as if it had been picked up off the floor, and trainers which, although top of the range, were hardly regulation. But that's how The Hawk would have described his brain.

'What a balls-up, sir,' were Ross's first words as William pulled the back door closed.

'Couldn't be much worse. In fact, you'd better get used to calling me William, as I have a feeling I could be calling you sir by the end of the week,' he said, before revealing the details of his telephone conversation with The Hawk.

'That bad?'

'Worse. He pointed out,' continued William, 'that we have more than enough evidence to arrest Christina Faulkner for assisting an offender, contrary to the 1967 Criminal Law Act.'

'Which would keep her out of harm's way for at least five years.'

'However, he felt we should concentrate on the bigger prize, while keeping her under surveillance. He believes she'll happily shop her husband in return for a reduced sentence, so we should, to quote him, keep our powder dry.'

'I wonder which party Booth Watson would end up representing, when it came to trial.'

'Both of them, if he thought he could get away with it,' said William.

'So what's our next move?'

'Some old-fashioned foot-slogging, as if we were back on the beat learning our trade. First, we have to reconstruct everything that took place yesterday in the hope of finding out where Faulkner ended up. Danny,' said William, leaning forward, 'head for that railway crossing where Faulkner took us both for a ride.'

During the journey to Limpton, William took Ross through the best-laid scheme he'd come up with during the night.

'Of mice and men,' said Ross.

'I know which I am,' said William. 'None of this would have been necessary if I'd used a squad car and not a taxi when we followed Faulkner. So The Hawk's right, there's no one else to blame. If I don't find Faulkner by the end of the week, I'll be back on the beat, and it's not hard to work out who'll be appointed to take my place.'

'Don't look at me,' said Ross. 'I'm a loner, not officer material. But I hear there's a job going in traffic control for a recently demoted sergeant. No experience required.'

'Don't joke about it,' said William, as Danny drove onto the motorway.

By the time they reached the level crossing, Ross had asked several insightful questions, and added one or two of his own ideas. William was quickly discovering why The Hawk held him in such high regard.

'Once Faulkner had seen you and Danny running towards the station, he would have had two choices,' said Ross. 'Turn back or carry on over the level crossing.'

'He carried on,' said Danny.

'How can you be so sure?' asked Ross.

'I didn't reach the train in time, so I had to return to the car. While I was crossing the bridge on the way back, I saw the barrier rise and a dark blue Mercedes drive through.'

'Why didn't you follow it?' asked Ross.

'The driver was wearing a chauffeur's hat, so I assumed

Faulkner was on the train. My first responsibility was to make sure there was a welcoming party waiting for him at the next station.'

'And there was, but Faulkner wasn't on it,' said William. 'It was some time before I cottoned on to the fact that his chauffeur had taken his place. From now on, let's start thinking like Faulkner. If I was driving over the level crossing, where would I head for?'

'He wouldn't have carried on into Limpton,' said Ross, 'because by then he would have realized there would be several ushers waiting for the groom.'

'There's only one other turning off the road before Limpton,' chipped in Danny.

'Then he must have taken it,' said William, as they approached a crossroads.

Danny ignored the signpost to Limpton, turned right and put his foot on the accelerator.

'Slow down,' said William. 'Keep a steady pace. Faulkner wouldn't have risked breaking the speed limit and being pulled over.'

'How long do you think he would have carried on for before he ditched the car?' asked Ross.

'Not for too long,' said William. 'He would have known that once we realized he wasn't on that train, every patrol car in the county would be on the look-out for a dark blue Mercedes.'

'Assuming it hasn't already been picked up, or stolen,' said Danny. 'We'd have a better chance of finding it if we'd been able to use the Met's helicopter rather than this ancient Austin Allegro.'

'I don't think the commander would have authorized that,'

said William, as Danny drove slowly through a small village before stopping at another crossroad.

'Help,' said Danny. 'Right, left or straight on?'

'Straight on,' said William. 'He wouldn't have turned left to Limpton. If we don't come across anything in the next fifteen minutes, we'll turn back.'

William became more and more pessimistic with each passing mile, but as they approached the next village, Danny shouted, 'Bingo!' and screeched to a halt beside a dark blue Mercedes.

Ross was about to get out of the car when William said quietly, 'Wrong number plate.'

No one spoke as Danny turned the car around and put his foot on the accelerator. He slowed down only when he was back at the crossroads. This time, he turned left and followed the signpost to Sevenoaks, being careful to keep his speed below thirty.

William couldn't help wishing he'd stayed in New York and was now visiting the Frick, rather than roaming around the countryside searching for an abandoned car.

'What in hell's name are they up to?' said Danny, when he spotted a couple of youths unscrewing the bolts on the wheel of a car. He threw on the brakes, but the two lads had fled in different directions long before he got out of the car, one of them with a wheel under his arm.

'Do you want me to go after him, boss?'

'No,' said William, staring at the number plate. 'They've left a far bigger prize behind. Call Inspector Thomas, tell him to send a tow truck, and to keep the car under wraps until I get back in touch with him.'

While Danny was on the radio, Ross, who had circled

the car several times, was now looking over a nearby hedge. 'Over here, sir,' he shouted.

William quickly joined him. They clambered through the hedge and into a muddy field, where William used a small branch to carefully pick up a chauffeur's hat.

'We'll only need one fingerprint to confirm that Captain Ralph Neville is in fact Miles Faulkner,' said William. 'But what I want to know is why he dumped the car here.'

'That might be the reason,' said Ross, pointing to a bus stop.

'Well spotted,' said William. They crossed the road and examined the timetable inside the shelter. 'There was a bus to Sevenoaks at two twenty on Saturday,' said William.

'That would fit in with the timing,' said Ross, as Danny joined them.

'Inspector Thomas is on his way, and a tow truck will follow shortly. What next, guv?'

'Seal this in an evidence bag,' said William, handing over the chauffeur's hat, before he checked the timetable once again. 'I'll take the next bus to Sevenoaks and meet you both there, at the last stop. Ross, when you get there, try to see everything through Faulkner's eyes. That might help us work out what he did next. I'll do the same while I'm on the bus.'

William watched as the two of them climbed back into the car and sped away. He sat down in the shelter and waited for the next bus to appear.

CHAPTER 10

THE LOCAL BUS TRUNDLED SLOWLY over the hill and juddered to a halt at the stop. A solitary passenger climbed aboard and took a seat near the front.

'Where to?' asked the ticket collector.

'Sevenoaks,' said William.

'Sixty pence.'

William took out his warrant card and asked, 'Were you working this run yesterday afternoon, around twelve, one o'clock?'

'No, sir, that's Rose's shift. She's off today, doesn't work Sundays.'

'Rose?'

'Rose Prescott. Been on this run for years,' he said with a chuckle.

'Thank you,' said William, then sat back and looked out of the window at the passing countryside, wondering if it was possible that Faulkner was still in England. His thoughts were interrupted by a siren, as a police car shot past them on the other side of the road. He made a mental note to call Inspector Thomas and thank him.

Although the bus made several stops on its slow interrupted journey to Sevenoaks, William saw nothing to make him think Faulkner would have got off before the final stop.

He checked his watch as a police pickup truck lumbered by. He wasn't confident there would be any of Faulkner's dabs on the Mercedes, but the chauffeur's hat? Ross was waiting for him when the bus reached its final stop, and he clearly hadn't wasted his time.

'The first thing Faulkner would have seen when he got off the bus,' Ross said, 'was the railway station and the cab rank directly opposite, on the other side of the road. Danny's already checking the station. So far I haven't had any luck with the cabbies. None of them recognized the photograph of Ralph Neville, but they told me quite a few of the regulars prefer working afternoons.'

'Then you'll have to keep on asking, while I pay a visit to Mrs Rose Prescott.'

'Who's she?'

'To be revealed later,' said William, as he left Ross to return to the taxi rank, while he walked across to the terminus.

'Rose,' said the supervisor, once he'd checked the Chief Inspector's warrant card. 'She hasn't done anything wrong, I hope.'

'No, nothing. I'm just hoping she'll remember a passenger who was on her bus yesterday afternoon.'

'On that route they're almost all regulars who she'd know personally.' He began to turn the pages of a large folder.

'She lives at number twenty-three Castle Drive.' Checking his watch, he added, 'She should be back from church by now.'

When William emerged from the terminus, he spotted Ross showing another taxi driver the blown-up photo of Neville, but the cabbie was shaking his head as William joined them.

'It's an outside chance,' admitted William, 'but don't let the odds put you off.'

Ross mumbled something unintelligible, as William climbed into the back of the cab and gave the driver an address in Castle Drive. As the taxi moved off, he asked, 'You didn't recognize the man in the photograph my colleague showed you?'

'No, guv. Yesterday afternoon I was watching Arsenal being stitched up by Chelsea.'

Now there's a surprise, William wanted to say, but decided not to reveal his true colours in case the cabbie decided not to speak to him again. He sat back and began to think about the questions he needed to ask Mrs Prescott, who he felt he already knew.

When the taxi drew up outside No. 23, William said, 'Can you hang about? I shouldn't be too long.'

'The meter will still be running,' said the cabbie with a grin.

William opened the little wicket gate, walked down a short path and knocked on the front door. Moments later, a young woman answered it.

'Is Mrs Prescott at home?' he asked, after he had shown her his warrant card.

'She's just got back from church. I'll go and fetch her.'

An older woman appeared a few moments later, dressed in her Sunday best. 'Do come in, Chief Inspector,' she said. 'I was just about to make a cup of tea. Would you like one?'

'Thank you,' said William, who closed the front door, and followed her through to the kitchen. Once she'd put the kettle on, she said, 'Please, sit down, young man, and tell me how I can help you.'

William took out the photograph of Ralph Neville and placed it on the kitchen table. 'When you were on the Sevenoaks run yesterday afternoon, did you see this man?'

'I most certainly did,' said Rose, as she poured William a cup of tea. 'Sugar?'

'No, thank you. What makes you so sure you recognize him?'

'Shouldn't think a gentleman like that travels by bus too often, at least not dressed as if he was going to a wedding.' William didn't interrupt. 'What I remember most was, when I gave him his ticket he didn't have any loose change on him, just a five-pound note. And what's more, Mrs Haskins, one of my regulars, told me later that he must have run out of petrol, because he'd left his flashy car by the side of the road.' She paused, took a sip of tea and said, 'Does he want his money back?'

'His money?' repeated William.

'The change from the five-pound note, although he did say I could keep it. Anyway, he's got a snowball's chance in hell of getting it back,' chuckled Rose, 'because I put it on the collection plate this morning, and I can't see the vicar giving it back.'

William laughed. 'I don't suppose you saw where he went after he got off the bus?'

'He walked across the road to the taxi rank.'

'Are you sure?'

'Oh yes. I thought he might be going to get some change, and would be coming back for his fiver, but he just got in the back of a taxi and off he went.'

'I don't suppose you'd recognize the taxi driver?' said William hopefully.

'No, sorry love,' said Rose, as the young woman reappeared.

'Any hope of you carting Mum off to jail, Chief Inspector?'

'Not quite yet, but if she tries to make a dash for it, I've got the handcuffs ready,' said William, as he finished his tea.

'Pity,' said her daughter. 'My boyfriend was hoping to spend the night.'

'You can forget it,' said Rose firmly. 'That's not going to happen until I see an engagement ring on your finger, and maybe not even then.'

'Thank you, Rose,' said William, as he stood up. 'I ought to get going.'

'Of course.'

William paused as she opened the front door for him. 'You've made my day,' he said.

'Mine too,' said Rose, 'because I wouldn't have wanted to tell the vicar he was going to have to give that fiver back. Mind you, I have a feeling the man in the photograph won't miss it.'

William bent and kissed the shrewd woman on both cheeks, which was rewarded with a warm smile. He walked down the path, climbed into the back of the waiting cab, and noticed the meter was still ticking.

'Back to the station, please.'

'She didn't look like a master criminal to me,' said the cabbie.

'You're right. But her late husband was a Gunners' fan.'

'Is that a crime?'

'It is if you support Chelsea,' said William, which created the silence he needed while he thought about what his next move should be.

Ross and Danny were waiting for him at the taxi rank, one smiling, one frowning. He took the frown first.

'Not a dickybird,' said Danny. 'The ticket collector let me know, ever so politely, that over a thousand passengers commute into London every weekday, and that on a Saturday, if the footy's on, it's even more. As far as he was concerned, the bloke in the picture looked like any other city gent, so how could he possibly be expected to remember him?'

'And you, Ross?'

'I also drew a blank, except that one driver had a strange experience you might want to hear about. He's just taking a customer to a local hotel, but should be back in a few minutes.'

'Time for a coffee break,' said Danny, hopefully.

William nodded in the direction of the station's café. Once they'd found a table, he said, 'I'll sum up where I think we are, and you can tell me if I've missed anything.

'We've found the car we believe Faulkner was driving, which is now on its way to the local pound. We'll probably have to wait a couple of days to see if they come up with any dabs. Somehow, I doubt it, but I haven't given up on the chauffeur's cap, which I'll drop into forensics as soon as we get back to the Yard.'

'Did Rose come up with anything worthwhile?' asked Ross.

'An eighteen-carat gem. Not only did she recognize Faulkner from the photograph, but saw him get into a taxi. Now we just need to find out which one.'

'That's him,' said Ross, looking out of the window. 'He's just pulled up outside the station.'

'I'll go and have a word with him while you finish your coffees,' said William. He drained his second cup of tea that morning, and crossed the road to join the last cab on the rank.

'Sorry guv,' said the cabbie. 'You have to take the one at the front.'

'I'm not looking for a cab, but one of yesterday's passengers. My colleague tells me you didn't recognize this man,' said William, showing him the photograph of Neville, 'but you had a fare who acted strangely?'

'An odd one that,' said the cabbie, 'but I never saw his face, so I can't be sure that's him.'

'What was odd about him?'

'He gets into the back before I have a chance to look at him. Nothing unusual about that, but then he tucks himself in the left-hand corner of the seat so I can't see him in my rear-view mirror. That sometimes means they're planning to do a runner without paying. But when I asked him where he wanted to go, he had such a toffee-nosed accent I relaxed.'

'Where did he want to go?'

'Luton airport, but he didn't say another word on the entire journey. When we got there, he pushed some cash through the hatch and was gone before I could give him his change.'

'What's unusual about that? He might just have been in a hurry.'

'Most of my customers who take a taxi to an airport want a receipt, so they can claim it on expenses. But not this one.'

'So you never got a look at him?'

'No, but he was smartly dressed and carrying a leather briefcase, which I thought was unusual for a Saturday afternoon. I wouldn't have thought anything of it if I hadn't seen him getting off the bus.'

William offered up a small prayer. 'What time was that?'

'Just after three.'

'Are you sure of the time?'

'I was listening to Match of the Day, wasn't I? Spurs versus Everton, and the Toffees scored in the first minute. The bastards.'

'Thank you,' said William, placing the photograph back in his pocket. 'That was very helpful.' He got back to the café just in time to pay the bill.

'Right, Danny, get your skates on, we're off to Luton airport.'

As they drove out of Sevenoaks and headed for the motorway, William briefed Ross about his conversation with the cabbie.

'A bit of a long shot,' said Ross, 'but enough coincidences not to be a coincidence.'

'We'll need to time how long it takes to get to the airport,' said William. 'Then we should be able to work out which flight he's most likely to have caught.'

'Why would he have chosen Luton, when Gatwick, Heathrow and Stansted are so much closer?' said Danny.

'He would have assumed we had them well covered.'

William and Ross had gone over various possible scenarios several times before Danny drew up outside the airport.

'One hour and twenty-five minutes, guv,' he announced.

'Wait here,' said William. 'We'll probably be going straight back to London, but who knows?'

He and Ross strode into the terminal and headed for the information desk.

'How can I help you, gentlemen?' asked the woman standing behind the counter.

'I'd like to know which flights took off after five o'clock yesterday afternoon?'

She began tapping away on her computer.

'The 5.05 to Dublin. Took off on time.'

'He wouldn't have made it,' said Ross.

'The 5.40 for Newcastle departed twenty minutes late.'

'That would have meant he was stuck in England overnight.'

'Moscow at 5.50,' said the woman, still staring at her console.

'I don't think so,' said William.

'The 6.10 to Brussels.'

'A possibility.'

'There was the 6.20 to Edinburgh.'

'No,' said William.

'Or the 7.10 to Copenhagen.'

'He wouldn't have wanted to hang about that long,' said William. 'It has to be Brussels.'

'I doubt if that was his final destination,' said Ross. 'Just the first plane that would get him out of the country.'

'Agreed,' said William, and thanked the woman before he and Ross made their way across to the Sabena booking desk. This time, William produced his warrant card before he asked his first question.

'I'd like to see your passenger list for yesterday afternoon's 6.10 flight for Brussels.'

'Are you looking for a particular name, sir?' asked the woman, as she tapped away, before checking the screen in front of her.

'Captain Ralph Neville.'

She double-checked the passenger list before saying, 'No one registered under that name is showing up on my screen for the flight.'

'Miles Faulkner?' suggested Ross, not looking at all confident.

'No,' she replied, her eyes still fixed on the monitor. Ross produced a photograph. She took a careful look and then shook her head. 'Can't say I remember him.'

William tried a long shot. 'Did anyone book in at the last minute and pay for his ticket with cash?'

'There was one gentleman who was quite late booking, and he wasn't pleased when we couldn't find him a seat in first class.'

'Do you recall his name?'

'I'm afraid not.'

'Are we going to risk it?' asked Ross.

'Is there a flight to Brussels this evening?' asked William, answering the question.

'The 6.10. Same time every day. I have two first-class tickets available.'

'I don't think so,' said William, giving her a warm smile.

'Two economy will be just fine,' he added, passing over his credit card.

'One-way or return?'

'One-way. We can't be sure where we'll be going next.'

This was one customer she wasn't going to forget easily.

'Hang about for the tickets, Ross, while I explain to Danny why we won't be going back to the Yard.'

Danny was pleased to hear he could return to London and take the rest of the day off. The Chief Inspector's idea of a joke.

'But not before you've handed in the chauffeur's hat to forensics. I've already told them to let me know if they find any dabs on it that match up with Miles Faulkner's.'

Danny touched his forehead with the fingers of his right hand and asked, 'Will you be needing me tomorrow, guv?'

'If I do, it will be to drop me off at the jobcentre,' said William, 'but I'll let you know.'

He strolled back into the airport to see Ross deep in conversation with another man, who was frowning.

'We've got a problem,' said Ross, as William joined them. 'Passports, or lack of them. This is Thomas King, head of security. He's happy to arrange a temporary travel visa, but he needs the authority of a commander or above before he can authorize it. I'm certainly not going to call The Hawk at home on a Sunday evening.'

William picked up the phone on the counter and dialled a number even Ross didn't know.

The Hawk listened with interest to how Chief Inspector Warwick and DI Hogan had spent their Sunday. 'Put him on,' was all he said.

William handed the phone to the security officer, who

said, 'Yes, sir' several times, before passing the phone back to William.

'If you come back without Faulkner, don't bother to put in a claim for your expenses,' were The Hawk's parting words.

'Thank you, sir,' said William, before he put the phone down.

'Are we still going to Brussels?' asked Ross.

'Yes,' said William, 'but only one of us may be coming back.'

Not long after William had fastened his seatbelt and the Boeing 727 had taken off, he fell asleep for the first time since he'd arrived back from New York.

Ross spent his time writing an update while considering the alternatives, which he accepted only threw up yet more questions for William to consider when he woke. That didn't happen until the wheels touched down on the runway at Brussels National Airport forty minutes later.

(a) Did Faulkner fly straight on to another airport?
(b) Did he stay at the airport overnight? Check every hotel within a two-mile radius.
(c) Is there a direct flight to Nice (Monte Carlo) from Brussels?
(d) Have we come to a dead end?

A uniformed security officer met them at the bottom of the steps as they disembarked from the plane. Clearly the commander hadn't been idle.

'How can I help?' he asked, after he'd shaken hands with them.

'How many flights took off from Brussels,' William asked as he checked his watch, 'after seven thirty yesterday evening?'

'Half a dozen, no more,' said the security officer. 'I'd need to check the log,' he added as they walked in a different direction to all the other passengers.

Once they were in his office, it took Mr King only a few moments before he pronounced, 'Paris, St Petersburg, Manchester, Helsinki, Luton and Barcelona.'

William studied the list for some time before concluding, 'My bet would be Paris, because he could have taken a domestic flight from there to Nice.'

'Barcelona could also be an outside possibility,' suggested Ross.

'Agreed. You check with Air France, while I talk to Iberia.'

'Were you both on duty last night?' was William's first question as he reached the check-in counter. He once again produced a large photograph of Ralph Neville and asked if either of them had seen him, but all he got was a shake of the head.

'Barcelona is Iberian Airways' last flight out of Brussels on a Saturday night,' said 'Blanca', 'and as usual it was packed with holidaymakers.'

'This man wouldn't have looked as if he was going on holiday,' said William.

They both took a closer look, but it elicited the same response.

'Can I check the passenger list?' he asked.

The security guard nodded, and one of the booking clerks swung the console around. William double-checked both classes, but there wasn't a name on the list that he recognized.

'Thank you,' Blanca said, as Ross walked across to join him, to report the same negative result for passengers flying to De Gaulle.

'Even if he was on one of those flights,' said William, 'it would still leave us with about three hundred suspects. We'll have to accept he's disappeared again.'

'He's beginning to make Houdini look like an amateur.'

'He's beginning to make me look like a raw recruit,' said William with considerable feeling.

'Do pretty girls always chase after you?' said Ross.

William turned around to see one of the young Iberian booking clerks running towards them.

'Can I take a closer look at that photograph?' Blanca asked.

William took the photo out of an inside pocket and handed it to her.

She studied the man's face for some time before she placed a hand over Faulkner's forehead and continued to look even more closely. 'Yes, I'm confident it's him. One of the first-class passengers on the flight to Barcelona was bald. When I queried the photo in his passport, he told me he'd just had his head shaved, even produced the bill,' she said, pointing to a barber shop on the other side of the concourse.

'His first mistake,' said Ross.

'Do you have a name?' asked William.

'Ricardo Rossi. I remember, because according to his passport he was a dress designer.'

'I'd kiss you,' said Ross, 'but I'm not allowed to.'

'How disappointing,' she said, and kissed him on both cheeks before returning to her desk.

'I wish I lived in Brussels,' said Ross. William didn't hear him because he was already on the move, having spotted that the sign on the barber's door was being switched from '*Ouvert*' to '*Fermé*'. The security man chased after him and quickly produced his pass. The door was reluctantly opened a few inches.

'Did you shave this man's head yesterday evening?' asked William, holding up a photograph of Neville.

'I wasn't here yesterday,' came the gruff reply. 'It would have been Carlo, and today's his day off. If the customer's got a complaint you can come back in the morning.' The door slammed and the blind was pulled down.

'Are we off to Barcelona?' asked Ross when they returned to join him at the check-in desk.

'Not much point,' said William. 'By now Faulkner will have flown on to his next destination and once again evaporated into thin air. We may as well go home and face the music.'

'Do you want to hear the good news or the bad news?' said Ross.

'I can't wait.'

'You're going to have to, because the last flight back to Luton has just taken off.'

William looked around at the rows and rows of hard plastic seats, before he asked, 'What's the good news?'

'I'm having dinner with Blanca.'

• • •

Danny picked up two dishevelled, yawning detectives off the first flight from Brussels the following morning. Neither of them had slept.

'Inspector Thomas has just called,' he said as they climbed into the back seat. 'They didn't find any of Miles Faulkner's prints in the Mercedes, but they found several of his wife's.'

'That would explain why there was no one to pick her up from the church.'

'But there's better news on the chauffeur's cap,' said Danny. 'One thumb and an index finger turn out to be a perfect match with Faulkner's right hand.'

'So,' said Ross, 'it appears that right now Miles Faulkner, aka Captain Ralph Neville, is holed up somewhere in Spain under the name of Ricardo Rossi, dress designer.'

'Though he's probably changed his name and profession yet again,' said William. 'I'll issue the latest photographic image we have of him to the Spanish police as soon as we get back to the Yard.'

'Do you want me to bring in Christina Faulkner for questioning?' asked Ross.

'No. Not while I've got my own undercover agent.'

CHAPTER 11

'YOU SHOULD HAVE STAYED IN New York with me,' said Beth as they strolled into the bedroom. 'Ella was fantastic, and we went back to the Met three times . . .'

'Although it was only a week, the children missed you terribly, and kept asking where you were,' said William, as he took off his jacket and hung it in the wardrobe. 'And it didn't help that I was roaming around the countryside looking for Christina's car.'

'While you somehow managed to lose her husband once again.'

'But I did find him again,' protested William.

'Well, let's be accurate. You found out which continent he was on, but you can't even be sure if he's still there,' said Beth as she unbuttoned her blouse.

'I know his name,' said William as he took off his tie.

'Ricardo Rossi flew in to Brussels but he may not be the same person who turned up in Barcelona.'

'Whose side are you on?' asked William.

'Yours, caveman,' said Beth as she slipped off her blouse. 'But only because I'll need your help if I'm going to get away with murdering Christina.'

'That's the last thing I want you to do. She's still my best chance of tracking down her late husband.'

'What can I do to help?' said Beth eagerly, as William threw his shirt onto a chair.

'Next time you see her, play innocent. I need you to find out whose side she's on,' said William, as Beth slowly unzipped her skirt. 'You may be surprised.'

'But she'll have worked out by now that you know Ralph and Miles are one and the same.'

'I agree, but is she the jilted bride,' asked William as he kicked off his shoes, 'or his partner in crime?'

'Why should I fall in with your plans, when all I want to do is strangle the damn woman?' Beth asked, as she undid his belt.

'Because if I put Faulkner back behind bars, half of his art collection will still be legally hers, so another masterpiece might well find its way onto the walls of the Fitzmolean,' he said as he fiddled with the clasp of her bra. 'There'd still be more than enough left over to keep her swimming in champagne for the rest of her life.'

'Along with endless toy boys to uncork the bottles,' said Beth, as she ripped off his trousers. 'While I was away, caveman,' she asked, as he bent down to kiss her, 'what did you miss most, my shepherd's pie or sex?'

'I'll need a little time to think about that,' he said as their lips parted. Beth fell back onto the bed as the door opened and a voice said, 'Daddy, you promised to read to us when you got home.'

Beth burst out laughing as Artemisia climbed up onto the bed and handed William her book. William quickly slipped on his dressing gown, as Beth jumped off the bed, pulled up her knickers and hurriedly put her blouse back on.

'Just one chapter,' said William, as Peter crept in through the open door and joined his sister on the bed. The twins snuggled up close to their father, who opened the book and began to read.

'PC Plod was a good and kind policeman. He liked to help grandmas and grandpas when they crossed the road, and if he caught a little boy riding a bicycle who wasn't wearing a helmet, he would tick them off, but not tell their parents, which made him very popular.'

Peter began to clap.

'But sadly, no one back at headquarters,' continued William, 'gave much thought to promoting PC Plod and making him a sergeant.'

'Why not?' demanded Artemisia.

'I expect we're about to find out,' said William as he turned the page, although his mind was elsewhere.

'Plod was, as he'd told his wife Beryl often enough, happy to be one of life's foot soldiers. Beryl didn't agree with him. "You're just as clever as Inspector Watchit, who always takes the credit for your ideas and then gets promoted," she said. "That's my job," explained Plod. "It's my responsibility to assist the public at all times while passing on any useful information to my superiors. In fact, Beryl, only today . . ."

he said, just as the phone began to ring. Beryl picked it up and listened for a few moments before she said, "But it's Fred's day off."

'"Not any longer it isn't," said Inspector Watchit. "Tell Plod to get himself over to the manor house, sharpish. There's been a burglary and a valuable pearl necklace has gone missing. Lady Doubtful wants the grounds searched while I question the staff."'

William glanced up from the book to see that Peter had fallen asleep, but Artemisia was still hanging on his every word.

'Time for bed, you two,' said Beth.

'No, no, no!' said Artemisia.

'Yes, yes, yes,' said William, before picking them up, one under each arm, and carrying them out of the room. When he reached the doorway he turned and smiled at Beth.

'I can't wait for PC Plod to return,' said Beth, as she once again slipped off her blouse.

• • •

'I'd like to begin this meeting,' said the commander, 'by officially welcoming DI Ross Hogan to our ranks.'

The rest of the team banged the palms of their hands on the table.

'Ross joins us not only with a formidable reputation as an undercover operative, but he previously served for four years as a Detective Sergeant with the murder squad. Invaluable experience that we can now put to good use.'

'And can I say,' interrupted Ross, 'before I accept my Oscar for best supporting role, how delighted and honoured

I am to be joining the team who were responsible for putting Miles Faulkner behind bars.'

'Only to let him escape again from right under our noses,' said William ruefully.

'Not your fault,' said Ross. 'Two bent prison officers were involved in that little fiasco. You'll be glad to hear they've both been transferred to Dartmoor, with no chance of an early release.'

'But the second time Faulkner escaped *was* my fault,' said William, 'and I won't rest until he's back in Pentonville on an extended lease, with no break clauses.'

'It shouldn't be long before Ricardo Rossi appears on our radar screen,' said Paul.

'To that end,' said The Hawk, 'I've briefed the Spanish police and Interpol, and supplied them with details of Faulkner's criminal record along with an identikit photo of what Neville would look like with a shaved head. But we'll have to put Faulkner on one side for now as the time has come for us to concentrate on our new assignments. DCI Warwick, perhaps you can bring us up to date.'

'As you are all well aware,' said William, 'the early stages of any murder inquiry are the most critical. The golden hour, that sixty-minute period immediately after the killing, is the best chance of recovering the evidence necessary to secure a conviction. CCTV, forensics, witnesses, and the likelihood that the murderer is still somewhere in the vicinity are a detective's best weapons. But in each one of these cases,' he continued, 'we didn't get the golden hour, or for that matter the silver or bronze. Truth is, these particular miscreants not only got clean away, but will now be convinced that their records have been gathering dust, in an unsolved crime cabinet, which they don't realize we're about to open.'

'And I think you should know,' chipped in The Hawk, 'the commissioner feels it will send an important message to the underworld if these villains are brought to justice. Not least because if even one of them were to be convicted and sent down, the others will be reminded that the prospect of a life sentence is still hanging over them.'

'There's a second, equally important reason to go after them,' said William. 'If they've got away with murder once, they might well consider doing it a second time.'

The Hawk nodded, before adding, 'With that in mind, each of you has been given a cold case to follow up, and although we'll still be working as a team, assisting each other whenever possible, you'll be the lead officer in your own case, reporting back to DCI Warwick at all times.'

'So let's begin by trading information,' said William. 'As you've been landed with the toughest assignment, DI Hogan, we'll start with you.'

'I've got two cases to investigate,' said Ross, 'which are interrelated. A couple of revenge gang murders, where one killed a member of a rival outfit, and, not long after, the other side retaliated in kind.'

'I've read about the Roach gang and their sworn enemies, the Abbotts, in the press,' said Rebecca, 'but I don't know much more about them beyond that.'

'There isn't much more to know,' said Ross. 'Two ruthless, highly organized East End gangs, like the Krays and the Richardsons, who've been at each other's throats for years. Between them they control the local drug scene, prostitution and gambling, and run a protection racket that's more efficient at collecting its weekly payments than the local council is with the rates. And even when we do manage to get one of them convicted and sent down, they're like cockroaches: stamp on one and two more creep out from under the floorboards to take their place.'

'Forgive me for being cynical,' said Paul, 'but do the public give a damn if these scum go on killing each other? Most people would be perfectly happy if they did our job for us and wiped each other out.'

'That may well be the case, DS Adaja,' said William. 'But if they're allowed to continue with their criminal activities, it won't be long before the East End ends up as a no-go area for the police, as well as law-abiding citizens.'

'I apologize,' said Paul. 'I should have thought it through.'

'No need to apologize, DS Adaja,' said Ross. 'Although I was working undercover at the time, I was made aware of your memorable contribution during the Trojan Horse operation.'

The rest of the team burst out laughing, while William recalled that Ross had given him a black eye on that occasion, so that no one other than the commander would know he was still working undercover.

'Could you brief us on your case, DS Roycroft,' said William, once the laughter had died down.

'Clive Pugh couldn't be more different from the Roaches and the Abbotts,' said Jackie. 'Although he's every bit as ruthless, he's far more cunning. As far as the outside world is concerned, he was a law-abiding citizen who ticked all the right boxes. Married with two children, both university graduates, deputy manager of his local branch of Barclays

Bank, and the local Rotary Club voted him businessman of the year.'

'So who did he murder?' asked Rebecca.

'His wife of twenty-seven years, and just months after he'd taken out a million-pound insurance policy on her life, with himself as the sole beneficiary.'

'How did he get away with it?' asked Paul.

'His story was that after he returned home from a Rotary Club meeting he found his wife hanging from a beam in the bathroom. He immediately called the police, who found a typewritten letter apologizing for what she'd done. It looked like an open-and-shut case of suicide, until the pathologist pointed out at the inquest that she'd been killed by a single blow to the head some time before she was strung up. The jury couldn't make up their minds if he was guilty, and ended up hung, which was somewhat ironic.'

'The judge was clearly convinced of Pugh's guilt,' said William, 'because he immediately ordered a retrial. But it ended up being thrown out of court on a technicality long before the jury had a chance to deliver a verdict, so Pugh got away with it a second time. The investigating officer announced from the courtroom steps later that afternoon that the case was closed and the police wouldn't be looking for any other suspects.

'The only good thing that came out of it,' said Jackie, 'was that the insurance company refused to pay up.'

'So he ended up penniless,' said Paul.

'Not quite. Pugh sued the insurance company, and they finally settled out of court for a quarter of a million.'

'I've known people who've been murdered for far less than that,' said Ross.

'When I checked through the evidence,' continued William, 'I noticed a couple of anomalies that might be worth following up. Pugh's brother-in-law gave a statement a few days after the murder took place that makes interesting reading.'

'But he backed down at the last minute,' Jackie reminded him, 'and refused to give evidence at the trial.'

'I'd still follow it up,' said William. 'Who knows how he might feel a year later?'

'And the other thing?' pressed Jackie.

'The suicide note was found on the floor below the wife's body, not on her writing desk. And it was unsigned, although we found a pen on her desk.'

'But the law of double jeopardy means that if Pugh was found not guilty,' said Jackie, 'he can't be tried again.'

'He wasn't found not guilty,' William reminded her. 'The first trial ended with a hung jury, and the second was thrown out of court on a technicality.'

'A fine legal point that Booth Watson would have a field day arguing in front of a judge,' suggested Ross.

'I'm sure Sir Julian Warwick would be up to the challenge,' said The Hawk.

'Let's move on to your case, Paul,' said William, 'which involves one of the most egregious individuals I've ever come across.'

'I couldn't agree more,' said Paul, as he opened a thick file in front of him. 'Max Sleeman is an unprincipled loan shark who lends cash at exorbitant rates, sometimes as high as ten per cent.'

'Per annum?' enquired the commander. 'That doesn't sound unreasonable.'

'Per month,' came back Paul. 'He also imposes unwritten penalties should his borrowers fail to pay up: a broken leg for the first offence, an arm for the second and, after a third, you simply disappear. A warning to his other customers of the consequences of not paying up on time. We're pretty sure that the three victims who went missing were murdered,' he added. 'But until we come up with even one body, we can't arrest Sleeman, let alone charge him.'

'How does he get away with it?' asked Rebecca.

'At the time the person goes missing, Sleeman always has an unimpeachable alibi. On the first occasion, he was attending the last night of the Proms, and was even seen on television for a brief moment waving a Union Jack. The second time, he was at centre court at Wimbledon watching the women's semi-final. During a break between matches, he dropped some cream on a woman seated at the next table. He paid to have her dress cleaned, and produced the bill as evidence.'

'And on the third occasion?'

'Sleeman was caught on a speed camera in Manchester doing forty-three miles an hour in a built-up area. He produced a photo of himself behind the wheel, along with a receipt from Manchester City Council.'

'Then someone else must have carried out the killings on his behalf,' said Ross.

'We think he employs a professional hitman, but I haven't come up with a name yet.'

'There still have to be three bodies out there somewhere.'

'I know,' said Paul. 'But where?'

'Find one of them,' said William, 'and you can be sure the other two will turn up.'

'Any leads?' asked the commander.

'The wife of one of the missing victims recorded a telephone conversation between her husband and Sleeman, in which he more than hints at what will happen to him if he misses another payment. I'm seeing her later this week.'

'Courageous lady,' said William. 'But will she be willing to appear in court?' he added, before turning his attention to DC Pankhurst. 'What have you got for us, Rebecca?'

'Darren Carter, a bouncer at the Eve Club, a sleazy establishment in Soho. He killed a customer with a single blow. Claimed it was the victim who threw the first punch. When it came to court he produced several witnesses to back up his story. It later turned out that the dead man was having an affair with the wife of the club's owner. However, that piece of evidence wasn't even raised during the trial. The defence counsel argued in camera that it was prejudicial and circumstantial, and the judge agreed. Carter pleaded guilty to manslaughter, served one year of a two-year sentence, and is now back working at the club.'

'I want that club closed down,' said The Hawk, 'and Carter locked up for life, so we send out a clear message to every other sleazy club owner in Soho.'

'I've got one lead,' said Rebecca, 'but I can't pretend I'm optimistic about my source's evidence being substantial, reliable or compelling.'

'What a right bunch of villains,' said William. 'And with one exception, they were all defended by our old adversary, Mr Booth Watson, QC.'

'Let me guess,' said Paul. 'For professional reasons he felt unable to represent both the Roaches and the Abbotts.'

'The Abbotts keep him on retainer,' said William.

'Perhaps someone should kill Booth Watson and solve all our problems,' suggested Ross.

The banging of palms on the table lasted for some time.

• • •

'What can I get you, Ross?' asked William.

'Half a pint of bitter please, guv. Any more and I'll fall asleep and be unable to keep up with your bright young turks.'

'I'm very fortunate,' said William, looking across at the rest of his team, who were sharing a joke. 'They're the new breed of professional coppers who don't believe in cutting corners or winging it. They prefer to rely on solid evidence before making an arrest, rather than jumping to conclusions that won't later stand up in court.'

'I look forward to working with them,' said Ross, 'though I've already experienced what they're like first-hand when I was working undercover. You included.'

'Creepy,' said William. He took a sip of beer before saying, 'You mentioned during the morning session that you might be able to help me with my unpaid overtime job of attempting to track down Faulkner and put him back in jail.'

'Yes, I've come up with one or two ideas. I'm now certain that ex-Superintendent Lamont is working as a consultant for both Booth Watson and Christina Faulkner.'

'A servant of two masters,' said William. 'But on this occasion, it's not a comedy.'

'Jackie tells me she sees Lamont socially from time to time, and reports any information she picks up back to you.'

'Along with stuffed brown envelopes she never opens.'

'Remembering that money is now Lamont's sole interest in life, I think I may have come up with a way of trapping both him and Booth Watson at the same time.'

William listened with interest to Ross's ideas while throwing in the occasional question. He ended with, 'I'm all for the idea, but we'd need to get The Hawk's approval.'

'I'll leave that to you,' said Ross, as he glanced over William's shoulder and became distracted by a young woman standing at the bar. She was elegantly dressed, her white pleated skirt falling just below the knee, and her blouse buttoned at the neck. No jewellery and just a hint of make-up. So understated, yet so alluring. He couldn't believe she was on her own. Their eyes met for a moment and she shyly turned away.

'The Hawk hasn't exactly given us the easiest of tasks,' William was saying.

'You should consider it a compliment,' said Ross, as he tried to concentrate on William's words, although his thoughts were elsewhere.

'But if we don't deliver, it won't be long before we're back investigating domestics, suicides and false confessions.'

Ross smiled before taking another sip of beer.

The woman returned his smile.

'Let's go and join the others,' said William, as he picked up his glass.

Ross reluctantly followed his boss across to the far side of the room. By the time he sat down the woman was no longer looking in his direction.

He paid little attention to the team's banter, making only the occasional bland comment. Jackie glanced across at the bar, and didn't need to be told why Ross was so uncommunicative. It crossed her mind that the woman was a younger version of herself. Men!

'We ought to get back to the Yard,' said William, looking at his watch.

'Must just go to the little boys' room,' said Ross. 'I'll catch you up.'

Once he was in the basement, he opened the lavatory door and grabbed a piece of toilet paper. He scribbled down his telephone number, folded the paper several times and hid it in the palm of his hand.

He walked quickly back upstairs, relieved to find the woman hadn't left.

'Hi,' he said, as he brushed past her and left the little square of paper on the bar. Out on the street, he soon caught up with the others. Only Jackie noticed that he hadn't been gone long enough to have a pee.

CHAPTER 12

BOOTH WATSON QUICKLY CLEARED CUSTOMS. He was carrying only a briefcase, as he planned on returning to London on the evening flight. Outside the airport he joined the short queue for a taxi and, when he reached the front, handed the driver an address.

As they approached the motorway, the driver turned left instead of joining the stream of heavy traffic flowing into Barcelona. Twenty minutes later, he drove onto a single-lane road which became a pot-holed path after a few miles.

Booth Watson glanced over his shoulder to check they weren't being followed, as the instructions he'd received couldn't have been clearer: 'If you think someone might be following you, turn around, go back to the airport and take the next plane to Heathrow.'

He had assumed that after his client had disappeared a second time, the Met might well have a detail tailing him, but had quickly concluded even their budget wouldn't stretch to that. Nevertheless, as Booth Watson was a man who left nothing to chance, he made an official complaint to the Home Office falsely claiming he had reason to believe his phone was being tapped, and that he was being followed. He had received a polite reply assuring him that neither was true, although he suspected it had been written only after Commander Hawksby had confirmed that 'the dogs had been called off'.

The car continued down a narrowing path before coming to a halt at the edge of a dense forest. Booth Watson got out and, as instructed, waited for the bemused driver to turn around and head back to the airport. Once the car was out of sight, an electric golf buggy appeared from out of the trees and drew up by his side.

A silent man drove the gentleman from London along an unmarked track through the forest before crossing a narrow bridge that spanned a fast-flowing river. It wasn't until they reached the other side that Booth Watson saw the house – although mansion, even chateau, would have been a more accurate description. It made Limpton Hall look like a suburban semi-detached.

Collins was standing by an open door waiting to welcome him. Oh good and faithful servant, he thought, as the butler gave a slight bow, saying, 'Good morning, sir,' as if he were a regular visitor, although this would be the first time he had seen Miles for several weeks.

'Mr Faulkner awaits you in the drawing room, sir.'

'No, he doesn't,' said Miles, as he came striding across the hall towards his guest. He thrust out his hand and said, 'Welcome to my country cottage.'

'More like a palace,' said Booth Watson.

Miles led the way down a long corridor, passing several familiar paintings Booth Watson had admired over the years. Finally, they entered a drawing room whose large bay windows overlooked a hundred acres of forested countryside on one side, and the calm blue of the Mediterranean on the other. 'Heaven on earth,' he said.

Miles sank into a comfortable armchair as a maid appeared carrying a large tray of coffee and biscuits. It was as if they were still in England and nothing had changed.

Miles waited for her to leave, before he said, 'Let's get down to business before I give you a tour of the house. What's Christina been up to?'

'She's still playing her part, but has absolutely no idea where you are at the moment, although she never stops asking.'

'And what do you tell her?'

'I let slip that you were last seen in Buenos Aires and had no plans to return to England in the near future.'

'Do you think she fell for it?'

'I can't be certain, but Lamont assures me that's what she tells anyone who enquires. And no doubt will continue to do so if she doesn't want her monthly allowance to dry up.'

'But surely Warwick and Hawksby must have worked out by now that I wasn't burnt at the stake in Geneva.'

'Indeed they have,' said Booth Watson. 'But Lamont informs me that you've fallen off their radar.'

'How can you be sure of that, when he's no longer on their mailing list?'

'Don't forget he still has someone who is, and she keeps the ex-Superintendent well-informed of everything Warwick is up to. It doesn't come cheap, but at least it guarantees you a no claims bonus on your life policy. Lamont tells me your file, MF/CR/76748/88, is gathering dust in the Met's general registry office at Hayes in Middlesex, where dead cases go to be buried, and are rarely exhumed.'

'That's good to hear,' said Miles, 'because I don't intend to spend the rest of my life locked up here, although I won't come out of hiding until you give me the all-clear.'

'Lamont's most useful function is to keep confirming that you're past history. However, it might be wise to lie low for a little longer.'

'But not for too much longer,' said Miles. 'Even heaven on earth becomes a prison after a while. And what's the point of a private jet, a yacht, a Swiss bank account and a pile of cash stashed in a vault in Mayfair if I'm trapped here?'

'Don't forget that Mayfair takes care of Christina, Lamont and his associate, as well as any other incidental expenses.'

'Including you.'

Booth Watson shrugged his shoulders.

'Perhaps the time has come to cut down on those expenses by removing Christina from the payroll,' suggested Miles.

'I wouldn't recommend that,' said Booth Watson firmly. 'She'd go straight to her friend Mrs Warwick and tell her you're very much alive, which would give her husband the chance to blow the dust off your file.'

'And we wouldn't want that,' said Miles. 'Not that they'd ever find me, even if they did discover I'd flown to Barcelona that night.'

'It may be the case that you're isolated and well-hidden,' said Booth Watson, leaning forward, finally unable to resist a chocolate biscuit. 'But if they were to find out that Ricardo

Rossi isn't a dress designer, but a criminal on the run, this palace would become a bunker, surrounded by an army, making it impossible for you to escape.'

'They still wouldn't catch up with me,' boasted Miles. 'Let me show you why.' He stood up and marched out of the drawing room, assuming that Booth Watson would be a pace behind. When he reached the end of the corridor, he unlocked a door and entered what was clearly his study. He sat down at a large partners desk while Booth Watson stared up at a life-size portrait hanging on the wall behind him.

'General Franco,' said Miles. 'He built this hideaway in 1937, at the height of the civil war. Even his closest confidants didn't know it existed. I've had to make some modifications,' he added. 'Which will prove my point. When you were picked up by the golf buggy, how long did it take you to reach the house?'

Booth Watson thought for a moment, before saying, 'Six or seven minutes. But a police motorbike would be a lot quicker.'

'Agreed. And how long did it take us to walk from the drawing room to this study?'

'A minute, a minute and a half at most.'

'I can assure you, BW, that anyone who sets foot on my land uninvited – and don't forget that this house is surrounded by a thick forest – would immediately set off an alarm. Even if they turned up in the middle of the night and I was fast asleep in my bedroom on the first floor, it would still take me less than three minutes to disappear into thin air.'

'Even if you had your helicopter waiting for you on the roof, I don't think they'd hesitate to shoot it down.'

'I wouldn't be heading for the roof,' said Miles. 'The helicopter is there simply to distract them.'

Twelve o'clock struck and a shrill alarm drowned out their conversation.

'Rehearsal time!' shouted Miles, as he got up from behind his desk and walked over to a vast iron door embedded in the wall. It had no handle, no lock and, as far as Booth Watson could see, no way of opening it. Miles tapped the face of his watch and waited for it to light up before entering an eight-digit code. Booth Watson watched, mesmerized, as the door swung open to reveal a large, empty space.

Miles stepped inside and beckoned Booth Watson to follow, while the deafening sound of the alarm continued. Booth Watson reluctantly obeyed, and Miles pulled the door shut, leaving them in complete darkness. He tapped his watch again and entered another eight-digit code. A moment later a second door on the far side of the safe swung open to reveal a well-lit staircase.

Miles stood aside to allow Booth Watson to step out. Miles then joined him at the top of the staircase and slammed the heavy metal door behind them.

'As you can see, BW,' he said, 'even if Chief Inspector Warwick and his plodders made it as far as my study, it would take them at least seven minutes, and they would still need my watch and the eight-digit code before they could open even the first door, let alone the second.'

Miles led his guest down the stairs into the basement.

When they reached the study, Booth Watson couldn't miss that the room was identical to the one on the ground floor above it, except that Franco had been replaced by a full-length portrait of Miles. The other half of Miles's art collection was also displayed on the walls – Christina's half.

'I have enough provisions down here to last me a month,' said Miles. 'I even have my own swimming pool.'

A green light began to flash on his desk, even before Booth Watson could reply. 'Daily rehearsal over. We can now return to civilization and have some lunch.'

'But your staff . . .' began Booth Watson.

'Only Collins is ever allowed to enter my study,' said Miles, as they walked back up the stairs, 'and even he doesn't know the security code.' He entered the safe's code which opened the first of the two heavy iron doors. When it swung open, he stepped back inside and waited for Booth Watson to join him, before he pulled the door shut. Once again they were plunged into darkness. Miles tapped his watch, entered eight new numbers, and the door that led back into his study swung open. Miles smiled when he saw the butler waiting for them, with two glasses of champagne on a silver tray.

'Luncheon is served, sir.'

• • •

Lamont didn't even attempt to shadow DI Ross Hogan, as he knew he would be noticed within moments by the sharpest undercover officer in the business. He satisfied himself with finding a spot where he wouldn't be seen, while he waited patiently for his quarry to appear.

As usual, Ross left Josephine Colbert's flat at around seven thirty. He was wearing a freshly ironed shirt and a silk tie, so Lamont knew he wasn't going home, but straight to the Yard.

Josephine Colbert appeared a few minutes after ten. She was dressed in a designer tracksuit and set off on her morning jog. She returned about thirty minutes later, and didn't appear again before lunch.

Her afternoon consisted of shopping, the florist, the grocer, the hairdresser, and the occasional visit with a girlfriend to a French cinema in Chelsea. Lamont had never once seen her with another man, other than when she attended her weekly meeting with Mr Booth Watson at No. 5 Fetter Chambers.

His final task was to hang about inside the entrance of the Army and Navy Stores on Victoria Street until Hogan left the Yard at the end of the day. If he turned right, he was taking the tube home; left, and he would be hopping on a bus bound for Chelsea. The trips to Chelsea had become more and more frequent.

Tonight, he turned right, so Lamont assumed he must be going home. However, to his surprise, Hogan walked straight past the entrance to the tube station and continued on walking. Aware that he couldn't risk following him, Lamont decided to head home, but changed his mind when he saw Hogan enter a shop. He took a closer look at the sign above the door – H. Samuel and Company, Jewellers. He stepped back into the shadow of a doorway until Ross reappeared twenty minutes later carrying a small bag, and headed back to St. James's station, where he disappeared underground.

Lamont walked quickly across to the jeweller's shop. He marched in to find a young man taking some necklaces out of the window in preparation for closing for the night. Lamont showed him his old warrant card, a thumb covering the expiry date.

'How can I help you, Superintendent?' asked the assistant nervously.

'A man came in here a little while ago, fortyish, six foot one, wearing a dark grey suit and a red tie.'

'Yes, sir. He left a few minutes ago.'

'Did he buy anything?'

'Yes, sir. An engagement ring.'

• • •

It had been the happiest month of his life. Ross couldn't believe how lucky he had been following that chance meeting. The very idea of falling in love had always been anathema to him. He was a hunter-gatherer, and always the one who decided to cast the latest conquest aside and move on. He considered it a compliment to be accused of playing the field.

That was until he met Josephine, and she didn't need to explain to him what the words head over heels meant. It wasn't just that she was beautiful, and far brighter than him; she was the first woman he had ever been fearful of losing. He couldn't understand why she had ever given him a second look, let alone a third. For the first time in his life, he was not always the first to arrive at work in the morning and the last to leave at night. Everyone else noticed. The loner was no longer alone. They didn't sleep with each other for a couple of weeks, another first. After that, he would have robbed a bank for her.

Jo had already told him about her unhappy marriage that had lasted for only a couple of years. The divorce settlement had meant she could live comfortably without having to work and, like him, she thought she could never fall in love.

Tonight, he was going to take her out to dinner and propose. He'd spent more than he could afford on the ring. Jo had once told him she would never marry again, but that was before she'd called Madame Blanche to tell her this was her last job.

When he got home that night, even earlier than usual, he found her sitting in the front room crying. He tried to comfort her, but nothing he said seemed to make any difference. She looked up, and he couldn't help thinking how enchanting she appeared even with tears streaming down her face. She tried to smile. 'I love you,' she said. The first time she'd admitted it.

'And I love you, too,' he replied. Another first. Unable to express how he truly felt in words, he decided he wouldn't wait any longer to prove just how much he loved her. He dropped to one knee, and fumbled in his pocket before extracting a small leather box. He opened it and said, 'I want to spend the rest of my life with you. Will you marry me?'

He waited for her reply, but none was forthcoming. She finally looked up, but still said nothing. He leant forward and gently took her left hand and tried to place the ring on the third finger, but she pulled her hand away.

'Don't you want to marry me?' asked Ross, sounding desperate.

'Yes, I do,' she said quietly. 'But after I've told you the truth, you won't want to marry me.'

CHAPTER 13

BETH PICKED UP THE PHONE on her desk.

'There's a Mrs Christina Faulkner in reception. She wonders if you could possibly see her.'

She was well prepared for this moment, though William had warned her it would come when she least expected it.

She took a deep breath. 'Send her up,' she said. While Beth waited, she repeated William's mantra whenever he was dealing with a suspect: *Listen, listen, listen, in the hope they'll say something they later regret.*

There was a gentle tap on the door. Usually, Christina came charging into the office unannounced, assuming Beth would drop everything for her. But not today.

'Come in,' said Beth, while remaining seated behind her desk.

The door opened slowly. The woman who entered her office was not the Christina she knew of old: self-assured, confident, in control. She stood hesitantly in the doorway, waiting for Beth to make the first move.

Beth didn't suggest she sit in the comfortable chair by the fire that Christina usually commandeered, but gestured to the seat on the other side of her desk, as if she were a junior member of staff. Christina meekly obeyed, and slumped down on the wooden chair, but didn't speak.

Listen, listen, listen.

'I don't know where to start,' she said in a faltering voice.

'By telling the truth for a change?' suggested Beth.

A long silence followed before it all came pouring out. 'I apologize for having behaved so badly, and would quite understand if you felt you could never forgive me.'

Listen, listen, listen.

'I'm not like you, straightforward, uncomplicated and scrupulously honest. It's one of the many reasons I admire you so much, and was proud to think I was your friend.'

Don't fall for the flattery, William had warned. *Listen, listen, listen.*

'I became used to a way of life that didn't always make that possible, but my farce of a marriage has finally made me come to my senses, whatever the consequences.'

Try to remember that she doesn't even know when she's lying, William had told her. *Next, she'll try to appeal to your better nature.*

'However, during the past few weeks, I've come to realize just how much I value your friendship, and hope it might still be possible for you to forgive me, although there's no reason you should.'

Listen, listen, listen.

'If I could tell you where Miles was, I would, but he's

made no attempt to contact me since the day of the wedding, other than through his mouthpiece, the loathsome Booth Watson, who simply tells me to keep my mouth shut if I want to continue receiving my monthly payment. He ordered me to come and see you today and try to find out if William knows where Miles is.' Christina looked up at Beth for the first time.

Listen, listen, listen.

'For the first time in my life, I've decided to do what William would call the decent thing.'

If she bursts into tears, William had added, *don't fall for it.*

She burst into tears.

Beth thawed. 'The gallery will never forget the invaluable role you played in securing the Rembrandt, a Rubens and a Vermeer, for which we will be forever in your debt.'

'You will never be in my debt,' said Christina. 'But I must warn you that if Miles is ever arrested and sent back to jail, Booth Watson has been instructed to claim the Vermeer back, and there'd be nothing I could do about it.'

For the first time Beth thought Christina might be telling the truth, but she continued to listen, listen, listen.

'Believe me, I'm determined to prove to you and William whose side I'm on. If there's anything I can do to prove . . .'

The moment she pretends to be on your side and asks what she can do to prove it, is when you strike. Start with something small, William had suggested, *and if she grants your request, you can then tempt her with something she won't be able to resist. Just before she leaves, ask her one final question that will reveal if she's telling you the truth, or is nothing more than a messenger carrying out her paymaster's orders.*

'What a kind offer,' said Beth. 'The museum is hoping to mount a Frans Hals exhibition next autumn. I know you have *The Flute Player* in your collection, and we'd love to borrow it for six weeks.'

If she turns down your request, William had said, *she's admitting that Miles still has control of the entire collection, and that's not something she'll want you to know, as it leaves her with no bargaining position.*

Christina hesitated. 'I'm sure that will be fine.'

'Thank you,' said Beth, before casting a far bigger fly on the water. 'That will compensate for the gallery not being able to afford Caravaggio's *Fishers of Men*, which we were recently offered, but couldn't meet the asking price.' Word-perfect.

'Is that public knowledge?' asked Christina, rising to the bait.

'No, it isn't,' said Beth. 'Lord McLaren approached us privately. It seems that following his father's untimely death, he's experiencing an inheritance problem and the tax man expects him to come up with twenty million by the end of the year. I had to tell him that sum was out of our league.' She paused for a moment, enjoying herself. 'That's confidential, of course.'

'Of course,' said Christina. 'But at least I can help you with the Frans Hals. That should prove which side I'm on,' she added, as she rose from her seat.

'You have nothing to prove,' said Beth, giving her a warm smile. 'But may I ask you one more thing before you leave?'

'Anything,' said Christina.

'Where is Miles at the moment?'

Christina didn't reply immediately, but eventually

murmured, 'Buenos Aires,' as if reluctantly revealing a well-kept secret.

'Thank you,' said Beth, not sure if Christina was lying, or genuinely didn't know where he was. William would have to make that decision.

Christina turned to leave the room, looking a little more confident than when she'd entered it.

Once she'd closed the door behind her, Beth picked up the phone on her desk, but hesitated for a moment before doing something she knew William normally wouldn't approve of. She dialled his private number at the Yard.

• • •

'You're being paid a thousand pounds a week to sleep with me?' said Ross in disbelief.

'Plus the rent on this apartment and a clothes allowance.'

'By who?'

'By *whom*.'

'By whom?'

'The escort agency in Paris that employed me to seduce you.'

'And what do they expect in return?'

'I have to report back everything you tell me, however inconsequential or irrelevant it might seem to me.'

'And have you?'

'Yes, but unfortunately you never talk about your work, so I can't be sure how much longer they'll keep me on.'

Ross remained silent for some time, before he finally said, 'Then we'll have to do something about that. You can now tell them that at last you've made a breakthrough.'

'But you'd never be disloyal to the man you call The Hawk.'

'You're right, but that doesn't stop me supplying you with lots of irrelevant information,' he said, clearly now enjoying himself. 'I'd have to brief the commander, of course, and he's bound to ask me who's paying the escort agency.'

'I've no idea,' said Jo, without guile.

'I'm pretty sure I know who it is,' said Ross. 'Have you ever come across a Miles Faulkner or Captain Ralph Neville?'

'No. All I can tell you is that I was introduced to a man who briefed me about you and told me I should report once a week to a Mr Booth Watson.'

'That clinches it,' said Ross, taking her in his arms. 'But there's one more thing I still need to know before you earn your next thousand pounds.'

'Yes?'

'Will you marry me?'

• • •

'So what did The Hawk have to say about my little exchange with Christina?'

'He couldn't have been more grateful for your "special constable" contribution. All we can do now is hope that she'll pass on your "highly confidential" slip of the tongue to Booth Watson. If she does, I have a feeling Faulkner won't be able to resist making a trip to Scotland so he can view the Caravaggio for himself.'

'That would also prove which side Christina's really on,' said Beth.

'I'm not sure even she knows which side she's really on.'

'But if she loans the gallery the Frans Hals . . .'

'If Faulkner goes along with that, you should try to convince Christina that you now trust her, and believe every word she says.'

'Even she doesn't believe every word she says,' replied Beth.

'You're learning quickly,' said William, 'and I'm fairly sure she'll tell Booth Watson about the Caravaggio. It will convince them she's still on their side.'

'I'm not cunning enough to follow that piece of logic.'

'If Faulkner does go to Scotland and tries to buy the Caravaggio, I'll be waiting for him, and he'll end up back in prison for a very long stretch. That will give Christina more than enough time to get her hands on the other half of his art collection. Which, to be fair, is legally hers under the divorce settlement.'

'I'm not sure which one of you is more devious,' said Beth.

'I only think like a criminal,' said William, as they strolled into the kitchen.

'So, who's cooking supper tonight?'

'My turn.'

'"My turn" rather suggests an equal division of labour, and you only have two dishes in your repertoire – spaghetti Bolognese or spaghetti pomodoro.'

'Al dente or overcooked, madam?' said William, pulling back a kitchen chair.

'You wouldn't know the difference,' mumbled Beth as she sat down.

• • •

'You asked to see me urgently,' said Booth Watson as Lamont walked into the room. 'I assume that means you have something worthwhile to report.'

Booth Watson never left his 'special consultant' in any doubt how he felt about him, but then the feeling was mutual.

'DS Roycroft has come up with some interesting intel about what Warwick and his new team are up to.' Booth Watson nodded. 'They're currently working on five murder cases that all went to trial but, for one reason or another, didn't lead to convictions. You appeared as defence counsel in four of them. I've written a full report on each case and how far their investigation has progressed.' He opened his Sainsbury's bag and extracted five files, which Booth Watson ignored. 'I've also recently come across another piece of information I thought you would want to know about.'

Booth Watson sat back. He could only wonder what Lamont could possibly tell him that he didn't already know.

'DI Ross Hogan has a new girlfriend, who clearly isn't short of money. She lives in a mews flat in Chelsea, and shops in Sloane Street.'

Booth Watson began to pay closer attention, while appearing uninterested. 'What's her name?' he asked, casually.

'Josephine Colbert. She's French, mid-thirties, recently divorced, but now living in London.'

'Any idea where her money comes from?'

'Certainly not Hogan. She must have got a generous divorce settlement to live in the style she does.'

'Interesting,' said Booth Watson, as Lamont handed him another file. This time he opened it and studied the contents for a few minutes. He was relieved to find that Lamont hadn't discovered Ms Colbert's profession, or the real reason she'd begun a relationship with Ross Hogan.

'Useful,' he conceded, before opening the top drawer of his desk and extracting a thick envelope. 'This also includes DS Roycroft's weekly payment of one hundred pounds,' Booth Watson said pointedly as he pushed the package across the table.

'Of course,' said Lamont, who only ever gave Jackie fifty pounds whenever they met, which wasn't once a week.

'Anything else?' asked Booth Watson to indicate the meeting was over.

'No, sir.' Lamont said, having decided not to tell Booth Watson about the engagement ring. That would be worth another brown envelope in a couple of weeks' time. He rose from his place, but didn't shake hands before he left the room and closed the door quietly behind him.

Booth Watson took his time studying the five files Warwick's team had compiled especially for him. He would have to get in touch with each of his former clients to warn them that their cases had been reopened, which would require several consultations after which he would advise them to do nothing.

He then returned to the Josephine Colbert file and read it a second time. He'd had a very productive meeting with Ms Colbert earlier in the week, which might just have produced the breakthrough he'd been waiting for. DI Ross Hogan was, as Lamont had suggested in his report, clearly besotted with her and, thought Booth Watson, long may he be so. She had also confirmed the five murder cases Warwick was working on and the two in particular that Hogan had been assigned. More importantly, she confirmed that Hogan had never once mentioned the name of Miles Faulkner to her, which he considered an added bonus. No news is good news, he would assure Miles when he next visited Franco's secret hideaway.

However, the triumph of the week had been his monthly meeting with Christina Faulkner, when she'd told him that the Fitzmolean had been approached by a Lord McLaren, who'd recently inherited not only his title, but also the death duties that went with it. As a result, he had been left with no choice but to sell his treasured Caravaggio, which he was hoping would fetch at least twenty million. Booth Watson would need to have a word with another of his 'special consultants' who worked in the tax office.

This could well be a golden opportunity to extract a percentage from both sides, as long as he was able to convince Miles to allow him to act as the go-between. He'd make sure his client was well aware how foolish it would be for him to visit Scotland to view the painting, however great the temptation.

Booth Watson was looking forward to his next trip to Barcelona; so much to report that would once again make him look indispensable.

He locked the updated file in his Miles Faulkner cabinet, which even his secretary didn't have a key to.

CHAPTER 14

'RIGHT, WHO'S GOING TO KICK off?' asked the commander. A hand shot up, and The Hawk nodded.

'I had another meeting with Lamont on Friday evening,' said Jackie.

'Where?' asked William.

'A little pub behind King's Cross station that neither the police nor any self-respecting criminal would consider frequenting.'

'Do you think he suspects which side you're on?'

'I don't think so. I ended up getting pissed and he had to drive me home.'

The rest of the team laughed.

'Mind you,' she continued, 'I'd discreetly emptied most of my double gins into a flowerpot behind me. I'm only surprised the poor plant survived the evening.'

'By which time,' said William, 'I assume you'd casually let slip what we've been up to.'

'No more than you wanted him to know. I told him about the five cold cases we're working on, but left enough spaces for him to fill in before he made his next report to Booth Watson.'

'Who will in turn pass the information on to his esteemed former clients, which will give them something to think about while they also hand over hefty fees for his services,' said William.

'Don't underestimate Lamont,' The Hawk chipped in. 'If he thought for one moment that you're setting him up, he'd not only report back to Booth Watson but turn it to his advantage. Who's next?'

'I've begun in-depth investigations into both the Roach and Abbott families,' said Ross, 'and what a right bunch of villains they turn out to be. Every family member has a specific role within the organization. Terry Roach and Ron Abbott are responsible for eliminating anyone who gets in their way. If Abbott was ever found guilty of murder, he could ask the judge to take at least five other cases into consideration. He's quite simply a professional hitman, and because his family is so feared in the East End, no witnesses are ever willing to come forward while they think they could be next in line.'

'That bad?' said William.

'Roach is even worse,' continued Ross. 'Abbott kills his victims with a single shot from a long-range rifle. But Roach's weapon of choice is a serrated kitchen knife. He's known as "the butcher", and considers death by a thousand cuts would be letting his victim off lightly. It's his calling card just in case anyone else should consider crossing the Roach family. He's been in and out of jail several times, but, thanks to Booth Watson, the longest sentence he's ever served is two years for GBH. So, while we don't have a budget stretched to a dozen highly trained officers watching him around the clock, he'll continue to get away with it. I have one or two ideas I'm working on, but it's too early to share them with you.'

'Understood,' said William. 'But if you could nail even one of them, Ross, it would be a feather in your cap.'

'Do you know where that saying originates?' interrupted Paul.

'Yes, I do,' said William. 'But this isn't the time to be discussing an ancient English custom that when a warrior had slain a foe in battle, he was allowed to wear a feather in his cap, which was later superseded by the award of medals. There are no awards for sprained ankles, DS Adaja, so may I suggest you get on with your report?'

'My loan shark, Max Sleeman,' said a chastened Paul, 'is still lending large sums of money to desperate people and resorting to violent measures if they fall behind with their payments. As you know, three of his customers have disappeared off the face of the earth after failing to cover their debts, which he later claimed from their estates. Another painful reminder to any other customers of what would happen to them should they fail to honour their unwritten contracts. But I think I may have come up with a way of not only sending Sleeman down, but bankrupting him at the same time. It's known as the Capone solution.'

'Tax avoidance?' said William.

'I think I can prove he's been avoiding paying any tax for years. A recent case in the high court resulted in a six-year sentence, but even more important, under the Tax Avoidance Act of 1986, the judge can award a fine of up to five times the amount the Revenue should have received. So not only would Sleeman end up in jail, but he'd be penniless, because the court could strip him of all his assets. A punishment to fit the crime, don't you think?' said Paul, looking rather pleased with himself.

'Possibly,' said the commander, 'but I'd still rather he ended up with a life sentence for the three murders he was responsible for. If that proves unrealistic, we may have to consider the tax route. But let me warn you Paul, that has its own problems. Tax trials can last for months, and juries never fully understand the details, while a half-decent lawyer can run rings around even an expert witness. So be warned, you'll have your work cut out, not least because it will be you who's standing in the witness box giving evidence for days on end.'

Paul no longer looked quite so pleased with himself.

'Jackie, what have you been up to when you're not getting pissed with our ex-Superintendent?'

'I've been continuing to investigate Clive Pugh, the insurance scam man who murdered his wife. I suspect he's now planning to become a widower for a second time.'

'But surely no insurance company would go anywhere near him,' said Paul, 'after he fleeced one of them for a quarter of a million.'

'He won't be bothering with insurance companies this time,' said Jackie. 'His sights are on a far larger prize than a quarter of a million.'

'So what's his new scam?' asked William.

'He's been escorting an older woman, whose main attraction seems to be that she's inherited a fortune from her late father.'

'But surely she must have worked out he's just another gold digger?' said William.

'Pugh's far too clever for that,' said Jackie. 'He's been putting his ill-gotten gains to good use. They eat at the finest restaurants, and when they go on holidays together they stay at five-star hotels and he always picks up the bill. I wouldn't be surprised if he proposes to her soon, as it can't be much longer before his cash runs out.'

'What makes you think he'll murder her?' asked The Hawk. 'Why wouldn't he be satisfied just to live off her for the rest of his life?'

'She may be ten years older than him, sir, but her father lived to a hundred and one. And, perhaps more important, Pugh's mistress, who I'm convinced was his accomplice for the first murder, is still hanging around. So don't be surprised if you open your morning paper one day to see "Wealthy heiress meets tragic death".'

'Surely he can't hope to get away with it a second time,' said Ross.

'He's far too bright not to have thought of a way around that.' Once again, Jackie had their attention. 'I've discovered he's already booked their next holiday, to South Africa.'

'Where only one murder in ten ends in a conviction,' said William.

'But we can always apply for an extradition order under section nine of the Offences Against the Person Act of 1861,' said Paul, which silenced them all except The Hawk.

'Not an Act the South Africans are all that familiar with,' he said. 'Especially when even the judges can be bought.'

'Maybe he'll think again, once Booth Watson tells him we've reopened the file on his wife's murder,' suggested Paul.

'I doubt it,' said The Hawk. 'Pugh's a gambler. He'll weigh up the amount of money he stands to gain against his chances of being caught, and back himself against the South African police.'

'It's too bad we can't afford to send you to the Cape for Christmas, Jackie,' said William, 'so you could brief us on what he's up to at our next meeting.'

'Where's DC Pankhurst?' asked the commander, pushing Jackie's file to one side. 'I was looking forward to finding out how she's been getting on with her nightclub bouncer.'

'She's on leave, sir,' said William.

'With the bouncer?' asked the commander.

'No, sir. A certain Captain Archibald Harcourt-Byrne.'

'Who's he?'

'He's an officer in the Grenadier Guards,' chipped in Jackie. 'She doesn't talk about him much, so I suspect it's quite serious.'

'I hope we're not going to lose her,' said The Hawk, his tone changing. 'She's a damn fine officer, with a promising career ahead of her.'

'I agree,' said William, 'but DC Pankhurst is every bit as independent as her suffragette ancestor, and I'm sure she's well capable of handling a Guards Officer while she continues to lock up miscreants on the side. So let's allow her to enjoy a well-earned holiday while we all get back to work.'

• • •

'Hurry up, old thing, or we might miss our flight,' said Archie.

'Relax. We've got more than enough time,' said Rebecca calmly.

'You're right,' said Archie, taking her hand. 'What's our gate number?'

'Sixty-three.'

'Why is my plane always parked at the other end of the airport?' grumbled Archie.

'And whenever I get back home,' chipped in Rebecca, 'I'm always stuck behind four hundred passengers who've just got off a jumbo jet. But I don't care. I've been looking forward to this holiday. It will be my first real break in heaven knows how long.'

As they passed the departure lounge for Gate 49, she spotted him seated in the far corner reading *The Times*. Rebecca took a second look to confirm she wasn't mistaken.

'I have to go to the loo,' she said, letting go of Archie's hand. 'You go ahead. I'll join you in a few minutes.'

As soon as Archie was out of sight she headed for the nearest phone. Would he still be at the commander's meeting, or back at his desk?

'DCI Warwick,' said his voice, just when she'd almost given up hope.

'Good morning, sir. It's Rebecca.'

'I thought you were meant to be on holiday.'

'I am, but I thought you'd want to know that I've just spotted Booth Watson waiting to board a plane.'

'He's allowed to take a holiday too.'

'Dressed in a three-piece suit and carrying a briefcase?'

'Where's he going?'

'Barcelona.'

'Then so are you, constable. Call me the moment you

land. By then I'll have worked out what your next move should be.'

'Can I remind you, sir, that I'm on holiday?'

'Were on holiday, DC Pankhurst. You're about to discover where Miles Faulkner is holed up.'

'But I . . .'

'No buts, constable. We may not get another opportunity like this.'

William put down the phone and dialled the commander's office, while Rebecca poured forth a stream of invective her mother would not have approved of. She walked quickly back to Gate 49, to see that the first-class passengers were already boarding the plane. She checked her watch; not enough time to return to the BA desk and exchange her ticket. She slipped into WHSmiths and waited until Booth Watson had presented his boarding pass and disappeared down the corridor that led to the waiting aircraft. She was hoping that Archie would come back looking for her, so she could explain what had happened. He didn't. She waited until the last few passengers were being cleared for boarding before she approached the check-in desk, where she took out her warrant card and showed it to the flight attendant.

'We've been expecting you, Detective Constable,' he said, once he'd checked her passport. 'We've just had a call from Scotland Yard warning us that you'd be wanting to travel on this flight. I've put you in the back row of economy. There's a rear door, so you can be the last on and the first off the plane.'

He handed her a ticket and said, 'Have a good flight, Ms Pankhurst.'

'Do I have time to go and tell my boyfriend why I won't be joining him?'

'I'm afraid not. The gate is about to close.'

Rebecca reluctantly headed down the long empty corridor, and was the last passenger to board the plane. She didn't relax during the entire flight. Her mind continually switched between Archie, wondering if he'd ever speak to her again; DCI Warwick, who she would happily have strangled; and Booth Watson, the root cause of her problems, who she assumed was seated up front in business class.

She began to consider her alternatives once the plane had landed in Barcelona. Was Booth Watson being picked up? Would he take a taxi, a bus or a train into the city? Had he already booked himself into a hotel? If so, was that where he would meet up with Faulkner? Or would he be driven straight to his new bolthole? And if that were to happen, what was she expected to do?

She'd gone over a dozen scenarios before the plane touched down, and was back in detective mode by the time it parked at the gate.

When the rear door was opened by a stewardess, Rebecca was first out of the blocks, not a moment to waste. She walked quickly down the steps and into the terminal, where she joined the throng of passengers heading for customs. Someone moving even more quickly caught up with her.

'Slow down and link your arm in mine, Detective Constable,' said a voice clearly used to giving orders. She glanced at the man by her side and carried out his instruction.

'Don't look back. Just keep walking, and leave the rest to me.'

'Yes, sir,' she found herself saying.

'I'm Lieutenant Sanchez of the Spanish National Police Corps,' he said without even glancing in her direction. 'My commanding officer had a call from a Commander Hawksby, who didn't leave us in any doubt how important your visit is.' He didn't speak again until they'd reached customs, where the desk officer didn't ask to see her passport, just saluted. Him, not her. The lieutenant chose a spot with a clear view of all eight customs posts and said, 'Just point him out the moment you see him.'

Rebecca kept her eyes on the stream of passengers joining the long queues to present their passports to a customs official. It was some time before she said, 'That's him, waiting in line at the sixth box. He's the only person who doesn't look as if he's going on holiday.'

'Three-piece suit, around fifty, slightly balding, carrying a leather briefcase.'

'You've got him.'

The lieutenant nodded to someone Rebecca didn't see. Once Booth Watson had cleared customs they followed him through baggage control – he had nothing to collect – and on into the arrivals hall. He hurried out of the airport and joined the taxi queue.

Rebecca noticed a young man slip into line behind him. When Booth Watson eventually reached the front of the queue and climbed into the back of a taxi, the young man made a note of the number plate, but didn't jump into the next cab.

'Isn't he going to follow him?' she asked, trying not to sound desperate.

'Can't risk it,' said the lieutenant. 'Your chief made it clear that if the man you're after thinks he's being tailed, he'll head straight back to the airport, and your journey will have been wasted. But don't worry, we have the details of the taxi driver, and we'll interview him later and report back to Scotland Yard to let him know where he dropped off your man.'

'What if he switches taxis?'

'He'll find the next available one is one of ours,' he said, looking across the road and nodding.

'So, I'm nothing more than a messenger,' said Rebecca.

'A very attractive messenger, if I may say so, señorita.'

'You wouldn't get away with that in PC England,' said Rebecca, smiling.

'Ah, but you are now in Barcelona, not England.'

'What am I expected to do now?'

'You have been booked on the next flight to Florence, where your boyfriend will be waiting for you in arrivals.'

'How did you manage that?'

'I think your boss felt guilty about interrupting your holiday,' the lieutenant said, as he handed her a first-class ticket to Florence. 'I hope you have an enjoyable time in Italy, Señorita Pankhurst. My grandmother was a great admirer of your ancestor, although it took my countrymen several more years before they finally gave women the vote.' He saluted, and had departed before she could say, 'In 1931.'

CHAPTER 15

'WERE YOU FOLLOWED?'

'No,' said Booth Watson. 'After we turned off the motorway I didn't see another car.'

'The day you do, I'll have to be on the move again.'

'Where to this time?'

'I already have somewhere lined up that I could move into tomorrow. But General Franco was here for twenty-seven years without anyone finding out about this place. By that time the commander will be dead, and DCI Warwick will have retired.'

'Amen to that,' said Booth Watson, as he opened his briefcase and took out several files. 'Where shall I start?'

'By proving Lamont is worth his exorbitant consultancy fee.'

'As long as he has someone on the inside, he's worth keeping on the payroll,' said Booth Watson, 'provided we remember that he'd plant drugs on his grandmother if he thought there was something in it for him.'

'Are he and Roycroft an item?'

'I'm fairly sure their relationship is based on nothing more than a mutual interest in money.'

'So they're not sleeping together?'

'Sleeping partners, yes, but sleeping together, no. The last time they met, Roycroft left the pub drunk, and Lamont dropped her off at her place before going home.'

'Did she have anything worthwhile to pass on?'

'She brought him up to date on the cold cases Warwick's team are working on.'

'Am I one of them?' demanded Miles.

'No. You seem to have been forgotten. Your name didn't even come up.'

'Long may that be so,' said Miles. 'Is Lamont also keeping an eye on Josephine Colbert?'

'Yes,' he said after extracting another file from his bag. 'It would appear that she and DI Hogan are an item. They're seeing each other three, sometimes four, times a week. It's begun to produce results. Or, more importantly, no results.'

'What do you mean?'

'She confirmed that Hogan is working on two of the five cold cases, Abbott and Roach. She's been told to report any other names he mentions and, so far, you're in the clear.'

'Has she asked Hogan if he's ever heard of Captain Ralph Neville?'

'Certainly not,' said Booth Watson. 'That would blow her cover straight away, as well as yours. As long as Hogan doesn't mention your name, or Captain Neville's, we can be confident your file's still gathering dust in Hayes, where it belongs.'

'I can assure you Hogan's wasting his time if he's trying

to finger Terry Roach,' said Miles. 'No one in the East End would ever consider giving evidence against that man.'

'You've come across Roach?' asked Booth Watson, sounding surprised.

'I was in prison with him. Not a man to cross, as two or three of my fellow inmates found out when they took a shower and discovered that blood is thicker than water.'

Booth Watson gave an involuntary shudder.

'So, you think Miss Colbert is worth a thousand pounds a week?' said Miles as he lit a cigar.

'Think of her as an insurance policy, even though the premium doesn't come cheap.'

'Women never do,' said Miles. 'Speaking of insurance policies, what's Christina been up to lately?'

'She's been keeping her side of the bargain,' said Booth Watson. 'After her meeting with Beth Warwick, she came back with two fascinating pieces of information.'

Miles looked interested.

'The Fitzmolean has recently been offered Caravaggio's *Fishers of Men* by a Lord McLaren, but they couldn't meet his asking price.'

'Which was?'

'Twenty million pounds.'

'Why's he putting one of Caravaggio's most famous works on the market when it's been in his family for generations?'

'Having to put, is the answer to that question. It seems that the seventh Lord McLaren has been saddled with extortionate death duties.'

'How extortionate?'

'Twenty-two million, seven hundred thousand pounds.'

'So now we know what he'll be prepared to sell the painting for,' said Miles.

'You're interested in buying it?'

'Of course I am, but I'll need someone to represent me because, unlike Christ, I can't rise from the dead.'

Booth Watson smiled, 'I'd be delighted to act on your behalf.'

'I'm sure you would, BW,' said Miles. 'You said Christina had come up with two pieces of information.'

'The Fitzmolean is mounting a Frans Hals exhibition next autumn, and Mrs Warwick has asked Christina to loan the museum *The Flute Player* for six weeks.'

'It's not hers to loan,' said Miles defiantly.

'Which is why I would counsel you to do so.'

'Your reason?'

'Mrs Warwick would then be convinced the collection is in Christina's hands and, more importantly, so would her husband.'

• • •

'*Fishers of Men* by Caravaggio,' said the tour guide, 'is without question the pride of the McLaren collection. Although the central figure in the painting is Christ, the eye goes immediately to the fishermen in the boat. The eminent art historian, Sir Kenneth Clark, wrote that the look of shock when the Apostles first see Christ walking on water can only be described as genius.'

'What's it worth?' asked a young man wearing a T-shirt displaying a Warhol.

'It's quite simply priceless,' said the guide, trying to hide his disdain, which raised a smile from an elderly gentleman seated in a wheelchair, his legs covered by a tartan rug.

'Although,' continued the guide, 'it may interest you to know that the first Lord McLaren purchased the masterpiece from a dealer in Milan in 1786 for fifty guineas, and on returning to Scotland he hung it here, in the dining room, where it has remained to this day.'

Not for much longer, thought the man in the wheelchair.

'That concludes the tour,' said the guide, 'which I hope you have all enjoyed.' The generous round of applause that followed suggested they had.

The guide gave a slight bow before saying, 'If you would like to visit our shop, enjoy some light refreshments in the café, or walk around the grounds, please feel free to do so. I hope you all have a safe journey home.'

The old man in the wheelchair thanked the guide and gave him a handsome tip, before his nurse pushed him slowly out of the dining room. 'I'd like to visit the shop,' he said.

'Of course, sir,' she replied, and followed the signs. The old man purchased a postcard of *Fishers of Men* and an illustrated catalogue of the McLaren family collection, before the nurse took him back to his waiting limousine. He spotted a young policeman in plainclothes who didn't give them a second look, as a chauffeur and the nurse helped the old man out of the wheelchair and into the back of the car.

As the limousine drove slowly out of the grounds, the old man turned to the first page of the catalogue, which displayed the McLaren family tree from 1736 to the present day. The first Lord McLaren, it seemed, had made his fortune in the early years of the Industrial Revolution, and his interest in art, which had begun as an amateur, became a passion during his middle age and, following 'the European Tour', an obsession: when he died in 1822, his collection was considered to be among the finest in private hands. By the time the limousine pulled up outside the entrance to Aberdeen airport, the old man had come to the end of the first Lord McLaren's life.

An attractive airport hostess took over from the nurse and wheeled the elderly gentleman to the front of the queue for customs. Once his passport had been checked, he was taken straight to the waiting aircraft.

During the flight home, he learnt how the second and third Lord McLarens had added Turner, Constable and Gainsborough to the collection, enhancing its growing reputation. The old man was among the last to leave the aircraft after it had landed, and by then he'd discovered how the fourth Lord McLaren had discovered the Impressionists, and acquired a Monet, a Manet and two Matisses before he passed away.

While he was being wheeled towards customs, he became engrossed in the fifth Lord McLaren's desire to purchase works by his own countrymen to hang alongside the Italian, French and English masters, so McTaggart, Raeburn, Peploe and Farquharson were added to the collection. Sadly, the sixth Lord McLaren showed no interest in art, only in fast cars and even faster women, which resulted in several of the paintings having to be sold to cover his extravagances. When he died of a heart attack at the age of sixty-three, he left his only son the title and no choice but to part with the Caravaggio if he hoped to keep the taxman at bay.

The old man progressed slowly through customs. By the time he reached the arrivals hall, he'd also reached the end of the book.

His chauffeur wheeled him out of the airport to his waiting car, which was parked in the disabled zone. He opened the back door for his master, who got out of his wheelchair, walked across to the car and climbed into the back seat. Lazarus would have been proud of him.

CHAPTER 16

'WHERE ARE THE TWINS?' ASKED Sir Julian, before Beth and William had even hung up their coats.

'They're spending the day with my parents,' said Beth, as they walked through to the drawing room.

'Lucky Arthur and Joanna,' said Marjorie.

'Strictly *entre nous*,' said Sir Julian, 'but when Artemisia last visited us she told me in confidence that I was her favourite grandfather.'

Beth smiled. 'The little minx repeated those exact words to my father when I dropped them off in Ewell this morning.'

'I shall have to rewrite my will in favour of Peter,' said Sir Julian, with an exaggerated sigh.

'Then my father will rewrite his in favour of Artemisia,' said Beth.

'As William never talks about his work,' said Marjorie, handing Beth a cup of coffee, 'and Julian talks of little else, I want to hear what your latest project is.'

'The museum's preparing a Frans Hals exhibition for next autumn.'

'I've often wondered what goes on behind the scenes before a gallery can open a major exhibition like that.'

'It's a long and tortuous process,' said Beth, 'that involves patience, resolve, bribery and corruption.'

Sir Julian suddenly looked interested.

'How many pictures will be on display?'

'If I'm lucky, sixty or seventy, including, we hope, *The Laughing Cavalier*.'

'Where's that at the moment?' asked Sir Julian.

'It's part of the Wallace Collection,' said William, 'so at least he wouldn't have far to travel.'

'One sometimes forgets,' said Sir Julian, 'that my son read Art History at an up-and-coming university and, had he not joined the police force, he might well have ended up as one of Beth's assistants by now.'

'That successful?' mocked William.

'Ignore the children, Beth,' said Marjorie. 'You were telling us about the preparations for an important exhibition.'

'Bribery and corruption,' Sir Julian reminded her.

'Most of Hals' works are in public galleries around the world. The best examples are to be found at the Rijks in Amsterdam, although the Met and the Hermitage have magnificent self-portraits, and there's another fine example, *The Merry Lute Player*, at the Mansion House in the City of London. But if you want to borrow a major work from another gallery, they'll expect a *quid pro quo* at some time in the future.'

'For example?' said Sir Julian, as he sipped his coffee,

'The Phillips Collection in Washington DC is planning

to mount a Rubens exhibition in two years' time, and they've already asked us if we'd loan them *Descent from the Cross* for three months. They have three Hals, and I'm after two of them.'

'Two Hals for a Rubens seems a fair exchange,' said Sir Julian.

'How many of Hals' pictures are in private hands?' asked Marjorie.

'Only eleven that we've been able to trace. When an important work by a major artist like Hals comes up for sale, quite often it's purchased by a national gallery, which guarantees it will never come on the market again.'

'Which only puts up the value of those works still held in private hands,' threw in William. 'Even more so if they're loaned out for a major exhibition.'

'I've approached all eleven private owners,' continued Beth, 'and asked if they'd be willing to support the exhibition. Three have agreed, but under the most stringent conditions, four have turned me down, and the other four didn't even bother to reply.'

'Why wouldn't they be willing to loan their pictures?' asked Marjorie, 'when, as William says, it would only add value to the works.'

'The Mellons and Rothschilds of this world are well aware of that and are always supportive of major exhibitions. The rejections often come from owners who are concerned their artworks might be damaged in transit. That's why I'm having so much trouble convincing Mr Morita to part with his magnificent Hals self-portrait that hangs in the Sony collection in Tokyo.'

'And those who haven't bothered to reply?' asked Marjorie.

'Often criminals who don't want to draw the taxman's attention to the fact that they own valuable works of art,' said William. 'The late Miles Faulkner is a typical example.'

'Or not so late,' said Sir Julian.

'Why do you say that?' asked William cautiously.

'Booth Watson doesn't appear in court as often as he used to, but as he still dines at the Savoy every day. He's either taken early retirement, which seems unlikely, or he's on a large enough retainer from a private client to be sure he doesn't have to seek regular work like the rest of us. You have to remember that few people employ a lawyer unless they have to.'

'Especially lawyers who continually interrupt their wives when they still have several more questions to ask about Frans Hals,' said Marjorie.

'Forgive me,' said Sir Julian. 'I'm becoming a legal bore.'

No one attempted to disagree with him.

'You mentioned that works sometimes have to be transported from one side of the world to the other,' said Marjorie. 'That must be very expensive.'

'Sometimes prohibitive,' said Beth. 'There are very few companies in Britain who are considered reliable enough to handle works of such importance. I know of one curator who insists that the painting is never let out of his sight, so, like him, it has to fly first class and not be put in the hold. That doesn't come cheap – and that's before you start worrying about the insurance premiums. The reason you can never borrow a Leonardo or a Michelangelo from the Vatican is because Lloyd's of London are unwilling to insure them, and the Pope has decreed no exceptions.'

'Can't the government help in those circumstances?' asked Marjorie.

'Sometimes they can be more of a hindrance,' said Beth. 'If the Foreign Office has reservations about the country you want to loan a picture to, they can refuse to grant you an export licence.'

'Understandably,' said Sir Julian. 'I can just imagine the outcry if the National Archaeological Museum in Athens asked to borrow the *Elgin Marbles* – just for six weeks.'

'And then there's the Jewish problem,' said William.

This silenced even Sir Julian.

'There are several major works hanging in public galleries that were stolen from their Jewish owners by the Germans during the Second World War. Some of them were later "liberated" by the Russians, and can now be seen in the Hermitage in St Petersburg, as well as several other well-known museums tucked safely behind the Iron Curtain.'

'Is there nothing the rightful owners can do about that?' asked Marjorie.

'Not a lot,' said Beth, 'while the authorities in those countries refuse even to acknowledge their claims. And they certainly wouldn't loan a looted work to an exhibition in a country where a civil action could be brought against them.'

'The Russians can't be the only culprits,' said Sir Julian. 'Hermann Göring assembled one of the finest private collections of old masters on earth, and I can't believe they've all been returned to their rightful owners.'

'Some of them have, but not too many. Most travelled east, not west, after the war. Don't forget the Red Army made it to Berlin before the Allies. So if you want to see those pictures they picked up on the way, you'll need a visa.'

'What about England?' asked Marjorie. 'Are there any paintings of dubious heritage hanging in our leading galleries?'

'Oh yes,' said William. 'Three of the Fitzmolean's finest works were donated by a well-known criminal.'

'On permanent loan by his generous widow,' insisted Beth.

'Who's almost as bad as her *late* husband,' said William, 'and if he is still alive, you can be sure Booth Watson will find a way of turning permanent into temporary.'

'Evidence?' demanded Sir Julian, tugging the lapels of his jacket.

'Christina Faulkner is represented by none other than Mr Booth Watson QC.'

'Not exactly proof, but . . .'

'Children, children,' said Marjorie. 'Desist.'

'Then there's my biggest problem,' continued Beth, 'which may prove insurmountable.'

'The bottom line, no doubt,' said Sir Julian.

'Exactly. You need to have at least sixty or seventy major works on display to be reasonably confident of good reviews from the critics who in turn will entice the public to visit in sufficient numbers, which in our case is a footfall of around ten thousand a week. Otherwise the gallery could actually end up out of pocket, as my boss continually reminds me.'

'Speaking of Tim Knox,' said Sir Julian. 'There's a rumour doing the rounds that he's going to be offered the post as Surveyor of the Queen's Pictures.'

'Let's hope it's only a rumour,' said Beth, 'because he'd be difficult to replace.'

'Does the Royal Collection have any Hals?' asked Marjorie, remaining on track.

'Three,' said Beth. 'And HM is always very generous when it comes to requests from public galleries.'

'I can't wait to see the exhibition,' said Marjorie.

'You'll both be invited to the opening night,' promised Beth. 'And now, despite Marjorie's misgivings, I'd like to hear about Julian's latest case.'

'Do you have an hour to spare?' said Sir Julian.

'Get on with it,' said his wife.

Sir Julian sat back, and paused for a moment before delivering the single word, 'Fraud.' He waited for as long as he felt he could get away with before adding, 'I shall be appearing on behalf of the Crown to prosecute a particularly devious and cunning individual who's been fronting a charity that rescues donkeys which have been ill-treated by their owners.'

'There are people who fall for that scam?' asked Beth.

'In their hundreds, it would seem. He only had to take out a quarter-page advertisement in the *Daily Telegraph* with a photo of a starving donkey, and the donations came flooding in. We are a nation of knaves and animal lovers, it would seem.'

'But if he saved the donkeys?' said Beth.

'There were no donkeys,' said Sir Julian, 'just hapless romantics only too willing to part with their money, which ended up in his back pocket. That's the reason he's able to afford the services of Mr Booth Watson, who will be making one of his rare appearances at the Old Bailey. Don't be surprised if several donkeys, of the two-legged variety, appear in the witness box to give evidence.'

It was some time before the laughter died down.

'When does the trial begin?' asked William.

'It should have been tomorrow at ten o'clock in the forenoon,' said Sir Julian, 'had Booth Watson not requested a postponement, which I reluctantly agreed to. It seems my unworthy opponent has a pressing engagement in Scotland, though he wouldn't say with whom.'

'He didn't say where, by any chance?' asked William.

'No, as always BW gave as little away as possible.'

Beth and William looked at each other, but didn't speak.

'Dad, could I make a phone call?'

'Yes, of course, my boy. Use the phone in my study.'

'Thank you,' said William, who stood up and quickly left the room.

'Was it something I said?' asked Sir Julian.

'No. Something Booth Watson didn't say,' said Beth.

'How intriguing.'

'I can even tell you who he's on the phone to.'

'The commander, no doubt,' said Sir Julian. 'And I can guess what he'll say when he returns.'

'"Sorry Mother, but we have to leave immediately,"' suggested Beth. '"Something unexpected has come up."'

The door opened and William came charging back into the room.

'I'm so sorry, Mother, but we have to go . . .'

'Something's come up that you have to deal with immediately?' suggested Sir Julian.

'How did you know that?' asked William.

'I didn't. But I could hardly help noticing that no sooner had I uttered the words Booth Watson and Scotland, than you suddenly needed to make an urgent phone call.'

William didn't rise to the bait. He kissed his mother on both cheeks and said, 'I'm only sorry that we can't stay for lunch.'

'Booth Watson isn't a man one should keep waiting,' said Sir Julian. 'When it's in his client's interests, he can move very quickly.'

'I look forward to seeing you in a couple of weeks,' said William, ignoring his father's remonstration.

'Only if you bring the twins with you next time,' said Marjorie.

'You can leave Artemisia at home,' said Sir Julian ruefully. 'She clearly has designs on another man.'

'I suspect she has designs on both of you,' said Beth, as Marjorie and Sir Julian accompanied them to the front door.

Once they'd said their farewells, William didn't speak again until they'd reached the road back to London. 'Do you think Faulkner will risk going to see the Caravaggio?' he asked.

'Collectors are passionate people,' said Beth. 'They don't usually allow representatives to make decisions on their behalf, especially when it's likely to cost them twenty million pounds.'

'Then let's hope Booth Watson will be accompanied by a dress designer by the name of Ricardo Rossi.'

'But if Booth Watson's doing no more than representing a client, and Faulkner doesn't make an appearance,' said Beth, 'it will be another wasted journey.'

'Not necessarily,' responded William, 'because when Booth Watson delivers the painting, he might just lead us straight to the front door of an obsessed collector who's standing on his front step waiting to welcome Christ with open arms and ends up with me.'

• • •

When Josephine woke the following morning, she found Ross sitting up at the dressing table writing a letter.

'A Dear John letter?' she teased as she stretched her arms.

Ross put down his pen. 'No. I've decided to resign from the Met,' he said, sounding unusually serious.

'But you've only just been promoted.'

'It's not the same since I stopped being a UCO,' said Ross. 'I can't just sit behind a desk shuffling paper clips around while two East End thugs go on running rings around us.'

'But if The Hawk won't let you go back undercover, what's the alternative?'

'I was in the SAS before I joined the Met, and my commanding officer was a Major Cormac Kinsella, a mad Irishman who used to eat cockroaches on toast for breakfast.'

'Fried or boiled?' asked Jo, trying to make light of it.

'They were still alive, which he said made it more of a challenge. His second-in-command, Captain Gareth Evans, thought the dragon was too soft a creature to represent the Welsh. They both retired from the SAS before the age of forty and set up a travel company, "Nightmare Holidays", that doesn't specialise in trips to Monte Carlo or St Tropez.'

'Where else is there?' asked Jo, with a sigh.

'Nightmare Holidays' slogan is "Survive a fortnight with us, and nothing will seem impossible". They offer their customers three different types of experience: "Uncomfortable", "Unpleasant" and, by far their most popular, "Unbearable".'

'I can't wait,' said Jo, 'do tell me more.'

'"Uncomfortable" is when they drop off a group of eight above the Arctic Circle and expect them to fend for themselves for a fortnight. They're supplied with one tent and enough food to last for a week. And each customer is allowed to take a thousand pounds in cash with them.'

'What's the use of money if you're stranded in the Arctic?'

'If you hand it to the ex-SAS officer in charge of the group, you'll be allowed to go home early.'

'This is becoming more enticing by the minute,' said Jo. 'I think I'll opt for "Unpleasant".'

'For that particular experience, twelve happy customers are dumped in the Brazilian rainforest a couple of thousand miles up the Amazon with half a dozen canoes and—'

'Enough food to last for a week,' said Jo.

'You're getting the idea. You then have to paddle down the river until you reach the next village some three hundred miles away, with only alligators, anacondas, piranhas and unfriendly natives to keep you company, so you don't get a lot of sleep at night.'

'I'll take your word for it.'

'You can still hand over your thousand pounds to the former SAS officer in charge of the trip, and a motor boat will appear from nowhere and drop you off at the nearest town. But you won't be reunited with your passport or given a plane ticket, so you'll have to make your own way home.'

'What's the point of that?'

'To make sure you think twice before leaving.'

'I'm not sure I want to know about the third option.'

'"Unbearable". You can't be considered a candidate for that particular challenge until you've already completed both "Uncomfortable" and "Unpleasant".'

'I can't wait to see the brochure.'

'You're dropped off in the port of Quellen in Chile, where you will join the crew of an ancient fishing vessel that sails around Cape Horn for the first week, before continuing on up the east coast to Brazil.'

'That doesn't sound too bad.'

'Until you discover you can't get off until you reach Rio, some two thousand five hundred miles away, and the waves regularly reach thirty feet during the voyage. Still, the good news is you can eat anything you catch.'

'And what do I get for my thousand pounds?'

'You'll be dropped off in the Falklands, and have to hope that the Governor's feeling sympathetic about the fact that you haven't got a passport or any money. Unfortunately, he's also a former SBS officer, so you'll probably finish your holiday locked up in a cell with half a dozen Argentinian bandits who haven't forgotten the Falklands invasion.'

'I'm only surprised that after handing over your cash, they don't make you walk the plank.'

'The mad major did consider that as an option, but in the end even he thought it was going a little too far.'

'And people pay to go on these holidays?' said Jo, in disbelief.

'There's a long waiting list of customers who'd be happy to take the place of any wimps who fall out at the last minute.'

'And dare I ask what role they have in mind for you?'

'I'd be in charge of selecting the ex-servicemen who will accompany the clients on each of the adventures. I'd only consider applications from the SAS, the Royal Marines and the SBS.'

'Now I understand why they chose you,' said Jo. 'Are you going to take the job?'

'I start in six weeks' time. The major has offered me almost double the salary I'm getting at the Met.'

'We're going to need every penny,' said Jo.

'Yes, because they're not going to pay you a thousand pounds a week to hear the private views of a mad major rather than a mad commander. Then it will be my turn to earn a thousand pounds a week, so the two of us can start a new life together.'

'The three of us,' said Jo, touching her stomach.

After a moment of realization, Ross leapt in the air, fell back down to earth, and said, 'We'll have to get married as quickly as possible.'

'Why?'

'My mother's an old-fashioned Irish Roman Catholic who uses words like wedlock, illegitimate and bastard as if they were still in fashion.'

'What will she say if she finds out I used to be a prostitute?'

'It would be a far bigger problem if you were a Protestant.'

CHAPTER 17

'THAT BRINGS US TO THE end of the tour,' said the guide. 'I hope you enjoyed it.' A warm round of applause followed. 'If you would like some mementoes of your visit, the shop on the ground floor is open, as is the café, should you require any refreshments. Do feel free to roam around the grounds, but please remember the gates will close at one p.m. today. Thank you.'

William and Ross followed the crowd out of the room, ignoring the shop and the café as they headed for the front door.

'Keep moving,' said William, as they strolled across a broad stretch of unmowed lawn towards a large clump of trees that overlooked the castle. 'Observations?' he asked, once they were safely out of earshot of any other visitors.

'The Caravaggio's still hanging above the fireplace in the dining room for all to see.'

'What else did you notice about that room?'

'A table had been laid for four. So they are clearly expecting Booth Watson for lunch,' suggested Ross. 'With or without his client.'

'Security?' said William, moving on.

'Virtually non-existent. The smaller paintings are all screwed to the wall, and there's only a rope barrier to prevent anyone getting too close to the pictures.'

'Alarm system?'

'Penfold, but years out of date.'

'And what didn't you see?'

'Any security guards, which you'd find in every room if it were a public gallery and not a private house.'

'Conclusion?'

'His Lordship can only afford to employ the bare minimum of staff, which you can be sure Faulkner will clock,' said Ross. 'That's assuming he turns up.'

'That's assuming he hasn't already,' said William. 'Don't forget the local police could only spare one constable to keep a lookout, 24/7.'

Ross didn't comment.

'However,' continued William, 'back to the dining room. What else did you notice?'

'A minstrels' gallery runs right around the upper level of the room.'

'Access?'

'A narrow spiral staircase leads up to it. The only security is a rope and a "No Entry" sign on the bottom step.'

'Any other observations?'

'There's a large window directly opposite the Caravaggio that looks out onto the courtyard. You can probably see the front gate from up there.'

'What else?'

Ross thought for a moment, but didn't respond.

'There's a small Hamburg organ on the left-hand side of the minstrels' gallery,' said William. 'Anyone hiding in the gallery wouldn't be spotted from the dining room below.'

'Is there room for both of us?'

'No. Only a choirboy,' said William, grinning. 'In any case, if both of us went missing, it's possible the guide would notice and come looking for us.'

'He didn't count us before he began the tour.'

'Well spotted,' said William, touching his forehead in mock salute. 'Nevertheless, when the tour ends, I want you to come back here and brief our boys, who will be waiting in squad cars ready to move at a moment's notice should Faulkner appear. Anything else the guide said that was particularly revealing?'

'The gates of the grounds will be closed at one o'clock.'

'Which suggests there'll only be one more tour today. So let's get moving, because we can't afford to miss it.'

They walked swiftly back down the slope towards the castle. Once they were inside, William purchased two more tickets from an elderly lady seated at the reception desk. They then joined a dozen or so people who were assembled in the hall waiting for the tour to begin.

Without a word, Ross made his way to the front of the group, while William remained near the back. Once the guide had given his introductory remarks, the tour began. William couldn't resist stopping to admire several of the collection's gems as they moved from room to room. He looked forward to telling Beth about a Farquharson, a Raeburn and a Peploe when he returned home that evening.

He didn't revert to being a detective until they were back in the dining room.

Ross remained at the front of the group while the guide told them how the first Lord McLaren had acquired *Fishers of Men* over two hundred years ago.

William pretended to be looking at a portrait by one of Caravaggio's less familiar contemporaries as he drifted casually towards the spiral staircase that led up to the minstrels' gallery. The guide concluded his remarks on the centrepiece of the collection, and began to walk towards the next room. A few worshippers couldn't resist one last look at the masterpiece before they rejoined the rest of the group.

Once William was certain he was alone, he stepped nimbly over the rope and made his way up the spiral staircase to the gallery. One or two creaks caused him to look back and make sure no one had spotted him. On reaching the gallery, he moved swiftly around the dogleg, then tucked himself up against the far side of the organ.

Although he had a clear view out of the large bay window, he couldn't see the dining room table below, or the Caravaggio. He settled back to do what he'd done so many times in the past: sit, wait, be patient and whatever you do, don't lose your concentration.

When the guide came to the end of the tour, Ross was among the first to break away from the group and quickly leave the castle. He noted that, although the guide mentioned the shop and the café, this time he didn't suggest that they should feel free to roam around the grounds. However, he did remind them that the gates would be closing at one o'clock.

Ross made his way back to the copse, from which he had

a clear view of both the castle's front door and the gates that led out onto the road. He pulled his radio out of an inside pocket and pressed the green button.

'DCI Warwick is still in the house. I'm outside stationed in the grounds about seventy yards from the front door. If Faulkner appears, I'll let you know immediately.'

'Understood,' said a voice that came crackling down the line. 'If we see a car approaching the castle, you'll be the first to hear.'

'All received,' said Ross, and placed the radio back in his pocket.

• • •

William peered through the large window and watched the remaining members of the tour group as they drifted towards the visitors' car park. When he heard footsteps in the dining room below he edged even further into the gap between the organ and the wall, tucking his knees up under his chin.

Two waitresses were chatting as they added the final touches to the place settings. They stopped talking when somebody else entered the room and a voice boomed, 'I don't have to remind you both how important his Lordship considers this meeting. We must all be on our toes. Is that understood?'

'Yes, sir,' piped up two voices in unison.

• • •

Ross watched as the gates closed the moment the last tourist had departed. Well, not quite the last. He glanced up at the large window on the first floor and wondered how William was getting on. If a car didn't appear in the next few minutes, how long would they have to hang about before he accepted it had been another wasted journey? Although he had no idea how William planned to get out of the castle, one thing was certain: the boss would have worked that out.

Ross's radio crackled into life, and he heard a broad Glaswegian accent on the other end of the line. 'A chauffeur-driven car is heading towards the castle, two passengers sitting in the back. They should be with you in about three minutes.'

'Message received.'

William stared out of the window to see the front gate edge slowly open. A moment later a BMW entered the grounds and headed towards the castle. He lost sight of the car long before it reached the front door, but Ross still had a clear view as the BMW came to a halt in the driveway. The chauffeur leapt out and opened the back door. Two figures appeared: a smartly dressed woman who headed straight for the door, followed by a man wearing a long black overcoat and carrying a briefcase.

They were greeted on the steps by his Lordship, who was dressed in a lovat green jacket, a kilt of the McLaren family tartan, heavy brown woollen socks and what his mother would have called sensible shoes. Standing by his side was an older woman who Ross thought he recognized. The front door closed and they all disappeared inside.

William was already stiff and needed to stretch, but he didn't dare move for fear of making the slightest sound. A few moments later a gong echoed in the distance, and shortly afterwards he heard a small group of people entering the dining room, chatting amicably.

'This is where *Fishers of Men* has hung for the past two hundred years,' said an aristocratic voice that could only have been Lord McLaren's.

Purrs of 'Magnificent', 'Superb', 'A masterpiece' followed.

'Why don't we take our seats for lunch,' William heard Lord McLaren suggest. 'I thought you would like to sit facing the painting, so you have a better view of it,' he said, addressing one of his guests, who didn't comment.

William heard chairs being pulled back while the waitresses scurried in and out of the room. Two of the diners' voices were quite clear, but one, who must have had his back to him, was almost indecipherable. Then a woman spoke, and William recognized her voice immediately. It certainly wasn't Lady McLaren.

• • •

Ross remained hidden in the copse, trying to imagine what they might be having for lunch on the other side of the castle's impenetrable walls. Smoked salmon and grouse from the estate, he guessed, considering the time of year. He licked his lips and resigned himself to a long wait before an unlikely minstrel would appear at the window. If William gave him a thumbs-up sign, he was to radio the waiting officers, who would immediately head for the castle, flashing lights not on, sirens not blaring. By the time they reached the front door William would have arrested Faulkner. A thumbs-down sign would mean Faulkner wasn't among the guests, and he would attempt to make a discreet exit.

• • •

William listened carefully to the conversation around the dining room table. He couldn't make out every word, and one member of the group hadn't yet spoken.

'Shall we get down to business?' said Lord McLaren once the main course had been cleared away.

'What figure did you have in mind?' said a voice, having dispensed with platitudes.

'I consider thirty million pounds would be a fair price.'

'Twenty million would be nearer the mark, in my opinion.'

'It's worth far more than that,' said McLaren.

'I'd agree with you, if it wasn't a fire sale.'

William would have liked to have seen the expression on his Lordship's face.

'While you have an inheritance problem, it's a buyer's market.' The voice paused. 'However, I would be willing to offer you twenty-two million, with an added incentive,' said the same voice.

'And what might that be?' asked McLaren, sounding flustered.

'My offer will remain on the table for one week. In the second week it will fall to twenty-one million, and twenty in the third.'

William realized that Faulkner knew the exact figure Lord McLaren needed to clear his death duties, and presumably also the date on which the full amount was due, after which he'd have to start paying interest to Her Majesty's collector of taxes.

'I'll need to think about it,' said McLaren, trying to sound relaxed and still in control.

'The clock is ticking,' said the same voice. The words of Faulkner, but delivered by his messenger.

'Let's adjourn to the drawing room for coffee,' said McLaren, ignoring the veiled threat. William heard chairs being pushed back from the table, and the lunch party making their way out of the room.

He now knew that the laboured, heavy steps belonged to Miles Faulkner's representative on earth.

William didn't move until the table had been cleared, the waitresses had departed and the door closed. Once there were no longer any voices to be heard, he crawled across to the window and gave a thumbs-down sign, just as the door opened again. He fell flat on his stomach and didn't move.

• • •

Ross cursed several times before he radioed the squad cars and delivered the simple message, 'Stand down. Mission aborted.'

'Sorry about that, laddie,' said a voice, before the radio went silent.

It must have been another hour before William and Ross both saw the gates open once again and the BMW disappear out of sight.

• • •

William didn't move until he was certain there wasn't anyone in the room below. He peeped over the gallery railing – no one to be seen – then tiptoed down the spiral staircase and headed across the dining room, unable to resist taking one last look at the Caravaggio. He opened the door just enough to peek through the crack, before stepping out into the deserted corridor, ready to slip into the café or gift shop should anyone appear. He walked cautiously towards the front door, growing more confident with each step he took. He was just about to turn the handle when a voice behind him said, 'Can I help you, young man?'

William swung nervously around to see the old lady behind the reception desk checking the morning's takings.

'Hello. Yes, I'd like a ticket for the afternoon tour,' he said, not missing a beat, while taking out his wallet and extracting a pound note.

'I'm sorry, but we're closed for the day.'

'Oh, that's disappointing. I was looking forward to seeing the Caravaggio.'

'Didn't I see you earlier this morning?' she said, taking a closer look at him.

'Yes. I'm going back to London tomorrow, and I was hoping to see the picture one more time.'

'You'll have to come back first thing in the morning, young man, because that may well be your last chance to see it.'

William risked, 'I don't understand. The guide told us it had been in the family for over two hundred years and was the pride of Lord McLaren's collection.'

'Indeed it was, but I'm afraid my son has no choice but to sell it,' said the Dowager Countess, as she came out from behind the counter, walked across the hall and opened the front door. 'Death duties, you know,' she added with a sigh, before closing the door behind him.

William now knew who the fourth person at lunch had been.

• • •

'Was Christina also at the lunch?' asked Beth, as William climbed into bed later that night.

'Yes, and she was posing as the interested buyer for the painting,' said William, 'although Booth Watson did most of the talking.'

'So, once again I've fallen for her lies. I promise you, I won't let her get away with it ever again.'

'Then you'll have to kill her, and just hope I'm the investigating officer in charge of the case.'

'I won't need you,' said Beth, 'because I know how to kill both of them without a drop of blood being spilled.'

'What do you have in mind?' asked William.

'If Tim Knox were to advise HMG to refuse Lord McLaren's request for an export licence on the grounds that *Fishers of Men* is a painting of national importance, it could be years before Faulkner would get his hands on it. And he'd have only one person to blame. Christina.'

'That's the last thing I want,' said William firmly. 'The commander has just sanctioned Operation Masterpiece, so I'll need you to find out who's been given the job of transporting the painting to its new owner.'

'That will only take me a couple of phone calls,' said Beth. 'But what do I get in return?'

'I'll bring Faulkner back in handcuffs, along with the painting.'

'If you pull that off,' said Beth, 'I'll ask Tim Knox to

recommend that the Chancellor waives his Lordship's death duties, in exchange for gifting the Caravaggio to the nation.'

'What do you mean by "the nation"?' asked William innocently.

'The Fitzmolean, of course.'

'I can't make up my mind who is more conniving and unscrupulous. You or Christina.'

Beth turned out the light.

CHAPTER 18

'ISN'T SHE GORGEOUS?' SAID BETH, when the bride and groom entered the room and she saw Josephine for the first time.

'And Ross is clearly besotted with her,' said William.

'Wouldn't you be?'

'I resigned myself to the fact some time ago that I'm stuck with you. *A poor virgin, sir, an ill-favoured thing, sir . . .*'

'*But mine own*,' said Beth, '*All's Well*.'

'No, *As You Like It*.'

'Your problem, is that you're semi-educated.'

'And your problem—'

'Shh,' said Beth as Ross and Jo took their places in front of the registrar.

'Welcome to Marylebone Old Town Hall,' said the registrar, addressing the assembled gathering.

'I don't think I'll ever get used to a woman performing the marriage service,' whispered Beth.

'You're so wonderfully old-fashioned,' said William, taking her hand.

'Which is how I ended up with you, caveman.'

'I have the pleasure of conducting this marriage service between Ross and Jo,' continued the registrar. 'I should begin by pointing out that the commitment they will make to each other today is for the rest of their lives, and just as morally and legally binding as any pledge taken in a church. So, let us begin the service.'

William had never seen Ross looking so relaxed and happy. The fashionable new suit, white shirt and even the cufflinks, complemented by a red carnation in his buttonhole, would have come as a surprise to the denizens of the underworld among whom he had mingled for so many years. None of whom had been invited to the wedding.

When the registrar solemnly asked, 'If any person present knows of any lawful impediment to this marriage, he or she should declare it now,' Beth gripped William's hand. He knew she was remembering how Miles Faulkner had crudely attempted to ruin their wedding day, and how Christina had come to their rescue.

No one raised a voice on this occasion.

William couldn't resist a smile as they took their vows. He still hadn't got used to one of the toughest men he'd ever come across being so hopelessly in love.

A warm round of applause broke out when the registrar announced, 'It gives me great pleasure to declare that you are now legally married. You may kiss the bride.'

Mr and Mrs Hogan kissed each other for the first time.

'I'm hungry,' whispered William.

'Patience. We've been invited to lunch at the Marylebone Hotel after the service.'

'I can't wait. I haven't had a good meal for weeks.'

Beth kicked him sharply on the ankle and he let out an exaggerated yelp.

The wedding party followed the bride and groom out of the room, down the Old Town Hall steps and onto the pavement. William held Beth's hand as they crossed Marylebone Road and headed for the hotel.

A man seated at the bus stop on the opposite side of the road was writing down the names of everyone he recognized. Only three of the guests were unknown to him. He took a closer look at the bride and groom, and wondered if Hogan realized he'd married a call girl. In any case, he'd be informing his employer immediately that the overpaid tart could no longer be relied on. Then he spotted DS Roycroft. Was she also no longer to be trusted? Had the information she'd been passing on to him already been vetted by Warwick? He'd have to assume the worst, while trying to turn it to his advantage. He would place the blame for any false information on the whore, and then take credit for exposing her. That would guarantee he didn't lose his only source of income.

Lamont didn't move as the wedding party drifted in the direction of a nearby hotel. Once they were all out of sight, he stepped inside the nearest phone box, dialled a number and waited.

'Fetter Lane chambers,' said a voice on the other end of the line. 'How may I help you?'

'I need to speak to Mr Booth Watson – urgently.'

• • •

'What a spread,' said William, joining the queue at the buffet table.

'Remember you're trying to lose a couple of pounds,' said Beth.

William ignored her protestations and piled his plate with coronation chicken, tomatoes and salad, before moving on to the other end of the table, where he filled any empty spaces with ham, cheese and new potatoes.

'You may drag a man out of his cave,' sighed Beth, 'but however hard you try to improve him, he'll always be a caveman.' She took a sliver of smoked salmon, half a boiled egg and a little salad, before strolling across to join Paul, who was chatting to the bride. His plate resembled an even larger mountain.

'This is Beth Warwick, William's wife,' said Paul between mouthfuls.

'Ross speaks so highly of your husband,' said Jo. 'But as I'm sure you already know he was always happiest working undercover. Otherwise he would never have considered leaving the force.'

'William's the exact opposite,' said Beth. 'He had a short time working undercover, but couldn't wait to get back to the Yard and be reunited with the team.'

'That's why they made such a good partnership,' said Paul.

'Am I allowed to ask where you're going on honeymoon?' said Beth.

'Ross offered me four choices,' replied Jo. 'Any one of the three Nightmare Holidays or touring the Loire valley vineyards, sampling their finest wines and enjoying the delicious local cuisine, before ending up in Paris for a long weekend at the Ritz Carlton.'

'You must have had to think long and hard about that,' said Beth.

'About a nanosecond,' admitted Jo. 'However, once we get back, Ross intends to experience all that Nightmare Holidays have to offer while I stay at home and make sure everything's ready for Josephine . . . or Joseph.'

'He invited me to join him on an "Unpleasant" holiday,' said Paul, 'but sadly none of the dates quite fitted in with my busy diary.'

They all laughed, as Beth glanced across the room to see an older woman deep in conversation with the commander.

'I must admit, I never thought my son would get married,' she was saying. 'So this all came as a complete surprise.'

'A pleasant one, I hope, Mrs Hogan,' said The Hawk. 'You can be very proud of your son, and I'm sorry we're losing him.'

'Praise indeed, commander. But as a good Roman Catholic, you can't have failed to notice that they've got married just in time,' said Mrs Hogan, glancing in the direction of her daughter-in-law.

'I fear I'm a lapsed Catholic,' the commander replied.

'Lapsed enough not to be concerned about her previous profession?'

The commander couldn't think of a suitable reply.

'Who's that chatting to William?' asked Jackie, as she joined Paul in the queue for a second helping.

'Major Cormac Kinsella. Ross's new boss. He's completely bonkers, so Ross should feel at home,' added Paul, as he grabbed the last chicken leg.

'When does Ross join you?' asked William.

'First of the month,' said Major Kinsella. 'So you'll only

have him for a couple more weeks after he gets back from his honeymoon.'

'Couldn't be better timing,' said William. 'We have one last assignment that can't go ahead without him.'

'Dare I ask?' said Kinsella. 'Ross refuses to tell me anything about what he gets up to at the Yard.'

'Neither will I,' said William. 'If I did, I'd lose my job.'

'Should that happen,' said Kinsella, taking a card from an inside pocket and presenting it to William, 'please get in touch.'

'Why would he want to do that?' asked Beth, as she appeared by William's side.

'We're most fortunate to have Ross joining us as the senior ground operative, Mrs Warwick,' said Kinsella, 'but it won't be long before I'll be looking for a new managing director to take my place. Frankly, I think your husband would be the ideal person to take the company on to its next stage.'

'What can there possibly be beyond "Unbearable"?'

'A salary of eighty thousand pounds a year, shares in the company and a percentage of the profits.'

'And what makes you think I'd be the right man for the job?' asked William. 'After all, you've only known me for ten minutes.'

'I know that you're the youngest DCI in the Met's history, and in Ross's opinion you're the finest officer he's ever served under. Frankly, I'd made the decision even before I met you.'

'Better not tell the commander,' said Beth.

'Better not tell me what?' demanded The Hawk, as he walked across to join them.

'Major Kinsella has just offered William a job,' Beth answered with relish.

'Over my dead body,' said Hawksby.

'Whatever it takes,' said Kinsella, grinning.

'And I'll do whatever it takes to stop you,' said The Hawk. 'I have higher things planned for DCI Warwick, and they don't include running a holiday camp. What's more, I'll happily murder anyone who gets in my way.'

'Don't the Gospels tell us that the thought of murder is every bit as bad as the deed,' said Beth, trying to lighten the mood.

'If that's the case,' said the commander, 'I'll have to ask our Lord to take about fifty other cases into consideration. And, frankly, you're not even top of my current list,' he said, glowering at the major.

William smiled, but then he knew exactly who was top of the commander's current list.

'And in any case,' continued The Hawk, 'I will also be retiring in the not-too-distant future, and someone's going to have to take my place.'

This silenced even Beth, while William was distracted by a voice whispering in his ear, 'Can I have a word with you before we leave for the airport?'

'Of course,' said William, leaving the commander to continue jousting with Major Kinsella.

'Will I be back in time for the big one?' asked Ross, once he was confident no one could overhear them.

'I've delayed everything by a week to make sure you are. I don't want to start this particular operation without you.'

'How did the specialised movers feel about the Yard joining them for the trip?'

'Not overjoyed, but they kept their counsel after The Hawk reminded them that most of their contracts have to be sanctioned by the government. They were still a bit bolshie for a few days, until the Home Secretary called their chairman. Not a long conversation, I'm told.'

'I can't wait,' said Ross.

'Don't let Jo hear you saying that,' said William, 'because I know she has other plans for you during the next ten days. So be sure to relax and enjoy your honeymoon. I'm going to need you at your sharpest when you return if we're going to pull off the biggest operation I've ever been involved in.'

'Bigger than Trojan Horse?' said Ross.

'That was the commander's operation. Masterpiece is mine.'

• • •

Ross spent the next week roaming around the Loire valley, sipping the finest wines, while not being allowed to empty his glass, then devouring several courses of nouvelle cuisine before going to bed feeling hungry. He spent the last three days of the honeymoon enjoying the sights of Paris, unaware that it wouldn't be long before he returned. He still managed a five-mile run every morning before joining Jo for a breakfast of croissant and coffee. Breakfast, he reflected, was clearly a meal the French hadn't come to terms with. In his absence, DCI Warwick and the commander spent the time fine-tuning every last detail of an operation that would require split-second timing.

By the time a suntanned Ross returned to work the following Monday morning, everything was in place, awaiting only the commissioner's imprimatur.

'If we pull this one off,' said Ross, after he and William had gone over the plan one last time, 'I'll leave the force a happy man. And not just because you won't be my boss any longer,' he added, laughing.

'If we fail,' said William, not laughing, 'I'll also be leaving the force, but I'll still be your boss.'

CHAPTER 19

It had never crossed William's mind how long it would take to pack a valuable work of art, and how many people were involved, even though Beth had tried to warn him.

The key person among the group was Ian Posgate, a senior broker from Lloyd's of London, who had insured the Caravaggio should it be damaged in transit, and for the full amount of £21 million if it failed to reach its destination. Posgate was delighted the police would be accompanying them on the trip in the guise of his assistants.

William and Ross stood to one side and watched the professionals go about their work. Mr Benmore, the senior fine art handler, could boast a Goya, a Rembrandt and a Velázquez in his catalogue raisonné. However, he'd recently left it to one of his assistants to pack a Warhol for the Tate. Mr Benmore didn't do modern.

The long process began with four technicians, two of them

half-way up ladders, while the other pair had their feet firmly on the ground. Between them, they walked the masterpiece off the wall in a slow, controlled descent, a few links of its chains at a time. William noticed that Lord McLaren appeared to age visibly as he stared up at the dark rectangular space that marked where the pride of his family's collection had hung for the past two hundred years.

When the bottom of the frame was at waist-height, the four techs lifted it off its chains and lowered it gently onto a set of foam bricks, then rested for a few moments before placing it into a specially prepared travel frame. This unique piece of craftsmanship had been constructed by a carpenter who'd never seen the canvas, but had been supplied with the exact measurements of its ornate gilt frame.

Once the painting had been fitted securely in place, a protective layer of polythene was stretched taut across the surface before the team of technicians, supervised by Mr Benmore, manoeuvred the travel frame into a fortified external crate, constructed by the same carpenter; a delicate undertaking that required skill and strength in equal measure. Mr Benmore's final responsibility, after checking there could be no internal movement during its long journey to Barcelona, was to securely fasten the crate's wooden lid with an electric screwdriver. Ross counted all twenty-four screws.

After a thorough inspection, Mr Benmore declared himself satisfied, and allowed his team a tea break.

Twenty minutes later, they were back in action. Two of them lifted the crate a foot off the ground, while the other two positioned a wide skateboard underneath. After the crate had been gently lowered onto the skateboard, it was wheeled slowly out of the dining room and along the corridor towards the front door. Correx sheeting had been laid out along the route to protect the marble floor.

When they reached the entrance hall, William glanced across at the laird, his arm around an elderly woman who he recognized. She was holding back tears for the dear departed.

He noticed that the painting remained upright from the moment it was packed into the crate, until it was strapped into place in a climate-controlled, air-ride suspended truck, to ensure that the *Fishers of Men* couldn't fall out of their boat.

They never exceeded thirty miles an hour on the twelve-mile journey to Aberdeen airport.

William and Ross followed behind in an unmarked police car. A private jet awaited them at an airport where private jets are more common than commercial aircraft.

Mr Benmore was the first out of the truck, and once again he supervised the technicians as they painstakingly transferred the painting into the plane's hold, where it was strapped in – still upright. He and the insurance broker never took their eyes off the wooden crate until the door of the hold was heaved into place. Four passengers climbed aboard a jet bound for Barcelona.

When the plane landed on Spanish soil a couple of hours later, they found Lieutenant Sanchez waiting to greet them on the tarmac.

He was equally well prepared. Under the anxious direction of Mr Benmore, four policemen in overalls unloaded the crate from the hold and strapped it upright into a padded, temperature-controlled van.

Ross sat next to Sanchez in the front, while Mr Benmore, Mr Posgate and William climbed into the back. William tapped the divide, and Sanchez set off at a funereal pace for the final part of the journey.

• • •

Booth Watson had flown in on an earlier flight that morning to keep his monthly appointment with his most valued client.

He found Miles in an unusually exuberant mood, as he waited impatiently for his latest acquisition to arrive. The two men sat in the drawing room facing a large empty space on the wall above the fireplace, where *Fishers of Men* would reside.

'While we're waiting,' said Faulkner, 'bring me up to date on what's happening in London.'

'Some good news, and some not so good,' said Booth Watson, as he opened his briefcase and extracted the inevitable files. 'I fear the reports your tart has been passing on to me can no longer be relied on. But then you never consulted me about her in the first place.'

'Get on with it,' said Miles, barely hiding his irritation.

'A couple of weeks ago at Marylebone Old Town Hall, Josephine Colbert married Detective Inspector Ross Hogan, the man you've been paying her to seduce so we'd be kept informed about what Warwick's team were up to. She's now clearly a fully paid-up member of that team.'

'Take her off the payroll immediately,' said Faulkner, his irritation turning to anger.

'I already have,' said Booth Watson. 'Is there anything else you want me to do about her?'

'Nothing you need concern yourself with. In any case I'm more interested to know how you came across this information, as I find it hard to believe you were invited to the wedding.'

'Lamont has had Hogan under surveillance for some time. I have to warn you that he suspects DS Roycroft is also in Warwick's pocket, not ours.'

'Tell Lamont to go on seeing Roycroft, so they don't realize we're onto her. Her next report should make interesting reading, now that we know where her true loyalties lie. Make sure you keep Lamont happy.'

'There's only one thing that keeps Lamont happy,' said Booth Watson, 'and the other side can't supply that.'

'That also applies to Christina. We certainly can't risk her jumping ship.'

'There's not much risk of that. She knows if she dumps you in favour of Mrs Warwick there will be no home in the country, no flat in town, no chauffeur to drive her around, no more dress accounts, or ladies who lunch, and certainly no more toy boys. She'd end up having to doss down in the Warwicks' spare bedroom and be satisfied with the scraps from their table. I don't think so.'

'Then why keep her on the payroll?' demanded Faulkner.

'While Christina's still in touch with Warwick's wife, she remains our best bet when it comes to discovering what her husband is up to, as she also seems to be susceptible to a different kind of bribery . . .'

'What are you getting at?' snapped Faulkner.

'Christina reported that her latest meeting with Warwick's wife went well. She was delighted that Christina agreed to loan her Frans Hals to the Fitzmolean for their exhibition next autumn.'

'My Frans Hals,' said Miles.

'You'll only be without it for a few weeks. Which is a small sacrifice to make when you weigh it up against the possible consequences.'

'Make sure you get the painting back the day after the exhibition closes. Anything else?'

'Yes,' said Booth Watson. 'The purchase of the Caravaggio has almost wiped out your assets in London.'

'They'll be replenished once the takeover of Marcel and Neffe goes through. And don't forget the cash I still have in Rashidi's safety deposit boxes.'

Booth Watson was loath to tell his client that particular source of funds was also running low, but for a different reason.

Faulkner checked his watch. 'If my private jet has landed on time, the painting should be with us in about an hour, so why don't we go and have some lunch?'

• • •

Lieutenant Sanchez switched on the engine, eased the van into first gear, and carried out Mr Benmore's repeated instructions to remain in the inside lane at all times and not exceed thirty kilometres an hour, even on the motorway.

Ross sat silently by his side, alert to everything around him, as he tried to anticipate the unexpected. He'd already spotted the four unmarked police motorbikes on the motorway. Two in front and two behind, who were trying to look as if they were on traffic duty. Once they'd turned off the motorway onto a country road, he switched on a video camera so he could record every step of their progress.

The lieutenant looked on enviously. 'Scotland Yard's standard issue?' he asked.

'Hardly. It was a gift from my wife.'

'The only gift my wife ever gives me is another daughter,' said Sanchez.

'How many so far?'

'Three. But I haven't given up,' he said as they reached the edge of the forest and had no choice but to come to a halt.

Ross switched off the video and slipped it into the glove compartment, while Sanchez banged firmly on the divide to let his colleagues in the back know they had arrived.

William glanced across at Mr Benmore, who looked anxious and was perspiring heavily.

Lieutenant Sanchez touched the van's horn and a few birds scattered from the tops of the tall pine trees. He was about to give a second blast when a golf buggy appeared out of the forest and came to a halt in front of the van.

Two muscle-bound men climbed out of the buggy and circled the van slowly. One of them opened the driver's door and exchanged a few words with Sanchez, who had a well-prepared script for every one of his questions. The guard gave him a mock salute, before joining his colleague at the back of the van. They examined the large wooden crate, counted the passengers, checked the clipboard and then slammed the door shut, before walking back to the buggy. One of them waved an arm to indicate that Sanchez should follow them.

Ross retrieved his video camera from the glove compartment, pressed a button on the side and began to record their slow, meandering route along an unmarked path until they reached a wooden bridge. He continued filming as they crossed a fast-flowing river before finally emerging into the open to see a palatial mansion dominating the landscape.

Sanchez followed the golf buggy across a finely cut lawn and onto a wide gravel drive that led up to the house. Ross went over Plan A in his mind one more time. If Faulkner appeared when the front door opened, Ross would go to the back of the van to reduce the chances of his former fellow prisoner spotting him, while he looked as if he was supervising the unloading.

As soon as Faulkner began to follow the crate inside, the four armed policemen would grab him and handcuff him. Sanchez would then arrest Faulkner and read him his rights.

If there was even a hint of resistance from the two bodyguards, the police motorcyclists who were impatiently patrolling the motorway would spring into action and be with them moments later.

The front door opened, and a butler appeared. But there was no sign of Faulkner. It was never that easy. Ross moved on to Plan B.

Sanchez and Ross got out of the van, made their way slowly to the back and watched as Mr Benmore oversaw the unloading of the crate. He'd already complained to William about the four amateurs who'd taken the place of his professional technicians, but to no avail. After much grunting and groaning, the crate was finally lifted out of the van, and the four policemen followed Sanchez and the butler into the house, accompanied by Ross and Mr Benmore, while William remained out of sight. Still no sign of Faulkner.

Once the front door had been closed, William pulled a

baseball cap low over his eyes, slipped out of the back of the van and took up his position behind the wheel, aware that he couldn't risk being seen by Faulkner who would have recognized him immediately. He would like to have been the arresting officer, but he assumed that when the front door opened again, a triumphant Sanchez would re-appear with the prisoner. Mr Benmore would no doubt become even more distraught when he discovered that the painting would be going straight back to Scotland; an agreement that had been brokered between the commander, the Home Office and the Spanish police.

The four policemen carrying their entry ticket made slow progress across the hall, while Sanchez chatted to the butler. Eventually they reached the drawing room, where a large, empty space on the wall above the fireplace marked the place where *Fishers of Men* would never hang.

The crate was carefully lowered onto the carpet, and the policemen stood back to allow Mr Benmore to set about his other job, which called on equal expertise. Unpacking.

As he began to extract the screws one by one, Ross slipped behind the open door so that if Faulkner made an entrance he would be ambushed.

Once all twenty-four screws had been removed, and the lid of the crate lifted, Mr Benmore removed the travel frame, followed by the layer of polythene that was stretched across it, protecting the surface of the canvas. After the job had been completed to his satisfaction, he instructed his untrained technicians to lift the painting gently out of its coffin by the four corners of its gilded frame. He must have repeated the word '*lentamente*' a dozen times. Mr Benmore wasn't used to repeating himself.

The four men bent down, took a corner of the frame each, and eased the masterpiece out of its travel box. Despite himself, Ross couldn't resist stepping forward to take a closer look, just as the butler re-entered the room, with his master following close behind.

Ross tried to duck back behind the door, but Faulkner spotted him immediately, and an expression of undisguised shock appeared on his face. He turned and began running back across the hall, followed closely by Ross, with Sanchez only a yard behind.

The butler stepped quickly into the doorway, but a straight arm tackle that would have had Ross sent off a rugby field felled him, though not before he'd gained his master a few vital seconds.

Ross chased Faulkner across the hall and down a long corridor, gaining on him with every stride. When he reached a door at the end of the corridor, Faulkner surprised Ross by stopping to check the time, before opening the door. He leapt inside and slammed the door shut behind him. Ross grabbed the handle a second too late. After one determined charge, he knew a rugby scrum could not have forced the door open.

Faulkner heard the shoulder charge and allowed himself a wry smile as he made his way across the room, coming to a halt in front of the heavy iron door. He entered an eight-digit code on his watch, and the massive door obeyed his command and swung open. He stepped inside, pulled the door closed and waited for the four heavy bolts to slide into place.

Once again, he tapped his watch and waited for the face to light up before he entered a second code, which immediately opened the far door. He stepped out and slammed the heavy metal door shut behind him. He breathed a sigh of relief, before descending the stairs to his other world. The well-rehearsed disappearance had gone to plan, but he knew that he would now have to think more seriously about moving on.

The first thing he did when he reached his study was make a phone call.

CHAPTER 20

THE BUTLER DIDN'T HESITATE TO hand over the keys to a furious Ross. After all, by now the boss would have had more than enough time to escape.

Ross ran back down the corridor to find Sanchez, William and a couple of his officers trying unsuccessfully to break down the door. All they had to show for their trouble were bruised shoulders.

He quickly unlocked the door, but it came as no surprise to any of them that Faulkner was nowhere to be seen.

'Take a closer look at this metal door,' said William. 'Tell me what you see, or more important what you don't see.'

'No handle and no lock,' said Ross immediately.

'And no dial,' added Sanchez. 'So how do you open it?'

'I suspect there's only one person who knows that,' said William, as the butler reappeared carrying a large tray of drinks, which only made Ross want to hit him even harder.

'How do we open that door?' demanded William.

'I have no idea, sir,' said the butler, placing the tray on the table. The blank look on his face suggested to William that he might even be telling the truth.

William was about to ask a follow-up question when the phone on the desk began to ring. He indicated to the butler that he should answer it.

The butler picked up the receiver.

'Good afternoon, this is the Sartona residence. How may I help you?'

William took a notebook and a Biro out of his pocket, wrote down the name Sartona and underlined it, as he listened to the one-sided conversation.

'Are they still there?'

'Yes, sir. I'm afraid Mr Sartona is abroad at the moment. Can I take a message?'

'Is Booth Watson still with you?'

'Yes, sir. He's looking forward to seeing you when you return.'

'Call me the moment you're certain that every one of those flatfoots has left and are on their way back to Barcelona.'

'Of course, sir. I'll let him know you called.' The butler replaced the receiver, turned to William and said, 'Can I be of any further assistance, gentlemen?'

Ross clenched a fist and took a step forward.

'No, thank you,' said William, quickly coming between them. 'In fact, I think it might be wise for you to leave.'

'As you wish,' said the butler, who gave a slight bow and left without another word.

William waited for the door to close before he said, 'If we're going to have any chance of finding out what's behind that,' he said, pointing at the impenetrable iron door, 'we're going to need some pretty heavy equipment.'

'Easier said than done,' said Sanchez. 'This place used to be Franco's secret hideaway. It's what you call in your country a listed property, so we can't touch anything without the authority of a court.'

'Then we'll have to get on with it without consulting the authorities, won't we?' said Ross.

'I don't think so,' said William, shaking his head. 'Try to remember, Ross, we're not in the back streets of Battersea. We don't have any authority here.'

'Who cares, choirboy?' said Ross, unable to hide his frustration.

'I do,' said Sanchez. 'Because we're not even in the back streets of Barcelona.'

'And in any case,' said William, 'you can be sure that by now Faulkner will be on the phone to his Spanish lawyer, who'll slap a restraint order on us before you can say acetylene torch.'

'We could always wait. After all, he has to come out eventually,' suggested Ross.

'I'll bet there's another world on the other side of that door,' said William. 'Heaven knows how long we'd have to twiddle our thumbs before he reappears.'

'And Faulkner's lawyer would have seen us off long before then,' added Sanchez.

William nodded, but Ross still didn't look convinced.

'And I'm pretty sure I even know the lawyer he'll be speaking to,' continued Sanchez. 'So there's nothing we can do until we get a court order overruling any objection.'

'How long will that take?' asked Ross.

'Days, weeks, could be months,' said Sanchez, as the phone on the desk began to ring again. After two rings it ceased, and William assumed it had been answered on another extension somewhere in the building.

Sanchez grabbed the receiver, to hear a conversation taking place between the butler and a woman with whom he'd crossed swords many times in the past.

'Who's the officer in charge?' said a no-nonsense voice.

'Lieutenant Sanchez,' said the detective, interrupting them.

'Good afternoon, lieutenant,' she said, as if addressing a junior colleague.

'Good afternoon, señora.'

'Let me make it clear from the outset, lieutenant,' she said, trying to sound reasonable, 'if I find that anything in my client's home has been tampered with, I will not hesitate to sue the police and hold you personally responsible. Is that understood?'

'Yes, señora.'

'So there can be no misunderstanding at a later date, Lieutenant Sanchez, I'll ask you once again. Is that understood?'

'*Absolutamente, señora,*' said Sanchez, and slammed down the phone.

'So, Faulkner's eluded us again,' said Ross.

'Not necessarily,' said Sanchez. 'I'll put a couple of patrol cars on the road between here and the motorway, so if he tries to escape we'll be waiting for him.'

'What about the other side of the house?' asked William.

'He'd be faced with a sheer cliff. Franco chose this location so he could never be taken by surprise. It doesn't help that Faulkner will know only too well I don't have the resources to mount a twenty-four/seven operation for too long. Everything is budgets nowadays,' he added with a sigh.

'Then we'll have to return when he least expects us,' said William.

'When you do, please keep me in the loop,' said Sanchez. 'Because Faulkner is someone I'd like to meet.'

Ross smiled, but didn't comment. The Spanish equivalent of turning a blind eye.

'But until then,' said Sanchez, 'there's not much more we can do today, so I may as well drive you back to the airport?'

William turned to see that Ross had dropped to his knees, and was carefully examining the bottom left-hand corner of the iron door. 'Anything of interest?' he asked.

'Nothing, sir,' replied Ross, getting slowly to his feet.

The 'sir' told William that Ross had spotted something he didn't want to share with Sanchez.

Ross and William followed the lieutenant out of the room. Half-way down along the corridor, William paused to take a closer look at *The Flute Player* hanging on the wall and frowned.

'Something special about that one, chief?' asked Ross.

'I'm afraid so. My wife's not going to be pleased when I tell her she can cross it off her list.'

• • •

Faulkner put down the phone in his basement study, satisfied that his Spanish lawyer would have dealt with the immediate problem, and it wouldn't be too long before the police were sent packing. But how long would it be before they came back in even greater numbers?

He flicked open the cover of his private phone book and leafed through the pages until he reached the Rs, only hoping the number wasn't out of date. Miles sat back in his chair and rehearsed exactly what he was going to say, before he picked up the phone and dialled the number.

The ringing tone continued for some time before the phone was eventually picked up and a voice said, 'Who's this?'

'Miles Faulkner. You may not remember me, but . . .'

'Mr Faulkner. How could I forget? To what do I owe this unexpected pleasure?'

'Who am I speaking to?'

'This is the head of the family.'

'I want to pass on a message to your son, Terry.'

'I'm all ears, Mr Faulkner.'

'I need him to do a job for me.'

'Understood. But first we have to agree on a price.'

'What's the going rate?'

'Depends on how high-profile they are.'

'The wife of a police officer.'

'That won't come cheap, Mr Faulkner.'

'How much?'

'Shall we say ten grand?'

'Fine,' said Faulkner, accepting that this wasn't a time to bargain.

'How will I be paid?'

'Ex-Superintendent Bruce Lamont will deliver the cash to you tomorrow morning.'

'He certainly knows where to find us,' said the voice. 'Now all I need is a name.'

• • •

'On balance, I preferred Faulkner's private jet,' said Ross, as they took their seats in the back row of economy.

'This was the only flight available,' said William, 'and frankly, we were lucky to get two seats at the last moment.'

'So where are Mr Benmore and Mr Posgate, dare I ask?'

'Sitting up front in first class, along with Christ and four fishermen.'

'Well, if we end up landing in the Channel,' said Ross, 'at least one of us will be able to walk on water.'

William waited for the plane to take off and reach its cruising height before he opened his notebook. 'What did you pick up that I missed?' he asked.

'We'd need a transatlantic flight to cover that,' said Ross, 'so you'd better go first.'

'Let's start with the butler's telephone conversation in the study,' said William, ignoring the demob-happy jibe. 'I'm pretty sure he was speaking to Faulkner.'

'What makes you think that?'

'When he picked up the phone, he knew exactly who was on the other end of the line.'

'How can you be so sure?'

'He said "Yes sir" twice, and finished with "of course, sir",' said William, checking his notes. 'The whole thing sounded to me like a well-rehearsed script prepared for that particular situation.'

'Speculation,' said Ross. 'You'd need something more solid than that to convince a jury.'

'All right. When Faulkner's lawyer phoned a few minutes later, it was the usual double ringtone you'd expect from an outside line, but the first time, it was just a single ring, so it had to be an internal call.'

'Not bad, but what did the butler purposely give away that I saw you make a note of?'

'Sartona. He obviously wanted me to think it's Faulkner's new alias, but I doubt it will be the name on his passport when he decides the time has come to make a break for it.'

'Well done, choirboy, but I'm about to trump your ace.'

William couldn't help smiling at the thought that Ross was one of the few people on the force who still dared to call him choirboy – to his face. He closed his notebook, sat back and listened.

'While you were having a kip in the van and I was chasing Faulkner down the corridor, he slowed down to look at his watch. What criminal, I asked myself, checks the time when he's being chased by a copper? When he touched the watch, the face lit up.'

'So what's the answer to your rhetorical question, Inspector?'

'He already knew his study door was unlocked, because that was all part of his escape plan should the police ever turn up.'

'And where does a wristwatch that lights up fit in with your "Rossonian" theory?'

'First, ask yourself why there's no handle or lock on the door of the safe.'

'What's your conclusion?'

'It wasn't a watch, but the key to opening the heavy metal door. All he needed to do when the face lit up was to enter a code and then the door would open.'

'That would explain how he managed to disappear into thin air but was still able to call the butler moments later.'

'And if you're interested,' continued Ross, 'I can tell you the name of the company that made that door.'

'NP,' said William, still in the game. 'The letters that were engraved in the bottom left-hand corner.'

'Not bad, choirboy, but do you know what NP stands for?'

'No, but I have a feeling you're about to tell me.'

'Nosey Parker. Colonel Parker is the one man who can tell us how to open that door.'

'But you've only got a week to go before you leave the force.'

'Then I may have to postpone my retirement for a little longer if I'm going to prove my theory is right.'

'Who needs an ex-copper who's going to work for a holiday company run by two complete lunatics?'

'You do,' said Ross, producing a small tin box from an inside jacket pocket. He flicked it open to reveal the plastic mould of a key.

'Faulkner's study door?'

'If I'd taken the key,' said Ross, 'he would have had the lock changed before we'd reached the airport.'

'Anything else?'

'Yes,' said Ross, producing his miniature video camera. 'I've recorded the only safe route through the forest to the front door. So you can't survive without me.'

William admitted defeat and shook hands with his partner as a stewardess leant over and handed each of them a plastic tray of dry rice and heated-up beef, with a sachet of brown sauce.

'Anything else?' asked William.

'Yes,' said Ross. 'I'd prefer to be sitting up front in first class next to Christ.'

'I think a choirboy is more likely . . .'

'It's better to save one sinner,' countered Ross.

• • •

Faulkner picked up the phone on his desk and listened.

'All clear, sir,' said the butler. 'Our man at the airport has just rung to say that he saw both of them board a plane for London.'

'Both of them?' repeated Faulkner.

'Chief Inspector William Warwick and his second-in-command, an Inspector Ross Hogan.'

'The Chief Inspector's wife is shortly to get an unpleasant surprise, and it's not just that she won't be getting her hands on my Frans Hals for her autumn exhibition,' Faulkner said, before he slammed the phone down. He left the room, climbed the stairs and, after tapping his watch, entered an eight-digit code. When the inner door opened, he stepped inside the safe, checked his watch again and entered a second code making it possible for him to return to his study on the ground floor.

When the door opened, he was greeted by the sight of Collins waiting for him with a freshly poured flute of champagne resting on a silver tray. He grabbed the glass on the move and said, 'Is Mr Booth Watson still with us?'

'Yes, sir. He's waiting for you in the drawing room.'

Faulkner glanced around the room, which had been ransacked. 'I see the Chief Inspector left his calling card,' he said, before heading for the drawing room, pausing only to straighten a picture in the corridor.

Booth Watson rose as his client entered the room.

Faulkner collapsed into the nearest chair and stared up at a redundant double picture hook on the wall.

'So, the Caravaggio was nothing more than bait to find out where I was holed up.'

'It would seem so,' said Booth Watson. 'And you won't be pleased to hear that they took the painting back with them.'

'Just make sure the cheque bounces.'

'I've already spoken to the bank. His Lordship presented the cheque this morning, and they were about to cash it when I called.'

'I'll still get hold of that picture,' said Miles, while looking up at the empty space on the wall.

Booth Watson didn't comment.

'How did you manage to avoid being seen by the police?'

'Collins took me up to one of the maid's rooms on the top floor and I hid under her bed.'

'Didn't the police check her room?'

'One of them came in, but found a gardener having sex with the maid. He apologized and quickly left. But you'll now have to face the fact this place will be under constant surveillance.'

'We always knew that was bound to happen sometime. At least I was well prepared,' said Faulkner. 'But now I need to plan my escape because it won't be too long before they're back.'

'When and how?' said Booth Watson. 'We have to assume they'll have patrols on the road out of here, twenty-four/seven.'

'But I won't be going by road.'

'But as you once told me, there's nothing on the other side of the house except a sheer cliff.'

'That would have been the case if Franco hadn't built a tunnel from his downstairs study all the way to the beach. However, I still can't afford to move until everything else is in place, so you'll be working overtime when you get back to London. First, I need you to get in touch with the captain of my yacht, and tell him to be ready to sail at a moment's notice.'

'And the collection?'

'Goes with me. Where I'm going, it may be the only asset I have.'

'May I suggest,' said Booth Watson, 'that in future you sleep in your study, with the door locked, so that if Warwick turns up in the middle of the night you'll have more than enough time to escape.'

'Good thinking, BW. I'll get Collins to make up a camp bed immediately.'

'Is there anything else you need me to do, once I'm back in London?'

'Just one more thing. Give Lamont ten thousand pounds in cash and tell him to deliver it to Terry Roach tomorrow morning.'

Booth Watson, like any experienced QC, never asked a question when he didn't want to know the answer.

CHAPTER 21

'So which European city have you been to this time, caveman?' asked Beth, as she poured William a second cup of black coffee.

'What makes you think I even left London?'

'I needed to borrow a couple of pounds yesterday, only to find your wallet was stuffed with pesetas.'

'Define the meaning of the word "borrow".'

'The full amount will be paid back at some time in the future.'

'How long in the future?' asked William, as he spread some marmalade on his toast.

'During my lifetime,' she said, giving him a kiss on the forehead. 'Stop changing the subject and tell me where you went after you'd visited Scotland.'

'What makes you think I was in Scotland?'

'Along with a thousand-peseta note, I also found a one-way

ticket to Aberdeen, and I don't think the peseta is the Scottish national currency yet.'

'You should have got a bit more than a couple of pounds for a thousand pesetas.'

'Stop changing the subject,' repeated Beth. 'I've already worked out you must have gone to Scotland to see Lord McLaren, or to be more accurate his Caravaggio. The only reason you'd have done that was in the hope Miles Faulkner would be there, and I suspect all you got for your trouble was his representative on earth.'

William buttered another piece of toast.

'It doesn't matter if you don't want to tell me,' said Beth, 'because I'm having lunch with Christina, and I'm sure she'll reveal all.'

William felt guilty at the thought that Beth was about to find out that the Frans Hals Christina had promised to loan to the Fitzmolean would not be hanging in their autumn exhibition, and he was to blame. 'Have to get moving,' he said, after downing his coffee, 'or I'll be late for the commander's meeting.'

'Do you have any pesetas left over?' asked Beth, following another kiss.

'My father warned me about women like you,' he said, as he handed her a five-pound note.

'I adore your father,' said Beth.

• • •

The commander took his place at the top of the table, pleased to see that every member of the team was present. He looked to his right and said, 'So now he knows that we know.'

'Yes, sir,' said William. 'Which means we don't have a lot of time to come up with a plan if we're going to trap him before he disappears again.'

'We?' said The Hawk.

'Ross has agreed to postpone his departure for a month, to make sure Faulkner doesn't get away a third time.'

'Is there nothing you won't do to go undercover again, DI Hogan?' asked The Hawk, switching his attention to the other side of the table.

'It would seem not,' said William, before Ross could reply. 'The Spanish police couldn't have been more cooperative. However, Lieutenant Sanchez thinks it would help if you had a word with your opposite number in Barcelona.'

'I'll call him later this morning,' said The Hawk. 'Just be sure to keep me fully informed on what you two are up to, and I mean fully.'

'Yes, sir,' said William, well aware that wouldn't be possible unless Ross kept him fully informed of what he was up to.

'What have the rest of you been doing while DCI Warwick and DI Hogan have been swanning around Europe at the taxpayers' expense? Let's begin with you, DC Pankhurst.'

'Darren Carter,' began Rebecca, 'is still working as a doorman at the Eve Club, and other than smoking the occasional joint in a back alley during his breaks, there's not much I can pin on him. Although loose talk after a couple of pints suggests he still thinks he's got away with it.'

'What about the owner of the club, who's equally guilty?' asked The Hawk.

'He's just made an application to extend his liquor licence until two a.m.'

'Have a word with the local magistrate and make sure it's thrown out. If he asks why, get him to give me a call.'

'Will do,' said Rebecca, making a note.

'Let me make it clear, Detective Constable,' continued The Hawk, his gaze still concentrated on Rebecca. 'I won't be satisfied until that club is closed down and both those villains are locked up.'

'Yes, sir,' Rebecca repeated, but she didn't make a note this time.

'Is your news any better, DS Adaja?'

'Yes and no, sir,' said Paul. 'Sleeman's still lending money at extortionate rates, while threatening to impose an unwritten default clause for anyone who doesn't pay up on time. But there's not a lot I can do about it.'

'Why not?' demanded William.

'Every victim I've interviewed so far has either clammed up completely, or denied ever having heard of Sleeman. Even the one who'd recently lost a finger.'

'They're obviously more frightened of Sleeman than they are of us,' said Ross.

'And who can blame them,' said William.

'Are you any nearer to tracking down any of the three who went missing?'

'No, sir. Still no sign of any of them. But that doesn't stop Sleeman's thugs turning up on their wives' doorsteps when the next payment is due, and extracting the widow's mite.'

'Perhaps one of those widows might become more co-operative in the future,' suggested The Hawk.

'I wouldn't be too optimistic about that, sir. Whenever I mentioned the name Sleeman, they all claimed they'd never heard of him.'

'Then our best hope is to catch him before the next victim disappears.'

'Easier said than done, sir. The next victim could be any one of a dozen people,' said Paul, looking down at a long list of names, 'and I've only got three Detective Constables to assist me, and one of them has only recently joined the force.'

'Don't give me the "I'm understaffed" excuse,' said the commander. 'I want to see Sleeman and his thugs sharing a cell for Christmas.'

Paul kept his head down.

'You're next, Jackie. How's your would-be ladykiller getting on? Has the woman he's planning to con finally seen the light?'

'Unfortunately not, sir. She became Mrs Pugh last week at a not-very-well-attended ceremony at the Chelsea Town Hall register office. The next morning, they flew off to Cape Town for their honeymoon. Don't be surprised if a grieving, even wealthier widower returns to England in a few weeks' time not wearing black.'

'I presume you've informed your opposite number in Cape Town and asked them to keep a close eye on Pugh.'

'It took a week just to find out who my opposite number was,' said Jackie. 'And when I finally did, he told me he already has forty-nine unsolved murders in his in-tray, so he didn't have much time to worry about one that just might happen at some time in the future. He said he'd call me the moment he heard anything. I haven't heard from him since.'

'Not exactly promising,' said William.

'Perhaps you should fly down to Cape Town and have a

quiet word with Mrs Pugh,' suggested Ross, 'and warn her that it might turn out to be a very short honeymoon, and she shouldn't be looking forward to living happily ever after.'

'If Jackie were to do that,' said William, 'Pugh would be certain to sue the Met, and he'd make a killing we wouldn't be able to charge him with.'

'Very droll, Chief Inspector,' said The Hawk. 'In any case, we don't have the resources to allow Jackie to swan off to Cape Town.'

'So, what should I do?' asked Jackie.

'Just wait for the time being. If they both return to England, you can reopen the file.'

'And if they don't?'

'We'll find you another file,' said William.

'Let's finally turn our attention to Ron Abbott and Terry Roach,' said the commander. 'Any news on that front, Ross?'

'Not much that you don't know already, sir. The two families are still at each other's throats. I fear it can't be long before it breaks out into open warfare.'

'We can't allow that to happen,' said The Hawk. 'Not least because it will give the press another opportunity to write about no-go areas and not enough bobbies on the beat. William, as the other three cases seem to be in limbo, and DI Hogan will soon be leaving us, I want you to take over responsibility for Abbott and Roach.'

'At the expense of Operation Masterpiece?' asked William. 'Because Ross and I are confident we've come up with a plan to bring Faulkner back to England so he can complete his ten-year sentence.'

'Plus whatever the court adds on following his escape,' threw in Ross.

'We're not bounty hunters,' said The Hawk. 'I'll need to be convinced you have a better than fifty-fifty chance of success before I would even consider sanctioning such an operation.'

'I have an appointment this afternoon with the company that constructed the metal door in Faulkner's study,' said Ross. 'That might well change the odds.'

'If they let you know how to open that door,' said The Hawk, 'I'll stand you a pint.'

'But you only gave me a half after our Trojan Horse triumph,' Paul reminded him.

'More than you deserved,' said William, 'considering you spent most of the evening in A&E with a sprained ankle.'

The rest of the team began to bang on the table with the palms of their hands, while Paul looked suitably chastened. He was rescued by the commander's secretary rushing into the room.

'A woman has just been murdered in South Kensington,' she said. 'They're asking for the Yard's assistance.'

'Tell them to get one of the local murder teams to handle the case, Angela,' said the commander. 'Don't they realize we have enough problems of our own?'

'Normally they would, the officer in charge assured me,' said Angela, 'but the woman was found with a serrated kitchen knife sticking out of her throat.'

'Roach,' said William and Hogan simultaneously, as they both leapt out of their seats.

'Tell them we're on our way,' said William. 'Jackie, make sure there's a squad car waiting for us outside the front door, and ask the duty officer to contact me on my radio, so he can brief me before I get there.'

William and Ross began running towards the door, but William suddenly stopped, turned back and said, 'Paul, put out an all-points alert for Terry Roach, with a warning that he'll be armed and dangerous. He can't be far from the scene, but in this particular case, it won't be the first forty-eight hours that are crucial, but the first forty-eight minutes. If we don't arrest him before he gets back to the East End, he'll have a cast-iron alibi along with a dozen witnesses who'll swear blind he hasn't set foot outside Whitechapel all day.'

Paul grabbed the nearest phone as William ran out of the room and into the corridor. Ross was already out of sight. He took the stairs down to the ground floor two at a time, not wanting to rely on the vagaries of the lift. By the time he reached the lobby, Danny was pulling up outside the front door.

William pushed his way through the swing doors, as Ross jumped into the back of the car, leaving the door open. William hadn't even closed it before Danny accelerated away.

They shot out of the Yard, siren blaring. Danny drove straight through a red light on the corner of Victoria Street, causing several vehicles to throw on their brakes, followed by irate horns blaring.

'Do we have the exact location?' William asked, clinging to the seat in front of him.

'Prince Albert Crescent,' said Danny, as he sped past the Palace Theatre in the direction of Hyde Park Corner. Several vehicles eased across to their right and left, allowing the car in their rear-view mirror to continue on its journey uninterrupted.

William's first thought was that the Fitzmolean was on Prince Albert Crescent. He tried to dismiss the idea from his mind. The radio buzzed, and William grabbed it. 'Chief Inspector Warwick,' he said.

'Inspector Preston, sir. I'm the duty officer at West End Central. DS Roycroft has just called to say you wanted to be briefed immediately.'

'Correct,' said William, not wasting a word.

'A young woman has had her throat slit in Prince Albert Crescent,' said Preston. 'It looks to me as if it was premeditated, and the killer knew his victim.'

'Any idea of her identity?'

'No, sir. A passer-by saw a car draw up by her side and a heavily built man wearing a stocking mask jumped out and slashed her across the face several times before finally slitting her throat. He then got back into the car which took off at high speed. It was all over in a matter of seconds.'

'Did anyone get the vehicle reg?'

'DS Adaja asked me the same question, but all we know is that the witness was pretty sure it was a black BMW.'

'Can you give me a description of the woman?'

'That's not easy, sir. She's been badly disfigured.'

'Skin colour, age?'

'Caucasian, I'd guess early thirties.'

William could hear his heart thumping.

'Weapon?' asked William, as Danny continued to weave his way in and out of the traffic.

'A small, thin knife with a serrated edge. He left it sticking out of her throat. It was almost as if he wanted us to know who'd done it.'

'He did,' said William, as he picked up the sound of

another siren in the distance. 'Don't allow the medics anywhere near the body before I get there.'

'Understood, sir,' he said.

As Danny shot past Harrods, pedestrians turned to stare, and as they got nearer, William offered up a silent prayer, trying to convince himself he was overreacting. Eventually, Danny touched the brakes lightly and swung left into Prince Albert Crescent, the speedometer still touching fifty. They couldn't miss the large police presence a couple of hundred yards ahead of them. A crowd of onlookers were gawping from the pavement on the opposite side of the road.

Danny screeched to a halt just feet away from the blue and white tape that surrounded the crime scene.

William was the first out of the car. He ducked under the tape and ran towards the lifeless body sprawled in a pool of blood on the pavement. As he approached it, he fell to his knees and screamed, 'No!'

Ross appeared by his side a moment later. When he saw who it was, he was violently sick.

Inspector Preston was surprised that two such experienced officers had reacted as if it were their first murder case.

'Do you know who she is?' he asked tentatively.

'Yes,' he replied, cradling his wife gently in his arms. 'And I'll kill him.'

CHAPTER 22

WILLIAM HAD ALWAYS WANTED TO take Beth to Paris for a long weekend. They'd talked so often of visiting the Louvre, the Musée d'Orsay, and of course the Musée Rodin. They would window-shop on the Rue de Rivoli, perhaps buy an oil from a pavement artist in Montmartre, recalling the story of the American woman who bought a painting from Picasso for a few francs because she liked it.

They would take a boat down the Seine, drink a little too much wine, and enjoy a coq au vin while sampling a cheese board they would never experience anywhere else in the world, before finally returning to their little pension on the Left Bank. They would resist climbing the Eiffel Tower, but in the end join dozens of other tourists in a crowded lift to witness the spectacular panoramic views of the most romantic city on earth. But not this weekend.

After stepping off the train at the Gare du Nord, William went in search of a taxi. He handed the driver an address in the outskirts of Paris, and twenty minutes later the taxi pulled up outside the church of St Mary the Virgin. After paying the driver fifty francs, William joined a trickle of mourners as they made their way up a path to the open door at the east end of the church.

The front three rows were occupied by a dozen or more of the most elegantly dressed women William had ever seen. He walked slowly down the aisle and took a seat in the pew behind his friend, whose head was bent in prayer.

When the hour struck on the clock tower above them, the priest made his entrance, coming to a halt on the steps in front of the altar. He conducted the funeral service with an air of quiet dignity, and although William could not understand every word, his schoolboy French allowed him to follow the proceedings, even the moving tribute given by an older gentleman, who William assumed must be a relation or long-standing family friend.

After the service was over, they all gathered in the churchyard. As the coffin was being lowered into the ground, William was glad that none of those standing around the graveside had seen her lying on the pavement moments after she had died, and would remember her only as a beautiful woman. The one saving grace was that her prematurely delivered daughter had somehow survived. She wouldn't have, if Roach had known that Ross Hogan's wife was pregnant.

The priest made the sign of the cross and blessed the mourners, after which the girls lined up and kissed Ross gently on both cheeks, leaving him in no doubt about the affection they shared with him for the only woman he'd ever loved.

William was among the last to pay his respects and found it difficult to express his true feelings. The hardened, cynical policeman broke down when William put his arms around him and simply said, 'I'm so sorry.'

'You won't be seeing me for a few days,' said Ross. 'I have some scores to settle. I'll be back once I've dealt with them.'

William thought about those words in the taxi back to the station, on the train to the airport and during the flight to Heathrow. He feared that Ross would be going back undercover and wouldn't be sharing the details with him, or the commander.

• • •

Ross had intended to take the first available flight back to London, as he didn't have a moment to spare before he carried out the first part of his plan. He would have done so, had he not been stopped by the elderly gentleman who'd delivered the eulogy, not a word of which he'd understood.

'Excuse me, Mr Hogan. My name is Pierre Monderan,' the old man said, with only the suggestion of an accent. 'I was your late wife's financial adviser.' He handed Ross an embossed card. 'Perhaps we could sit down, as what I have to tell you might take a few moments.'

'I wish I'd been able to follow your kind words about Jo,' said Ross, as he took a seat on the bench next to Monsieur Monderan. 'They were so clearly appreciated by her friends.'

'It's kind of you to say so,' said Monderan, taking an envelope out of his overcoat pocket and handing it to Ross. 'I've translated my eulogy. I admired your wife greatly, and thought you might like to read it at your convenience. Your wife's untimely death has left me with one last duty to carry out. For some time, I took care of Josephine's personal finances, as I do for all the other girls in the syndicate.'

'The syndicate?'

'The joint holdings of their company were registered under the name of The Vestal Virgins. Twelve of them in all, each of whom invested ten thousand francs a month in a joint enterprise, which I administered on their behalf. Quite successfully, I think you will find. The object was that when the time came for them to retire, they would have sufficient financial reserves not to have to be concerned about their future. Sadly, in Josephine's case, she will not benefit from what I believe you would call her nest egg. As her next of kin, that now passes to you.'

He took a second slim white envelope from an inside pocket and handed it to Ross.

'But what about her family, or close friends? Shouldn't they take precedence over me?'

'She never spoke of any family and, let me assure you, her friends are well taken care of.'

'Then a favourite charity, perhaps,' said Ross, not wanting to open the envelope.

'That is not for me to decide, sir,' said Monsieur Monderan. 'However, if you were my client, I would politely remind you you have a daughter who might benefit from her mother's prudence.' Without another word, Monsieur Monderan rose from his place, gave Ross a slight bow and departed, having carried out his fiduciary duties.

Ross looked down at the unopened envelope and felt guilty that he had not considered his daughter's future. It was some time before he finally tore open the envelope and extracted a cheque made out to Mr Ross Hogan QGM. He smiled at the thought of how Jo had pressed him on several occasions to tell her what he had done to be awarded the Queen's Gallantry Medal. He had always managed to subtly change the subject.

He stared at the cheque and had to look at the noughts a third time before he realized that, for the first time in his life, he was a rich man. Though in truth, he felt like a poor man, and would have torn the cheque up without a second thought if it would have brought Jo back.

• • •

Beth didn't have to ask William which foreign city he'd spent the day in when he returned home that night, because she already knew. She had wanted to accompany him to Paris, and would have done so if Artemisia hadn't caught chicken pox, which meant that Peter almost certainly would follow her, as he always did. But Josephine had been in her thoughts all day.

She was just about to read the twins their bedtime story when she heard the front door close. She ran downstairs to find William hanging up his coat. They clung to each other for some time before William managed, 'How's Artemisia?'

'Recovering. But now Peter's gone down with it, as expected. They're hoping you'll read them their bedtime story.'

'Of course I will, and then over supper I'll tell you about everything that happened in Paris.' Although he still hadn't decided just how much he would tell her.

William walked wearily upstairs, but his spirits were lifted the moment he entered the children's room and the twins scampered out of bed and clung onto a leg each. His thoughts turned once again to Ross and the joy he knew his daughter would bring him. Those thoughts were rudely interrupted when Artemisia reminded him, 'We've reached Chapter Three, and we want to find out what's going to happen to PC Plod.'

He smiled at her, pleased to see her spots had nearly disappeared; but the smile turned to a frown when he saw that Peter's were just appearing.

'Don't forget,' said William, 'that PC Plod always tells his children not to pick their spots.'

Peter nodded as William opened the book. 'Where did we get to?'

'PC Plod has just been told to go to the manor house,' said Artemisia. 'Immediately!'

'Do you remember what was missing from the house?'

'A pearl necklace belonging to Lady Doubtful.'

'And what's the name of PC Plod's wife?'

'Beryl!' said Artemisia. 'She thinks he ought to be an Inspector.'

William nodded, and began to read.

'When PC Plod arrived at the manor house, he propped his bicycle up against the shed and joined the other policemen, who were searching the grounds for clues. He doubted they'd find any, as he was sure it was an inside job.'

'What's an inside job?' asked Peter.

'PC Plod thinks someone who lives or works in the house must have stolen the pearls.'

'Who?' demanded Artemisia.

'I've no idea,' said William, stifling a yawn as he turned the page.

'But you're a detective, Daddy, so you must know,' said Artemisia, with the unquestionable logic of a child.

'PC Plod noticed the front door of the manor house open,' continued William, ignoring her, 'and saw a scullery maid who'd served the Doubtfuls for years being led out of the house by Inspector Watchit, who looked rather pleased with himself. Plod frowned. He knew that Elsie wouldn't have stolen a chocolate biscuit from a tea trolley, let alone a pearl necklace. He would have to go back to the station and put Watchit straight, before he charged the poor girl with a crime she hadn't committed. He left the lads to get on with their job, and walked back to his bike. He was about to put on his safety helmet when he spotted a fishmonger's van coming up the drive to deliver the catch of the day. Plod was surprised to see Mr Nettles the fishmonger park his van right outside the front door and not at the back of the house by the kitchen entrance. Nettles got out of the van and strolled up the steps to the front door which was opened by Lady Doubtful even before he had a chance to press the bell. Her Ladyship handed the fishmonger a large cardboard box, then quickly disappeared back inside.

'Why hadn't Nettles gone to the tradesman's entrance and delivered the fish to the cook as he did every Friday, wondered PC Plod. It didn't make any sense, so he decided to investigate. Plod plodded across to the van, where Mr Nettles had left the cardboard box on the passenger seat and was now sitting behind the wheel about to leave.

'Plod tapped on the window and said, "What are you up to, my lad?" Nettles turned as red as a traffic light. He quickly switched on the engine, crunched the gear lever into third, and shot off towards the front gate. Plod dashed up the steps to the house and banged on the front door. When the butler opened it a few moments later, he told him to quickly close the electric gates. The butler touched the switch just in time to prevent Nettles from getting clean away.

'I think that's enough for tonight,' said William.

'No, Daddy!' screamed Artemisia and Peter in unison. 'More!'

'All right, just a couple of pages,' said William, with an exaggerated sigh. 'The other three policemen quickly surrounded the van while PC Plod opened the passenger door and took out the cardboard box. He opened it to find it was full of oyster shells, and when he prised one open, he found a pearl in it. Plod knew that pearls were normally found at the bottom of the ocean and not in cardboard boxes.'

The phone in the corridor began to ring. William put down the book and said, 'Can you take that, Beth, Mr Plod is about to arrest the real criminal?' He looked back at the children and continued, 'He immediately arrested Mr Nettles and told two of the constables to escort him back to the local police station, along with the evidence. "What shall I say when Inspector Watchit asks me what you're up to?" asked one of the constables. "Tell him I will be paying a visit to the manor house and arresting the real culprit," said Plod. "And he may be surprised who . . ."' William was about to continue when Beth poked her head around the door.

'It's James on the phone,' she said.

'James?'

'James Buchanan, he's calling from New York.'

'Mum will carry on reading,' said William, 'while I take the call.'

'But then you won't discover who Mr Plod arrests,' said Artemisia.

'I feel sure Mum will tell me later,' William replied, as he climbed off the bed, left the room and exchanged a book for a telephone. 'What a pleasant surprise,' he said, before James had been given the chance to speak.

'You may not feel so, when I tell you the reason I'm calling,' said James, 'because I need to seek your advice on an embarrassing situation.'

'I'm at your disposal,' said William calmly.

'I've recently discovered that my closest friend at Choate got someone else to sit his entrance exam papers for Harvard.'

'Proof?' said William.

'He asked me first, and I refused. However, when the names of the successful candidates were announced, to my surprise my friend was among the top half a dozen on the list.'

'In which case, someone else must have failed, someone who everyone else in your class would have expected to be offered a place.'

'You're right, and I can even tell you his name. He's a scholarship boy from a one-parent family, who's always short of money.'

'And you want to know,' said William, 'whether you should pass on your suspicions to a higher authority.'

'Yes. I was curious to find out what you would do, if you faced the same dilemma.'

William remained silent for so long that James eventually said, 'Are you still there, sir?'

'Yes, I am,' said William. 'I confess that I faced almost the same problem when I was at school. I caught a friend, not my best friend, stealing from the school tuck shop once too often.'

'Did you report him to your headmaster?'

'Yes, I finally did,' said William, 'but not a day goes by when I wonder if I should have turned a blind eye.'

'But why,' asked James, 'when you were obviously doing the right thing?'

'He was moved to another school the following term, and was expelled a year later for taking drugs.'

'Were there any repercussions for you?'

'It didn't exactly endear me to my classmates, who labelled me a sneak and a traitor, and not always behind my back.'

'Sticks and stones,' said James.

'It happened again more recently,' said William thoughtfully, 'when I had to investigate a fellow officer, who I'd been at police college with. We had reason to believe he was accepting backhanders from a local drug baron on his patch. In his case stones were involved.'

'Were you able to come up with enough evidence to arrest the subject?'

'More than enough. He's now serving a long prison sentence, which once again hasn't endeared me to my colleagues, but if you're still thinking about doing this job, you can't make one rule for your friends and another for those you don't know or, worse, don't like.'

'I'll make an appointment to see my headmaster first thing in the morning,' said James, 'and tell him my misgivings.'

'Misgivings aren't proof,' William reminded him, 'but it will certainly test his moral compass, especially in this case.'

'Why especially in this case?' enquired James.

'The future of two boys is involved, and their whole lives will be affected by your headmaster's decision. However, do let me know how it turns out.'

'I will, sir, but for now I'll let you get back to Mr Plod, because Beth tells me he was about to arrest the real criminal.'

'Yes, and that also has a surprise ending. But one more question before you go, James: should I assume you've also been offered a place at Harvard?'

'Yes, sir. I won the John Quincy Adams open scholarship.'

'Now there's a man who wouldn't have turned a blind eye.'

• • •

'Anything I should know following your trip to Paris?' asked The Hawk.

'Ross somehow managed to get through the funeral, but I'm a bit concerned about something he said to me after the service.'

'Enlighten me.'

'I wrote down his exact words while I was in the taxi back to the Gare du Nord.' He opened his notebook. '"You won't be seeing me for a few days. I have some scores to settle. I'll be back once I've dealt with them."'

'Scores to settle can only be Faulkner,' said The Hawk. 'Any ideas about what he's got planned for the next few days?'

'I think he intends to kill Roach.'

'And who can blame him?' mumbled the commander under his breath.

'But that won't be easy, even for someone with Ross's particular expertise,' said William, ignoring The Hawk's comment.

'Don't forget he spent four years in the SAS, four years with the murder squad, and has been undercover for the past three. There can't be many people better qualified to kill someone.'

'I think I should pull him in,' said William, 'and spell out the consequences.'

'Agreed,' said The Hawk. 'But if you're going to stop him doing something he'll later regret, you'll have to find him first. And if he does manage to kill Roach, we'll have an even bigger problem on our hands.'

'Namely?'

'He'll come back to work in a few days' time and tell you he's been in mourning or looking after his daughter, but now he wants to get on with the job of putting Faulkner back behind bars. But all he'll really have on his mind is how he's going to kill him.'

CHAPTER 23

THE TRAMP WALKED SLOWLY DOWN the road pushing an ancient pram, a cigarette butt drooping from the corner of his mouth. He wore an old army greatcoat that almost touched the ground, along with four combat medals – the only parts of his disguise that were genuine – suggesting he was a veteran of some long-forgotten war. His dark hair was matted and stuck out from under a woollen hat that looked as if it had been a tea cosy in an earlier life. His face was unshaven and you could smell him from several feet away. He clocked the varying reactions he received from those who passed him in the street: sympathy, usually women; disgust, tattooed youths; and some even handed him a pound coin to relieve their guilt.

He approached a pub out of which was blasting 'I Can't Get No Satisfaction'. Don't worry, he promised those inside, it will only be a matter of time.

As he passed the pub, he kept an eye on the two bouncers

who'd been posted on the door to make sure no uninvited guests intruded on the birthday boy's celebration. He'd arrested one of them several years ago, but the man didn't give the old git a second look as he shuffled past. If he'd glanced into the pram, all he would have seen was a torn packet of cornflakes, a dented tin box that had once contained 'Edinburgh's finest shortbread biscuits', an empty Kleenex box and a Marlboro packet with one cigarette butt sticking out. A couple of threadbare blankets that Oxfam would have rejected were stuffed into one corner.

When he reached a set of traffic lights, he pressed the button and waited for the little green man to appear before crossing the road. He kept up his slow pace until he came to a crossroads: the demarcation line that unofficially marked the boundary dividing the two empires controlled by the Roaches and the Abbotts. Two aggressive-looking youths were patrolling the pavement on the far side, their sole purpose to ensure a Roach didn't stray onto the Abbotts' territory. The tramp stopped and asked one of them for a light.

'Bugger off, you stupid old fart,' was the immediate response. So he did. He kept on walking until he reached an unlit alley that even the most passionate young lovers would have avoided, and the police didn't venture down on their own after dark.

He pushed his pram half-way down the alley, then, checking that no one was taking any interest in him, he removed his tea-cosy hat and put it in the pocket of his greatcoat, which he folded and placed under the blankets in the pram. The hair was still matted, the face still unshaven, the smell still nauseating, but the man dressed in a black tracksuit and black trainers now drew himself up to his full height and took one more look up and down the alley. Not even a stray cat to observe him.

He reached into the cornflakes box and pulled out the stock of a rifle. Next, he flicked the lid off the 'Edinburgh's finest' and extracted a small night-vision telescope. Finally he unscrewed the handle of the pram, tapped it gently on the top, and a slim, perfectly weighted barrel slid out. It took him only moments to piece together a Remington M40 sniper rifle. It wouldn't have been his first choice, but it was the model Ron Abbott favoured. He finally grabbed the Marlboro packet and slipped it into a tracksuit pocket. Moving swiftly towards the building at the end of the alley, he began to climb the drainpipe on its rear wall with the ease of a cat burglar, bringing back memories of the Iranian Embassy siege when he'd been a young lance corporal serving with the SAS, later mentioned in dispatches.

When he reached the top floor, he looked down once again to check if anyone had spotted him. No one had. He'd chosen his vantage point carefully: he was overlooked only by an old warehouse that closed its doors at six o'clock every evening.

He clambered up onto the roof, then crawled slowly across until he reached the other side, where he studied the gap between the two buildings. Ten feet and nine inches divided him from his chosen vantage point. That wouldn't be a problem. He'd practised the jump several times with the rifle slung over one shoulder, and his average had been just over fourteen feet.

He retraced his steps, then crouched down for a moment before bursting out of the blocks and sprinting towards the edge of the building, reaching top speed on the last stride. With inches to spare, he leapt into the air like an Olympic long-jumper who knew exactly where the take-off board would be, and landed on the roof of the next building with several feet to spare. He knelt down on one knee and caught his breath, not moving again until his heartbeat had returned to a steady fifty-four.

He then crawled across to the edge of the building, but didn't look down. He'd never told Colonel Parker, his old commanding officer, that he had a fear of heights. After a few more minutes he stood to take in everything around him, and was well satisfied. But then he'd chosen the spot carefully. He was directly above Ron Abbott's flat, and Abbott, he'd quickly discovered, was a creature of habit. Something that was considered a deadly sin by the SAS, as it made you an easy target for the enemy. Abbott spent every Thursday evening with members of his family at the dogs in Romford, where they were regularly separated from some of their ill-gotten gains. That was invariably followed by dinner at a local nightclub, not known for its cuisine. He usually arrived back at his flat around one o'clock in the morning with a girl on one arm, sometimes on both.

The other reason Ross had selected that particular spot was because it gave him a clear view of the pub where the birthday celebrations were now in full swing. Two hundred and forty yards – well within the range of the high-powered precision rifle – as the crow flies.

He eased the butt of the rifle gently into his shoulder, and lined up the crosshairs on the telescopic sight on the forehead of one of the bouncers. He held the rifle in that position for two minutes before he lowered his arm and rested.

Ross suspected it would be a long wait before the real target appeared. After all, it was his thirty-fourth birthday. He took the Marlboro packet out of his pocket, extracted six highly polished bullets and stood them up in a straight line like soldiers on parade. Then he settled down to wait, but didn't for a moment lose his concentration.

The first reveller emerged from the pub just after midnight. Not someone he recognized. The second, who spilled out onto the pavement a few minutes later, was Terry Roach's uncle Stan, who had been in and out of jail for the past twenty years, and was now rumoured to have been pensioned off by the family.

Ross raised the rifle once again and centred the crosshairs on Uncle Stan's lined forehead. He pulled the trigger. A small click followed, allowing Stan to go on his way, blissfully unaware he'd been target practice.

Although he didn't expect the real target to appear for at least another hour, he loaded six bullets into the magazine. Just in case.

Over the next hour a stream of inebriated guests made their way out of the pub and started walking unsteadily in the direction of their homes. Taxi drivers avoided that street, even in the middle of the day.

Then, without warning, the birthday boy appeared. He staggered out of the pub, accompanied by two of his mates who were in no state to assist him.

Ross calmly took out his phone and dialled 999. When an operator asked, 'Police, fire or ambulance service?' he said firmly, 'Police,' as Terry Roach lurched forward and grabbed at a window ledge to steady himself.

'Police. How may I assist you?'

'There's a gun battle going on in Plumber's Road, Whitechapel,' he said, trying to sound breathless.

'Can I take your—' But he'd already switched off the phone. He would dispose of it later.

He nestled the butt of the rifle back into his shoulder, and steadied the barrel with his left hand. He centred the crosshairs of the telescope on the enemy's forehead, just as he had done in Oman, and now in Whitechapel. He lowered his sights to the birthday boy's right kneecap, his old sergeant major's words ringing in his ears: *Concentrate, breathe normally and squeeze the trigger smoothly in one movement, don't snatch*. He carried out the order and the bullet whistled through the air towards its target. Seconds later Roach sank to the ground in agony, clasping his right leg.

As Ross had anticipated, the stricken man's two mates tried to drag him back into the pub. He lowered the crosshairs an inch and steadied himself before pulling the trigger a second time. This time, the bullet headed for Roach's groin, and the sudden agonized movement of Roach's hands from his knee to his balls rather suggested Ross had hit the bullseye. One of his mates continued to drag Roach back towards the pub, screaming for help at the top of his voice, while the other ran off in the opposite direction.

The pub door suddenly swung open and a crowd of Roach family and other gang members came rushing out. A finger pointed up in his direction, and every available body began charging across the road towards him. Ross lined up the rifle for the last time, not aiming at Roach's forehead to end his agony, but a few inches lower. The third bullet struck him just above his Adam's apple, passed right through his neck and ended up embedded in the pub's wall.

Ross looked over the side of the building to see lights appearing in the windows of the flats below. He was interested only in one particular flat and moments later he was rewarded.

He placed the rifle next to the three spent cartridges, turned, and took a deep breath before running flat out across the roof and once again launching himself into the air. This time he flew even higher than before, but then he was no longer carrying a rifle. He landed safely, rolled over and was quickly back on his feet. As he made his way to the far corner of the building, he could hear a siren in the distance. He began the long climb down, always slower and more challenging than climbing up, as any mountaineer will tell you.

When his feet touched the ground, he jogged back towards the alley where he retrieved his hat and greatcoat from the pram and pulled on his tea-cosy hat. He'd just reached the end of the alley when he heard voices close by. He continued heading towards the battlefield, a risk, but he couldn't afford the owners of the voices, whichever side they were on, to think he was running away from the scene. One of them slowed down as they passed him, hurled the pram onto its side and took a cursory look at its contents before he ran on. But then, he no longer had anything to hide.

After he'd thrown everything back into the pram, Ross continued walking towards the pub. There was no longer a demarcation zone. It was all-out war.

The first squad car screeched to a halt outside the Plumber's Arms, and within moments the street was swarming with armed police in protective gear and carrying riot shields. They began rounding up members of both gangs before hurling them into the nearest Black Maria.

He couldn't resist a smile when he saw the choirboy standing outside the pub, directing operations. He walked straight past him, and wouldn't have looked back had he not heard the thud of a body landing in the middle of the road behind him. His only mistake.

CHAPTER 24

ALTHOUGH HE HADN'T GONE TO bed until after two that morning, Ross was up again by five, as he had an appointment with Jimmy the dip. Not that the dip was aware that a police inspector from Scotland Yard would be joining him for breakfast.

Ross took a long, cold shower, washed his hair and, with the help of a razor, removed four days of non-designer stubble. He checked his watch, confident he could be at the Putney Bridge Café long before Jimmy turned up. Once he'd completed his business with the old lag, he would make his way back across the bridge to keep an even more important appointment in Chelsea.

The one thing Ross knew about the dip, other than that he was unrivalled in his profession, was that he didn't like to go to work on an empty stomach. Jimmy had served a couple of terms in the nick, but had managed to charm more than one jury into believing he was a victim of a deprived upbringing who, if given a chance, would mend his ways and lead a new life. He would have spent far longer in prison had those same juries been made aware of his past criminal record, but the British have always believed in fair play, and giving a chap the benefit of the doubt.

Ross turned up at the café just before seven, ordered a black coffee and sat on a stool at the far end of the counter. The dip arrived just after seven thirty, took his usual place by the window and began to read the *Sun*.

Ross didn't make his presence known until the waitress appeared carrying Jimmy's daily plate of two fried eggs, bacon, beans, mushrooms, tomatoes and hash browns. It was clear that Jimmy would have agreed with Somerset Maugham's observation that 'To eat well in England you should have breakfast three times a day.' Not that Jimmy had ever heard of Somerset Maugham.

'To what do I owe this honour, Inspector?' asked Jimmy nervously, when Ross sat down opposite him. 'You're not going to find anything incriminating on me at this time in the morning.'

'I need your help, Jimmy.'

'I'm not an informer. Never have been, never will be. Not my style.'

'I'm no longer in the force,' said Ross. 'I've quit.'

Jimmy still looked doubtful, until Ross took a roll of banknotes out of his pocket and placed them in the middle of the table.

'What would I have to do to earn that much dosh?' said the dip, looking at the notes longingly.

'I need you to put something back for a change,' said Ross, before explaining exactly what he had in mind.

By the time Jimmy had finished his breakfast, the two hundred pounds had also disappeared.

'You'll get another two hundred, but not before you've completed the job.'

'Then all I need to know is when and where.'

'I'll be in touch,' said Ross, 'now I know where to find you.' He got up, and was about to check the time to make sure he wouldn't be late for his next appointment, only to find he no longer had a watch. He stretched out his hand and waited.

Jimmy the dip shrugged, handed him back his Rolex and said, 'I wouldn't want you to think I'd lost my touch, Inspector.'

• • •

'Congratulations, Chief Inspector,' said the commander, when William entered his office later that morning.

'What for, sir?'

'Finally cleaning up the Roach/Abbott problem.'

'But did I?' said William thoughtfully.

'What do you mean? Your team rounded up fourteen gang members, and the two worst offenders conveniently ended up in the graveyard.'

'A little too conveniently, perhaps?'

'All the evidence tells us that Ron Abbott killed Terry Roach. We even have the rifle, the spent cartridges and the body. You don't often get that lucky.'

'Unless the odds are stacked in your favour before you turn up,' said William.

'By whom?' said The Hawk.

'Whoever it was who left the murder weapon and three spent cartridges on the roof of the building Abbott just happened to live in.'

'But two of the Roach gang caught Abbott on the roof, and our lads got there just in time to see them throwing him off the top of the building.'

'Just in time,' repeated William. 'Don't you find it a bit of a coincidence that a member of the public just happened to phone 999 at one thirteen this morning, and our boys somehow got there in time to hear the third shot being fired? Roach was still alive when I turned up. So I suspect that phone call was made before the first shot was fired.'

'What are you getting at?' said the commander, his tone changing.

'As the officer in charge of the investigation, I'm trying to get at the truth.'

'And have you reached any conclusion?'

'My gut feeling tells me it was someone who was on compassionate leave who fired all three shots, but was in no mood to be compassionate himself. However, I concede it was the two Roach gang members we found on the roof who threw Abbott off the building. But then I suspect that was all part of Ross's plan.'

'If Abbott didn't kill Roach, how come they found him on the roof?'

'I think he heard the shots from his flat, and went up to see what was going on. Don't you find it strange that we later found an identical rifle to the murder weapon in his flat? Why would he have two, I ask myself.'

'Do you have anything more to go on than your gut feeling?'

'An empty Marlboro packet was also found on the roof.'

'A lot of people smoke Marlboros, me included. You'll have to do better than that, Chief Inspector.'

'While the lads were rounding up the other gang members, Ross walked straight past me, disguised as a tramp and pushing an old pram.'

'Why didn't you ask him what the hell he was doing there?'

'I was trying to question Roach at the time before the medics put him in the ambulance.'

'He was still alive?' said The Hawk, in disbelief.

'He survived for another twenty minutes, which I suspect was all part of Ross's plan.'

'But you can't prove the tramp you saw was Ross.'

'He was wearing four combat medals.'

'Then you'll only need to interview about ten thousand possible suspects.'

'I could eliminate the 9,999 of them who haven't been awarded the Queen's Gallantry Medal.'

'Ross wouldn't make a mistake like that.'

'I don't think it was a mistake. I think he wanted me to see it.'

'Then why didn't you arrest him?'

'Because at that moment Abbott's body landed on the pavement just a few feet away, which I confess distracted me.'

'Will you call him in for questioning?' asked The Hawk.

'What's the point? He'll have all his answers off pat, and will be well aware we don't have anything that would stand up in court.'

'Do you still want him to be a member of your team when you go after Faulkner?'

'We wouldn't get as far as the front door without him,' said William, 'let alone beyond Faulkner's study.'

'If you're right and he did murder Roach, you'd better make sure he isn't carrying a gun when you enter the house, because he won't give a damn who sees him kill Faulkner.'

• • •

The door was opened by a man who towered over him, arms folded, fists clenched, 'HATE' tattooed on the knuckles of both hands.

'What can I do for you?' said a voice.

He looked past the doorkeeper to see a wizened old man who was seated behind an oak desk in a large leather chair that seemed to gobble him up.

'I need to borrow a grand, Mr Sleeman,' he said anxiously, as he stared at the diminutive figure, who looked even more odious than his gormless bodyguard.

'Why?' demanded Sleeman, his thin lips hardly moving.

'I need to buy a car.'

'Why?' he repeated.

'I've been offered a job as a sales rep with a pharmaceutical company and I told them I had my own car.'

'Do you have any form of security?'

'The car, and I'll be earning two hundred quid a week, plus commission.'

'Where do you live?'

'I have a small mews house in Chelsea.'

'Do you own the house?'

'No, I have a short lease.'

'How short?'

'It's still got sixteen years left on it.'

'I'll need the car's log book and the lease, which my man will collect this evening,' said Sleeman, nodding to the giant by the door. 'Both will be returned to you, but not before I get every penny of my money back. Plus the usual interest, of course.'

'What are your terms?'

'You'll get your grand,' said Sleeman, 'and in return you'll pay me six hundred pounds a month for the next three months.'

'But that's nearly a hundred per cent interest,' he protested.

'If you want the car, those are my terms. Take it or leave it.'

He hesitated long enough for Sleeman to unlock the drawer of his desk, take out a wad of fifty-pound notes and push them across the table without bothering to count them.

The man stared at the money. His hand shaking, he hesitated before he finally picked up the cash and turned to leave.

'Before you go,' said Sleeman, 'let me warn you that my collector will be calling on the first day of the month, for the next three months. If you fail to pay up on time, I don't send out written reminders, but he will leave you with something to remember.'

The man shuddered and dropped one of the fifty-pound notes on the floor, which landed at the feet of the door-keeper who bent down, picked it up and handed it back. 'I look forward to seeing you on the first of the month,' he grunted, as he opened the door. 'Make sure you're there.'

'I'll be there,' promised Ross.

CHAPTER 25

'I MAY HAVE HAD A breakthrough in the Sleeman case,' said DS Adaja, as he sat down in the chair by William's desk.

'Walk me through it,' said William, putting down his Biro and leaning back.

Paul handed him a see-through evidence bag that contained a single fifty-pound note. 'An anonymous person left this for me at the front desk.'

'Presumably you had it checked for fingerprints – did they find any?'

'Mine,' admitted Paul.

'Idiot. Anyone else's?'

'Max Sleeman's.'

'Better. And, from the smug look on your face, they must have come up with someone else even more surprising.'

'Leonid Verenich.'

'The psychopath who was thrown out of the Russian mafia because he was too violent?'

'The same.'

'I thought he was serving a life sentence in Dresden prison.'

'He was until he met a certain Colonel Putin, and became more useful on the outside,' said Paul. 'What I can't work out is how he got past immigration control.'

'That wouldn't have proved difficult for someone with the connections Sleeman has, in both underworlds,' said William. 'So now all you have to do is find him.'

'That won't be easy. In Moscow he was known as "whispering death".'

'Whoever left that note at the front desk must know how to find him.'

'But I have no idea who that was.'

'I do,' said William.

• • •

Ross had never travelled business class before, but as he'd barely slept for the past few nights and would need to be at his sharpest when he arrived in Cape Town, he reluctantly paid for an upgrade, looked up to the heavens and touched his wedding ring, once again thanking Jo, who was rarely out of his thoughts.

He knew he could spare only a couple of days to warn Mrs Pugh of her pending death, while Miles Faulkner remained his overriding priority. If the choirboy were to summon him, he'd have to drop everything and come running. That was assuming the choirboy could find him.

He leant back in his comfortable seat and looked forward to a long uninterrupted sleep, thankful that the place next to him was unoccupied.

The steward was just about to close the aircraft door when an overweight, out-of-breath man rushed onto the plane and lumbered down the aisle checking each seat number. Ross stared out of the cabin window and watched as the airbridge was pulled back, hoping the latecomer would pass by, but then he heard a squelch of leather as the man collapsed into the seat next to him, still breathing heavily.

'Just made it,' he said between gasps.

Ross glanced at his new neighbour, who could have lost a couple of stone and still been overweight. Certainly not a candidate for Nightmare Holidays.

He decided that as soon as the plane reached cruising altitude, he would recline his seat, cover himself with a blanket, put on his eyeshade and not take it off until the steward announced, 'Ladies and gentlemen, please fasten your seatbelts, we are about to begin our descent.'

'Hi,' said his eleven-hour travel companion, thrusting out a hand. 'Larry T. Holbrooke the Third. What takes you to Cape Town?'

The last thing Ross needed was a chatty American who looked as if he'd already had a good night's sleep. He wondered what the reaction would be if he gave a truthful answer: 'I'm hoping to prevent a very unpleasant individual from murdering his wife, inheriting her fortune and living happily ever after.'

'Ross Hogan. I'm on holiday, and off to watch the Test match,' he replied as they shook hands. This stopped any further conversation for a moment, but only for a moment.

'Lucky you. I'm on business. Can't remember when I last had a vacation. Tell me, Ross, what's your line of business?'

Ross didn't respond immediately. When he had first enlisted in the SAS, he'd had to sign the Official Secrets Act, so he couldn't tell anyone what he did. Since he'd joined the police force, he was bound by the same law.

'I work for a travel company. And you?' he said, immediately regretting the words.

'I'm a financial broker. I collect short-term debts. So if someone owes you a large amount of money that you need collecting, I'm your man.'

Suddenly, Ross was wide awake. 'How does that work?' he asked, as he clicked on his seatbelt.

'Let's imagine the travel company you work for has a cashflow problem. You have reliable customers, but they often take sixty, sometimes ninety days to pay their bills, while you have your costs to cover, like rent and your payroll. I buy those debts, so you can carry on your business without having to worry about any temporary financial embarrassment.'

'Where's the profit in that?' asked Ross.

'I wait for the sixty or ninety days to pass before I collect the full amount owed, and then take a commission of between two and three per cent, depending on how long your company's been a customer.'

'But if the customer doesn't pay up after ninety days,' said Ross, 'wouldn't you lose the full amount?'

'You're right, but I only deal with companies that have a high Standard and Poor's credit rating. I'm not in the risk business, which means I don't make a fortune, but I'm doing just fine. My grandpa, who founded the company, used to say if you treat folks right, they'll come back and do business with you again and again.'

'Mr Holbrooke . . .'

'Larry, please.'

'Larry. I have a problem you just might be able to help me with. But first I have to admit that I don't work for a travel company, and it's the wrong time of year for a Test match. I'm a Detective Inspector with the Metropolitan Police.' He produced his warrant card, which Larry studied carefully.

'Scotland Yard, no less! I'd be happy to assist you, detective, but what can I offer that your redoubtable police force can't?'

'For starters, you might be able to advise me how to deal with a loan shark your grandpa wouldn't have done business with.'

'Will you be taking dinner, gentlemen?' asked a stewardess, as she offered them both a menu.

'Sure will, miss,' said Larry.

'Me too,' said Ross.

'OK,' said Larry, once she'd taken their orders. 'Walk me through your problem slowly, and don't leave out any details, however mundane they might seem to you.'

Ross took his time telling Larry everything the police knew about Max Sleeman, his associates and the methods they used to make sure his customers repaid their debts punctually.

The stewardess had cleared away their trays and was serving coffee before Larry T. Holbrooke the Third offered an opinion.

'Fascinating,' said Larry, as he dropped three sugar lumps in his coffee. 'With two words you revealed Sleeman's Achilles heel, which you can now take advantage of.'

'As long as I can identify those two words.'

Larry began to stir. 'You have the bow, detective, all I can do is supply the arrows.'

'Detectives rely on clues,' Ross reminded him.

Larry took a sip of coffee, before drawing an arrow from his sheath. 'When did Sleeman tell you he'd be collecting the first payment of six hundred pounds?'

'On the first day of the month, without fail.'

'"Without fail" are the two words you have to take advantage of. Because you now know the time and the place when his collector will appear.'

'I can't be certain of the time,' said Ross.

'You'll be the first call he makes that morning,' said Larry, as a steward topped up their coffee.

'How can you be so sure?'

'First payments are always the easiest to collect. It's later, when the borrower gets deeper and deeper into debt and can't pay up, even if he wants to, that the real trouble begins. I always give my customers a few days' grace, but then I'm not just interested in a single transaction. That's not possible for the Sleemans of this world, who deal in threats and deadlines. So you have to make sure that when his collector turns up on the first day of the month, you have the six hundred pounds ready to hand over. Then you'll be in the driving seat.'

'I know you're going to tell me why,' said Ross.

'Don't forget, he'll be spending the rest of the day collecting money from less willing customers. You can be sure he'll leave the most difficult one to last, and I have a feeling you'll want to be present when that happens.'

'How dumb of me,' said Ross.

'Not at all. I've been in the debt-collecting business for over thirty years, and during that time I've come across crooks every bit as ruthless as your Sleeman guy. You'll be pleased to hear they usually end up dying alone with no one attending their funerals.'

'What if I don't get that lucky?'

'Then you'll need to be on top of your game on the first day of next month.'

Ross was already thinking about where he would park his car. How he would . . .

'One last question before I grab a couple of hours' shut-eye,' said Larry, as the steward removed his coffee cup, and stored away the tray table. 'How recently did you lose your wife?'

Ross was so taken by surprise it was some time before he recovered sufficiently to say, 'A few weeks ago. But how did you know?'

'I lost Martha six years ago,' said Larry, 'and I still never stop touching my wedding ring. Don't listen to people who tell you it will get easier as time goes by. It doesn't. I wouldn't be fifty pounds overweight and living on aeroplanes if it did.' With that he reclined his seat, pulled his blanket up to his chin and closed his eyes.

'Thank you,' said Ross, delighted this shrewd and decent man had slumped down in the seat next to him, and not moved on.

• • •

'The head of Heathrow airport security on line one, chief,' said Paul.

William picked up his extension to hear a familiar voice. 'Good morning, sir. It's Geoff Duffield. You asked me to let you know if DI Ross Hogan booked himself onto an overseas flight.'

'I'm listening,' said William.

'He boarded flight BA027 to Cape Town at nine thirty last night. It touched down at nine o'clock this morning, local time.'

'Thank you,' said William. 'Has he booked a return flight?'

'No, sir. His ticket was open-ended. But I'll let you know as soon as he makes another booking.'

'He'll be back before the end of the week,' said William, without explanation.

CHAPTER 26

'WOULD YOU BE KIND ENOUGH to sign the visitors' book, sir?' said the receptionist, swivelling round a large, leather-bound volume just as the phone on the desk began to ring. She picked it up and announced, 'Good morning, the Mount Nelson Hotel. How may I assist you?'

Ross began to flick back through the pages of the visitors' book in search of Mr and Mrs Clive Pugh, who he knew had planned to check in earlier that week.

'Can I help you?' asked the receptionist as she put the phone down and caught him looking closely at a particular page of the log.

'Yes,' said Ross, not missing a beat. 'I was just checking to see if a friend of mine, Larry T. Holbrooke the Third, had booked in.'

'We have no one under that name staying with us,' said the receptionist. Ross looked suitably disappointed, as she handed him a large metal key. 'You're in room thirty-three on the third floor. A porter will take your bag up. I hope you have a pleasant stay with us.'

Pleasant wasn't what Ross had in mind. 'Thank you,' he said, before following the porter across the hall to the lift. On the way they passed a photograph of Winston Churchill sitting on the veranda of the hotel smoking a cigar and clasping a large brandy.

When the lift reached the third floor, Ross followed the porter down a wide, thickly carpeted corridor, the walls cluttered with sepia photographs of the Queen Mother, Jan Smuts and Cecil Rhodes, reminding the hotel's guests of a bygone era it seemed reluctant to let go. The porter unlocked the door to room 33 and placed Ross's suitcase on a stand at the end of the bed. Ross thanked him and handed him a tip.

Ross walked across to the bay window and was stunned by the breathtaking panoramic view of Table Mountain, with the clouds resting above it like a fluffy eiderdown. He turned back to see the king-sized double bed and once again thought about Jo, before slipping off his jacket and lying down just to find out how comfortable it was. He closed his eyes and immediately fell into a deep sleep.

• • •

'It's for you, chief,' said Paul, handing over the phone. 'A Lieutenant Sanchez calling from Barcelona.'

'Hi Juan,' said William as he grabbed the phone. 'Any progress?'

'Yes. My wife's pregnant again, and this time we're hoping for a boy.'

'Congratulations,' said William, laughing, 'but that isn't what I had in mind.'

'On that particular front, I also have some good news,' said Sanchez. 'Following Commander Hawksby's call to my boss, he's given the next stage of Operation Masterpiece his blessing, but with several caveats.'

'Do we have a date?' asked William.

'Yes, next Sunday. I don't think you can afford to wait much longer. We'll need to get together before then to go over the details. I could fly to London on Wednesday afternoon, if that's convenient for you.'

'That's fine,' said William, turning a page of his diary. 'Where do you plan on staying?'

'I was hoping you could recommend a cheap hotel near Scotland Yard.'

'London's not known for its cheap hotels,' said William. 'Why don't you stay at my place? It will give you a chance to meet Beth and the twins.'

'Thank you,' said Juan, 'but wouldn't that be . . .'

'Then that's settled. Just call up from reception when you get here.' William put down the phone, looked across at Jackie and said, 'Find Inspector Hogan. I need him back here for a full briefing with Lieutenant Sanchez by nine o'clock on Thursday morning, otherwise we're all wasting our time.'

'Where will he be, sir?' asked Jackie. 'Because I know he's not at home.'

'At the same hotel as Mr and Mrs Pugh in Cape Town.'

'Do you know the name of the hotel?'

'No, DS Roycroft, I don't. I thought I'd leave you something to do.'

• • •

Ross woke from a vivid dream to find he was still fully dressed, and for a moment he wondered where he was. He glanced at his watch, 6.18 p.m., and moved into first gear. He climbed off the bed, stripped off his clothes and threw them over a chair before going into the bathroom and taking a long shower.

Jets of cold water quickly brought him back to life, and helped him to move into second gear as he went over a tentative plan in his mind. By the time he'd stepped out of the shower and dried himself, he was in third gear, but still no nearer to working out how he could arrange to bump into Mrs Amy Pugh without her husband realizing what he was up to.

If he did manage to spend even a few minutes with her, his story was well prepared. He was an insurance broker, and felt he should warn her that her husband had taken out a policy on her life for one million pounds. He would then ask her if she was aware of the circumstances of his first wife's death. He had his next question ready if she replied yes, and a short well-prepared speech if she said no.

He put on a clean white shirt, a golf club tie and a suit that made him look like someone who was at home in a five-star hotel rather than a deserted back alley. He picked up his room key and moved into top gear as he left for the dining room.

The hotel might well have had a folksy charm about it, what Jo would have described as quaint, but when he entered the Nelson Room it only took one look at the maître d' for Ross to know he was dealing with a pro.

'May I ask for your room number, sir?' enquired the tall,

thin man dressed in a long morning coat and pinstriped trousers.

'Thirty-three,' said Ross. He glanced around the room, his eyes settling on a couple seated in a small alcove on the far side of the restaurant. He noticed that, although the banquette on their left was occupied, the one on the right was empty.

The maître d' interrupted his thoughts. 'Are you dining alone this evening, sir, or will someone be joining you?'

'I'll be on my own for the next two days. I wonder if I could have that alcove seat by the window.'

The maître d' checked his table list. 'I'm sorry, sir, but it's already booked for this evening.'

Ross took out his wallet, extracted a fifty-rand note and placed it on top of the reservation list.

'Please follow me, sir,' said the maître d', giving Ross a warm smile. Nothing folksy or quaint about the maître d', thought Ross, as he watched him pocket the note like Jimmy the dip.

Ross picked up a copy of the *New York Times* from a side table as he followed the head waiter across the room to his alcove seat. He sat down with his back to the Pughs, opened the newspaper and began to read. If they were even to glance in his direction, they would assume he was an American. He leant slightly back, and although he could catch only the occasional word from Mrs Pugh, he could hear almost everything her husband was saying.

A wine waiter appeared. 'Can I get you something to drink, sir, while you're deciding what to order?'

Ross studied the long wine list. He remembered that Jo had once told him the South African vineyards were now producing wines that were second only to the French, not that the French would ever admit it. The list confirmed another of Jo's nuggets, that the local wines would be far cheaper than the French imports. He selected a half bottle of Malbec from the Western Cape, and after the wine waiter had left he took a cigarette case out of an inside pocket and placed it on the table.

Ross glanced at the headline in his newspaper: *Peace talks to begin in Geneva between Iraq and Iran.* He would have read the article if he hadn't been trying to concentrate on the conversation taking place behind him.

'Have you decided what you'll have, sir?' asked his table waiter, notepad open, pen poised.

'The vegetable soup, followed by a rump steak, medium rare.' He looked across at the empty seat on the other side of the table, but no one was sitting there.

He waited for the waiter to leave before opening the cigarette case and adjusting the mirror inside to an angle that allowed him a perfect view of Pugh, although he could see only the back of his wife's head. NP had been happy to supply the silver cigarette case, originally commissioned by a customer for a sum of money that would have impressed Cartier.

It was clear that Pugh was taking pains to appear solicitous towards his new spouse, while giving the impression he was listening attentively to a story he must have heard several times before, keeping a fixed smile on his face the whole time.

The wine waiter returned, and Ross flicked the cigarette case shut, but continued to listen to what was being said on the next table as the sommelier uncorked the half bottle of Malbec and poured him a small amount to sample.

'Excellent,' Ross said, and the wine waiter filled his glass.

Ross reached the sports pages to discover that the Yankees had beaten the Oakland Athletics. He looked into the mirror to see the Pughs had finished their meal. The only important piece of information he'd picked up was that Clive Pugh would be visiting his bank in the morning, having suggested to his wife they should open a joint account. It was clear from her body language that she wasn't at all enthusiastic about the idea. Ross recalled that at the last team meeting he'd attended, Jackie had told them Pugh must be fast running out of money if several unpaid bills were anything to go by.

Pugh told his wife to expect him back around twelve, reminding her that they would be taking the cable car to the top of Table Mountain to have lunch at a café, more famous for its view than its cuisine.

Ross would have to decide whether to take advantage of Pugh's absence while he was visiting the bank and attempt to set up a meeting with his wife, or to follow him to the bank in the hope of finding out just how bad his financial situation was.

As the Pughs rose from their table, Ross pocketed the cigarette case, but continued to read his paper as they left the restaurant. He waited for a few minutes before he left. As he passed the maître d' he slipped him another fifty-rand note, not for services rendered, but for services he might require at some time in the future.

• • •

'He's in Cape Town,' said William.

'What's he doing there?' asked the commander.

'Keeping a close eye on Mr and Mrs Pugh would be my bet. He probably intends to warn the blushing bride about her husband's long-term plans for her before it's too late. But I'm confident he'll be back in time for Thursday morning's meeting with Sanchez.'

'Why?' asked the commander.

'He has an appointment on the first of September that he can't afford to miss.'

'Who with?'

'Max Sleeman's debt collector, Leonid Verenich, who Paul assures me always starts his rounds with new customers on the first day of the month.'

'So Ross will be waiting for him. But what do you think he has in mind, because whispering death isn't a man you'd go looking for if you could possibly avoid it.'

'I've no idea, sir, but I intend to put a stop to Ross's plans before I end up having to arrest him.'

'He'll see you coming.'

'I'm hoping he'll be so preoccupied with Verenich that I can take him by surprise.'

'Don't count on it,' said The Hawk. 'Since his wife's death, he's been like a man possessed. First Abbott and Roach, now Pugh, next Sleeman, and he's probably also got Darren Carter in his sights. Where will it all end?'

'With Miles Faulkner would be my bet, sir.'

CHAPTER 27

Ross woke at five the next morning in London to find it was already seven o'clock in Cape Town. Not long before he would have to make a decision.

He was among the first to come down for breakfast, but he chose to sit on the other side of the dining room to reduce the chances of Mr and Mrs Pugh remembering him.

Like Jimmy the dip, Ross began the day with a hearty breakfast, starting with a bowl of porridge, followed by a pair of lightly grilled kippers that would have passed muster in a Highlands hostelry.

While he waited for the Pughs to appear, he read the previous day's London *Times*.

He took his time reading a long article on page three below a photograph of the choirboy. 'The officer who brought the two most feared gangs in the East End of London, the Abbotts and the Roaches, to their knees,' the crime correspondent informed his readers. Ross was relieved to find no mention in the article of a mysterious tramp who'd been seen pushing a pram through the middle of the battlefield, and the crime correspondent concluded that 'this was an internal feud between the two rival East End gangs and no one else was involved'. Ross doubted that William had come to the same conclusion when delivering his report to The Hawk.

He was beginning to wonder if the honeymoon couple were having breakfast in their room, when Clive Pugh strolled in and went straight to their usual table. He also ordered kippers before turning his attention to the *Financial Times*, but there was still no sign of his wife by the time he'd reached the latest stock market prices. If she didn't make an appearance, the choice of which one of them Ross should pursue would be academic.

Pugh eventually rose from his place, left the dining room and, after a short chat to the receptionist on the front desk, walked out of the hotel. Ross was not far behind. He was never happier than when working undercover, and keeping an eye on this particular target was not difficult. Pugh was wearing a dark blue blazer, open-neck cream shirt and neatly pressed grey flannels, but it was the white panama hat that made him hard to miss. Jo had once told him you could tell the quality of a panama hat by how small the weave was, and that way she'd know if the client could afford her. I don't have a hat, he had told her. Now, dressed in a non-branded grey T-shirt, jeans and a pair of trainers, Ross melted into the crowd on the busy streets of the bustling city centre.

He took care not to get too close to Pugh. He might have been shadowing an amateur, but he couldn't risk being spotted, especially as he was still planning to sit behind him at dinner again that night.

The first stop Pugh made was at a chemist's, but he came back out moments later. He covered another block before making his second stop, at an upmarket department store. Ross followed him inside, and hovered in the background pretending to be interested in a silk scarf while Pugh was shown a box of Montecristo cigars by an assistant at the tobacconist's counter.

'I'll take a couple of boxes,' said Pugh, passing over his credit card. After a few minutes, the embarrassed assistant handed him back his card and whispered a few words Ross couldn't hear.

'There must be some mistake,' said Pugh angrily. 'Why don't you ring the bank.'

The assistant obliged, but when he put the phone down he looked even more embarrassed, and placed the cigars back on the shelf.

Pugh, red in the face, turned and strode towards the nearest exit. Ross followed.

'Excuse me, sir,' said a young woman chasing after him, 'will you be purchasing that scarf?'

An equally embarrassed Ross handed back the scarf. Fortunately, Pugh had already left the store.

Out on the pavement, Ross quickly spotted the white panama bobbing up and down on the far side of the road. He'd nearly caught up with Pugh by the time he entered the Cape Bank, where Pugh headed straight for the nearest teller.

'I want to speak to the manager,' he demanded in a loud voice. 'Immediately.'

Ross hovered behind a desk on the far side of the banking hall, picked up a Biro and began filling in a form to open a savings account while they both waited for the manager to arrive.

A tall, smartly dressed man appeared a few moments later. It wasn't difficult for him to work out which was the irate customer who had demanded to see him.

'How can I help you, sir?' he asked politely.

'Are you the manager?' said Pugh, unable to hide his surprise.

'I am, sir. Mr Joubert,' he said, offering his hand. Pugh ignored it.

'My name is Clive Pugh and your bank has just caused me some considerable embarrassment.'

'I'm sorry to hear that, sir,' said the manager. 'Perhaps you would like to discuss this matter in the privacy of my office?'

'I don't need to be patronized by you, Joubert. All I want to know is why my credit card was rejected.'

'Are you sure you wouldn't prefer to come to my office and talk about the problem?'

'There isn't a problem,' said Pugh, almost shouting. 'An explanation and an apology is the least I expect if you want to keep your job.'

Ross noticed that he was no longer the only person in the banking hall who was taking an interest in the encounter between the two men.

'I'm afraid,' said the manager, almost whispering, although everyone could hear his words, 'your account is well over its limit, so I was left with no choice.'

'Then I am also left with no choice,' said Pugh, 'other than to transfer my account to another bank. I expect you to have all the necessary paperwork ready when I return tomorrow.'

'As you wish, sir. May I ask when that might be convenient?'

'It will be convenient when it suits me,' said Pugh. 'It's clear to me that you boys aren't yet ready to do a man's job.'

Ross was about to break another golden rule and knock out the person he was meant to be shadowing, and might have done so if Pugh hadn't turned on his heel and marched out of the bank.

Ross followed him onto the street, but lost him when it became clear he was returning to the hotel. He couldn't wait to hear his version of events over dinner that evening.

• • •

'If Ross isn't back in time for our meeting tomorrow,' said Juan, as the three of them sat around the kitchen table after dinner, enjoying a second bottle of wine, 'I'm going to have to call the whole operation off. We won't even reach Faulkner's front door without him.'

'He'll be back in time,' said William, sounding more confident than he felt.

'Let's hope so,' said Juan, 'because my boss won't allow me to hang around on the off-chance he'll turn up. We've got enough of our own criminals to deal with, I can hear him reminding me.'

'Sounds just like The Hawk,' said Beth.

'Cut from the same cloth,' said Juan, 'if that's the correct English expression.'

'How come your English is so good, Juan?' Beth asked.

'My mother married a Welshman, and he lost the toss. However, he still thinks the only saint is David, the only flower a daffodil, and the only game rugby.'

Beth smiled, and asked innocently, 'If Ross does turn up in time for your meeting in the morning, does that mean William will be going back to Barcelona?'

'What makes you think I've ever been to Barcelona?' said William, grinning.

'A plane ticket was the first clue, even more pesetas were the second, and Juan coming to stay with us finally clinched it.'

'Ignore her,' said William in a stage whisper.

'If you don't feel able to answer my question,' said Beth, pouring her guest another glass of wine, 'perhaps I can ask you, Juan, if you've actually seen *Fishers of Men*.'

'A planted question,' interrupted William. 'Trying to draw you in without admitting how little she actually knows. Just ignore her, and she'll eventually give up.'

'Yes, I have seen it,' admitted Juan. 'But, sadly, I was distracted, and didn't have much time to appreciate it.'

'Distracted by its would-be owner, perhaps?' asked Beth, still fishing.

Both men were silenced for a moment, until William said, 'Let's just say that Faulkner had even less chance to appreciate it than Juan. And, sadly, I doubt if any of us will ever set eyes on it again.'

'Unless, of course, you two resourceful gentlemen manage

to arrest Faulkner and put him back behind bars where he belongs. In which case, with the help of my close friend Christina, the Fitzmolean may yet get its hands on the masterpiece, and you'll be able to return and admire it without fear of being interrupted.' Neither Juan nor William responded, but Beth didn't give up. 'Which would at least make up for you two preventing the museum from being able to borrow Frans Hals' *The Flute Player*, which I suspect was in the same house.'

'Clever woman, your wife,' was Juan's only comment.

'You don't know the half,' said William. 'Just wait until breakfast tomorrow, when you'll meet Artemisia.'

• • •

Just as William was heading upstairs to bed, the phone rang. He picked it up to hear James Buchanan's unmistakable Boston accent on the other end of the line.

'I took your advice, sir,' he said, not wasting a word, 'and reported my findings to the headmaster, who promised me he would look into the matter.'

'And did he?' asked William.

'He can't have done,' said James, 'because my friend has a study on the same corridor as me, at Harvard.'

'You will, no doubt, have come up with a convincing explanation for why he ignored your findings.'

'Yes, but it's only circumstantial, and wouldn't stand up in court.'

'I'll be the judge of that,' said William.

'One of my class, who should have sailed into Harvard, failed spectacularly.'

'That's not proof, unless he'll admit his involvement to the headmaster, with at least two witnesses present.'

'My friend's father was chairman of Choate's fundraising committee, and they had a record year.'

'Still not proof, but adds to motive.'

'He was also at Choate and Harvard at the same time as the headmaster.'

'So were several other people, I suspect,' said William, dismissively.

'You're sounding like my headmaster,' said James, 'who, when I finally asked him what decision he'd made simply said, "There was absolutely no solid evidence to back up your accusations, Buchanan."'

'And he's right,' said William wryly, 'though I'll be fascinated to know where your friend ends up.'

'In prison along with your friend probably,' said James.

'While you've learnt the importance of gathering irrefutable evidence before you even consider presenting your case. A lesson that will stand you in good stead if you still want to be the Director of the FBI rather than chairman of the Pilgrim Line.'

'My father's now chairman of the company,' said James, who paused before adding, 'but he's not my grandfather.'

After William had put the phone down, he thought about that sentence for some time.

• • •

Ross was already seated in his place, head buried in the *New York Times*, when Mr and Mrs Pugh entered the dining room and were shown to their usual table by an attentive maître d'. Pugh was still spluttering angrily to his wife about what had taken place at the bank that morning while she appeared to listen sympathetically. Ross couldn't help noticing that he didn't mention the fact that his credit card had been rejected when he tried to buy two boxes of Montecristo cigars.

Pugh tried once again to persuade her that they should open a joint bank account, but Ross needed to catch only the occasional word drifting his way from the next table to realize that she still wasn't convinced. When he told her he would be returning to the bank in the morning to close his account so the same bank could take care of both of their affairs in future, she nodded, but didn't comment.

Ross had already decided he wouldn't be following Pugh to the bank in the morning, but would remain at the hotel in the hope of detaining his wife for a few minutes in order to, in the commander's words, enlighten her.

The conversation at the next table turned to a proposed visit to the theatre the following evening. Pugh confirmed that the hotel had managed to get them front-row seats in the dress circle for a performance of *Les Misérables*. Mrs Pugh seemed delighted by the news, and although Ross could catch only the occasional word coming his way, the laughter and clinking of glasses suggested that the atmosphere between the newlyweds had changed. After they had given the waiter their orders, Pugh leant across the table and said something in a stage whisper that took Ross by surprise.

'Your wig has gone a bit skew-whiff, my love.'

Mrs Pugh rose slowly from her place and said, 'I'll only be a few moments, my darling,' and left without another word.

Ross readjusted the mirror in his cigarette case, and watched as Pugh took a cigar holder out of an inside pocket, which struck Ross as strange, as the Pughs hadn't yet been served with their main course.

Pugh unscrewed the holder, removed a cigar and placed it on the table in front of him. He looked cautiously around the crowded room, before tipping the tube upside down and emptying some white powder into his wine glass. He stirred the wine with the handle of his fork, before placing the cigar back in its holder and returning it to his pocket. Pugh glanced around the room once again, before he switched wine glasses with his wife's. The whole deception had taken under a minute.

Ross caught the eye of the maître d', who was showing some guests to their table. He scribbled a few words on the back of his menu and put a finger to his lips as the maître d' approached him. He read the message before moving casually to the next table, where Mr Pugh was staring intently towards the entrance of the restaurant.

'I'm sorry to bother you, sir,' said the maître d', 'but you have an overseas call. If you could go to reception, the caller is holding on.'

'Did they give you a name?' demanded Pugh.

'No, sir. It was a lady. She said it was urgent.'

Pugh quickly got up and scurried out of the restaurant. As soon as he'd left the room, Ross dropped his copy of the *New York Times* on the floor. He bent down to retrieve the newspaper and, as he stood up, he switched back the Pughs' wine glasses with a sleight of hand that would have impressed Jimmy the dip.

Ross was walking towards the bar when an angry Pugh

stormed past him. He had only just sat down when his wife reappeared.

Ross climbed onto a stool at the far end of the bar, ordered a coffee and continued to read his newspaper. He looked up to see Pugh raising his glass in a toast, to which his wife happily responded. He drained his glass, and she took a sip from hers, as their main courses were placed in front of them.

No sooner had Pugh picked up his knife and fork than his face turned ashen. He began to shake and fell forward onto the table, foaming at the mouth.

'Fetch a doctor!' shouted Mrs Pugh hysterically. A man seated a few tables away jumped up and hurried across, but after only a cursory examination it was clear to everyone watching that there was nothing he could do to help.

Ross watched as events unfolded in front of him. A few moments later two waiters appeared carrying a stretcher, accompanied by the maître d'. Some of the guests turned away, while others looked on with morbid fascination as the lifeless body was lowered onto the stretcher and carried out of the room, followed by the distraught widow.

Ross took advantage of the commotion and quietly left the restaurant. As he passed the maître d', he slipped him a hundred-rand note which he acknowledged with a slight bow. From the foyer Ross watched discreetly as the stretcher was carried out to a waiting ambulance, where two redundant paramedics took over. Mrs Pugh burst into tears as one of them checked her late husband's pulse, closed his eyes and gently pulled a sheet over his head.

Ross had come across many grieving widows over the years, and he wasn't in any doubt that Mrs Pugh's tears were genuine, which took him by surprise. Was it possible she really had loved that odious creature? Perhaps she would have felt differently had she known it should have been her, not him, being whisked off to the morgue. As the ambulance drove off, he strolled across to the reception desk to pick up his key.

'You have a message,' said the receptionist.

He unfolded the little slip of paper, and after reading it he said under his breath, 'You're good, choirboy. Very good.'

'I beg your pardon?' said the receptionist.

'Can you tell me the time of the next flight to London?'

'The first flight in the morning is at nine o'clock,' she said, before glancing at her watch. 'But if you were to hurry, sir, you might just catch the red-eye which leaves in a couple of hours.'

'Please have my bill ready, and book me one business-class seat on that flight. I'll also need a taxi to take me to the airport.'

Ross bounded up the stairs to the third floor, where he quickly opened his door and began throwing all his possessions into his suitcase, before he ran back down to reception and paid his bill. A porter put his bag into the boot of a waiting taxi, its engine turning over. The promise of a hundred-rand tip if he made it to the airport in time ensured that the driver ignored every speed limit. Ross was the last person to board the plane that night.

'Will you be wanting dinner tonight, sir?' asked the steward, once they'd taken off.

'No, thank you,' said Ross. 'Just a pair of eyeshades.'

'Of course, sir.'

As there wasn't a Larry T. Holbrooke the Third seated

next to him, Ross looked forward to a good night's sleep. He should be back in time to have breakfast with Jimmy the dip at the Putney Bridge Café, before reporting to Chief Inspector Warwick at the Yard. He could only wonder how much the choirboy already knew.

CHAPTER 28

'ARE YOU PC PLOD?' ASKED Peter, when Juan came down for breakfast the following morning.

'No,' said Juan, taking a seat opposite the twins. 'My youngest daughter tells me I'm not as clever as PC Plod, because I don't solve every one of my cases immediately. She thinks I'm more like Inspector Watchit.'

Artemisia giggled, as Beth placed a plate of bacon and eggs in front of their guest.

'My father will be jealous when I tell him what I had for breakfast this morning,' said Juan, picking up his knife and fork.

'Doesn't your daddy have breakfast?' asked Artemisia.

'Don't talk with your mouth full,' said William.

'Who stole the pearl necklace?' asked Peter.

'I don't know,' admitted Juan.

'We'll find out when Daddy gets back tonight and reads us the last chapter,' said Artemisia.

'If Daddy gets back tonight,' said William as the phone in the hall began to ring.

'Who can that possibly be at this time in the morning?' said Beth.

'Probably The Hawk,' said William as he got up and headed for the door.

'It's PC Plod,' whispered Juan.

'I hope so,' said Artemisia, 'then he can help you solve—'

William closed the door behind him and picked up the phone on the hall table. 'William Warwick.'

'Good morning. Geoff Duffield from Heathrow security. DI Hogan flew in from Cape Town first thing this morning, and has just passed through passport control.'

'Thank you, Geoff. At least that's one of my problems dealt with. Thank you,' he repeated before hanging up the phone and returning to the kitchen.

'Have you met PC Plod?' Peter was asking Juan.

'No, but I'd like to, because your father and I could do with his help at the moment.'

'That was him on the phone,' said William, joining in the game. 'He's on his way to the Yard, so we'd better get going.'

'Naughty Daddy. Grandpops says you must always finish your breakfast before going to work.'

'I agree with your grandpops,' said Juan, who continued to enjoy his eggs and bacon, as William gave in and sat back down.

'I apologize,' said Beth. 'Artemisia tends to repeat the last thing she's heard.'

'No need to apologize,' said Juan. 'Don't forget I have three daughters.'

'And another on the way, William tells me.'

'What can I possibly have done to deserve that?' said Juan.

• • •

'Good morning, Inspector,' said Jimmy the dip. 'Will you be joining me for breakfast?'

'Haven't the time,' said Ross, staring enviously at Jimmy's empty plate before it was whisked away. 'But if you're still hoping for the second two hundred, make sure you're outside the Queen's Theatre in Wardour Street at ten thirty tonight.'

'I'll have to check my diary,' said Jimmy, as he dropped a third sugar lump in his tea.

'If you're not there,' said Ross, 'I'll be joining you for breakfast every morning until you've paid back the first two hundred.'

'You've persuaded me, but then there's no disguising your Irish charm, Inspector,' said Jimmy, spooning a large blob of marmalade onto a slice of toast. By the time he had picked up his knife and begun to spread it, the Inspector had left.

• • •

Lieutenant Sanchez spread out a large map of Catalonia on the table in front of him, and the team gathered around to take a closer look.

'Once Chief Inspector Warwick and Inspector Ross have landed in Barcelona,' he began, 'they will be driven to a safe house on the outskirts of the city, where I'll carry out the final briefing, before we all change into the appropriate gear for a night operation.'

'When is the witching hour?' asked the commander.

'Midnight, sir,' replied Sanchez. 'We'll leave the city in an unmarked car, and be dropped off a couple of kilometres from the boundary of Faulkner's estate.'

William nodded as Sanchez pointed to an 'X' he'd marked on the map. 'Can you be sure he's still there?' he asked.

'We've got cameras on the road leading up to the estate and patrols on the beach at the foot of the cliff, and so far there's been no sign of life, so we're fairly confident he's still holed up in the house.'

'Don't forget, we know Booth Watson has a flight booked to Barcelona on Monday,' interjected Rebecca. 'Why would he bother to make the trip if Faulkner wasn't there?'

'Fair point,' said William. 'But I suspect the reason for Booth Watson's visit is to put the finishing touches to his client's unscheduled departure, so this may be our last chance before he disappears again.'

'We'll need Detective Inspector Hogan to get us from here,' Sanchez's finger rested at the edge of the forest, 'to here,' he said moving it across to the front door of the house.

William shook his head. 'No. Ross is convinced our best hope of getting into the house unobserved is through one of the windows in the servants' quarters on the fourth floor. When we were last there, he noticed three of them were left open during the day. Here, here and here. This one,' he added, his forefinger moving across the plans, 'is next to the fire escape.'

Sanchez nodded, but suggested, 'We still need to know what DI Ross has planned once we reach the edge of the forest. I suspect we'll find it's full of alarms, traps and other surprises for unwelcome visitors.'

'He should be with us in the next few minutes,' said William, checking his watch.

'What makes you so sure of that?' asked The Hawk.

'His plane landed at Heathrow a couple of hours ago. In fact I'm surprised—' continued William as the door burst open and Ross strode in.

'Sorry I'm late. Something held me up.'

Or someone, thought William, but satisfied himself with, 'Lieutenant Sanchez was just taking us through what we'll be up against once we arrive in Barcelona.'

'I can only get us as far as the end of the road leading to the estate before you'll have to take over,' admitted Sanchez.

Ross took his place at the table and began to explain in detail how he planned to get the three of them from the edge of the forest to the fire escape on the far side of the house without setting off any alarms. No one interrupted him. William finally brought the meeting to a close when they began to ask the same questions a third time.

'That still leaves the problem of the impenetrable door,' said The Hawk, as they rose from their places.

'I have an appointment this afternoon with the only person other than Faulkner who knows how to open that door,' said Ross. 'I'll report back.'

'Then let's all meet again at eight tomorrow morning,' said William, 'and go over the plan one last time.'

'I have a meeting at eight tomorrow morning that I can't afford to miss,' said Ross without explanation. 'But I'll call you later this evening with an update.'

'Fine,' said William, to everyone's surprise. But then, he knew exactly where Detective Inspector Hogan would be the following morning at eight o'clock, because he intended to be there as well.

• • •

'What do you know that I don't?' asked Beth, as Christina took a seat on the other side of her desk.

'Not a lot,' admitted Christina, 'except that I'm convinced that wherever the Caravaggio ended up is where you'll find Miles.'

'As well as the Frans Hals?' said Beth.

'I'm afraid so,' said Christina, 'and if I had any idea where that was, I would tell you, believe me.'

Beth didn't believe her, so she took William's advice and continued to listen, listen, listen.

'All I know for certain is that Booth Watson plans to fly to Barcelona on Monday morning. It can't be a coincidence that Miles's yacht will be sailing out of Monte Carlo on Saturday night. I wouldn't be surprised if they both ended up in the same place.'

'Which can only mean Miles must be on the move again,' said Beth.

'Agreed,' said Christina. 'And if his yacht's involved, the collection will also be on the move.'

'Where are you getting your information from?' asked Beth.

'Ex-Superintendent Lamont, who's only too happy to have more than one paymaster.'

'Let's hope Miles never finds out,' said Beth, 'because he

doesn't believe in golden parachutes, unless he has control of the release cord.'

'So now you know as much as I do,' said Christina, as she got up to leave.

Beth doubted that, but still intended to call William the moment she'd left. She could already hear her husband's response when she passed on the information Christina had just revealed.

'I'm still not sure whose side that woman's on.'

• • •

Nosey Parker was the name displayed above the door of 114A Charing Cross Road. An establishment that rarely served more than one or two customers a day, and then only by appointment with the proprietor. Ross marched into the shop five minutes early and nervously approached the counter.

'At ease, corporal,' said a voice he could never forget. He hadn't been addressed that way for almost ten years, but he still couldn't relax in the presence of his old boss.

'I was sad to hear of your wife's death,' said Colonel Parker in a far gentler tone than Ross had ever heard during his four years with the SAS. 'But for now, corporal, we must consider the future,' he said, the voice of authority returning.

'Were your boffins able to install the modification I requested for my video camera?'

'A relatively simple task,' replied the colonel, producing an unmarked box from under the counter. 'This will allow you to detect any alarms or booby traps while still videoing the whole operation in real time.'

Ross was going to enquire about the locked door with no lock, when the colonel said, 'How did my 1950s Silver Cross pram work out?'

'Couldn't have been better, sir. I walked straight past the target area without anyone giving me a second glance. I carried out the operation as planned, and escaped unnoticed by either gang or the police.'

'I enjoyed reading *The Times*' report of the incident,' said the colonel, smiling for the first time. 'And the cigarette case?'

'Worked like a charm. Although I'll never trust a woman when she's powdering her nose.'

'Never trust a woman, full stop,' said the colonel.

An observation Ross would have agreed with until he'd met Jo.

'Now you've dealt with those particular problems, should I presume you now need some help with your next mission?'

'Yes, sir,' said Ross. 'When I was on an assignment abroad recently, I came across a large iron door that had no handle, no lock and no dial. The letters "NP" were engraved on the bottom left-hand corner.'

'The Sesame Safe,' said the colonel. 'Perfected by a former member of the Stasi who escaped from East Germany and joined the firm.'

'But how do you open the safe when there's no code?'

'There is a code, corporal, but only when the owner is in the same room.'

'Then it has to be the watch,' said Ross, now realizing why Faulkner had tapped on its face just before he entered his study.

'You could be right,' said the colonel, failing to answer

his question. 'Mind you, I regret ever having dealt with that particular gentleman. He claimed to have been a naval captain who'd served in the Falklands campaign, but frankly I doubt it, as he turned out to be the sort of bounder who doesn't pay his mess bills.'

A cad, Ross had wanted to add, but thought better of it.

'In fact, he still hasn't paid the final invoice for the Sesame Safe we installed for him a couple of years back. However, given time he'll need to replace the batteries in the watch, and then he'll have to pay up, because they're also unique.'

'How much is his outstanding mess bill?' asked Ross, expecting to be court-martialled for even raising the subject.

'A bit out of your league, I'm afraid, old chap.'

'Try me.'

'Five thousand pounds would settle the account.'

Ross took out his chequebook, picked up a Biro from the counter and began writing.

'Won the pools, have we?' ventured the colonel.

'No, sir. Lost a wife,' said Ross, as he handed over the cheque.

'I apologize,' said Parker, genuinely contrite. He turned around, entered a code that unlocked a small safe in the wall, extracted a watch with a blank face and tapped it. The dial immediately lit up and flashed the time in bold numerals for a few seconds, before the light went out. He handed the watch to his former comrade in arms.

'This isn't much use to me,' said Ross, 'if I don't know the code.'

'What time is it, corporal?'

'Twenty past three,' said Ross, glancing at a clock on the wall behind the counter.

'Think like a soldier!' barked the colonel.

'Fifteen twenty,' replied Ross.

'Month and year.'

'Nine eighty-eight.'

'Correct. 15 20 09 88.'

'The time, date and year,' said Ross. 'It couldn't be simpler.'

'And the beauty of it is that the time changes every minute, which means the code does as well. But corporal, don't forget that although your adversary may be neither an officer nor a gentleman, you'll still need to get up very early in the morning to catch him asleep.'

'That's exactly what I plan to do,' said Ross, as he strapped on the watch.

• • •

DC Pankhurst was seated at a table by the window of a wine bar overlooking Wardour Street. She had selected the spot carefully. The little bar, on the first floor above a restaurant, was packed with young people enjoying a night out, although she was still on duty. From her vantage point she had an uninterrupted view of Darren Carter as he went about his work. After fourteen days of surveillance, she not only knew his routine, but also his job description (unwritten). Carter was first and foremost the Eve Club's gatekeeper. He, and he alone, decided who should be allowed to enter the club, and his prejudices had become only too obvious to Rebecca over the past fortnight.

He welcomed stray middle-aged foreigners who looked as if they had money and could be seduced into parting with it. If they'd had a little too much to drink, that was a bonus. 'Undesirables' – tattooed youths wearing jeans, especially if they were in groups – were politely rejected, and occasionally not so politely. 'Sorry sir, this is a private members' club' was usually enough for them to move on, and if they didn't, the suggestion of what might happen next persuaded the more determined. One or two didn't give up quite so easily, which was met with a menacing look, and if they were still stupid enough to push their luck, a firm shove followed, although Rebecca hadn't yet witnessed anything that could have been described as GBH, and therefore warranted an arrest.

Rebecca accepted she would have to be like a patient angler, prepared to wait for hours in the hope of landing a catch. At least she was sitting in a warm bar enjoying a drink, and not perched on a river bank in the pouring rain. But she was painfully aware her written reports were becoming shorter and shorter by the day. In fact, lately, only the date changed. She wondered how much longer it would be before the chief moved her on to another assignment.

At least she had plenty of time to think about Archie. She loved her job and being part of a highly trained elite team, but she knew she would soon have to make a decision about her future. Archie had started talking about their life together as a shared partnership. He was currently doing a spell in Northern Ireland, and she was well aware that, as a young army officer, he could expect to be regularly posted abroad. 'Goes with the territory, old thing,' he'd once told her, making it clear in his own sweet way that he assumed she would want to resign from the Met, as she obviously couldn't be in two places at once.

If she were to marry him, it would mean giving up the job she loved to become an army officer's wife, produce the regulation 2.2 children, while her greatest thrill would be helping the CO's wife organize cocktail parties for visiting 'bigwigs' (Archie's word). As she was musing on this vision of her future, she became distracted by a lively bunch of theatregoers pouring out of the Queen's Theatre to begin wending their way home. The usual reminder that she should also be thinking about calling it a day.

'Another glass of wine, miss?'

• • •

'Good evening, Inspector,' said Jimmy the dip, who had appeared out of nowhere. 'If you've got the gear, I'm ready to earn the other two hundred nicker.'

Ross turned his back on the passing crowd and without a word slipped Jimmy three small packets and a bundle of used notes. Jimmy melted back into the crowd.

A few moments later, Ross spotted him on the far side of the road mingling with the audience coming out of the theatre, before he stopped outside the entrance to the club and asked the doorman the way to Leicester Square.

'What do you think I am, mate, a fuckin' tour guide?'

'Sorry to bother you,' said Jimmy, who bent down and picked up a watch from the pavement. 'Is this yours by any chance?'

'Yeah,' said the doorman, grabbing his watch and slipping it back on his wrist without a word of thanks.

Jimmy the dip moved on, while Ross stepped into a nearby phone box and dialled a number.

Moments later a voice announced, 'Inspector Watts.'

'I've just come out of the Eve Club, and the doorman tried to sell me some drugs. I thought you'd want to know.' He hung up before the call could be traced. Four minutes was considered by the Met's crack drivers to be a fast response to an emergency call, so when a squad car swept into Wardour Street three minutes and forty-two seconds later, Ross allowed himself a smile.

• • •

At first Rebecca didn't take much notice of the police car as it sped into the street below her. Hardly surprising, she thought, as there were regular disturbances in Soho every night. But she began to take a closer interest when it screeched to a halt outside the Eve Club. Four uniformed officers leapt out and surrounded Carter, whose shocked expression appeared to be genuine.

A small crowd began to gather on the opposite side of the road as two of the officers pinned him against the wall, while a third searched his overcoat and extracted several small packets and a bundle of used notes. The fourth officer, an Inspector Rebecca didn't recognize, arrested Carter and cautioned him, before he was handcuffed and led away. She could still hear his cries of protest as he was bundled into the back of the police car.

She began to write down everything she had witnessed, pausing only when the owner came rushing out of the club and shook a fist at the squad car as it disappeared out of sight. The crowd had dispersed by the time Jimmy the dip reappeared by Ross's side, unable to hide a smirk.

'You did well, Jimmy,' said Ross, palming him the other two hundred.

'Happy to oblige,' said Jimmy. 'That's exactly the sort of lowlife what ought to be locked up.'

Ross was about to make a comment about pots and kettles when Jimmy added, 'Like the flash new watch, Inspector. But how do you tell the time?' Before he could answer, Jimmy had disappeared into the night. Ross checked his wrist, relieved to find the watch was still there.

• • •

Once Rebecca had completed her report, she emptied her glass, settled the bill and left. She would have called the chief at home if it hadn't been so late. That would have to wait until tomorrow morning. Then she remembered where she would be at six o'clock the next morning. She corrected herself. This morning.

CHAPTER 29

SIX PIPS WERE FOLLOWED BY the news headlines, but neither of them was listening.

'I don't enjoy spying on a colleague,' said Jackie. 'Especially one I like and admire.'

'Couldn't agree more,' said William. 'But when you're your own worst enemy, you need friends.'

'You're still convinced he was involved in the Roach and Abbott killings?'

'You have to admit,' said William, 'that his wife's death gave him a pretty strong motive. Let's just be thankful the Abbott/Roach file has been closed. But the Sleeman case hasn't, so it's important we try to stay one step ahead of Ross. And of Verenich too, for that matter.'

'My latest intel on Clive Pugh might also interest you,' said Jackie, as the two of them continued to stare out of the car window at a red door at the far end of the mews.

'Enlighten me,' said William, sounding like the commander.

'I had a call from my new buddy in the Cape Town police department yesterday. He told me I'd got it completely wrong, and I needn't worry about Mrs Pugh any longer.'

'How come?'

'Because her husband keeled over during dinner a couple of nights ago and died before the ambulance reached their hotel. At least we know Ross can't have been involved in that one.'

'So Pugh didn't get his hands on her money after all.'

'Now there's the irony,' said Jackie. 'It seems that Mrs Pugh failed to mention to her latest husband that she'd been married twice before, and between them they'd bled her dry. She assumed that, as Pugh always paid the bills, he had to be a rich man. She was devastated to discover that he was also penniless. It turns out she can't even afford to pay her hotel bill.'

'The Mount Nelson doesn't come cheap,' said William.

'How did you know where they were staying?'

'Do the local police think Mrs Pugh might have been involved in her husband's death?' asked William, avoiding the question.

'No, sir,' said Jackie. 'In fact, they've issued a statement confirming there were no suspicious circumstances, and allowed the bereaved widow to accompany the body back to England. Tourist class. So you'll have to find me another impossible case to solve.'

'Concentrate on this one,' said William, as a light went on in Jo's house, and others continued to go on and off during the next hour, but then William had learnt over the years that surveillance was a cat and mouse game and patience was the cheese in the trap.

They both listened to the seven o'clock news on the radio, and nothing had changed by the time the eight o'clock news followed an hour later. During that time the milk, the papers and the post were delivered, but the front door remained closed.

William was beginning to think that 'the first day of the month' might not have been as important a clue as one of Paul's informants had suggested, until a black Toyota pulled up outside the house and parked on a double yellow line.

When the passenger door opened, neither of them needed an identikit picture to know who it was heading for the front door.

'Christ, he's built like a tank,' said Jackie.

'Six foot four, two hundred and twenty pounds, and he practically lives in the gym,' said William, as the giant knocked on the door.

Verenich waited for a short time, casting an occasional glance up and down the mews, before knocking again. This time a little more firmly. A few moments later Ross appeared, dressed in a tracksuit.

'Doesn't look as if he's planning to come in to work today,' said Jackie, as Ross handed a thick wad of notes to Verenich, who took his time counting them.

'I still intend to put a stop to whatever he does have planned,' said William, as Verenich gave Ross what passed for a smile, pocketed the money and returned to the car.

William switched on a radio that connected him to the rest of the team.

'Verenich's car is heading towards the traffic lights at the junction with Merton Street. I'll let you know which way he turns. Remember to keep your distance.'

'Understood,' said three alert voices, who had also been waiting impatiently to go to work since six o'clock that morning. William was about to follow the Toyota when Ross came running out of the house, jumped into his car and immediately drove off.

'The mark is turning left,' said William, 'so he's yours, Danny, and DI Hogan isn't far behind. Keep me briefed, but ditch Verenich when he reaches his next customer. Paul will take over.'

'Understood,' said two voices, as the Toyota drove past a taxi that never picked up a paying passenger.

William smiled when he saw Ross turn left at the lights and continue to follow Verenich. 'Constable Markham.'

'Sir.'

'He's driving a dark blue Volkswagen . . .'

'Clocked him, sir.'

• • •

Ross could see the Toyota up ahead, and tucked in behind a taxi. The traffic light at the next junction was green, but he wasn't sure he would make it in time. He put his foot on the accelerator.

Verenich's driver turned right and the taxi followed, but the lights began to change as Ross approached them. He drove straight through, only to be met by a policeman who stepped out into the road, raised the palm of his right hand and with an exaggerated wave of the arm indicated that Ross should pull into the kerb. As he came to a halt Ross voiced several Anglo-Saxon expletives behind the car's closed windows.

The young officer walked slowly towards him, as Ross wound down the window, his engine still running.

'How can I help you, constable?' he asked, as Verenich disappeared around the next corner.

'Do you realize, sir, that you just drove through a red light?'

'I did nothing of the sort,' said Ross, breaking a golden rule.

'My colleague and I,' said the constable, looking to his left, 'witnessed you breaking Section 36(1) of the Road Traffic Act 1988. Could I see your driving licence please?'

Ross handed over his warrant card.

'This is not your driving licence, sir,' said the constable, handing it back.

'I don't have my licence with me.'

'Then I'll need to take down your particulars, sir,' said the constable as he extracted a notebook and Biro from his top pocket.

'Which I suspect you already know, constable,' said Ross.

'This shouldn't take long,' replied the officer, ignoring the comment.

'How long?' said Ross.

'I beg your pardon, sir?'

'How long did they tell you to delay me?'

'I've no idea what you're talking about, sir.'

'How long?' repeated Ross.

'Ten minutes, sir,' admitted the constable.

Ross had to grudgingly admire Warwick. He might have had the face of a choirboy, but he didn't take prisoners. He was beginning to believe he was, as Jackie had suggested, the natural successor to The Hawk. However, he still had a surprise in store for the Detective Chief Inspector before the day was out.

'Can I go now you've served your purpose?' Ross asked, innocently.

The constable checked his watch. 'Yes, of course, sir. But perhaps you could drive more carefully in the future.'

• • •

Paul called in to report that Verenich had only had to clench a fist to ensure Sleeman's second client coughed up.

'Take advantage of it,' said William. 'Interview the man and see if you can get a statement from him that would stand up in court.'

'On my way,' said Paul.

'The Toyota's just driven past me,' said Rebecca. 'I'll call back when he reaches his next collection point.'

'What's your position, Danny?'

'I'll take over from DC Pankhurst when he comes back out.'

'What I can't work out,' said Jackie, as William switched off the radio, 'is why they're always at home when Verenich turns up.'

'If they weren't, it would be their wives who answered the door,' said William, 'and then they'd get grief from both sides.'

A red light began flashing. William flicked a switch.

'Good morning, sir. It's Inspector Watts of the drug squad. Do you have a moment?'

'I'm a bit preoccupied at the moment, Inspector, so unless it's important . . .'

'It concerns a certain Darren Carter, sir, but I can call back later.'

'You have my attention, Inspector.'

'I arrested Carter last night while he was on duty outside the Eve Club, and charged him with possession and intent to supply three ounces of heroin, four wraps of top-grade cocaine and several bags of cannabis.'

'He can't be that stupid,' said William.

'He's swearing blind we planted the gear on him, but we were given the tip-off by a member of the public, and we have it all on tape.'

'Did the call come to you direct, Inspector, or from the 999 switchboard?'

'Direct, sir.' Watts paused. 'Why do you ask?'

'I'll tell you when I've listened to the tape. So, where's Carter now?'

'Locked up in the local nick, where he'll stay until he appears in front of a magistrate later today and applies for bail.'

'The Beak will tell him to get lost,' said William.

'I'd agree with you, sir, if he wasn't being represented by Mr Booth Watson QC. I confess that came as a bit of a surprise.'

'It doesn't surprise me,' said William. 'Carter's no more than a side-show. Booth Watson's fees will be covered by a Mr Staples, the owner of the Eve Club, who'd lose his licence if his doorman was convicted of selling Class A drugs. Make sure you take every opportunity to refer to the defendant's previous record, including his conviction for manslaughter, because I'm hoping to end up with two for the price of one. Keep me briefed.'

'Will do, sir.'

'Do you think it could have been Ross who planted the drugs on him?' said Jackie, after he'd switched off the radio.

'Not a risk he'd take,' said William. 'But he knows a dozen dips who could have carried out that job at the drop of a hat, quite literally.'

'I just can't believe . . .' began Jackie.

'You don't want to believe,' said William, as the radio crackled into life again.

'DC Pankhurst, sir. Verenich's just made his third collection. He had to force his way into the house, and he came out a few minutes later carrying a large television under one arm and a bulky plastic bag under the other. No sign of the previous owner.'

'Pay him a visit, Rebecca, and try to charm him into making a statement. I need this case to be watertight. Danny, where is he now?'

'On his way back to Sleeman's office, with a large amount of dosh and a boot full of plunder. Should I head back to the Yard, sir?'

'No, stay put,' said William, 'because you can be sure Verenich hasn't yet made his final call of the day.'

'What now, sir?' asked Jackie.

'We have to be patient, because the more vulnerable clients, the ones who can't pay up, will come later in the day, when it's dark and there's less chance of any witnesses. We still have to gather enough evidence to make Booth Watson's job as difficult as possible. And what's more . . .' he said as the red light on the radio began flashing once again.

A soft Irish lilt meant he didn't have to ask who it was on the other end of the line.

'I now know how to open the door in Faulkner's study,' said Detective Inspector Hogan. 'I would have told you earlier, sir, if an overzealous young constable hadn't held me up. Still, no doubt we'll meet up at the cemetery after Verenich has made his last call of the day.'

'Which cemetery?' demanded William.

'The one where you'll find DC Pankhurst's campaigning ancestor is no longer bothering the police,' said Ross, before he severed the connection.

'What the hell was that all about?' asked Jackie.

'He knows something we don't,' said William, as he flicked a switch. 'Rebecca?'

'Yes, sir.'

'Where are you?'

'I'm with the gentleman you asked me to interview at his home in Kensington.'

'Where is Emmeline Pankhurst buried?'

'Brompton Cemetery. Why do you ask?'

'Wrap up the interview and go straight there. Report back if you come across anything suspicious.'

'What am I looking for?'

'I don't know,' admitted William.

'Now I'm completely lost,' said Jackie, as William switched off the radio.

'It's not difficult to stay a yard ahead of Sleeman and Verenich,' he commented, 'but it's a damn sight harder keeping up with Ross.'

'Particularly when he's dealing with you, sir,' said Jackie.

William was about to respond when Danny came back on the line.

'He's just made his fourth call, sir. After he left, Paul moved in to interview the client.'

'Good. Stay on the line. There may well be a change of plan.'

• • •

Sleeman slipped out of his office soon after Verenich had left to make his final call. He would be passing through Swindon by the time the body was buried.

He walked for a couple of blocks before hailing a taxi and climbing into the back. 'Euston,' was all he said.

Once he'd been dropped off outside the station, he joined a queue in the booking hall and purchased a first-class sleeper to Edinburgh. Before he paid, he asked the woman behind the counter in a loud voice how she had the nerve to charge sixty-three pounds.

The man standing behind him witnessed the unpleasant altercation, but said nothing. Sleeman then made his way across to Platform 7, and was about to board the train when two police officers blocked his path and arrested him.

'On what charge?' he demanded.

'Threatening a railway employee will be enough to be going on with, although I have a feeling there will be more to follow,' said the commander, who couldn't remember when he'd last arrested someone.

He reported back to DCI Warwick.

• • •

Two lines were going at once.

'It's DC Pankhurst, sir. There's a recently dug grave at the back of the cemetery, which the chief gravedigger tells me he didn't authorize.'

'Stay out of sight,' said William. 'We'll be with you shortly. Danny, where are you?'

'Verenich has just turned up outside a house in Chiswick and is knocking on the door.'

'Keep me briefed,' said William. 'The rest of you head for Brompton Cemetery in Kensington. Once you get there, make sure you keep out of sight, because Verenich won't be far behind.' He switched off the radio and said, 'Let's get moving.'

Jackie eased the gear lever into first and accelerated away.

'I presume you know where you're going,' said William.

'No, sir. But I'm hoping you do.'

• • •

Hiding ten plainclothes detectives in a cemetery didn't prove difficult, especially when they were aided and abetted by the chief gravedigger. There were more than enough monuments, private vaults and large memorial piles to hide an army.

Once everyone was in place, the more difficult challenge was to remain silent. A sneeze at that time of night would have sounded like a volcano erupting. The silence was broken only when Danny called in.

'Verenich has just come out of the house in Chiswick and right now he's shoving a protesting client into the back of the Toyota. They should be with you in about twenty minutes. Just say the word, chief, and I'll ram the bastard and then the boys can move in and arrest him.'

'No,' said William. 'Stay put. If he spots you, the whole operation will be scuppered,' he added as Jackie drove into the cemetery, turned off the headlights and tucked the car behind a clump of trees.

'But if you're wrong about where they're taking him . . .'

'That's a risk I'm going to have to take,' said William, reminding Danny why he'd never wanted to be promoted.

'Maintain radio silence,' was William's next order.

As the minutes passed, William kept glancing at his watch. He still wasn't certain if Ross was on the side of the angels who were currently surrounding him, or if he was somewhere else the other side of London, preparing a different burial of his own. Either way, he wouldn't be satisfied with making an arrest while explaining to Verenich his right to remain silent.

William let out a long sigh of relief when he spotted a black Toyota entering the north end of the cemetery. No lights to guide the driver on a moonless night, but then he knew where he was going. Ten testosterone-filled young officers awaited his command, but William didn't move until he saw the car pulling to a halt.

The back door was opened by the driver, while Verenich pulled his whimpering victim out and began dragging him towards an open grave.

'Oh my God,' said Jackie, 'they're going to bury him alive.'

William leapt out of the car and began running towards the grave, while ten officers appeared from every direction.

DS Adaja quickly overtook DCI Warwick and crash-tackled the driver, who'd dropped his spade and tried to make a run for it. Paul held him down long enough for two other officers to pin him to the ground, while DS Roycroft handcuffed him.

William kept heading towards Verenich, who hurled his screaming victim to one side and defiantly stood his ground.

Just as William was about to launch himself at Verenich a spade appeared out of the grave, and with a practised golfer's swing it came crashing into Verenich's ankles, causing him to drop on his knees. As he tried to get up, a second blow hit him full on the side of his face, and he toppled forward and fell head first into the grave. Ross raised the spade high above his head to administer the final blow, but William grabbed its shaft with both hands and was pulled into the grave, landing on top of Verenich.

Ross could only look on as a couple of officers unceremoniously yanked Verenich back out, laid him flat on the ground and handcuffed him. William then clambered out, still clutching the spade. He looked down at the prostrate body, relieved to see Verenich's eyes flicker open and stare blankly back up at him.

DS Adaja informed the two prisoners that they were under arrest on suspicion of conspiracy to murder, and cautioned them before they were led away. As Rebecca tried to calm the traumatized victim, Ross drew William's attention to three unmarked graves.

'All in good time,' said William, aware that he would need a court order to exhume the bodies, which he felt confident would give them all the evidence they needed to charge Verenich with murder and Sleeman with being an accessory.

Ross managed a curt nod, as the two prisoners were led away.

'You should have let me kill him,' he said.

William ignored the comment and simply asked, 'Can I assume, Inspector, that your thirst for revenge has finally been quenched?'

'No, you can't, sir,' said Ross. 'Not while Faulkner is still alive.'

The Hawk, who was standing alone in a dark corner of the cemetery, had watched with interest as the scene unfolded. When the curtain finally came down, he realized he had two choices: he could either suspend DI Hogan pending a full inquiry, or recommend to the commissioner that he be awarded a second Queen's Gallantry Medal. He didn't need to toss a coin.

CHAPTER 30

WILLIAM BOARDED THE CROWDED PLANE to find Ross already seated by the window. He sat down next to him, but to a casual observer it would not have been obvious they were colleagues. They didn't once discuss Caravaggio on their flight to Barcelona, nor Beth, Jo, the twins, or Jo Junior – as Ross called his daughter – nor the upcoming Frans Hals exhibition at the Fitzmolean, nor even the frailty of West Ham's defence or the brilliance of Chelsea's attack, depending on their point of view.

They fell into a companionable silence. William would have liked to ask Ross how he had managed to creep into that grave unnoticed, but suspected that no answer would have been forthcoming.

However, he did notice that Ross was no longer wearing the Rolex Jo had given him as a wedding present. The anonymous, black-faced watch that had taken its place wasn't, in William's opinion, a worthy replacement, but with Ross there was always a reason.

As the plane touched down on Spanish soil and taxied towards its stand, William looked out of the window to see Lieutenant Sanchez standing next to an unmarked black car by the side of the runway, its back door already open.

The two detectives were the first passengers off the plane, each carrying only an overnight bag, although they had no intention of staying overnight.

Juan greeted them, and their car had driven through the security exit and was on the motorway before most of the other passengers had reached the airport terminal.

William wasted no time in taking Juan through the latest refinements to the plan and answering all the lieutenant's questions, with Ross making the occasional observation.

The safe house turned out to be an inconspicuous two-up two-down in a quiet back street on the west side of the city. Juan led William and Ross through to the operations centre, a large room with a circular table surrounded by half a dozen chairs, along with the inevitable corkboard covered in maps, diagrams and photographs taking up almost a complete wall.

Juan began the final briefing by drawing their attention to several aerial photographs of Faulkner's estate. Ross took the opportunity to refamiliarize himself with the unmarked tortuous route through the forest and across the bridge to the front door of the house that the golf buggy had taken when they'd delivered the *Fishers of Men* on their first visit.

Having satisfied himself that he knew every inch of the route, Ross walked across to join William and Juan, who were studying a large cardboard model of the house that had been placed in the centre of the table. Juan pointed to the kitchen steps on the west side of the house, and then the fire escape that led up to the fourth floor, where the three bedrooms whose windows had previously been left open were marked with large red crosses.

'We only need one of them to be open tonight to make it from here to here,' said Juan, his finger moving along a corridor and down a wide staircase to the landing outside the master bedroom.

'Let's hope the bedroom door's locked,' said William, 'because then we'll know he's inside.'

'Even if he's somehow made it downstairs to his study,' said Ross, his finger taking a path down the staircase and along the corridor on the ground floor, 'I should be able to reach his study before he has time to open the metal door.'

'Whether he's in bed or not,' said Juan, 'my back-up squad will already have surrounded the house by then.'

'We also have to consider the possibility that he'll already be in his study,' said William, 'and that by the time Ross arrives he'll have opened the metal door and disappeared into thin air once again.'

Ross said nothing. If Faulkner escaped while his colleagues were still on the first floor, he intended to open the metal door and join him on the other side, before they could catch up with him. A detail he'd neglected to mention to William.

'What if he isn't in the bedroom or his study,' said Juan, 'but has already left the house?'

'That's unlikely,' said Ross. 'Booth Watson is flying in to Barcelona tomorrow morning, and the latest sighting of Faulkner's yacht was about three hundred miles away, giving him an ETA of around seven o'clock tomorrow evening, which is when I expect he plans to sail off into the sunset.'

'We need to have Faulkner safely locked up long before Booth Watson arrives,' said William, 'because that man will find a dozen ways of setting him free.'

'Let's go over the timing once again,' said Juan. 'We'll leave here at midnight, so by the time we reach the house Faulkner and most of his staff should be sound asleep.'

'But not the guards,' William reminded them.

'There are six of them in all,' said Juan. 'They work around the clock in eight-hour shifts. One pair will be on patrol from ten o'clock tonight until six tomorrow morning. We know that it takes them fourteen minutes to carry out a complete circuit of the house, and they take a fifteen-minute break around two in the morning.'

'How did you get hold of such valuable intel?' asked Ross.

'One of my men still can't make up his mind if he wants to be a gardener or a policeman, so for the past three weeks he's been both.'

A rare look of respect crossed Ross's face.

'Right,' said William, 'let's go over the plan one last time. Juan, don't hesitate to query even the slightest detail you're unsure about, because, one thing's for certain, we won't be given a third chance.' He felt this must be what it was like to be a mountaineer attempting to conquer Everest. He had planned the expedition and would lead them to base camp, at which point Ross, as climbing leader, would take over, with the task of getting them to the summit, in this case an open window on the fourth floor of the house. Once they were inside the building, William would resume command.

After everyone had been briefed yet again on their individual responsibilities, they took a break for a meal they barely touched, as heightened anticipation, accompanied by a rush of adrenaline, took over.

Finally, they changed into outfits more suited to criminals than upholders of the law. Sleeveless black T-shirts, black tracksuits, black socks, black trainers, even black laces.

'Not on my watch,' said Juan, as Ross took off his jacket to reveal a gun in its holster. 'My boss has made it clear there will be no firearms on this operation.'

'I hope your boss has mentioned that to Faulkner's guards,' said Ross.

'They won't be any trouble when they realize we're police officers,' said Juan.

'Right,' said Ross. 'So once you've pointed that out, they're just going to stick their hands in the air and say, "Fair cop, guv."'

'DI Hogan,' said William sharply, 'don't forget we're guests in this country, and the success of this operation is entirely dependent on the local police's cooperation.'

'Yes, sir,' said Ross, as he reluctantly handed his gun to Sanchez. But it was all he could do to prevent himself from adding, *Then I'll have to strangle him, won't I?*

They spent the next half hour pacing around the room like caged animals desperate to be released, especially Ross, who when the curtain rose had no intention of keeping to the script.

'Let's move,' said Juan, when the first of several church clocks began to strike twelve times, reminding William they were in a Catholic country.

The same unmarked black car was waiting for them in

the street outside. They sat in anticipatory silence as they headed towards the target, no longer needing to discuss the plan.

The driver turned off the motorway at exit 9, and after a few miles he pulled over to the side of the road. The three black-clad men climbed out of the car and watched silently as the driver turned around and left them.

William had calculated that, on foot and in the dark, it would take around forty minutes to cover the five kilometres before they reached the edge of the forest. He took the lead, while Ross brought up the rear. None of them spoke as they progressed slowly down the narrow road, alert to the slightest danger. Only a startled hare paused to take a closer look at the passing strangers, while an owl didn't stop offering his opinion.

When the dense barrier of the forest loomed up in front of them, William raised a hand, the sign for Ross to take over. He moved quickly to the front, taking NP's modified video camera from his backpack. He switched it on and stepped cautiously into the thick undergrowth. The three of them advanced one step at a time, like soldiers on a slow march, aware that a single foot fault could trigger an alarm, light up the grounds and give Faulkner more than enough time to escape.

The long circuitous route demanded by the video camera took them nearly an hour to complete. When they reached the river, they crossed the bridge cautiously, and not long afterwards the forbidding grey stone building came into view, sharply silhouetted in the moonlight.

As they were about to emerge from the forest, Ross gestured firmly to his cohorts with a wave of the hand to get back down. Two guards were patrolling the north side of the building, the wide beams of their torches making sweeping circles that illuminated the deserted grounds.

Ross watched every step the guards took before they turned left at the west end of the house and continued on their way. Thanks to Juan's research, he knew how long it would be before the guards returned. He pointed silently to a small clump of bushes fifty yards from the house that had been highlighted on the map supplied by the zealous gardener. They set off again, this time crawling through the undergrowth, reaching the copse only moments before the guards reappeared. They passed by them so closely that even in the dark Ross could see they were armed. One had a cigarette dangling from the corner of his mouth. Colonel Parker would have put him on report and confined him to barracks.

Ross watched carefully as the guards kept to a designated path so as not to set off an alarm that would wake their paymaster. He knew roughly how much time they had to make it to the kitchen where they could hide beneath a steep flight of stone steps, allowing the guards to pass a second time before they attempted to enter the house. They began to weave their way across the lawn towards a well-trodden path, aware they'd left themselves only seconds before the guards would reappear. They wouldn't have needed a torch to spot the uninvited trio frozen like rabbits in their headlights.

Once the guards were safely out of sight, Ross, closely followed by William and Juan, sprinted towards the building. They knew exactly where their next stop would be, as the kitchen staircase was imprinted on their minds from the model back at the safe house. But this was anything but a safe house. Once they reached the staircase, Ross descended the steps, closely followed by William and Juan, before crouching down opposite an entrance marked '*Entrada de servicio*'.

William held his breath, hearing only the sound of his heartbeat which wasn't seventy-two to the minute, as the guards passed by a few feet above them, before once again disappearing around the far corner of the building.

The next step was the fire escape. Ross glanced up at the fourth floor and was relieved to see one of the three windows that had been marked with red crosses was open. As he approached the fire escape, he no longer needed to look back and check his two bloodhounds were still in pursuit.

He gripped the two sides of the iron ladder and began his ascent with the skill of an experienced cat burglar. William and Juan, not quite so practised, followed several rungs behind.

When he reached the fourth floor, Ross stepped nimbly across to the nearest windowsill, and in a single movement swung himself through the open window and landed noiselessly on the wooden floor. His eyes quickly focused on a bed on the far side of the room, in which a young woman was sleeping contentedly. She was about to have a bad dream, thought Ross, as he advanced cautiously towards her.

William clambered through the open window just as Ross placed a hand over the young woman's mouth. Even in the faint moonlight, he couldn't miss the look of horror in her eyes as she began to shake uncontrollably.

Juan, who had landed in the room with a thud, ran quickly across to the bed and spoke to the young woman in her own tongue, which appeared to calm her, as she stopped shaking. She nodded when Ross indicated he was going to remove his hand, again helped by Juan who assured her she wouldn't come to any harm if she remained silent. But Ross wasn't taking any chances. He bound her wrists and legs while William firmly gagged her with one of her own stockings.

Juan returned to the window and peered down from behind the curtain as the two guards sauntered by once again, their torchlights flashing in every direction except the house. When he could no longer see them, he joined William and Ross at the door. William cautiously opened the door a few inches and waited for a moment before poking his head out into the unlit corridor. No one in sight. Closing the door silently behind them, the three of them turned right and headed for the top of the stairs.

William led them slowly down the thickly carpeted stairs, though each of them knew the layout of the house as if it were his own home. They came to a halt when they reached the landing that led to the master bedroom. William and Juan stayed put while Ross continued on down the sweeping marble steps to the ground floor.

As he and Juan tiptoed along the corridor, William didn't even glance at the magnificent paintings that adorned the walls. He paused only for a moment before placing a hand on the doorknob. He turned it slowly, noiselessly, to find it was unlocked. He pushed the door open, but the moment he stepped inside the room a deafening alarm screamed out, and vast arc lights immediately illuminated the grounds outside, flooding the house with light. William switched on the bedroom light and stared at a large, empty bed that hadn't been slept in. Faulkner had clearly anticipated Plan A. Juan was quickly on the radio to his waiting team.

Downstairs in his study, Faulkner leapt out of his make-shift bed the moment the alarm sounded. It didn't worry him when he heard loud footsteps echoing along the marble corridor that led to his study. He had more than enough time. He walked across to the metal door and tapped the face of a watch that never left his wrist. When the dial lit up he entered 03 43, the first four numbers of the timecode. He had just tapped in 09 88, the month and the year, when he heard a key turning in the door behind him. But how could that be possible? He quickly stepped into the safe just as Ross burst into his study and came charging towards him.

He was only a stride away when Faulkner slammed the massive door shut, breathing a sigh of relief as he heard the heavy steel bolts slide into place.

Ross was about to tap his own watch and enter the code that would open the safe door when he heard footsteps running along the corridor. He decided to wait for the choirboy and the lieutenant to appear before he performed the opening ceremony.

• • •

Faulkner was also smiling, but then he assumed that time was on his side. Booth Watson would be arriving later that morning, and if the interlopers hadn't already left by then, one phone call from his Spanish lawyer and they would quickly be dispatched. And what his pursuers didn't know was that General Franco had built a tunnel from his underground study through the cliff that led to a tiny cove where his yacht would be waiting for him. This time the captain would take him somewhere that didn't have an extradition treaty with Britain.

He touched the face of his watch to check the time: 03.45. The code that would open the outer door and allow him to descend to the safety of his other world. This time the year came first, 88, followed by the month, 09, and finally the time, which had just flicked over to 0346. He would have to wait for a moment before he could enter the new code. He waited for the light to go out before he touched the face again so he could begin the whole process once more. He tapped the face of his watch and entered 88, but the light immediately flickered, grew dim, and faded. He touched the face again, but only had time to enter 03 before the light went out again. He tapped the watch more firmly than before, but it refused to light up. He jabbed at it repeatedly, but still no response. He then pulled it off his wrist and shook it violently, but it made no difference. The battery was spent.

• • •

William ran, panting, into Faulkner's study to find Ross staring at the closed metal door. 'I didn't get here in time,' he said.

William cursed as Juan rushed in to join them.

'My boys have surrounded the building and are rounding up the guards,' gasped an out of breath Juan. 'So he can't hope to get out.'

'But we can't get in,' said William, staring at the metal door.

Ross said nothing, just pulled up the left sleeve of his tracksuit and touched the face of his watch, which immediately lit up.

He checked the time, 03.48, and was about to enter the code when Collins calmly entered the room, dressed in a tailcoat, striped trousers, stiff white collar and grey silk tie.

'Good morning, gentlemen,' he said. 'I'm afraid Mr Sartona has not yet returned from his business trip. If there is anything I can do to assist you, please don't hesitate to ask.'

Ross swung around, his fist clenched, and advanced towards the butler, but Juan stepped quickly between them, just about managing to keep the two men apart, while Ross hurled a string of expletives at Collins, who just stood there, impassive.

'Quiet!' William suddenly shouted. He walked over to the metal door, fell on his knees and pressed an ear against its surface.

Tap.

They strained to hear the faint sound, which was repeated a few seconds later.

Tap, tap . .

'My God,' said Collins, the surface veneer finally crumbling. 'Mr Faulkner's locked himself inside.'

'Then for God's sake tell us how to get him out,' said Juan, 'before it's too late.'

'I don't know,' admitted the butler. 'He's the only person with the watch.'

Ross smiled.

Tap, tap, tap . . .

'There must be a spare one,' insisted Juan.

'No, there isn't,' said the butler. 'The only other person who even knows who made it is Mr Faulkner's lawyer, Mr Booth Watson, and he's not expected to arrive until twelve o'clock.'

Tap, tap, tap . . .

They all stared at the safe.

'How long can he hope to survive in there?' William said, almost to himself.

Tap . . . tap . . .

'Four, maybe five hours at the most,' said Ross, lowering his arm and letting the sleeve of his tracksuit fall over his wrist.

Tap . . .

Tap . .

Tap.

'We're going to have to call in a specialist,' said William turning to Juan, 'if we're to have any chance of getting him out before he suffocates.'

'It's not that simple,' said Juan. 'Señora Martinez obtained a court order that prevents anyone other than Faulkner or his lawyer from even touching it.'

'Then get her on the line immediately,' pressed William. 'Explain exactly what has happened and the consequences if we can't get the door open.'

'But she won't be in her office much before nine, and by then it will be too late,' said Juan.

'Collins will know her number,' said William, looking around, but the butler was nowhere to be seen.

'Where the hell's he got to?' said Ross as a red light began flashing on the phone on Faulkner's desk.

'One step ahead of us again,' said Juan. 'It's just lucky

that Faulkner doesn't trust anyone,' he added as he placed a finger to his lips and pressed the speaker button.

'What do you mean by waking me up at this time of the morning, Collins?' boomed a voice William immediately recognized.

'I'm sorry to wake you, sir,' said Collins, 'but Mr Faulkner's locked himself into the safe, and I don't have any way of getting him out.'

'Call Isobel Martinez immediately,' said Booth Watson, suddenly wide awake. 'She can get the court order lifted. Then ring the fire brigade. They'll have the right equipment to drill a hole in the door so at least he can breathe, which will give us a little more time. But what the hell was he doing in there in the first place?'

'Inspector Warwick, Lieutenant Sanchez and a third policeman turned up in the middle of the night.'

'DI Hogan no doubt,' said Booth Watson. 'Señora Martinez will have to take care of them too. Tell her I'll be on the first flight to Barcelona.'

'I'll have to go back to the study and look up her number in the boss's contacts book,' said Collins. 'What do I tell Warwick if he—'

'Tell him you're calling your lawyer. They can't stop you doing that,' said Booth Watson as he slammed down the phone and clambered out of bed.

'I can get him out of there,' said Ross, looking at the door, 'but I need Collins out of the way,' he added without explanation, as the butler came back into the room and headed straight for Faulkner's desk.

Sanchez immediately stepped into his path. 'You're under arrest, Mr Collins.'

'On what charge?'

'Preventing the police from carrying out their duties,' said Sanchez, as two uniformed officers stepped forward and grabbed Collins by the arms. 'Take him to the station and lock him up. Make sure he doesn't speak to anyone before I get there.'

'I'm entitled to phone my lawyer,' protested Collins. 'That's the law.'

'You already have,' said Juan as the two officers bustled Collins out of the room.

William waited for the study door to close before saying, 'So tell me Ross, how do you propose to open that door?'

'All in good time,' said Ross as he flicked through the telephone book on Faulkner's desk. He found the name he was looking for and dialled a number.

'Who is this?' asked a sleepy voice.

'I'm Mr Faulkner's private secretary. He asked me to let you know there's been a change of plan. He's been taken ill, nothing serious, but he wants to get back to London as quickly as possible so he can see his own doctor. How soon can you have his plane ready for take-off?'

'A couple of hours, three at the most,' said a voice no longer asleep. 'I'll alert the crew immediately, but our departure time will depend on when we can get a landing slot in London.'

'Tell them it's an emergency,' said Ross. 'We'll meet you at the airport.'

'Understood,' said the pilot, who was already out of bed before Ross had put the phone down.

'It's the watch, isn't it?' said William, remembering the anonymous black dial that had taken the place of Jo's Rolex.

Ross smiled. 'Now Collins is out of the way, I'll get Faulkner out and we can take him to the airport and fly him back to London on his own plane.'

'That's kidnapping,' said William, 'which, in case you've forgotten, is against the law, in both countries.'

'You've obviously forgotten, Chief Inspector,' said Ross, 'that Faulkner demanded to see his doctor. I distinctly remember him mentioning the words Harley Street.'

'The Spanish authorities certainly wouldn't be applying for an extradition order to bring him back,' said Juan, matter-of-factly.

'We can have him safely locked back up in Pentonville by the time Booth Watson lands in Barcelona,' added Ross.

'I'm still not sure—'

'Of course you're not, choirboy, but as you recently reminded me, we're not in Battersea, but Barcelona, so it's not your decision to make.'

They both turned to face the lieutenant. Juan nodded, but didn't speak.

Ross raised his left arm, pulled up his sleeve and tapped 04 11 09 88 on the face of the watch.

• • •

Booth Watson's mind was working overtime even before he'd turned on the shower. He didn't wait for the jets of water to warm up before he began to formulate a plan. Should he go to his office first, and call Isobel Martinez before he went on to the airport? Not that he was even sure he had her home number in chambers. He decided he would have to trust Collins to track her down and carry out his instructions, while he went directly to Heathrow and caught the first available flight to Barcelona.

Once he dried himself, he put on a clean shirt and yesterday's suit and tie, while his thoughts turned to Warwick and how the damn man never gave up. Once dressed, Booth Watson went down to his study, picked up his briefcase and put on an overcoat. He opened the front door to be greeted by a cold crisp morning. He double-locked the door then stood on the pavement and waited for some time before he spotted the words 'Taxi' glowing in the distance.

• • •

An unmarked police car came to a halt outside a private entrance to the airport. When a guard appeared, Lieutenant Sanchez produced his warrant card. The guard saluted, barely giving the three men in the back a second look, before pointing the driver in the right direction.

The car headed towards a long line of private aircraft, one of which was being refuelled and had its steps down waiting for its owner.

William and Ross helped Faulkner out of the back of the car. He was still unsteady, not having fully recovered from spending three hours locked in a safe. They guided him towards the aircraft's steps. The pilot was waiting in the plane's doorway, and couldn't hide his surprise when he saw his boss being accompanied by three men all dressed in black, who he'd never seen before.

Juan took him to one side and explained that Mr Faulkner had insisted on being flown back to England immediately, as he wanted to see his own doctor.

'But look at the state of him,' said the pilot. 'Shouldn't you have taken him to a local hospital?' he demanded, as Faulkner was almost carried up the steps and into the aircraft.

'I couldn't agree more,' said Juan. 'If you want to tell him, be my guest.'

'If he doesn't make it to London,' said the pilot, 'on your head be it.'

'I have a feeling you might be right about that,' said Juan, as the pilot quickly returned to the cockpit. William shook Juan warmly by the hand, before he left the aircraft.

Ross lowered Faulkner into a comfortable leather chair and fastened his seatbelt, while William placed a small package in an overhead locker before they both took their places on either side of the prisoner. The stewards slammed the aircraft door closed and moments later the plane began to taxi towards the south runway.

• • •

'Damn,' said Booth Watson, as the taxi came to a halt by his side. 'Damn,' he repeated before telling the cabbie he'd forgotten his passport, but would be back in a few minutes.

The cabbie smiled. A trip to Heathrow with a sober passenger wasn't his usual fare at that time in the morning.

As Booth Watson unlocked his front door, he tried to remember if he'd left his passport in chambers. He almost ran to his study. The next word he uttered was also four letters, and it wasn't damn.

• • •

Once the plane had reached its cruising height, William picked up the phone in Faulkner's armrest and called Danny at home.

'Get yourself to Heathrow, sharpish,' he said, before Danny had a chance to speak.

'Which terminal, sir?'

'Number one, the private aircraft stand. We should be there at,' he checked his watch, 'around five o'clock.'

'The taxi or a squad car?'

'A squad car,' said William. 'I'm not taking Faulkner back to prison in a taxi.' After hanging up, he glanced across at the prisoner, who looked as if he was about to emerge from a deep sleep.

'Which one of us will be calling the commander?' asked Ross innocently.

'I will,' said William. 'But not until Faulkner's safely locked up.'

• • •

When Booth Watson's taxi dropped him off at Heathrow fifty minutes later, the first thing he did on entering the airport was to check the departure board. The first flight to Barcelona was due to leave in forty minutes, and there wasn't another scheduled until a British Airways flight took off in a couple of hours' time.

He headed for the Iberia desk to be told by the booking clerk that the only seat available was near the back of the plane. He reluctantly handed over his credit card, aware that he couldn't afford to hang around and wait for a first-class seat on BA.

Once he'd settled in his seat, he tried to concentrate on the problems he'd be expected to deal with once he landed in Barcelona, but a screaming child with its mother on one side of him, and a man on his other who kept up a running conversation with someone across the aisle on whether Arsenal should sack their manager, made that impossible.

• • •

'Where am I?' demanded a waking voice as the Gulfstream jet touched down at Heathrow and began to taxi towards the far end of the runway.

'Back where you belong,' said Ross, without further explanation.

William looked out of the cabin window as the plane taxied to a halt, relieved to see Danny standing by a squad car waiting for them.

'Stop them, stop them!' shouted Faulkner at the top of his voice as he was yanked out of his seat and unceremoniously propelled towards the exit. The stewardess ran to the front of the plane and banged on the cockpit door as Faulkner was pushed down the steps, stumbling onto the tarmac, where Danny caught him in his arms like a long-lost lover. William and Ross quickly followed and bundled the prisoner into the back of the car as Danny climbed back behind the wheel.

'Good morning, sir,' said Danny, glancing in his rear-view mirror. 'Should I wait and see what those two gentlemen want, before we leave?'

William and Ross looked out of the back window to see the pilot and an airport official running towards them.

'No,' said William firmly. 'Get moving.'

Danny didn't need any encouragement to shoot off, siren blaring, lights flashing.

• • •

When Booth Watson's flight finally landed in Barcelona two hours later, he was reminded just how long it could take to disembark when you didn't travel first class. The same queue was waiting for him at passport control, and it was some time before he got through customs and emerged out into the morning sun, only to be greeted with another long queue standing in line for a taxi.

When Booth Watson eventually reached the front, he climbed into the back of a cab and checked his watch. His first thought was: would Miles still be alive? His second: what he would do if he wasn't.

• • •

'Booth Watson's flight from Heathrow has just landed,' said Sanchez as he put down the phone. 'So you can release Collins and take him back to the house. Make sure they both arrive around the same time.'

The watch *agente* unlocked the cell door and stood aside to allow the irate prisoner out. He'd left his breakfast untouched. When Collins reached the top of the steps, he found Lieutenant Sanchez waiting for him. He looked him in the eye and said, 'If he dies, on your head be it.'

Collins was the second person who had told him that this morning, and Juan suspected that, when he reported to his captain later, he might hear the same opinion expressed for a third time.

• • •

Faulkner didn't stop protesting as the squad car shot out of the airport and onto the main road. It took all of William's and Ross's strength just to restrain him. Ross finally decided on a delaying tactic, and thrust an elbow sharply into Faulkner's groin with all the strength he could muster. Faulkner doubled up, and his protests turned to a whimpering moan.

'Was that necessary?' asked William.

'Possibly not, sir,' replied Ross, 'but I had reason to believe you were about to be attacked.'

William looked out of the window to make sure Ross couldn't see him laughing.

Faulkner had fully recovered by the time Danny reached Pentonville Road, siren still blaring. The vast wooden gates began to slowly open as they approached the prison.

'You've made a dreadful mistake,' protested Faulkner. 'I'm Captain Ralph Neville RN.'

'And I'm Mother Teresa RC,' said Ross.

This time William couldn't stop himself laughing.

Danny drove through the prison gates to find a reception party waiting for them. When he came to a halt, the governor stepped forward.

'Welcome back, 0249,' he said as the prisoner was dragged out of the squad car. 'I'm afraid your old cell is currently occupied, but we've found you a larger one, which you'll be sharing with a couple of lifers. One murdered his mother, and the other's a heroin addict, who just can't get to sleep at night, poor fellow. Still, you should be safely out of harm's way on the top bunk.' He gave Faulkner a warm smile, before adding, 'Just be thankful you're not in solitary. But do let me know if that would be your preference.'

'I demand to speak to my lawyer,' said Faulkner.

'I'm afraid he's out of the country at the moment,' said William, as two guards grabbed the prisoner's arms and led him into the high-security wing. 'But I'll be sure to let him know the moment he gets back.'

• • •

Collins got out of the police car just as a taxi drove through the front gates.

'Did you get him out of the safe in time?' were Booth Watson's first words as he climbed out of the cab.

'I was about to call Señora Martinez when I saw your taxi coming up the drive.'

'But I told you to do that hours ago,' said an exasperated Booth Watson as he waited for Collins to unlock the front door.

'I would have done it hours ago,' snapped Collins, 'if Sanchez hadn't arrested me on spurious charges. I've only just got back from what was so obviously a set-up.'

'Then we haven't a moment to lose,' Booth Watson snapped back as Collins ran into the house and along the corridor, coming to a halt outside the study door. The butler waited for a breathless Booth Watson to join him before they both entered the room. Neither of them could help noticing that the solid metal door was still firmly closed.

Collins walked quickly over to the boss's desk and started leafing through his private telephone book.

'How long has he been in there?' asked Booth Watson, pointing at the safe door.

'Over four hours,' Collins replied. 'We might still be able to save him, but we'll have to move quickly.'

Collins began dialling the number of Faulkner's Spanish lawyer, when Booth Watson asked, 'What were Mr Faulkner's instructions before the police turned up?'

'He told me I was to pack up every one of his paintings and put them in the hold of the yacht as soon as it arrives this evening.'

'Then you should carry out those orders, and leave me to speak to Señora Martinez.'

The butler reluctantly handed the phone over to Booth Watson. 'Should anyone ever ask you, Collins, you will tell them that Mr Faulkner died in Switzerland last year, where he was cremated, which I can confirm, as I attended the funeral along with Inspector Warwick.'

'Señora Martinez's office,' said a voice as Collins closed the door behind him.

Booth Watson quietly replaced the receiver.

• • •

'I told you to brief me on everything you two were up to, Chief Inspector,' said the commander at the top of his voice. 'And I meant everything.'

'I didn't think you would want me to wake you in the middle of the night, sir,' replied William unconvincingly.

'Then you were wrong, Chief Inspector. Both of you will

report to my office immediately – immediately!' repeated The Hawk, before he slammed the phone down.

His wife turned over, blinked and looked across at her husband as he climbed out of bed. 'What are you smiling about?' she asked, but he'd already closed the bathroom door.

The Hawk clenched a fist and punched the air several times, the smile not leaving his face.

ACKNOWLEDGEMENTS

My thanks for their invaluable advice and research to:
Simon Bainbridge, Michael Benmore, Jonathan Caplan QC, Kate Elton, Alison Prince and Johnny Van Haeften.

Special thanks to:
Detective Sergeant Michelle Roycroft (Ret.)
Chief Superintendent John Sutherland (Ret.)
and Detective Chief Inspector Jackie Malton (Ret.)

If you enjoyed *Over My Dead Body*, why not go back to where it all began?

Read on for an extract from the first William Warwick book, *Nothing Ventured*

CHAPTER 1

14 July 1979

'You can't be serious.'

'I couldn't be more serious, Father, as you'd realize if you'd ever listened to anything I've been saying for the past ten years.'

'But you've been offered a place at my old college at Oxford to read law, and after you graduate, you'll be able to join me in chambers. What more could a young man ask for?'

'To be allowed to pursue a career of his own choosing, and not just be expected to follow in his father's footsteps.'

'Would that be such a bad thing? After all, I've enjoyed a fascinating and worthwhile career, and, dare I suggest, been moderately successful.'

'Brilliantly successful, Father, but it isn't your career we're discussing, it's mine. And perhaps I don't want to be a leading criminal barrister who spends his whole life defending a bunch of villains he'd never consider inviting to lunch at his club.'

'You seem to have forgotten that those same villains paid for your education, and the lifestyle you presently enjoy.'

'I'm never allowed to forget it, Father, which is the reason I intend to spend my life making sure those same villains are locked up for long periods of time, and not allowed to go free and continue a life of crime thanks to your skilful advocacy.'

William thought he'd finally silenced his father, but he was wrong.

'Perhaps we could agree on a compromise, dear boy?'

'Not a chance, Father,' said William firmly. 'You're sounding like a barrister who's pleading for a reduced sentence, when he knows he's defending a weak case. But for once, your eloquent words are falling on deaf ears.'

'Won't you even allow me to put my case before you dismiss it out of hand?' responded his father.

'No, because I'm not guilty, and I don't have to prove to a jury that I'm innocent, just to please you.'

'But would you be willing to do something to please me, my dear?'

In the heat of battle William had quite forgotten that his mother had been sitting silently at the other end of the table, closely following the jousting between her husband and son. William was well prepared to take on his father but knew he was no match for his mother. He fell silent once again. A silence that his father took advantage of.

'What do you have in mind, m'lud?' said Sir Julian, tugging at the lapels of his jacket, and addressing his wife as if she were a high court judge.

'William will be allowed to go to the university of his choice,' said Marjorie, 'select the subject he wishes to study, and once he's graduated, follow the career he wants to pursue. And more important, when he does, you will give in gracefully and never raise the subject again.'

'I confess,' said Sir Julian, 'that while accepting your wise judgement, I might find the last part difficult.'

Mother and son burst out laughing.

'Am I allowed a plea in mitigation?' asked Sir Julian innocently.

'No,' said William, 'because I will only agree to Mother's terms if in three years' time you unreservedly support my decision to join the Metropolitan Police Force.'

Sir Julian Warwick QC rose from his place at the head of the table, gave his wife a slight bow, and reluctantly said, 'If it so please Your Lordship.'

William Warwick had wanted to be a detective from the age of eight, when he'd solved 'the case of the missing Mars bars'. It was a simple paper trail, he explained to his housemaster, that didn't require a magnifying glass.

The evidence – sweet papers – had been found in the waste-paper basket of the guilty party's study, and the culprit wasn't able to prove he'd spent any of his pocket money in the tuck shop that term.

And what made it worse for William was that Adrian Heath was one of his closest pals, and he'd assumed it would be a lifelong friendship. When he discussed it with his father at half term, the old man said, 'We must hope that Adrian has learnt from the experience, otherwise who knows what will become of the boy.'

Despite William being mocked by his fellow pupils, who dreamt of becoming doctors, lawyers, teachers, even accountants, the careers master showed no surprise when William informed him that he was going to be a detective. After all, the other boys had nicknamed him Sherlock before the end of his first term.

William's father, Sir Julian Warwick Bt, had wanted his son to go up to Oxford and read law, just as he'd done thirty years before. But despite his father's best efforts, William had remained determined to join the police force the day he left school. The two stubborn men finally reached a compromise approved of by his mother. William would go to London University and read art history – a subject his father refused to take seriously – and if, after three years, his son still wanted to be a policeman, Sir Julian agreed to give in gracefully. William knew that would never happen.

William enjoyed every moment of his three years at King's College London, where he fell in love several times. First with Hannah and Rembrandt, followed by Judy and Turner, and finally Rachel and Hockney, before settling down with Caravaggio: an affair that would last a lifetime, even though his father had pointed out that the great Italian artist had been a murderer and should have been hanged. A good enough reason to abolish the death penalty, William suggested. Once again, father and son didn't agree.

During the summer holidays after he'd left school, William backpacked his way across Europe to Rome, Paris, Berlin and on to St Petersburg, to join long queues of other devotees who wished to worship the past masters. When he finally graduated, his professor suggested that he should consider a PhD on the darker side of Caravaggio. The darker side, replied William, was exactly what he intended to research, but he wanted to learn more about criminals in the twentieth century, rather than the sixteenth.

At five minutes to three on the afternoon of Sunday, 5 September 1982, William reported to Hendon Police College in north London. He enjoyed almost every minute of the training course from the moment he swore allegiance to the Queen to his passing-out parade sixteen weeks later.

The following day, he was issued with a navy-blue serge uniform, helmet and truncheon, and couldn't resist glancing at his reflection whenever he passed a window. A police uniform, he was warned by the commander on his first day on parade, could change a person's personality, and not always for the better.

Lessons at Hendon had begun on the second day and were divided between the classroom and the gym. William learnt whole sections of the law until he could repeat them verbatim. He revelled in forensic and crime scene analysis, even though he quickly discovered when he was introduced to the skid pad that his driving skills were fairly rudimentary.

Having endured years of cut and thrust with his father across the breakfast table, William felt at ease in the mock courtroom, where instructing officers cross-examined him in the witness box, and he even held his own during self-defence classes, where he learnt how to disarm, handcuff and restrain someone who was far bigger than him. He was also taught about a constable's powers of arrest, search and entry, the use of reasonable force and, most important of all, discretion. 'Don't always stick to the rule book,' his instructor advised him. 'Sometimes you have to use common sense, which, when you're dealing with the public, you'll find isn't that common.'

Exams were as regular as clockwork, compared to his days at university, and he wasn't surprised that several candidates fell by the wayside before the course had ended.

After what felt like an interminable two-week break following his passing-out parade, William finally received a letter instructing him to report to Lambeth police station at 8 a.m. the following Monday. An area of London he had never visited before.

Police Constable 565LD had joined the Metropolitan Police Force as a graduate but decided not to take advantage of the accelerated promotion scheme that would have allowed him to progress more quickly up the ladder, as he wanted to line up on his first day with every other new recruit on equal terms. He accepted that, as a probationer, he would have to spend at least two years on the beat before he could hope to become a detective, and in truth, he couldn't wait to be thrown in at the deep end.

From his first day as a probationer William was guided by his mentor, Constable Fred Yates, who had twenty-eight years of police service under his belt, and had been told by the nick's chief inspector to 'look after the boy'. The two men had little in common other than that they'd both wanted to be coppers from an early age, and their fathers had done everything in their power to prevent them pursuing their chosen career.

'ABC,' was the first thing Fred said when he was introduced to the wet-behind-the-ears young sprog. He didn't wait for William to ask.

'Accept nothing, Believe no one, Challenge everything. It's the only law I live by.'

During the next few months, Fred introduced William to the world of burglars, drug dealers and pimps, as well as his first dead body. With the zeal of Sir Galahad, William wanted to lock up every offender and make the world a better place; Fred was more realistic, but he never once attempted to douse the flames of William's youthful enthusiasm. The young probationer quickly found out that the public don't know if a policeman has been in uniform for a couple of days or a couple of years.

'Time to stop your first car,' said Fred on William's second day on the beat, coming to a halt by a set of traffic lights. 'We'll hang about until someone runs a red, and then you can step out into the road and flag them down.' William looked apprehensive. 'Leave the rest to me. See that tree about a hundred yards away? Go and hide behind it, and wait until I give you the signal.'

William could hear his heart pounding as he stood behind the tree. He didn't have long to wait before Fred raised a hand and shouted, 'The blue Hillman! Grab him!'

William stepped out into the road, put his arm up and directed the car to pull over to the kerb.

'Say nothing,' said Fred as he joined the raw recruit. 'Watch carefully and take note.' They both walked up to the car as the driver wound down his window.

'Good morning, sir,' said Fred. 'Are you aware that you drove through a red light?'

The driver nodded but didn't speak.

'Could I see your driving licence?'

The driver opened his glove box, extracted his licence and handed it to Fred. After studying the document for a few moments, Fred said, 'It's particularly dangerous at this time in the morning, sir, as there are two schools nearby.'

'I'm sorry,' said the driver. 'It won't happen again.'

Fred handed him back his licence. 'It will just be a warning this time,' he said, while William wrote down the car's number plate in his notebook. 'But perhaps you could be a little more careful in future, sir.'

'Thank you, officer,' said the driver.

'Why just a caution,' asked William as the car drove slowly away, 'when you could have booked him?'

'Attitude,' said Fred. 'The gentleman was polite, acknowledged his mistake and apologized. Why piss off a normally law-abiding member of the public?'

'So what would have made you book him?'

'If he'd said, "Haven't you got anything better to do, officer?" Or worse, "Shouldn't you be chasing some real criminals?" Or my favourite, "Don't you realize I pay your wages?" Any of those and I would have booked him without hesitation. Mind you, there was one blighter I had to cart off to the station and lock up for a couple of hours.'

'Did he get violent?'

'No, far worse. Told me he was a close friend of the commissioner, and I'd be hearing from him. So I told him he could phone him from the station.' William burst out laughing. 'Right,' said Fred, 'get back behind the tree. Next time you can conduct the interview and I'll observe.'

Sir Julian Warwick QC sat at one end of the table, his head buried in the *Daily Telegraph*. He muttered the occasional tut-tut, while his wife, seated at the other end, continued her daily battle with the *Times* crossword. On a good day, Marjorie would have filled in the final clue before her husband rose from the table to leave for Lincoln's Inn. On a bad day, she would have to seek his advice, a service for which he usually charged a hundred pounds an hour. He regularly reminded her that to date, she owed him over £20,000. Ten across and four down were holding her up.

Sir Julian had reached the leaders by the time his wife was wrestling with the final clue. He still wasn't convinced that the death penalty should have been abolished, particularly when a police officer or a public servant was the victim, but then neither was the *Telegraph*. He turned to the back page to find out how Blackheath rugby club had fared against Richmond in their annual derby. After reading the match report he abandoned the sports pages, as he considered the paper gave far too much coverage to soccer. Yet another sign that the nation was going to the dogs.

'Delightful picture of Charles and Diana in *The Times*,' said Marjorie.

'It will never last,' said Julian as he rose from his place and walked to the other end of the table and, as he did every morning, kissed his wife on the forehead. They exchanged newspapers, so he could study the law reports on the train journey to London.

'Don't forget the children are coming down for lunch on Sunday,' Marjorie reminded him.

'Has William passed his detective's exam yet?' he asked.

'As you well know, my dear, he isn't allowed to take the exam until he's completed two years on the beat, which won't be for at least another six months.'

'If he'd listened to me, he would have been a qualified barrister by now.'

'And if you'd listened to him, you'd know he's far more interested in locking up criminals than finding ways of getting them off.'

'I haven't given up yet,' said Sir Julian.

'Just be thankful that at least our daughter has followed in your footsteps.'

'Grace has done nothing of the sort,' snorted Sir Julian. 'That girl will defend any penniless no-hoper she comes across.'

'She has a heart of gold.'

'Then she takes after you,' said Sir Julian, studying the one clue his wife had failed to fill in: *Slender private man who ended up with a baton.* Four.

'Field Marshal SLIM,' said Sir Julian triumphantly. 'The only man to join the army as a private soldier and end up as a field marshal.'

'Sounds like William,' said Marjorie. But not until the door had closed.

Extract reprinted with permission from Pan Macmillan